Primale POSSESSION

REESE GABRIEL

ELLORA'S CAVE
ROMANTICA PUBLISHING

What the critics are saying...

❧

SERIA'S STAR WARRIOR

5 Stars "Reese Gabriel continues her *More Than Male* series with the story of two people fighting the attractions they feel for each other. Seria is not supposed to have submissive desires, but Raylar brings out her desire to submit. She wants him more than she wanted any other male. Raylar is fighting his own demons, and Seria distracts him from his pain. He wants to dominate her even though he knows he should not have those feelings for a Fem. The love scenes are ultra hot. I cannot wait for the next book in this series." ~ *Sensual EcataRomance Reviews*

AZAR'S PRIZE

5 Stars "Reese Gabriel reintroduces the original characters from the first book in this series, *Theron and Nyssa*. Now they have a grown daughter with a destiny of her own to fulfill. Will Azar and Theryssa agree to become a part of the plans that Theron and Nyssa map out for them? Read the book to get the answer. I loved these characters and I hope Ms Gabriel will include them in future stories." ~ *Sensual EcataRomance Reviews*

An Ellora's Cave Romantica Publication

www.ellorascave.com

Primale Possession

ISBN 9781419957864
ALL RIGHTS RESERVED.
Seria's Star Warrior Copyright © 2006 Reese Gabriel
Azar's Prize Copyright © 2006 Reese Gabriel
Edited by Pamela Campbell.
Cover art by Syneca.

This book printed in the U.S.A. by Jasmine–Jade Enterprises, LLC.

Trade paperback Publication June 2008

PRIMALE POSSESSION

 හ

SERIA'S STAR WARRIOR
~11~

AZAR'S PRIZE
~211~

SERIA'S STAR WARRIOR

ജ

✦

Chapter One

જી

Seria was lost the moment she saw the Guardian's image, larger than life, floating before her face in holoid form. Even in a society of genetically engineered people, flawless and beautiful, the man was in a class all his own.

He was just that breathtaking and captivating in his pale blue Guardian Corps uniform, the one-piece coveralls revealing a firm, hard body with well-defined muscles, perfect-sized shoulders and a narrow waist. His eyes were hauntingly blue, a shade nearly as light as the robin's egg hue of his uniform.

"He's so..." Seria lacked the words. Her twenty-five solar passings had done nothing to prepare her for such an experience.

"He's quite a specimen," agreed the mysterious woman with the blue and yellow feathered dress and mask who had invited Seria here to this super-luxurious dwelling unit, five thousand floors up in one of the finest anti-grav cylinders under the dome of Arcos City.

Seria found her voice way too familiar. Was it off the Hologrid, maybe? Was she one of the special class of entertainers who broadcast themselves over the galactic virtual reality beams? Could that explain all the secrecy? It had all happened so fast. She had been trying to stay awake for a briefing at Diplomatic Corps Headquarters on the social customs of Borian Slime Worms, when her supervisor had handed her a digigram, requesting her presence at this unknown address.

The woman with the holostar voice was right, of course— there was no mistaking the Guardian's handsomeness, the perfect cut of his features. He was a primale, after all, part of that special class of men designed to be superior in every physical and mental aspect. But it was the intensity of his gaze, the haunting quality of his expression that caught Seria's attention.

Though he appeared to be about her own age, there was something very deep and ancient about him. Something that kept him apart from others. Had he ever been in love? she wondered.

Unlike the mems, that more easygoing, less intensely engineered type of male, primales were incapable of casual relationships. They knew only possession. One woman. For life.

The main group of females, called fems, could not bear this kind of relationship. The fems, of which Seria was one, were genetically engineered to create sexual harmony through polyamorous relationships. A different kindof woman was needed for the genetically superior primales. These were the obedients, designed for beauty...and submissiveness to their single partner whom they often addressed as Lord or Master.

Seria had mixed feelings thinking about this particular Guardian having an obedient of his own. On the one hand, it was right and fitting, because she could never be all the things a man like that needed. On the other hand, a part of her was a little jealous, thinking how she could never even have a chance to try to please such an interesting-looking man.

The idea was nonsense. Primales were only happy with complete, mindless surrender. The only way an obedient got the last word with her man was by opening her mouth to say, "Yes, Sir."

Seria's fem girlfriends all liked to make fun of primales, because they were so serious and really so naïve when it came to dealing with the deeper complexities of womanhood. A fem worth her salt would bring the toughest primale to his knees in a matter of minutes. Or so they liked to tell themselves. The way Seria saw it—the obedients these men claimed were not exactly doormats. Many a mem, for example, would try his hand at claiming one of the special little beauties only to find himself shut out in the cold. Obedients might seem weaker, but that was only because they were engineered to walk straight into the fire. Would a fem be any less consumed by such fiery male heat?

Every now and then you heard tales, tall tales, perhaps, of fems who got a little too close and ended up falling for primales. It was a sad sight to see a woman begging for something she could never have.

It was the same now, looking at this Guardian—twin impulses to either find him and bare her soul completely or else run like hell.

"You'll forgive me." Seria shook out her long, golden curls. "But I'm still not sure what all this has to do with me."

The woman's eyes smiled a little behind the mask. The look seemed more ironic than anything else. "Suppose you begin by telling me what goes through your mind when you look at Raylar." She turned off the holoid projector.

Raylar. His name was Raylar.

"A lot of things," she tried to keep her voice steady. "Mostly I'm just trying to figure out why I'm here."

"You're here, Seria, because you've never quite fit in. Never been like your fem girlfriends. Relationships mean more to you. You want to please men, too, don't you, in ways they don't understand?"

She didn't do a very good job of hiding her shock. "Who are you?" she demanded. "You don't know me. Not at all."

"I'm someone who cares. You needn't be embarrassed," the woman soothed. "Have you ever heard the story of the ugly duckling?"

"No," Seria said, reeling.

The woman was right about her, absolutely right. She was far too weak-kneed for a fem. Males got to her. They did things to her belly that took away her strength. Dealing with regular males, the garden-variety mems were hard enough, but the few times she had crossed paths with a primale, she had suffered near meltdowns. Her girlfriends—engineered with one-hundred-percent fem blood—were able to laugh it off. Sure, they wanted to go to bed with the primales—as if any female in existence could resist the appeal of a sub-gender of human male bred for super strength, desirability and beauty—but they hadn't been drawn like moths to a flame.

Behind Seria's own joining laughter was pain, and a good deal of confusion.

"A mother duck has a brood of ducklings," the woman explained. "One doesn't quite fit in. Always a half-step behind, never quite on key. Then one day it finds out why—it's not really a duck at all, but a swan."

Seria blinked, still thinking about Raylar, wondering if she could do anything for him, to ease that pain in his eyes.

There it was again, the desire to soothe and please, to know him to his core, to let him touch her own, just like always, only more so—so much so that she could barely contain her whirling emotions. Comets and stars, was she falling in love…with a holoid?

"You, Seria, are a beautiful swan. A creature totally unique in the world. A work of genetic art, half fem…and half obedient."

Seria snapped from her dreamy passions. Surely she had misheard? "No one can be…half anything," she gasped, unable to imagine such an act of social sacrilege. "The sub-genders were designed pure."

"Ordinarily, yes," the woman agreed. She was obviously beautiful, with her silver sandals, legs crossed on the hover couch. Seria felt awkward and ugly by comparison in her own plasticite chair. "The Council made an exception in your case. Your genes come not from the harvest pool but from two specific donors."

Seria had to get out of here. The woman was mad, she had to be. "I've listened to all I care to," she declared.

Before she could make a move to leave, the woman took off her mask. Seria's jaw dropped. It was Nyssa. Not just a holostar, but also the newly named Head of the Council. If anyone could be in a position to know of the Council's secret activities, it was she.

So it must be true. All of it...

Seria tried to keep her voice steady. "If I believe you then that makes me a freak. The victim of some kind of a horrible joke on the Council's part."

"Not a freak." The beautiful Nyssa shook her head. "A new kind of human being. An experiment, yes. But hardly a joke. The basic idea, Seria, is to create new types of people, individuals whose DNA comes from the intermix of two specific genetic parents, and not a general formula."

This was the topper. "What do you mean genetic parents?" she demanded. "Are you talking about some kind of...of *natural* birth?"

The very idea that she could have been fertilized in the body of a woman and delivered like some kind of animal in this day and age was beyond disgusting.

Nyssa, her hair short and straight and neon blue, shook her head. She had blue eyes to match her hair and pink highlights in her bangs. "No, you were grown in a lab like everyone else, don't worry. It's just that your DNA was chosen deliberately so as to create a hybrid offspring. In your case, you had an obedient mother and a primale father. The resulting balance makes you most similar to a fem, though you have some submissive tendencies, too. Perhaps you have already discovered this for yourself."

Now there was an understatement.

The reality slammed Seria hard as she thought of how hard her life had really been when it came to the opposite sex, how dangerous it was for her to be kissed or touched by males.

Even the look of a man upon her could stir the deepest feelings and needs, a desire to bond with him, to find his deepest heart—to belong to him. Seria's friends had rolled their eyes at how dramatic she seemed to be and how easily she became entranced. Most of the mems in her cluster became afraid to date her, claiming she was too intense. They just wanted to have fun—she was looking for much more.

Seria had never been able to figure out what was wrong with her. Everyone else seemed to handle the aspects of sex-making so easily, moving blithely from partner to partner. But once she became interested in a mem, she wanted to be with him exclusively, until she lost all sight of reality. Sadly, there had been mems who had taken advantage, allowing her to pour endless amounts of love and attention on them while they had happily continued their polyamorous ways, so she had never been able to commit to the sex-making. To experience what everyone else had taken for granted.

That was the thing—fems and mems were engineered to love multiple people, to spread sex-making wherever they went. Seria, by contrast, had always been obsessed with finding just one all-consuming relationship. Having never found it, and upon reaching the age of twenty-five this year, she had made a decision. Since the only men who took women monogamously were primales, and since they basically took their women as slaves, she would no longer pursue that elusive dream. She was left with only one possibility.

Celibacy.

Which is why she'd made the decision to sign up for the Diplomatic Corps. Three years schooling followed by one year of protocol work at Headquarters. Nothing really exciting yet, but these things took time. She had a bright career ahead of her, by all accounts. Only now she wondered if there was much point to anything. She scarcely knew who she was anymore, much less what her life's goals should be. "If it's all the same to you," she said, "I'd like to go now. I need to spend some time…thinking."

"Of course," said Nyssa. "But there are a couple more things you should know first."

Wonderful, thought Nyssa glumly. As if enough damage hadn't been done already.

"I didn't drop this bombshell on you with the intention of leaving you to deal with it alone, Seria. As it so happens, there is an added side benefit — if you could call it that — of having individual progenitors. You, my dear, have an actual biological family. Beginning with me. Your elder sister. By five solar passings."

Seria stared blankly. The concept was so foreign. She tried to compare it to the notion of being related to her girlfriends in their common cluster. It was like a family, but there were no blood ties. Everyone's genes came from the computer. "My...sister?"

"I was as surprised as you are, trust me. Technically, we are half-sisters. We share the genes of Morax, the former Commander of the Guardians. My mother is Dekalia, recently retired Head of the Council. As you probably know, my mate Theron is the new Commander."

Seria did know this. The fact that a primale would take a fem for a lifemate, and that a fem would agree to such a thing, had astounded everyone.

"I am half-fem, half-primale. I'm designed for leadership. You — you have a different destiny."

"But wait!" Seria exclaimed. "Who is my mother?"

Nyssa's lovely features grew troubled for a moment. "I'm sorry to tell you, Seria, your mother is no longer alive."

Seria felt a lump in her throat, suddenly mourning the life of a woman she never knew. "But she couldn't have been that old..."

"No," Nyssa agreed. "She wasn't. She died of a broken heart, to put it bluntly. I wish I could tell you more. In time it will all be clear. I promise. For the moment, I have to talk to you about the Guardian in the holoid."

"Raylar."

"Yes, Raylar."

Seria braced herself. "Don't tell me he's our brother?"

Nyssa laughed. "Oh, stars, no. Not by a long shot. Although you were worried he might be off-limits, weren't you?"

Seria flushed red. "Is it that obvious?"

"It's written all over your face, actually."

"I never have been good at playing it cool," Seria sighed.

"That's the obedient in you," Nyssa reminded. "It's a charming characteristic, especially mixed with your fem spunkiness."

"I always thought it a curse," Seria mused.

"That's ugly duckling talk. You're the swan, remember? And Raylar, by the way, to borrow another old story, is your prince."

Seria's blood surged. "My…prince?"

"Raylar is your lifemate," she confirmed as though the information were quite matter-of-fact. "You belong to him. Soul and spirit…and body."

Her nipples tented under the loose silver top. She shifted on the seat, the heat building between her thighs. "But I don't even know him."

"That doesn't matter. The Council stacks the deck for us hybrids. We are designed ahead of time with mates, like pairs of shoes. That's part of what makes us strong. That and the DNA pairing that occurs in our own offspring. We are even experimenting with having direct contact and influence over our progeny to further the effect of hybridization. Theron and I are quite involved in the life of Theryssa, our five-year-old daughter, for instance."

By the stars—now there were children being raised outside of clusters? *Biological* children? Seria was trying her best to absorb it all. The holoid, the sister she never imagined having, their little girl, not to mention the biggie—the idea of her producing genetic reproductions with a primale, their DNA in exclusive combination, like the animal kingdom. And not just with any primale, but with one who was destined to be her lifemate.

"Your own daughter," Seria said, her voice a little strained. "You must be very proud."

"We are, thank you. Theryssa is quite a handful, but rather adorable just the same. You'll have to meet her. She is, if I recall the term from the historical lexicon, your niece."

"Yes…thank you." There was one question in all of this that begged to be asked. "Nyssa?" she ventured.

"Yes, Seria."

"Does he know?"

Nyssa pursed her lips. Her brow wrinkled a little. Damned if she didn't do that herself from time to time, in just the same way. Was that a trait of their father's? "Raylar is not, in our opinion, in a good position to hear the truth, start to finish."

Like Seria was?

"So when *will* he be told? Before the wedding, I hope."

Nyssa smiled wryly, presumably appreciating the wit of her little sister. She was so gorgeous, thought Seria. Maybe she ought to be jealous?

"That's where you come in, Seria. We are rather hoping you will be able to convince the man on your own that you are the one for him."

Seria laughed. "You can't be serious? I can scarcely accept it myself."

"You will. You both will. I saw how you reacted to the holoid. He makes you wet, doesn't he? He's under your skin already. And I promise you it won't get any better. I know. I went through this with my husband. You're already Raylar's, and he is yours."

Seria drew a breath, trying not to think of Raylar in the flesh, his hand reaching to touch her, his lips uttering the magic words "You are mine". How would her body respond? His image alone managed to so unnerve her. She pushed the possibilities back in her brain. It was too much to think of. "No offense, Your Honor, I'm not sure you have the right to make anything happen between us. Just because we were engineered and manipulated does not make us robots or slaves."

"Please, call me Nyssa. Yes, what you say is true. But you are both under Council orders, you by virtue of your pledge to the Diplomat Corps and him by his oath to the Guardians. Call it unfair, call it what you like, we intend to engineer your lives one more time, putting you both in a confined situation which will lead to your making sex, frequently and steamily. This will result in bonding. And life mating."

Seria couldn't believe it. A half-hour having an honest-to-goodness sister and already she hated her. "I won't do it," she fumed.

"You won't have a choice, Seria. You're not programmed to resist such a serious command, even with your partial nature. Besides, this is a matter of galactic security. Raylar is being groomed to lead the next war against the Narthians. He has just twenty-six solar passings, but he has been given special genes that will make him a warrior as great as or greater than my husband, who at thirty-eight solars is looking to retire from combat. But Raylar is brooding at the moment, blaming himself for the death of some of the men under his command. The fact that what happened was not his fault and that he defended the rest of them, saving them against overwhelming odds, consoles him not at all. Unless he has the love of his woman to sustain him, he will fall into depression, or worse, into treachery."

Nyssa's words rendered an invisible swath across Seria's heart. So that was it—she knew she had seen something in Raylar's face. He had held life and death in his hands. He had faced the impossible. And lost. But it was more than just what

Nyssa was talking about. There was something else troubling the man's soul, something she could not put her finger on. She wasn't sure even Raylar himself knew what it was, but there was no mistaking its reality.

All of a sudden, backing away was not an option for Seria. She didn't think it was her genetics compelling her into service, or even her own patriotism, truth be told. Rather it was him. A man she already knew without knowing. Whose true soul and spirit, she believed, were hidden behind an expression of worry and self-blame.

She had to go to him, help him. The only question was, what did the Council have in mind? What sort of mission required repeated steamy sex-making? It sounded contrived to her, not to mention a good recipe for disaster. Even assuming she held up through the command performances, how would he react? A man like that would not take well to being cornered, or forced to make sex with any half-breed obedient.

Then there was the deeper problem of what to do if she actually succeeded? Suppose he did want to make her his forever? Then what?

"Let's say I did agree," Seria ventured. "And let's say you make Raylar do this...this thing with me—whatever you have in mind. What's to stop him from just rejecting me? No matter what genetics you gave him, he is a primale. One look at him tells you how strong his will is. He would die first."

Nyssa smiled. "Your view of him is already colored by passion and personal devotion. That's a good thing," she said approvingly. "But you needn't fear. Your sexual submission will work its charms on him. Once you have given yourself over to his power and mastery, completely and helplessly, body and soul, he will not have it in his heart to reject or betray you. He will stand by you. Until his dying breath."

Seria felt the crimson burning up and down her chest. "You speak as if it's a certainty," she balked, "and yet you only just met me."

21

"In one sense, yes, I have only just met you," Nyssa agreed. "But in another sense, I have always known you. I see parts of myself in you. And this Raylar of yours, I have met him a few times and he is my husband all over again. Trust me, woman, you are about to be drowning in a sea of testosterone…and loving every minute of it."

Seria still wasn't sure. "It's just so much to absorb. There's so much I don't understand. This situation, as you call it, that we are going to be put into. What is that all about? You do realize, don't you that I am scheduled to take a posting on Alphus Six, as Assistant Ambassador?"

Nyssa nodded. "I know, you are leaving tomorrow. Raylar has been assigned to take you there, as your military escort. That is all he will know. It will be your responsibility to take advantage of your opportunities."

Seria's sex pulsed. "You mean seduce him," she said flatly.

Nyssa winked. "Just think of it as doing what comes naturally."

Tempting a primale into sex? That wasn't "natural". That was like considering jumping into a slag hole full of Narthian egg bearers. Down right dangerous.

"He won't like having to do this," Seria predicted.

"No, he will hate it," Nyssa agreed. "That will make things all the more challenging for you."

Seria sucked on her lower lip. Her confusion and doubt and indignation were giving way to another emotion, far more primal. She fought it hard, for what it represented—not strength and fem independence, but obedient dependence. "Nyssa?"

"Yes, Seria?"

"What if…" She steeled her courage to make the hardest statement of her life. "What if I can't do it right?"

"Do what right?"

"You know," she hedged, "the submission part. What if I can't make him want me? A man like Raylar could have any submissive he wanted. Or a hologrid star, for that matter."

"Oh, sweetie," Nyssa cooed, sounding more like a mother than a sister. "How could he not want you? One look at you and he will be slain. Don't you realize how lovely you are?"

"Not exactly."

Nyssa laughed. "Well, you are. You are positively gorgeous, though you don't seem to know it. I promise you, he will be hard as a rock the moment he sees you. And once he tastes you, he will be hooked forever."

Seria lost eye contact. She focused on her bare, sandaled feet, which were now as red with embarrassment as the rest of her.

"There!" exclaimed Nyssa. "That's the expression we want. Approach him with that look on your face and he will never want another woman again as long as he lives."

Good, she thought. Raylar didn't need to want other women. He needed to want and pursue her. Wait a minute, though. By the Moons of Vega, what was she really saying? If he put his mark upon her and claimed her that would satisfy her obedient side, yes, but what about her fem side? Wouldn't that entail an inevitable backlash and rebellion on her part?

Presumably time would tell. That's how it went with impossible government missions. Or so her teachers at the Diplomatic Academy had warned her. It's just that she hadn't expected hers to be quite so...personal.

The Diplo Corps was supposed to get her away from sex, not get her thrown headlong into it. With a sexy as hell, downright irresistible primale no less.

"Yes, I'll do it," said Seria, though she hadn't a clue what she was agreeing to.

"That's the spirit. I guarantee, Seria, you won't be disappointed."

Disappointed? No. Devastated—that was another story.

"Thanks," Seria managed to say.

Nyssa breathed deeply. "Well, that's a relief. Now, do you still want to go, or would you like to come with me and meet the rest of our family first…such as it is?"

A relief for one of us, thought Seria, pasting on a smile. "I'd like that, yes."

Nyssa took her hand, pulling her close for a hug. "Oh, I know I am being too pushy. And you probably hate me by now, for what I'm telling you, and for not telling you sooner. Just know that the Council and our father kept our identities secret for reasons he felt were valid. I only learned who I was a few years ago, when I was close to your age. I only discovered you existed a week ago."

"It's okay," Seria assured her.

Nyssa laughed. "You're lying through your teeth, and you're sweet to do so. Just trust me, if you hang in there, it will get easier."

Seria didn't see how it could, but she had no alternative but to trust Nyssa. She was family. Whatever that meant.

* * * * *

Raylar frowned at the invitation to sit down. It was his preference to remain standing at attention in the presence of the Guardian Commander.

"Sit," Theron repeated more firmly. "That's an order."

Raylar obeyed, conforming his body to fit the austere, thinly upholstered olive green seat in front of the Commander's desk. Raylar was a well-built man, six feet, two inches tall and extraordinarily fit, even by primale standards. He maintained himself in top form through a regime of extreme discipline. When at all possible, he slept on the floor, ate simple, uncooked foods and maintained a regimen of six hours a day of exercise, in addition to his already demanding daily routine. To his way of thinking a soldier was never truly off duty, but should be in a state of combat readiness at all times.

He had always been this way, but he was even more so now, following his experience on Rensus Nine. He was technically in post-combat restorative period, and while he was meticulous in following all the required programs and procedures, he took the liberty of filling every free moment with hard discipline. The psycho-combat doctors had urged him to rest more, to play, but with all due respect to their profession, none of them had been there that fateful dawn on Rensus Nine to see what these new Bug Hordes could do. How they could obliterate a young officer's command, taking down a dozen fine men with a single spray of their hideous poison juices.

In short, no one in the history of the Guardians had experienced quite the failure and agony that Raylar had. Losing his men in the field was only the beginning. The pain stayed and ate at him. Though they were Special Forces and therefore had no lifemates to bring the news to, still, all felt their loss. The entire Corps had suffered. Because of his errors in judgment.

"So," the General began, laying his palms flat on the clear surface of the plasticite desk, "Colonel Mazrat informs me you have kept yourself...occupied during your restorative period?"

"Yes, Sir." Raylar noted the careful choice of words. Mazrat had probably passed along the reports of the therapists, chiding Raylar for not letting his guard down, for remaining so much on edge. "Sir, permission to speak freely?"

"Certainly."

"I am already fully restored, Sir. I know myself better than any doctors or therapists. I would like to be returned to the front. As soon as possible."

Theron studied him, his expression unreadable. The General was a good man and a fine soldier. He was obviously making the best of having to sit behind a desk and tend to administrative duties. Raylar admired him all the more because he did it from sheer duty.

"You do know, Lieutenant Raylar that the post-combat restoration program is an injunction directly from the Council? All Guardians must participate. You are only halfway through your scheduled time."

"Yes, Sir." The General's wife was head of that body. Raylar did not envy the man having to balance the responsibilities of running the Corps and submitting to the authority of his own lifemate. There were some among the Guardians who questioned why the General was mated to a fem in the first place. They did not understand why he had not taken an obedient, to serve and delight him and make his life easier.

Raylar was not among them. In his opinion, it was contrary to the principles of the Corps to question the wisdom and judgment of a superior, except under grave life-and-death circumstances, and even then there were procedures to be followed, by which a man might be relieved of command.

Theron exhaled, steepling his fingers. "I know you are frustrated with having to wait to go back to the battlefield. Frankly, as a soldier, I do not appreciate the delays myself at times. But I recognize the Council's wisdom. They take things into consideration that we cannot. Certain aspects of psychological functioning and so on. The bottom line is we are not a military dictatorship, Raylar. We take our orders, too."

"Understood, Sir."

The General was pursing his lips, like he wanted to say something else, something harder and more personal. "Raylar, your commanding officer has reported to me that you have refused to accept the Star Cluster for your heroism on Rensus Nine."

"Yes, Sir."

"Would you mind telling me why?"

"I don't deserve it, Sir. I lost twelve men. Fifteen more wounded. I led us straight into a Narthian ambush."

"You also saved fifty more. Including the fifteen wounded you pulled one by one from the bug nets, facing a constant barrage of fire."

"I did my duty. Too little too late."

The General leaned back in his seat. Despite the relaxed position, it was obvious he was a man of great strength and power. "So you question the judgment of your superiors in giving you this recognition?"

Raylar tensed. He hadn't seen it that way. "Sir, I meant no disobedience. I only sought to not dishonor the Corps any further."

The General sighed. "Son," he addressed him, "I am not insensitive to what you feel. But I am going to remind you of some things, and they will not be pleasant to hear."

"Yes, Sir." *Good. The more unpleasant the better.*

"You are not the first officer to lose men. I don't have to tell you that. Can you imagine what would happen if they all reacted as you have? Pulling into yourself, displaying stubbornness bordering on insubordination? The fact is, officers sent back out too soon, officers with chips on their shoulders, officers with too much too prove are useless officers. There isn't room for ego in the Corps. You're a perfectionist, Raylar, and that's as bad or worse as being a slacker."

"Is it perfectionism to want to keep my men alive?" The words came out of Raylar's usually guarded mouth before he could stop them.

Theron's response gave good evidence he was Commander and not Raylar. "No," he said evenly, not reacting to the younger man's sudden anger. "Perfectionism is trying to turn yourself into some kind of wooden idol instead of learning to accept and work with your inevitable imperfections as a human being. When your men are under fire, they must turn to the real you, and they must know you well—good and bad. Otherwise they will never trust or respect you."

Raylar felt warm with shame. "Forgive me, Sir."

"Apologies aren't necessary. Being a goddamn pain in the ass perfectionist is part of what makes you who you are. Tempered, your character will make you a fine soldier. Far better than you can even imagine yourself capable. That's the other problem with perfectionism. It is the surest way to prevent actual growth."

Raylar's admiration for the man only grew. "I think I understand, Sir. I will work on this. With every ounce of my strength."

The General laughed. Seeing Raylar's concern, he said, "Don't worry, I'm not laughing at you. I'm laughing at me, about ten years ago."

"Yes, Sir."

"Raylar," he smiled, "I'm prepared to make you an offer. I think it's one any Guardian officer would relish."

"Sir?" Raylar was wary because frequently the treats enjoyed by others proved tedious to him.

"How would you like to get out of restoration limbo and back on active duty? Not combat, but vital nonetheless?"

"Sir," he sought to contain himself, "anything, Sir."

"It involves escort duty. For the Diplomatic Corps."

"Yes, Sir." Raylar wasn't thrilled with diplomats, but he'd take a bunch of gray-haired eggheads over another hour in therapy any day. "I would be honored. Is it the new delegation to Sarsus?"

"Alphus Six, actually. You'll be escorting a special envoy to the embassy there. We'll outfit a small cruiser for you. A two-seater."

"Alphus Six?" There couldn't be a more remote, unknown point. Nothing of any cosmic consequence had ever happened there and likely never would. As far as he was concerned, the native intelligence on the planet, in the form of sentient fungi, hardly qualified as life at all. Basically, it was an embassy for rock collectors and frustrated biologists who enjoyed talking to rotted plant matter. "I wasn't aware there was any pending diplomatic activity on that planet, Sir," he noted dryly.

"You'd have to ask the Diplomatic Corps," he shrugged. "Apparently there is a message of some sort to be delivered there, in person. Here's the diplomat you'll be escorting, by the way."

Raylar looked to the right. The wall disappeared, transforming itself into a three-dimensional image of a blonde woman in her mid-twenties, wearing a low-cut formal turquoise gown, sewn with miniature sparkling crystals. The gown hugged her narrow waist and accented her perfectly proportioned hips. Not to mention what it did for her bosom.

"Sir, *this* is the diplomat?" he questioned, his pulse racing.

"That's correct."

"But she's female."

"You noticed that as well?" quipped the General. "Indeed she is. And a rather well put together one, don't you think? Her name, incidentally, is Seria. She has no mating attachments and she's into health foods and exercise like you."

"Sir, surely there is some kind of mistake here?"

"A mistake?" said Theron innocently. "What sort of mistake?"

"Sir, you can't possibly mean for me to travel through deep space alone with...with a *female*?"

"Why not, my good man? She's had her shots."

Incredible! The General was making light of it. As if this weren't a violation of a half dozen Guardian Corps regulations, at least. "Sir, I respectfully remind you of Section Eight of the Code, forbidding prolonged, possibly stimulatory contact between active duty personnel and —"

29

"I know the regulations, son. I helped write them."

Raylar shifted in his seat. There was no getting around what he had to say next. "Sir, permission to speak freely once again?"

"Granted."

"Sir, I must recuse myself from this mission, regulations or not."

"Why is that, Lieutenant?"

"Because," he managed with as much dignity as possible. "I find her attractive. In a...physical way."

"You'd like to make sex with her?"

Raylar's primale cock was awakening from a very long slumber, in spite of his best efforts to keep it at bay. He was known as the Iron Monk by his comrades for his ability to resist sexual urges, but this little honey-haired blonde, with her bright eyes, perky smile, expressive lips and button nose, the way she carried herself so gracefully, yet confidently, the very epitome of femininity in his estimation—might change that. Who was she? She had to be fem to be in the Diplo Corps but he had never before found a fem even remotely attractive.

"Lieutenant, I asked you a question."

"Yes," replied Raylar, responding stiffly to his superior, "I would."

"You're afraid you'd fuck her in deep space, is that it?"

By the Code—what had gotten into the General? This was hardly the way for a man of his station to speak. Still, there was no evading the truth of his words. Yes, he was afraid of precisely that. "Sir, things happen to a man's mind out there, you know that. Inhibitions are lowered. Judgment can be impaired in the middle of all that blackness, so far from Earth."

Theron inclined his head. "Fair enough. Suppose I told you, though, that the Corps would look the other way? That whatever happened consensually between you and this Seria would never be held against you? That it would be considered part of your restorative therapy?"

"Sex-making with a *fem*? While on duty?" Raylar attempted to keep his voice steady. This couldn't be any more wrong. Under no circumstances should a primale touch a fem, much less when both were in service. "Sir, is this some kind of a test? To see if I am worthy to stay in the Strike Force? Because if that's the case, I can assure you I am committed to maintaining the required celibacy."

"I don't doubt your commitment, son. But celibacy isn't right for everyone. Especially not for commanders and generals. Great warriors need women. Mates to go home to."

Raylar's confusion continued to mount. He was anything but a great warrior. "Are you ordering me to mate, Sir? Am I being transferred from the Strike Force? If so, than why do you not send me for an obedient?"

"Slow down, Raylar. Your mind is racing too far ahead. All I am saying is that I want you to let nature take its course. If Seria does nothing for you, then there is no harm. But if you do feel something, if you find someone to be happy with, what loss can that be?"

"Sir," he pleaded, "I already feel things. Inappropriate things."

"I'll bet you do." He smiled. "Ah, to be young as you again, Raylar. I can tell you the things I would do to Seria in your place. I would sweep her right off those pretty feet of hers. I'd make love to her like there was no tomorrow until she couldn't even think the name of another male. She's something special, son. I've met her. She's sweet, smart as a whip, loyal as hell. Has a lot in common with my lifemate, actually."

Raylar's eyes kept drifting back to the holoid. Life-size, perfect, and sexually appealing. Just the kind of body he'd always had a weakness for. Willowy, lush, but not too lush. Shapely, but lean at the same time. And fit—she looked very fit. Like she could make sex for hours at a time. Or run through a jungle, nude, the dew and sweat collecting on her perfect skin. He'd always had that fantasy, of tracking down a female for capture and sex. Running her to the point of collapse, or wrestling her to the ground, pinning her panting body underneath his.

His primale eyes and primale erection letting her know he meant business. One word on his lips.

Submit.

His pretty, naked capture, spreading her legs, wet and ready to take him, on his terms...for their mutual pleasure.

"Sir, I really don't think I'm right for this."

"I think you're perfect, Lieutenant." The General's tone brooked no argument. "You will leave in the morning. You may consider Seria formally in your charge, as of this moment."

His cock throbbed at the possibilities. "In my charge? Now?"

"That's what I said. She will be meeting you in the lounge of the Comestitorium, along with Nyssa. I'll join you presently. They will be late of course because they're women. We'll all have dinner and then you will take Seria out dancing on your own, show her a nice time. A room has been reserved for you in Cylinder Prime. You'll leave from there first thing tomorrow morning for the rocket port. Any questions?"

Yes, he felt like replying. *Why are you suddenly acting like a sorry version of a primale matchmaking robot instead of a Guardian?*

"No questions, Sir."

"Good. You may consider yourself dismissed."

Raylar saluted crisply and spun on his heel. He was grateful for this simple action to perform, rote and military and predictable. So unlike the situation he was about to be plunged into.

"Lieutenant, one more thing."

Raylar spun back around at the door, at attention. "Sir?"

"You'll have fun with Seria, but when it comes to the mission, you're in charge. You're security liaison. She takes orders from you, start to finish."

He tried to imagine a fem taking orders. Never mind, the General had said his piece—the rest was Raylar's problem. "Yes, Sir."

"And you have my permission to do what you need to enforce that."

"Sir?"

"She's a woman, Raylar, use your imagination."

"I prefer not to, Sir. It gets me in trouble."

"Blast it, man, must I spell everything out for you?" the General growled, his eyes still lit with a sparkle of mischief. "If the lassie gets out of hand, you put her over your knee."

Spanking. He was talking about spanking an officer of the Diplomatic Corps.

"Ten or so good smacks will get a woman in line. Works wonders on my Nyssa—makes her hot as hell, too, but I'll have you court-martialed if you repeat that to a living soul, got it?"

"No, Sir. I mean yes, Sir."

This was a dream, that was it. Any minute he would wake up on his bunk at the restorative center, fresh and ready for a ten-mile cyber resistance run.

There wasn't only the dream of the crazy General to contend with, though. There was the other dream, centered on that holoid, smiling at him from where the wall was supposed to be. The image of beautiful Seria, whom he would soon meet in the flesh, and who would soon be in his charge. Under his command and subject to his discipline.

Sexually available, too, if he could manage her seduction.

How easy was the General making this? He was practically ordering him to make sex with her, throwing in every kind of tantalizing enticement. Her ass, no doubt as gorgeous as the rest of her, literally was his. If she did not conform to mission requirements, as he defined them, she would find it reddened, and promptly.

He would spank her until she said she was sorry and promised to do better.

Seria…over his knee, his hard-on raging, pushing up against her pelvis, letting her know of his power and his desire. Ten strokes, the General had said. She would probably beg him to stop before then. She would squirm. That would feel good. Athletic Seria, lean and healthy, a good, fit woman, finding her place. Under his hand.

I'm sorry, Raylar. I'll try to do better.

Those sweet lips, offering a humble apology. Would he dare to order her to kiss him? Primales were magnets for women's lips. She wouldn't resist him. That was a fact, not a boast. Fem or not, he could have her. The question was why? Was he supposed to find happiness with a woman who could be his equal or superior?

His cock was going in and out of her hot, open sex in his mind. Seria was moaning to him, and none of the rest mattered. His teeth were sunk into one of those nipples, hidden under that turquoise, slinky dress. What would she sound like in orgasm? Better even than she would sound being punished.

"All right, then," Theron nodded, "off with you. Your woman is waiting. And put on something appropriate, like your dress uniform."

"Yes, Sir." *His* woman. What was the General saying? And why did he feel like he had just been hit by an iceberg—a conversation where only ten percent of what was really going on was actually being said?

Here he had been summoned for what he'd thought was a simple debriefing with the CO on the new Narthian weapons and instead he would be playing babysitter to a female diplomat and going to dinner with the Head of the Council.

Talk about a strange turn of events.

Things had gotten so strange, in fact, that he was beginning to wonder if he wouldn't be better off back in therapy with the nagging doctors at restorative care.

Then again, he could look at all this as punishment—part of what he deserved for being such a poor officer. Even worse than he'd imagined, according to the General.

But the General didn't want him punished. He wanted him having a good time. With a blonde named Seria who had managed to do something no other woman ever had. Namely give him a full erection without physical contact.

And in a meeting with the highest of his bosses, too.

That might not be the stuff lifemating was made of, but it sure promised some good times in bed. If he actually got her that far without taking her.

Maybe he would get lucky and the holoid would prove old or out of focus. Maybe she would look like a Narthian queen up close.

Yeah, and maybe primales would learn to beg their women for sex instead of seducing them with utter dominance.

Either one was a complete and utter impossibility.

By the Code, he prayed to the ancient Spirit of the Guardians, *let me get through this mission alive. And back to the battlefield. Where I belong.*

Chapter Two

ຄວ

Seria felt naked in the ruby gown. She was not entirely sure it would even be legal in every star system. With every breath she feared the crossed swaths of material that constituted the front of the thing would slip to the sides, exposing her breasts. There were also the slits to be considered, and the plunging back that exposed her nearly to the buttocks.

"Now *that* will make Raylar sit up and take notice," Nyssa approved as her newfound sister emerged for the tenth time from the auto-dresser.

So far Nyssa had rejected every outfit she had chosen for herself out of the dressmaking machine, claiming it was too "blah" or too "camp", or too something else. Finally she had gotten Seria to agree to let her design one and this was the scandalous result.

It would never do. Clearly it was too sexy, and therefore far too dangerous to wear around a primale. Red-blooded and single.

"What do you think?" Nyssa asked, as Seria looked herself up and down in the mirror.

Seria turned redder than the gown at the sight of her own reflection. What kind of woman would Raylar think she was? He might think she wanted to please him with her figure, or even entice him into sex-making with his hard, muscular, perfect primale body.

"What I think, Nyssa, is that I am going to change again or else have the machine make a wrap to go over this."

"Where's your sense of adventure?" Nyssa pouted.

"I don't have any. I'm in the Diplomatic Corps. We do things by the holobook, remember? I don't see why I can't just wear my dress uniform, anyway."

"Stop being such a prude, sis. You're not trying to wow him with career skills, you're supposed to be making him want to have you naked at his feet, your hair balled up in his fist—a hot, needy little obedient."

"That's a disgusting image," said Seria, though it made her pussy warm and tingly and turned her spine to mush nonetheless. "Besides, I'm only half obedient, so we definitely don't want to go getting the man too riled up."

Nyssa re-crossed her legs over on the nearby grooming seat, allowing the small pedicure robot access to the toes of her other foot. "Don't we, sis? So you can honestly tell me it doesn't arouse you to think of Raylar so out of his mind with desire for you that he pushes you against a wall, rips that fabulous rag off your trembling body and has his way with you, right there in the restaurant?"

Seria's pussy clenched. She was overcome with a wave of pleasure so intense it was as if Raylar had his hands all over her, imprinting, marking. Owning. Hastily, she scooted back under the dome of the machine and ordered a wrap to cover her trembling skin under the provocative garment.

"And don't think a primale wouldn't do it," warned Nyssa when she came back out. "I may rule the Council, but Theron rules my body. To love he must own and when he wants me, I am his. Anytime, anywhere. Raylar will be no different. In bed you'll be his slave, Seria, so you might as well get used to it. But it's worth it, trust me. The way he will look at you, the way he will touch and possess. He will revere you, cherish you, and oh, stars, will he turn you on. I resisted the full depth of primale treatment at first, but my man broke me down. Trained me. I know, it sounds animalistic. But trust me, on the other side of your shattered pride, in the heat of your sexual humiliation there is an ecstasy beyond words, like all your deepest fantasies come to life as he makes you feel like the only woman in the galaxy. The only one he's chaining and disciplining, anyway."

"Disciplining?" Seria's cheeks turned a shade paler, inducing the miniature hovering makeup robot to spray on a little more rouge.

Nyssa laughed. She had two drinks in her hands, rainbow sparklers—a whirl of bubbly colors in fluted glasses. "Primales are hands-on with their women, sis." She handed Seria one of the flavorful, intoxicating beverages—something Seria desperately needed. "I can argue until the cows come home and sometimes I win, but when it comes to matters in our personal sphere, my hubby won't hesitate to take me over his knee. I've been paddled and caned on occasion, too, but that's pretty rare. Still, I know he won't hesitate if he thinks I deserve it."

Seria's jaw dropped. The fluted glass nearly went with it. "But that's...so demeaning for a woman in your place."

Nyssa offered a catlike grin. "I know. And it turns me on like hell. He takes advantage of that, too, the rogue. He's really a big pussycat, but all he has to do is say my name in that certain tone of voice, and I'm totally helpless, space putty in his hands. I know he's gone totally primale on me and there's nothing to do but obey the man completely and perfectly and hope he will give me relief without teasing me too terribly first."

Seria gulped down her drink and pushed images of herself submitting to Raylar from her mind. She hadn't even met the man. She didn't even know what he looked like in person or what it might be like to shake his hand. How could she think about having to obey him as his sexual possession— cherished and adored, but still owned nonetheless? What if she didn't want to be taken anytime or anywhere? What if she didn't want to have to be accountable to his will? What if she couldn't bear to be spanked, or stars forbid, paddled?

Never mind that she was practically squirming thinking about Raylar having that kind of power over her and wanting her so much as to accept nothing less than her ownership.

Something occurred to her. "Nyssa, you have primale blood. Doesn't that make it hard for you to be in the role of sexual obedient?"

"It makes me fight harder, sure. Theron loves the challenge. He also says it makes it ten times sweeter when he conquers me. And it's something he gets to do again and again, too. I'd be lying if I said I didn't love it. Drives me right out of my mind. The most excruciating thing is when he tells me ahead of time what he's going to do. Like when we're sitting or standing there, engaged in some high-level meeting or negotiation and he will lean over and whisper in my ear that in half an hour I am going to be naked, bound and on my knees sucking his mammoth erection. I know how much he wants it, and how he loves that power and I just get off on it. And stars, if he ever says what he intends to do to me while I'm bound up, well, I don't even want to go there."

Seria didn't either. "Another drink, please, Nyssa?" She held out her empty glass.

It was a good thing they were alone right now in Nyssa's specially reserved apartment getting ready for this dinner. Seria really couldn't face anyone else now. Least of all Theron, or precocious little Theryssa. The child would have way too many questions about why she was shaking and flushed and so on and she would have no answers to offer that were appropriate to her age.

As it was, from the very first introduction earlier today, Theryssa had talked her ear off about how they were related and how there was going to be a mating ceremony soon for Seria and "a very handsome Guardian". Could she be a flower girl? the five-year-old had wanted to know, and could she dance with the bride *and* the groom?

"Don't pester your aunt," Theron had said with an attempt at paternal sternness, his tone indicating that his daughter probably had him wrapped around her little finger. "She's only just met us and she hasn't even met her fiancé yet."

Theryssa grinned mischievously and jumped into the arms of her tall, uniformed father. "Okay, Daddy. Can I pester you?"

Nyssa, who had finished her own drink as well, produced two more from the objectifier on the wall. It took but five seconds for the machine to produce the beverages, glasses and all, using nothing but raw molecules.

"My relationship with Theron has been unique," Nyssa speculated, offering Seria the replacement. "His love for me has meant he has had to compromise like no other primale in history. I worry sometimes, if I truly give him all he needs, but he tells me he would have no other woman on the planet. If I am not satisfied, he says, he would die. And I have no reason to doubt him."

"He must really love you." That much Seria could envy. She had always wanted a man who would put her above everything. Who would love her so much that he would move heaven to see to her fulfillment. Even as he had his way with her…ravishing her very soul.

Nyssa glowed like a bride on her wedding night, all this despite her sophistication, worldliness and wit. "I like to think so. I'm kind of fond of him, too. Even when he's being a sadistic bastard, pulling his little primale mind games on me."

"Mind games?" Seria's nipples tightened under her dress. This was an area that turned her on and frightened her at the same time. Though she had shared this with no one, she frequently had fantasies where boyfriends and older men took control of her in certain ways. Manipulating, and teasing.

"They all do it, the primales do," explained Nyssa. "Although I have no clue how Raylar's tastes go. I suspect you'll learn a lot together, as he discovers your vulnerabilities, your hot buttons. Mine is loss of sexual control. I fucking hate it, but I need it. Theron's developed this absolutely diabolical way to control my orgasms. I like to think it's my gift to him, because I love him, but he makes me acknowledge that I have been trained, like some kind of freaking pet osilox. I can't even come when I masturbate, even if I wanted to, because he's inside my head so much making me need him.

"I can be right there on the edge of the biggest climax of my life, and I'll be stuck, without that little nod of approval. On the other hand, he can make me climax without touching me, whether or not I happen to want to at the time. It doesn't matter what I feel—once the trigger word hits his lips I am down for the count. And don't think he won't do it to me in public, either. I have had to get real good at hiding them. I've often wondered over the years how many people have seen me squirming in my seat at meetings wondering what was the matter with me."

Seria was laughing in spite of herself. She couldn't help it, all the emotion of this incredible day was catching up to her. "Oh...god..." she exclaimed, on the verge of hyperventilating.

"What is it, sis?" Nyssa asked, a bit concerned. "Are you all right?"

"I'm...fine," she cried, the words coming in short bursts. "It's just that...here you are telling me...I am about to be thrown to a wolf...and you are making me look so sexy. But the truth is...I'm a..."

"You're a virgin," Nyssa finished the thought. "I gathered as much."

"Yes...that's it." She was practically in hysterics, though deep down, her belly was roiling and she was more eager, scared and lightheaded than she had ever felt in her life. "Isn't that silly...at my age?"

It wasn't the artificially composed alcohol getting to her, either. It was him. Raylar, the gorgeous, intense as a supernova Guardian, who somehow had managed to plant himself in her mind. And loins.

Nyssa gathered her sister into her arms. "You are such a delight, you know that, Seria? And of course it's not silly. It's your destiny. Raylar is to be your first. And your last. Now how about we finish getting you ready? What would you say to a new hair color? Something a little more daring?"

Seria nodded, stunned. Why not? What did she have to lose?

Just her independence, her virginity…and her heart.

All in one night, too, if Nyssa and Theron had their way.

"I have another idea, too," said the mischievous, matchmaking Nyssa. "The perfect accessory designed to send the perfect message."

Seria looked at the beautiful gemmed necklace, a fortune in cut stones of every color fused together into a breathtaking whole.

"You like?" Nyssa asked.

"Like" didn't begin to cut it. "It's…it's gorgeous," she said. Seria did have one question, though. The length of it was far too short for a conventional necklace. "Is it what I think it is?"

"Lift your hair," said Nyssa, coming up behind her.

Seria held her breath as her newfound sister encircled her throat with the fabulous choker. Her blood raced at the implications…

So like a collar, marking her, bonding her. She let her fingers stray to her throat. Her pussy spasmed as if she had touched herself there instead.

"Let me see." Nyssa had her turn around.

Seria reddened under the woman's gaze. Nyssa was seeing her as Raylar would, or any other primale.

"Yes, that's just what we needed," Nyssa concurred. "Raylar won't be able to help having ideas for you after seeing you like this."

Seria shivered ever so slightly in anticipation. *That's just what I'm afraid of,* she thought as Nyssa took her to the grooming machine for her promised hair change.

* * * * *

Raylar could barely breathe. Seeing Seria walk into the lobby of the Comestitorium was like a sucker punch to the heart. He had thought seeing her ahead of time in holoid form would protect him to some extent from the effects of her beauty, but he was dead wrong. She was ten times the woman in person, and a hundred times more dazzling.

She had certainly gone to a lot of trouble for the occasion. Her hair, changed from gold to shimmering silver and swept high on her pretty head was like a goddess's and that dress—it was like something off a hologrid play. She was wearing a choker, too, giving a subtle but very real indication of what she might look like in a collar.

Any man would kill for a woman like this—that was the bottom line.

He did not read her as a femme fatale, however. If anything, she was shy as hell, completely vulnerable. In fact, he was virtually certain the dress, incredibly sleek and revealing and red, was someone else's idea. Which would explain why she was hugging herself to death, trying to hide everything under that wrap.

Well, it wasn't working. She could be wearing an old sack or a tarp and still raise the dead. In fact seeing her try to conceal her sexiness so much only made him want to grab her all the more, to sweep her into his arms and try out those pouting red lips.

"Lieutenant Raylar," the General said in introduction. "This is Fem Seria, of the Diplomatic Corps."

"It is my honor to serve, Fem Seria." He took her hand, offering the standard greeting.

Seria was redder than her dress. "The service is mine, Primale Raylar," she murmured.

By the Code, she was as timorous and exciting as an obedient. He found himself holding onto her warm little hand, so very vibrant and alive. She offered no resistance as he held onto her hand just a little too long. Was he only imagining this lightning zap in their interchange—a deeper meaning in her reply that went beyond mere formula?

The service was hers...

Exactly what service was she prepared to render and for how long?

"And this other beauty is my wife," said the General. "The Honorable Fem Nyssa, Head of the Council."

"I don't think your young officer is much interested in me at the moment," teased Nyssa. "He seems otherwise occupied."

Raylar tore himself from Seria's gaze. She had the most complicated and alluring expression he had ever seen on a woman. She was a wide-open holobook, her beautiful cobalt blue eyes totally defenseless and yet their depths were so great he doubted he could sort it all out in a hundred years.

What was going on? She wanted to be here...then again she didn't. She seemed to be debating spilling her guts about something or running away to the nearest deep tunnel. The pieces didn't add up. Had she been given the same sort of bizarre instructions about the mission as he had received? Was she supposed to be looking at this as a sex-making opportunity, too?

If so this was going to be one long, hopelessly mixed-up night. Not to mention the space flight tomorrow.

"It is my honor to serve, Fem Nyssa." He took the slightly older woman's hand. No spark now, only the firm, polite grip of a fellow citizen.

"The service is mine." She smiled cheekily. "Now, how about we get right to dinner so we can get it over with and let you and Seria move on to the fun stuff? Theron, I trust you have a table ready?'

Raylar winced. Obviously the General's wife was as direct as he was. Looks like the dinner battle would be fought on two fronts, he thought grimly.

The robot *maitre d'* led them to a fine corner table, right against the window. They could see the entire bottom of the city from here, clear across to the far side of the dome. The dome was just settling into twilight colors, yellow swathed with red and orange. The stars would be up soon, a complete laser replica of the Earth's sky at night. There was no telling the difference with the naked eye, though Raylar always felt a little trapped beneath these domed cities. It might have been the effect of having spent so much time in the freedom of deep space or maybe it was just his personality.

The table was a floating disc, the latest piece of autoserve technology. The chairs floated up silently behind them to relieve their buttocks and push them underneath. Raylar was next to Seria, close enough to touch her.

"Welcome," the table said in a smooth, ringing baritone. "Would you like to start with some drinks?"

Nyssa ordered first, selecting a glass of wine. She convinced Theron to order the same. Raylar went next, choosing a simple glass of cran-beer instead. The desired beverages appeared instantly in front of them. Autoserve tables had objectifiers built in, which meant you could have absolutely anything, no waiting.

"I'll have a cran-beer, too," said Seria, declining to follow Nyssa's choice of wine.

Raylar's cock, already half aroused, stiffened a little more. Whether she realized it or not, this fem diplomat was sending out strong submissive signals. Her gestures, the way she carried herself and now this—effectively deferring to him for her choice of drinks.

"A toast," pronounced Nyssa. "To fate...with a little helping hand."

All four held up their glasses in tandem. The High Councilor really was a beautiful woman, he thought, with her slinky black dress and jet-black hair. General Theron, sitting in his gold-buttoned dress uniform with more medals than he could count was certainly a lucky man. But Nyssa didn't do it for Raylar, not like Seria.

Raylar observed Seria stiffen, subtly, but perceptibly at the toast.

"To fate," they all repeated.

Raylar was doing it again. Reading Seria like an open holobook, seeing below that incredible exterior to her hidden soul. She was decidedly uneasy. Wrestling with something. Once again, he had the distinct feeling there were things she knew about this mission that he did not.

He didn't like that feeling one bit. If she intended to hold out on him, leave him dangling while they traveled through the dark depths of space, she was sorely mistaken.

Raylar felt a little jolt at the word sorely. Theron's injunction came to mind. He could take this woman in hand if need be. Seria was his. To punish. That pert little bottom, no farther away than the range of his own breath, could be rendered as red as that tantalizing dress of hers anytime he designated.

"Another toast," declared Theron.

Seria's glass was still touching Raylar's. Their fingers were nearly in contact, so close to intertwining. He couldn't take his eyes off them, so slender, and that delicately extended wrist, too, so different from his own, so dainty. What would it look like, along with its companion, bound in leather or locked in polysteel? At his mercy, along with the rest of her, every incredible curvaceous inch of her fem-flesh.

"To duty and to service."

"To duty and to service," they all agreed.

The rest of dinner went smoothly. Theron ordered on their behalf, choosing a selection of delicacies from across the galaxy. Nyssa was clearly proud of her husband's ability to orchestrate such a feast. Raylar made a point of complimenting the general on a job well done.

"Oh, yes, I agree," said Seria, softly echoing his words.

Raylar clenched his teeth. If she had any idea how much her acquiescence made him want to throw her down over the table this instant and have his way with her...

Did she want that at some level, he wondered, despite her initial shyness and reticence? It was definitely puzzling. Seria obviously had a mind of her own, carrying on a wonderful conversation with them, but why did she keep throwing off these signals to him, casting little glances to determine his reaction to things before reacting herself? And why the hard nipples, which seemed to be ending up more and more aimed in his direction as the cran-beers disappeared and the wrap slipped imperceptibly down over her creamy shoulders?

At a certain point, Nyssa—who had partaken liberally of her wine—announced her intention to go to the "little fems' room" and inquired as to whether Seria would like to come. Women always went in packs, so he was hardly surprised when she said yes. What caught him off guard was how she said it.

"Okay, sis." She grinned. "Sounds like a plan."

Theron frowned heavily as soon as she said it, confirming Raylar's suspicions that it was no mere idle reference to their common gender. "I didn't realize they were in the same cluster as children, Sir," Raylar said as soon as the ladies were out of range.

"Their backgrounds aren't important," he said, ending the conversation. "Just focus on the present. And what you intend to do with your lovely date before morning."

Or do to her...

47

"Yes, Sir," he replied, fearing that he might be blushing as much or more than Seria had.

He had ideas, all right. The question was would he be bold enough, or foolish enough, to carry them out.

* * * * *

Nyssa was playful and randy all the way home from the restaurant. Theron gave her leeway, allowing her to kick off her shoes and sidle up against him in the two-seater aircar, though he denied her contact with his already straining cock. Blast the woman and her deviously sexy ways. How was he supposed to remain stern and give her the punishment she deserved?

"Don't Raylar and Seria make a fabulous couple, baby?" she crooned, nibbling at his neck in that way that always drove him crazy.

His hands stiffened on the wheel. Theron was one of the few officers, not to mention one of the few citizens, who insisted on driving his own vehicle. He took it as a point of independence. Nyssa claimed he was just stubborn. "Obviously, they do, Nyssa. The geneticists intended it that way."

She ran her hand over his chest. "Why so grumpy, General?"

"That's enough," he said sharply. "Put your hands in your lap and we will discuss the matter."

Nyssa complied, though she was anything but chastised. "Did I forget to line up your socks again this morning?" she teased, the most delicious pout on her face. "Is the big bad primale going to spank me?"

"You know perfectly well I have the domestic droids line up my socks, woman. This is far more serious. I want to know what you told Seria about her background."

"Just what we talked about," Nyssa said. "More or less."

"I'm thinking more," he grumbled, angling the aircar to the right, cutting an invisible path through the quiet, cool pseudo-night blackness. He had a detour in mind, one he would keep to himself. "In particular, the part about you being her biological sister."

Nyssa, too tipsy to notice the deviation in course, moved to kiss him again, her wicked female hands back out of her lap and looking for mischief. "It might have slipped, honey. But I thought she had a right to know."

Theron resorted to a simple but effective primale technique. "Hands in your lap, woman." He found her nipple through the sleek black dress out of sheer instinct. "Now."

Nyssa gasped. It wasn't just the immediate pressure he was applying, but all the sense memories it evoked from their long, complex history. The domination, the impressing of his sexual will on hers, the intimate connection they shared that no other would ever understand.

"Theron..." she sighed, leaning back in her seat, back arched, her body paradoxically lax and tense at the same time. Her eyes were liquid and wild. He could smell her heat, like an alley cat. His very own tigress, tamed as much or as little as he desired.

"We agreed to tell the two of them only that there was an opportunity being presented, if they wished, to mate," Theron confirmed. "I followed my part of things, but you went further, in direct violation of our agreement, you let Seria know our secret plans."

"I did," Nyssa moaned as he rolled the nipple between thumb and forefinger, keeping his eye on the open air in front of them. He knew from the feel of her, from the sound of her breathing she was close to coming already. He also knew she would wait.

Because she belonged to him and him alone. "Remove your dress, Nyssa."

"Yes, Theron." There was no place for argument or debate here. A primale's woman, Council Head or not, remained clothed only by his whim. If he wished to display her beauty, stripping her in an aircar a quarter mile above the city or in a crowded robo-ball stadium, that was his affair.

So were all matters of punishment, corporal or otherwise.

Nyssa wore no undergarments. Theron didn't allow it. He wanted her accessible at all times, her mind as close to the idea of being taken, as was her body. She balked on occasion, but what woman really hated knowing that she was being outfitted to match her mate's constant, uncompromising sexual desire for her?

And want her Theron did, night and day, near and far. He wanted her when she was good, and even more when she was bad and willful. Like now. Oh, she had her reasons. They had gone over this before. Nyssa had felt that for Seria to be an effective seductress she needed to know the full score. She also felt it wasn't fair to completely blindside both of them.

As a matter of public policy, the decision would have been hers, but he had trumped her, citing the matter of blood connection. This was ultimately a family matter and as such, the sway was his.

Or so he'd thought.

His vixen pulled the black dress up to her waist and lifted it over her head. He nearly crashed, so distracted was he by the sight of her lithe body, contorting deliciously in the process. Nyssa was as enticingly fit as the day he had met her. Each added year only brought out her beauty more, like a fine wine. He could not wait to see her reach her prime. She would be truly regal, like her mother, the Former High Councilor Dekalia.

"Throw it in back," he instructed as she held out the slinky piece of cloth.

She did so, rendering herself completely exposed and helpless. Never had she looked so stunning in his eyes, so soulfully lovely and erotic.

"What are you going to do to me?" she asked, her eyes a mix of trepidation and wild eagerness.

"I'm going to remind you who is the male in this relationship and who is the female."

"Yes, husband." Her lips curled, just at the corners, as if to say, bring it on.

Theron did not need any further encouragement. He peeled the opening in his dress uniform trousers, the one covering his crotch. His primale cock emerged, hard as polysteel. Nyssa sucked her lower lip as she saw he had expanded it to full size. Admittedly, the ability to control the size of his erections was not one of the most noble of his primale superpowers, but it was one of the most fun to use.

"Suck," he commanded.

"Yes," she whispered, devotion and awe in her eyes. "My husband."

Nyssa rarely applied this title to him. It was an old one, not often used anymore. She had chosen it herself, as a way to convey what she felt at times like this—not the full slavish attachment of an obedient, but something much more intimate and biological than the mere mating of equals.

Theron groaned softly as she applied that silver tongue of hers. One long lick around the head of his cock, like an ice-cream cone. He knew how much she loved this, so it was a little hard to justify it as punishment. If anything it was a reminder of his power. Nothing put a woman more quickly in her place than reddening her behind and putting her on her knees in front of a monster hard-on, one she could never dream of taking fully into her throat. Sometimes she would beg him to get this big, so she could worship at his temple, as he called it. Mostly, he kept to a more moderate size, so he could get deeper.

The oral sex was not one-way, of course. Primales also had excellent tongue muscles and a capacity for muscular control that was capable of blasting any female into orbit and keeping her there.

Nyssa applied herself well, her belly heated by the wine and her mind heated by the anticipation of some devilish new torture ahead. He had to be careful not to come too quickly and spoil the fun. He let her lick him up and down, nibbling along the vein on the underside. He caressed her silky hair, long and black for the occasion. Tomorrow it might be short, blue, or gold, depending on her mood. By the Code, how he adored this woman. So very alive and fiercely proud and smart.

He would never admit it, but if Nyssa's instincts had told her she should tell Seria about her lineage, than she was right to go with them. Nyssa was a wise woman. Though he would by law have to obey any Council Head, he sincerely believed she was the best qualified, the one person worthy of following.

Frankly, this whole business between Seria and Raylar had him a little uneasy. He was supposed to be running a military Corps, not a matchmaking service. But Raylar was an important man, much more important than he realized, and his happiness was vital to his ability to utilize his unique gifts as a battlefield commander. Like it or not, having Seria as his own would make all the difference.

If only there was some more open, straightforward way to introduce Raylar to his destiny. Theron's own mentor and superior General Morax had had no such qualms, of course, in setting him up with Nyssa. Was he sorry for that? Of course not. Would he have mated with Nyssa otherwise? Probably not. He had planned on military celibacy, like Raylar. Obviously, they had done him the best favor of his life, but the ethics still troubled him a bit.

Even more disturbing was the fact that he had actually enjoyed himself in dealing with Raylar. The young man really would be lucky to have Seria and it was fun to have a bit of a helping hand. In effect giving the straight-arrow lieutenant permission to play the part of predator.

Were he a different sort of general, he might simply order the Guardian to mate for life. He had suggested this, but Nyssa had pitched a fit. She'd called him pigheaded, unimaginative and insensitive to Seria's feelings.

So telling her everything was better? Giving her the blunt, almost cynical truth that she would never really have a choice as to who to feel for in life?

There was the fact of Seria's hybrid background to consider, though. This was something only Nyssa could truly understand. Theron had been specially engineered from anonymous donors, but the mix was a standard primale one. Seria was a combination of sub-genders, just like Nyssa.

Theron had taken much time with his lifemate, helping her to feel fully secure in this. He would never permit her to feel like a freak. He had single-handedly hunted down the members of the secret society opposed to hybrids, eliminating all except Malthusalas himself, the ringleader. This one failure on his part haunted him, night and day.

It was a reminder of several things, including his own imperfection. No, he could not fault his wife for going against their agreement and revealing herself to her sister. She had suffered the loneliness of being the only one of her kind too long. And she could not bear to see another suffer, even if only out of ignorance of her true nature.

Still, he had his authority to consider.

Besides, if he backed down on punishing Nyssa now, she would kill him.

"We are going to the woods," he told her.

She shivered slightly. Her mouth slackened and she took him deeper. They had been to the woods—in various locations—many times before. As much as anything it was a metaphor for that part of their relationship where she was most in the position of slave and he in the position of Master.

Things happened in the woods. Primal things. Sexual conquests, sweating and heaving in the dirt, heavy bondage over rocks and hanging from trees, and the delicious sting of the switch, the fresh, whiplike branches cut down with Theron's own knife.

He had seen Nyssa go half mad with lust in settings like this, breasts heaving as she begged to be thrown down and taken. Hard—primale hard.

Theron moaned, letting her know she was pleasing him. Taking hold of her mane of hair, he balled it up lightly, lovingly. Up and down, the rhythm passionate, intense.

He resisted climax, holding out until landing.

Theron set the aircar down in a dirt clearing, surrounded by tall pine trees. Small branches crunched under the flat pads of the landing gear. An owl hooted as he slid the bubble open, exposing them to open air.

Nyssa stopped sucking his cock and cuddled against his chest. There was a light chill, perfectly in keeping with the climate of a deciduous forest in springtime. Everything here was synthesized, of course, though it would take a damn fine biologist or molecular physicist to tell the difference.

This particular mini-forest was reserved for Council use. He gave the verbal order, announcing to the unseen computer that it was now occupied. Anyone else flying overhead would see only gray clouds.

Theron thought of Seria and Raylar again. They would be out right now, enjoying the awkward thrill of first meeting. Would passion ignite there, under the bright lights of the Dome, before morning? Or would it occur in the depths of space, as they found themselves unable to resist entwining, mentally and physically, until ultimately, they combusted, as he and Nyssa had.

Maybe they would be strong enough to resist all that. In which case, they would resort to more desperate measures. The backup plan involved a false stranding at their destination, a created situation of Adam and Eve type isolation. For as long as needed, the two would remain in splendid isolation until they had bonded.

Did Seria know every detail? He would have to ascertain this. He doubted Nyssa had gone that far. One thing he was sure she would never divulge was the real cause of the urgency of getting these two together.

It wasn't just about true love and happiness — it was a matter of galactic security. They needed Raylar sharp and ready to go, cured of his trauma. For unbeknownst to all but a select few, the small Narthian force Raylar had encountered on Rensus Nine with its super-weapons was the vanguard of a new attack army. A test force, designed to probe the humans' weaknesses.

Raylar's force had fought them off, but they would be back. And if the Guardians were not ready, they would have a new war on their hands that they might not be able to win.

Theron shut off the aircar and climbed out of the driver's side. Nyssa was waiting for his direction, eyes imploring. He knew how badly she wanted to touch herself right now, almost as much as she needed to be denied. Helping her from the vehicle, he allowed her to plant her feet, one by one on the dirt. The earthiness always turned her on. It was a part of the package.

"Fuck me," she begged, pressing her bosom against his chest. "Right here on the ground. Use me."

"No." Theron spun her about, pinning her arm up behind her back. "Not until I say."

"Yes…" she hissed, her own subjugation arousing her all the more.

He pressed her over the hood of the machine, smooth and warm. "Spread," he ordered, giving her a firm smack on the ass.

She inched her feet apart, exposing her pussy and delicate anal opening. Unable to resist himself, he slid a finger against her clitoris, maneuvering it to erection. "You'll take my hand, Nyssa, against your ass, then you'll take my cock."

"Oh, god…yes, please," she groaned, extending her arms in front of her, palms down on the metal. "Do it."

"You disobeyed me." He cracked his hand hard against her firm flesh. "You need discipline."

"Fuck, yes…discipline me," she egged him on.

What a glorious creature she was. How utterly suited to meet his every need, and challenge his every male impulse. He never tired of this, never tired of her. Each time was like the first as he probed ever deeper into her infinite, incredible soul.

She squirmed hotly as he continued his lover's assault, warming her posterior, his spanking intermixed with teasing of her dripping pussy. By the tenth smack, she was twitching, her ass pushed out in delightful confusion, unable to distinguish pain from pleasure.

"Oh, Theron," she begged penetration from his cock, "put me in my place. Teach me obedience."

He had to smile at this. His Nyssa would never obey. She was fem and primale, in a most volatile mix. Defiance was in her nature and he would have it no other way. His job was to protect and encourage her bold femininity. But there would always be this between them, too. The dance, the endless play. The give and take. They needed each other, their bodies, and their different wisdoms.

Each without the other would be lost. Nyssa needed to feel the power of a strong man, but it had to be one who loved and cherished her absolutely and understood her uniqueness. And Theron needed to know his was the finest woman in the universe, the most wonderfully delightful and exasperating. The only one truly worth having.

"You are my world, Nyssa," he sighed, falling into her. "You and Theryssa." Theron's cock was hard and ready and magically exposed from the work of his fingers. He had barely been aware of what they were doing, not until he had found his way to her labia.

"You're mine, too, baby." She turned her head back, reaching for him.

Theron slid commandingly and satisfyingly into the depths of Nyssa's sex. She took him straight to the hilt.

"Am I good for you, baby? Am I good?" She needed to know.

He pulled her upright, encircling her breasts from behind. "You please me very much, sweetheart."

Nyssa melted against him, as enveloped as she was impaled. He knew how she never tired of hearing those words. To the rest of the world she was the strong leader, doing what suited her own will and judgment and requiring others to follow. But with Theron she was free to express that other part of herself — the flesh and blood woman who wanted to turn her man on, who wanted to be the little sexual toy who provided him endless amusement.

He cherished this side of her, as he did a million others — childish, proud and selfish, generous, silly, and all the rest.

"Come inside me, husband?" Her arm snaked behind his neck. He was inhaling her fragrance, tasting the silky hair at the back of her head.

"Yes," he hissed, swelling his cock in anticipation. "I will come inside you, my love. And you will come with me. At the same time."

Even were she not trained so completely to the lead of his voice and body, she would never have been able to resist. Nyssa said it was her love that made her this way now, though he sometimes wondered if some of it still wasn't about his powers.

That was one of the drawbacks of being primale. Always wondering if a woman is subdued truly by you, or only by your abilities in bed.

Nyssa would help him with this, telling him often how she loved him. Thus did they work on each other's insecurities. They were breathing so tightly against each other, their heartbeats so frantic, he didn't know if he would be able to let go of her long enough to establish a rhythm. He might just spill his seed this way, with no strokes at all.

But no, she was starting to move her body, just enough to pass the hint. Still standing, front to back, he retracted his cock, to the halfway point and then a few inches past that. She moaned at the emptiness. Quickly, feverishly, he filled her, once more burying his shaft in the sweet heat of her pulsing depths. It was the kind of sex that only came with practice, with knowing intimately the motions and intricate realities of the other person. It was mutual fantasy made reality.

Their bodies talked to one another, telling what each would like next, the spaces to be filled, the little aches to be created and dissipated.

Their sighs merged as he maneuvered himself into just the right position, comfortable and true and then drove himself home. With measured strokes he brought them to the point of combustion.

A dozen times he penetrated, in and out, until he could no longer hold back his climax. With his thick, familiar spurts came the rivulets of her own ultimate pleasure. Nyssa screamed out as she orgasmed. He cried out with her, the male equivalent. The artificially projected moon above them, nearly full, seemed to shine just for them. So, too, the glowing stars.

As the passion subsided, he held her close, nibbling at her neck. He waited for the telltale sigh, indicating she was passing over the threshold into that post-coital state of sweet vulnerability that inevitably followed their lovemaking.

At this point he swept her up into his arms. She nuzzled close, sleepy-eyed. His woman. Theron looked to the artificial sky, his primale blood surging. He would kill a thousand men barehanded to protect her. He would guard her to his dying breath, suffer a million wounds, or crawl across a desert of fire or a continent of ice to be by her side.

She was what made him whole. Without her, he could no longer be any of the things he was — or even be at all, for that matter. Could he begrudge the younger Raylar from having this experience with Seria?

Of course not. No more than he could ever deprive her of the experience of having the love of such a good, strong man. They deserved one another and once they were settled — once the Narthians were repelled yet again — there would be the experience of child rearing to share.

A baby, produced from their shared genetics. The ultimate sign of their unity and friendship and love. If their child were half the miracle for them that Theryssa was for him and Nyssa, they would be blessed indeed.

But first there were the Narthians to quell. Clutching his naked, well-ravished and sleeping wife to his chest, Theron breathed deep of the night air. The Guardians must succeed. Raylar must succeed.

And succeed they would, he laid her gently in her seat, covering her with the blanket folded in the backseat. The alternative was quite simply unthinkable.

He kissed her forehead before getting back in the driver's side.

What was it about being with his wife that made each time more familiar and comfortable than the last but also more exhilarating? Almost frightening in a way, when he considered how much more he needed her with each passing day.

Once he had thought battle to be the final frontier, the ultimate challenge. But now he knew better. The real courage in a man's life came from daring to love.

Nyssa, mother of his child and his mate for life, murmured in her sleep and put her head against his shoulder. The emotions overwhelmed him as they frequently did since Theryssa's birth. He wiped the tears away as the aircar lifted off. Guardians were not supposed to cry. Especially not Generals.

But this one did.

And he wouldn't trade it for the world.

Chapter Three

✆

Up to the last possible second, Seria had hoped he might chicken out, or otherwise tell her the whole thing was some kind of a joke. The very idea of a man like Raylar trying to dance was like imagining a group of obedients going out on strike for the right to control their primale mates.

"This really isn't necessary," she told him yet again as he held out his hand to lead her onto the dance floor, center stage of the starlit floating disc known as the Mandollo Yummy Happy Waltz Emporium.

It wasn't that she didn't want to dance. She just didn't want it to feel so horribly awkward, what with him just marching them over here from dinner without a moment of get-acquainted time. Another part of her was scared, too, of how she might react, if she were in the man's embrace, locked there, albeit in the guise of dancing.

"It is necessary, Seria," he countered. "Very much so." The look on his face was one of pure military determination. She could see there was no way he was going to back down.

"Raylar, be honest with me," she queried, the cran-beer making her unusually bold. "Are you dancing with me because you want to or did someone put you up to this?"

By someone, of course, she meant Theron, because she had gotten the distinct impression a couple of times at dinner that the older man was coaching him.

Raylar raised a brow. "I could ask you the same about that dress."

Seria's cheeks heated. "What's wrong with my dress?"

"Nothing. I just don't think you designed it yourself, that's all."

"Really? And what about that getup you have on?"

"This? It's a standard dress uniform for a Guardian lieutenant."

He did have a point there. But Seria was not ready to give in yet. "So? I bet you only wore it because Theron told you to."

Raylar's mouth moved slightly. She'd scored a direct hit, she was sure of it.

"That's enough talking," he grumbled. "Let's dance."

Seria felt a wave of heat as he took her hand. It was like the first time, when they'd been introduced, only much more potent. She was floating, her body lighter than air.

Her pulse quickened as he took control. He wasn't supposed to know she was half obedient, but was he picking up signs from her and acting on them? She wasn't even sure what she was transmitting. She was crazy desperate to please him, but mostly that was nerves.

Deep down, she was just confused. Who was this man and why was she supposed to like him? For that matter, who was she, now that she had a sister and a secret mission? Should she really expect to be commanded like a slave—induced to absolute sexual surrender at his whim? Would he expect her to obey, and to face the consequences if she could not?

Beneath the terrible scandal of the red dress—the dress she hadn't wanted to wear—Seria was wet, her thighs slick and open. Raylar was so damn attractive and manly in that dress uniform. All through dinner she had to fight to keep control of her senses. With his every move, she wanted to reach out and grab him, to touch him and rub against him.

What must he think of this outfit? She was embarrassed…but also titillated. Was he aroused? Did he want her body? She didn't think of herself as especially attractive, but Nyssa had begged to differ, calling her a knockout.

"Trust me," she had told her. "Raylar will lose control and that primale blood will take over quick enough."

Seria had never had the experience of being swept into a man's arms, though she had dreamed of it, like every other young woman. Raylar certainly did not disappoint her expectations as he quickly assumed the lead, moving them artfully into the center of the circle of dancers, gracefully waltzing to a piece by Thromodius Bach, the classical Martian composer.

A dozen or so couples surrounded them, mems and fems mostly, with a few uniformed Guardians mixed in, each of them clinging tightly to an adoring obedient. The others had eyes only for their dates, but Raylar's concentration seemed divided, like he was simultaneously competing with every other couple.

He was beating them, too. His pacing and posture absolutely perfect, like some sort of computer program.

"Have you danced often?" she asked.

"Never," he replied.

Seria blinked as he dipped her. "Then…how—"

"I studied the others, while you were freshening up. Using primale absorption powers, combined with intuition, I obtained the level of a grand master in under two minutes."

Seria looked at him, waiting for the punch line. When none came, she decided to laugh anyway.

"Is there something funny about that? I am actually pleased with my accomplishment," he said.

She had to stop in her tracks. "Oh, Raylar, I know you are…and that's what's so funny." She put her hand on his chest, steadying herself. "Please forgive me, I don't mean to laugh. It was so kind of you, really."

"I just don't see the point of doing something if you aren't going to do it correctly," he said. "It's how I'm built."

Seria stood on tiptoes and touched his cheek. There was something so darling about the way he furrowed his brow. So very serious and grumpy. Not to mention the fact that he had taken the time—albeit a scant two minutes—to learn something just for her. "I know that," she said softly. "And I thank you, from the bottom of my heart, for doing this."

"It's not that big a deal," he shrugged.

Seria was fighting the urge to kiss him. "Can we sit down? I'm feeling a little woozy."

"You had too much cran-beer," he said, taking her hand protectively.

She let him lead her to a small table, liking that he was fussing over her. She was curious, though, what would happen if she pushed her limits. "Two champagnes," she called to a passing serving robot.

Raylar helped her sit down and took a seat across from her.

"So...am I as easy to figure out as the waltz?" she wondered a few moments later, fingering the fluted stem of her champagne glass, newly delivered by the spindly, multi-armed auto-robot in his antique tuxedo.

Seria should have known better than to expect sly, witty banter. As with the dancing, he went for the jugular.

"You're lonely, deep inside," he told her. "You pour yourself into your work to take away the pain. You're ambivalent about your body, about sex, about me. Plus you are burdened with a dark secret that threatens to upend all that you know and believe."

"Is that all?" she retorted, hiding the sting of his unwanted analysis. "Gee, with that act, you should be a traveling robo-psychic."

"You've never made sex with a man, have you, Seria?"

Seria squirmed slightly. Damn, talk about being made to feel naked.

"No," she attempted to fend him off. "Only women."

"That's a lie," he shot back.

Seria licked her lips. She'd gotten a little emotion out of him that time. "What makes you so sure?"

Raylar's voice took on a slight edge now, barely perceptible...except to her pussy. "Because you are far too passionate in your responses to men. Your body is curious...and overdue."

"You have a vivid imagination, Primale."

"I have even more vivid environmental preceptors...*Fem*."

Seria shivered inwardly. She'd forgotten that these super-male types could sense a female in heat, like a lion senses prey. Was that what she was to him now? "So I'm horny." She gulped the rest of her champagne. "What of it?"

"No more drinks for you," he dictated, his jaw firm and full of resolve.

She promptly raised her hand to order another.

"I said no," he repeated, speaking in a tone that made her want to open her legs for him right there at the table.

"All right." She tried to clear her head. "How about if we play a game instead? We'll tell each other fun things about our childhood. I'll go first. When I was a little girl, I used to tell everyone I could talk to the dog in our cluster house. I would run around pretending to translate for it. I guess that's why I ended up a diplomat. Okay, now it's your turn."

"There isn't anything fun about me," Raylar said.

"Oh, come on. You must have done something cute when you were a wee lad. Trying to attack Narthians in your closet, or rescue princesses from pretend pirates?"

"I'm a primale. Primales don't play silly games, not even as children." Abruptly, he shifted back to sex. "We need to talk about your hormones, Seria."

65

"My hormones?" She laughed at the absurdity. "What on earth for?"

"We're going to be in tight quarters in space," he explained. "I need to know what to expect from you, sex-wise."

"Not much," she quipped. "If this is your idea of charm."

"I'm not trying to be charming."

"No shit."

"It's a matter of biology. You'll be responding to my primale testosterone. Even as a fem, you will have strong desires to submit for copulation. If we're going to be dealing with specific desires and sexual fantasies you have about me, we have to discuss them up front."

She couldn't believe her ears. How had this perfect gentleman managed to turn into such a complete prick? "What you're dealing with, you arrogant bastard," she let him have it with both barrels, "is a flesh and blood woman with feelings. Not some interstellar bimbo who airs out her dirty laundry for you."

Raylar remained placid, incredibly oblivious both to the outrageousness of his words and the ferocity of her reaction. "So you'll keep yourself under control?" he pressed. "I will be able to count on you not to distract me with overt bodily displays?"

"You mean, will I come on to you like a two-bit whore?" She picked up his glass and took aim, splashing it into his chiseled, gorgeous face. "Does that answer your question, Lieutenant Raylar?"

Raylar didn't flinch. "Seria, I am not going to tolerate that kind of disorderly behavior under my command."

Anger mixed with arousal. A most dangerous combination when it came to maintaining one's rationality. "What command?" she snorted. "I'm not in your stupid army."

"But you are under my protection. You must follow my orders, and submit to my discipline until we reach our destination."

Discipline...damn, he'd used that word that meant spanking. And paddling. It was a damn good thing they weren't going to be sexually involved, or her ass would be in serious trouble pretty soon.

"Well, you can kiss my fucking ass before I follow any orders from you," she fumed.

"I don't allow profanity, either."

She glared at him in disbelief. The man was unreal. "You can't be serious? What are you going to do to stop me? Give me a court-martial?"

"General Theron offered a much more straightforward approach," he said meaningfully.

Seria saw that look in his eyes and knew at once what he was talking about. "Oh, no," she exclaimed. "You can't do that. We're not mates, or even lovers."

Yet...

"As your temporary commanding officer, under the Guardian Code, I must administer discipline according to the leeway I am given. General Theron was specific in including corporal punishment as part of the regimen. That means spanking. The paddle if need be. You may also be put in bondage at my discretion."

"Like hell." She tried to rise, but her knees were far too weak for her own good.

"Don't test me, Seria. This may seem harsh now, but in space, following my orders could mean life and death. What if we encounter pirates, for example? Or Narthians?"

"In that case, I will be only too happy to go with them to get away from you."

"You don't mean that." He looked slightly ridiculous, the champagne dripping from his face. This would be a really poor time to laugh, she decided.

"Why not? They couldn't insult me any worse than you already have."

"My words might be blunt," he acknowledged, "but they are intended to protect you. Pirates would seek only your abuse and degradation."

"So? I'd probably enjoy it, right? According to you I'm just a sex-seeking, manipulative little wench."

"I said no such thing."

It was true, he hadn't. Why was she putting words in his mouth like this? He was stirring things up in her, things she couldn't control. "You don't need to say it. It's written all over your face—you're not the only one who can read minds, you know."

"Really?" He arched a brow. "What am I thinking, then?"

Seria felt a chill down her spine. The challenge of the gesture made her squirm in her pants. It was a toss-up whether she would shoot off a smart-aleck reply or beg for his touch. The man was just so infernally desirable. She could lick and kiss every inch of his naked body. She could tear those clothes off and devour him whole, worshipping at the temple of that fine, primale body, beautifully bronzed and so very powerful.

Stars…if he was just toying with her, why didn't he claim his prize? She stood no chance against him, and they both knew that. Damn the man and his apparent sense of duty.

"What was it I heard before from Swami Superman? Oh, yes, you're…deeply lonely. You're conflicted. About sex. About me."

"We're nothing alike." He rejected her effort to turn the tables on his earlier analysis of her. "Primales don't experience emotional conflict."

Yeah, right.

"You're a terrible liar, Raylar. I've never seen someone as uptight and unavailable as you. It's like you're an iceberg, nine-tenths of you hidden, so tied up in emotional conflict it's gone. Where is it, I wonder? Back in combat someplace?"

His face tensed. Finally, she had hit him back. "You need to be taken over a man's knee," he told her. "Followed by a night of gagging to teach you how to better use your tongue."

She pictured the various ways he might gag her, including with his cock. "You're not man enough," she spat, not sure if she was trying to put him off or goad him.

"Seria, I told you already, don't challenge me. You'll lose."

"Prove it." This time she made it to her feet. She had no idea what she was doing, except that she was about to play the rabbit, wagging its cottontail in front of the wolf.

Raylar caught her wrist from behind, his grip like polysteel as he whipped her back around to face him. "Where do you think you're going?"

Her heart was pounding. She could feel the adrenaline surging through her body. She had awakened the beast, all right. "Wherever I bloody well please," she defied.

His hand crashed down on her ass. Hard. "You will go where I decide, Seria, as long as you are assigned to me. Is that clear?"

Her head was swimming. She had been spanked—*spanked*. "That hurt," she whimpered.

He smacked her again, harder. "The next time will be on bare flesh, Seria. I swear it by the gods."

"All right," she yielded, the fire surging through her body. "It's clear. I go where you tell me."

"And you take my orders."

She swallowed. Here it was, the moment of destiny. She could scarcely believe this was happening, in a public place, with onlookers calmly dining and dancing. Seeing his uniform, they no doubt took this as a standard primale domestic situation. She was his little obedient, being dealt with in the manner she was genetically designed for.

Except she wasn't an obedient at all. At least not completely.

"Raylar, please don't make me…"

His hand moved to the back of her dress. Would he really tear it off her?

"Wait, don't! I'll take orders! Please, I promise!"

His breathing was heavy, his eyes glazed, his nostrils flared. She could tell she had pushed him to some other place, with its own rules. Rules she could neither control nor fully understand. One thing was certain, it was a place of domination and submission, where a man's emotions…and his will were not to be toyed with by the likes of her.

Seria's response was as deeply erotic as it was instinctive. "Please," she whispered. "Sir?"

It came as a hot and tiny plea, scandalous, with a power all its own. What had possessed her? Did she not know what such a concession would mean to a man like this?

Raylar made her wait, as exposed in her affirmation of him as if she had slipped her dress from her body and offered herself for his sexual pleasures. Each second was like an eternity, pulsing between her legs, making her burn for his answer, for his hard, hot hands, and his equally hard cock.

Seria could understand now, just a little of what Nyssa had meant, about how she fucking hated to lose sexual control, but how she needed it so desperately at the same time.

Fucking giving me an order, she wanted to scream. *Call me a bitch, tell me you'll fuck me or not the whole damn trip, or lock me in a cabin, whatever the hell you want, so long as I get the message…you're in charge and not me.*

She had nearly fainted from the tension, when he seized her lips for a kiss so fierce it stole her breath and nearly sucked the life from her.

Being kissed by a primale, it was said, was like being branded and Seria believed it now. He didn't just make contact with her lips — he morphed them into the absolute shape of his desire. There was no mistaking as his tongue bid entry into her mouth that she was to be what he desired, no more, no less. She would be allowed to hold nothing back. There would be no protection, no pretense. He would have her naked, here and now to the core.

Seria melted to his lusting purpose, reforming against him, her body molded to his. There was no mistaking what was happening in her mouth, as he explored every inch of her curious softness. It was sex-making. And she was yielding, every bit as much as if he were working himself down below, cock between her legs.

She had no more strength to stand. His powerful chest and heartbeat were her world. She was a mere moon, glowing in orbit. He was the planet. And the sun. His hand moved to her neck, caressing her hair, teasing the skin beneath with his fingertips. Her back arched, her nipples peaked in instant response. He could kiss them, too. He could pinch them, or if he wished, slap them.

She was his.

Another hand moved over the small of her back and now she was moaning blatantly into his victorious mouth. Signaling her own vanquishment, her own readiness for more. Whatever he desired.

Did he want her on the floor? Spread wide? Would he push her to her knees? Order her to strip? Strip her himself? Nothing was impossible. Nothing would be denied him. Everything about her said "fuck me", everything said "my virginity is yours".

Oh, stars, she was shaking, shivering, her pussy releasing little waves. Was she going to come this way — just from a kiss?

He released her before she could find out. She was terrified to let him go and begin breathing her own air again.

"Raylar," she said, pronouncing the only words that felt right on her lips, "I'm yours."

"What you are is drunk."

"Only a little." She pinched two fingers together. "See?"

Before he had a chance to object, she kissed him, offering him the fullness of her female charms, her barely covered breasts against his chest, flat smooth belly against rock-hard abdomen, recessed delta against protruding hardness.

He did not resist or cast her aside. She proffered herself, licking, nibbling with her lips. The only thought in her mind was of the space in the Star Ring Hotel that Nyssa had said was reserved for them tonight. She had dreaded being alone with him, but now she craved it more than anything in the universe. "I really am yours...all night," she reiterated, her leg provocatively moving between his. "Take me to our room...make sex with me."

She thought his shaft would burst free of the smooth, gold material of his tight trousers—he was that aroused. But his face still showed imprisonment and torment. She would drop to her knees right here and now, unfasten his pants and rub her face over the entire surface of his erection if that would tip the balance.

If only it were that simple. In truth, only Raylar could do the freeing. And that would not happen until he had the chance to redeem himself. She could not imagine the ransom he had set on his own soul. A normal male, even a primale would never meet it. But Raylar was not any other man. He was a man who could dance after only two minutes.

And be the best at it to boot.

He'd redeem himself, all right. And when he did, the world would tremble at his feet. Then they would see, he was no martyr, no masochist. Seria wondered if even Nyssa and Theron knew this much about him.

Certainly there was no reason she should, after such a short period of time.

Unless she really was the key to his destiny.

"Seria...you don't know what you're saying. You're a virgin."

"You make it sound like a disease." She put her hand to his chest, like a moth to the flame, full of crazy confidence, never more certain of anything in her life. "And it doesn't matter, because I know that I want to be in your arms. I know that I want you...to be my first...please?"

The frown and crinkled brow returned with more intensity, but this time he took her hand. "Come with me."

Was it the tone of her voice, she wondered, the imploring in her eyes, or maybe just the implications of her pleading that had tipped the scales? Whatever it was, it was happening, he was taking the reins.

"Yes, Raylar," she sighed.

Stars, yes.

Raylar stopped on the way out just long enough to instruct an auto-server to charge their drinks to the Guardian accounts. Hailing one of the egg-shaped bubble transports lined up in front of the restaurant, he helped her in. As she slid across the smooth, luxuriant seat to make room for Raylar, she got a new idea.

A devilish one at that.

Seeing as how their room was minutes away in the cross-dome traffic and the bubble transport was here and now, incredibly cozy and intimate with its rounded, smoky roof, why not take advantage? So what if they would be zipping past thousands of other bubbles, not to mention the countless rockets, aircars and ped floaters? Why not sex-making suspended, as it were, above the entire population? This little bubble could be their own little world. And unless she missed her guess, the seat in a transport bubble reclined pretty far.

"Destination?" inquired the mechanical voice of the bubble's guidance computer as Raylar took his place.

"The Star Ring Hotel," he said, his voice husky.

"Destination acknowledged. Estimated time of arrival will be twenty-one minutes."

Actually, she planned to be arriving a lot sooner.

Seria waited until the bubble top slid over them, hiding them, partially at least, from the rest of the world.

"Please secure yourselves in a safe position," chimed the mechanical voice of the bubble's guidance computer.

Seria chose Raylar's lap.

The sudden move caught him off guard. "What are you doing, woman?"

"I'm getting in a safe place." She squirmed, her giddiness half from alcohol and half from him.

"Safe for who?" he growled.

"For me," she beamed. Her hands found the opening to his uniform. Hungry, starving, she pulled at the material, baring as much of his chest as she could manage. So much skin and so much powerful, primale muscle. Her small fingers did their work, sliding with electric intensity over his pectorals and down to his rock-hard abdomen, outstandingly ribbed.

Stars, he was like a drug. She could barely keep from biting as she leaned in and pressed her lips to the hollow of his neck. She wanted to be touching, licking, consuming him everywhere at once. She wanted inside his mind. She wanted him inside her body.

Curious, she dabbed her tongue at his nipple. He jolted. "Ooo, did I hurt it?" she exclaimed.

"No, they're just sensitive."

"Oh, good." She dove in to bite it.

"Hey, easy." Raylar seized her hair, pulling her head back.

"I'm sorry," she cooed. "You want to get me back?" Her hands moved to the front of her dress, fumbling for the opening.

74

The material gave way, allowing her breasts to spring free. Ready. Nipples erect, swollen with desire. "Do you like them, Raylar? Nyssa said I have very nice ones."

He responded with a lionlike growl, immediately taking one of the morsels into his mouth. She cried out in soft, deep affirmation as he suckled, working his tongue greedily over the nipple, clamping deliciously with his teeth. She kept on saying "Yes", her fingers running through his short, bristling hair.

"Darling, darling..." moaned Seria. "Don't make me wait. Fuck me now."

She was wriggling, trying to pull her dress up to her waist.

"Seria, not in the bubble. Are you crazy?"

"Why not now?" She thrust her breasts against him, rubbing her hands over his cock. Artless as she was, she had the right biology to get the job done.

In a moment or so he was groaning, ready to rip the thing off her.

"Here, let's try it like this." She tried to guide his hands. Lifting her ass, she pulled at the hem of the thing, hiking it higher and higher. Her breasts posed a tempting target, especially with all the movements she was making. He kept reaching for them. His actions were a two-edged sword, because as good as it felt it was also slowing things down.

"Ow," he grumbled, bumping his head on the roof.

Seria couldn't keep from laughing. It was a nervous habit.

"It's not funny," he insisted.

"Oh, baby, I'm sorry," she breathed.

Gathering the material at her waist, she managed to bare her pussy and her ass both. Now there was Raylar's uniform to contend with. The opening at the crotch was one of those micro-magnetic mini-locks. His cock emerged completely erect, larger than any she had ever seen on the hologrid. Her heart skipped several beats. It was reddish-purple with veins protruding. At once beautifully smooth, there was also a kind of primal roughness to it. A hardness, like super-metal. From anatomy lessons she knew his balls would be tight and full, containing the semen that a male shot into the female upon ejaculation.

Oh, stars, was she ready for this? Was his cock really going inside her? *Her first one.*

Raylar saw her nervousness. "We should wait," he grimaced, his hands at her waist, attempting to keep their sexes from fusing.

She could see in his face how it was hurting him to hold back. She could also see how he would do anything in the world not to hurt her. This one expression, more than anything, sealed her confidence. None of the rest, not Nyssa and Theron's great speeches, not even her supposed destiny mattered compared to this.

"It's all right," she assured him. "I don't want you to hold back." She was so wet already, and so hot. She could no more keep this tide at bay than she could stop a sunrise. Whatever abyss they were plunging into, they were fated to do so together.

Raylar mouthed a mild curse. There was no resisting her power, no fighting the call of raw lust. The bobbing transport bubble provided them a cushion of sheer air even as he lowered her down onto the tip of his red-hot cock. He moaned, his head thrust back with the sheer male joy of a warrior. She sucked in a breath, her body trembling all over as he filled her, inch by inch, a glorious, slow-motion descent. It felt like eons, her heartbeats stretched to eternity. At a certain point she felt a slight tearing, the rupturing of her hymen. There was a trickle, warm and wet. For barely a second, it was uncomfortable, but then the pleasure came back with a vengeance. Down the slippery slope into a cool jungle valley. A million times yes, a million tiny explosions up and down her spine. *So this is what it's like*, her mind kept telling her. *I'm making sex…making sex…*

It was all so very exhilarating, almost frightening, but she knew she was safe. Raylar had perfect control of her body. Indeed she had never felt safer and more at home than she did now in his grip, her weight effortless in his powerful arms. She could scarcely believe they had only met today. The way he handled her body was amazing, like they'd known each other all their lives. Or maybe before. It was as if instinctively he knew how much she could take and how fast.

"Got to…go slow," he grunted, the sweet tension evident on his handsome face.

"Yes, lover. Yes." She didn't mind him dragging it out. His cock felt so good. It was as hot as fire, but it caused no pain, it occupied every open part of her, but it did not overfill her.

"Oh, Seria," he said her name, the reverberations extending all the way to her pussy.

She clawed at his bared chest, wanting to be in his skin and under it. "Raylar…" she said his name back, the single time a down payment on the million times she wanted to pronounce it.

He took her down, all the way until she was fully impaled. Her pelvis touched his. She couldn't believe she had taken so much of him inside her. It was at this point she remembered the power primales reputedly had to control the size of their erections. Was he being merciful and keeping his to a minimum? If so, what would he be like fully expanded? The very thought made her head swim.

She was at his mercy. And she had put herself there, freely.

Seria looked at him, the awe obvious in her eyes. He cupped her cheeks in his hands, drawing her in close to deliver a kiss. His lips burnt, like parching her soul, and yet he was the water, too, the cool liquid she needed to survive. She gave access to her mouth, allowing him to probe. To explore. To possess. It was all so silently beautiful, their hearts attuned, connected, excited, and sublime.

Meanwhile the bubble continued to purr along, like a tiny star hung on the firmament of the dome heavens. Its computer, oblivious to the lust being enacted by the craft's occupants, kept on plotting their course, a plodding, miniature electrobrain operating the engines that would take them to their hotel.

And more sex-making.

The city was oblivious, too. A pulsing mass of millions outside the bubble, a teeming host that might as well have been a galaxy away.

"We won't consummate here," Raylar declared, releasing her lips at long last. "We must build the anticipation."

His level of control both inflamed and frustrated her. She didn't have it in her to wait, though she secretly marveled at a man who could. "But we can do it again when we get to the room," she offered. "Can't we?"

He freed her hair from his grip, allowing it to cascade over her shoulders, shimmering, artificially altered to silver by the machine. She liked it better than her own color. She wondered if he did, too.

"Yes we can," he agreed, running his fingers through it. "But the first time—your first time—must be perfect."

Seria felt a surge of frustration.

Why? Why did he care so much about the quality of her experience? Anyway, that was up to her to decide. It was her body, after all.

"This is perfect already." She rocked her hips, reminding him that he had already breached her hymen, making this the first time, here and now.

Raylar took hold of her shoulders, his fingers pressing firmly, not painfully. "Be still, woman."

Seria felt the gush in response to his touch, warm and fresh from between her thighs. Something in her body kept responding to this man. It was an instant link, almost primal in its heat. "Yes, Raylar."

She was not in control.

The implications were sexy, a little unnerving, but totally exciting. She wanted him now. She wanted *it* ten times as bad. But it would come at his pace. Her body's deep pleasures would be unlocked at his discretion, according to his timetable. She ought to rebel, but that wasn't what she felt. Instead she had this insane desire to offer herself even more, to seek to make him want it, to want her to the point of losing control.

Was this a means to sexual power, though, or just a road to further weakness and helplessness? Stars, did it matter? It certainly felt good. She decided to play her hand, to see if she could push things further along.

"Does it arouse you," she whispered, making sure not to move a muscle, "when I obey you?"

His eyes narrowed. He was obviously too smart to fall for any feminine trap. "Obedience is a prerequisite, Seria. It is understood."

Seria felt hot tingles. Something in the tone of his voice. Not threatening, but quite firm. The question was begged, of course, what would he do if she did not obey? She knew what he *could* do, at least with regard to issues of ship's discipline. But was she subject to spanking for sexual peccadilloes?

Her pussy was spasming, still occupied, and conquered. Clenching and unclenching on its own. There was the distinct possibility, strange as it might seem that she could come right now, just like this, filled with cock, not the least bit of actual fucking going on. If she wasn't careful to stop turning herself on with this conversation...

"If you had a mate," Seria speculated, wondering for the millionth time what to do with her hands, how to keep them off his body, so luscious and strong and touchable. "She would have to obey you...in bed, I mean."

"And outside of it," he replied, not one sign of sexual strain showing on his face. "But I don't have a mate, Seria. And I am not looking for one."

Amazing. The more worked up she became, the more sexually consumed, the more self-possessed he became. She could see this was his element. Domination.

"I'm not either." She was painfully aware of her breathing and what it did to her breasts. Her rapid intake of air made them rise and fall quickly, rendering them very tempting targets.

Or so she thought. He couldn't keep his hands or mouth off them a few minutes ago. Why wasn't he itching to touch and grope and suckle her now? And how could he endure being inside her without needing to move, to come?

"Raylar?"

"Yes?"

She knew it was a losing proposition, asking questions that only highlighted her own growing insecurity and weakness, but she couldn't help herself. It was part of the deal somehow. "Do you find me attractive...really?"

"Why are you asking me?"

There. He'd done it. Pinned her to the wall, leaving her no choice but to reveal her weakness. And she did not have it in her to do anything but squirm. And hope he would enjoy the show. She could hate herself for all this later with her more dignified fem half. For now she was just another obedient, though, offering up everything for scraps of male pleasure. "I...I've not been able to tell before, that's all."

He eyed her suspiciously. Her behavior was aberrant and he knew it. No fem should ever doubt that. No fem should ever care. Fems looked out for what they could get *from* men, not what they had to receive in order to feel whole.

"You're a beautiful woman," he said simply. "That's obvious."

Her heart sang. "I'm not looking for flattery," she offered quickly, trying to hide the surge of emotion.

It was too little, too late.

"You're not like the others." He shook his head.

He seemed worried, concerned. For a split second she feared he was going to change his mind about making sex with her. "I can be like them, though. I can be like anyone you want, if you teach me."

Stars, what had made her say that? That was downright mentally unhealthy, taking that kind of attitude.

"You must be you and no one else," he said firmly. "I have no say in the matter."

She shook her head. That wasn't so. What he said, what he felt and what he wanted did matter to her. Much more than she wanted to admit. He must know that, too, so why wasn't he going to take advantage? Tears formed in her eyes. So many strange feelings. Where were they all coming from?

"You're pretty thin-skinned," he observed, "for a diplomat."

When it came to romance, yes, she thought, though ironically enough, she was considered quite skilled at her profession. She had graduated top of her class and finished her trials in record time. Looking at it now, she wondered if it wasn't that half-obedient mix that didn't make her such an effective, yet humble negotiator, ideally suited for interplanetary affairs, where being overly thick-skinned was a definite drawback.

"I'd say in your case, I didn't do a very good job staying objective," she teased.

Raylar lifted her, removing her from his cock and setting her back down beside him. He did so in a single motion— smooth, effortless and efficient. "We will be landing in a few moments," he said. "We need to prepare ourselves."

He meant they needed to remove the sexual evidence and cover themselves. She had to smile a little at his tact. He would make a pretty good diplomat himself, she decided.

"There's a little blood," she whispered, looking down at her thighs.

"I know. I'll take care of it," he said, removing the small, handheld molecular cleaning device from the door panel of the bubble. All vehicles, and most residential rooms, had these. They were designed to remove stains, by molecular zapping.

"Open," said Raylar, indicating her legs.

Seria's pulse quickened. Her thighs parted, baring her sex, glistening and throbbing. Zappers didn't emit any sort of energy a person could feel, but Seria swore she could sense the charge nonetheless as he skimmed the small nozzle gently over her thighs.

There was no mistaking the symbolism. Fems did not spread their sex blindly for primales, giving them full and total access, no matter what the purpose.

The blood was dealt with easily, but to her shame they found they could not dry her sex. With each removal came fresh liquid, from deep inside her needy pussy.

"I feel so cheap and tawdry," she blurted.

"Nonsense," said Raylar, putting her instantly at ease. "You're a normal, healthy female. Look at me. I can barely control my reactions around you—and I'm a primale."

She smiled weakly. He had no idea the infinite gratitude he had just won.

His hand was gentle on her shoulder, though it sent rivulets of white flame to every nerve ending. "Put your clothes back on, okay, Seria?"

Seria nodded, her belly in flames. He had phrased it as a request, but as she sought to pull the skimpy gown back over her heated breasts, she was exquisitely aware that he was in charge here, by her own wishes. Which meant that everything he said was an order and every response on her part would be an act of obedience, pure and simple.

The idea struck her fancy, though at the moment, she wanted different orders to follow. Sexual orders. Things she must do to him, and for him. To give him pleasure, ultimately leading to orgasm. And through this, to find her own release in the very acts he commanded.

Her fingers trembled as she tried to work the complex straps. She was useless at the task of dressing. "Raylar," she whispered, her voice painfully feminine and sweetly naked in the tiny metallic bubble. "Will you..."

He didn't need her to finish the thought. "Sit forward," he said.

His hands were so gentle, his fingers so amazingly delicate. She swooned as the tips of them brushed her skin. How could the same touch be like fire and ice and soothing water all at once?

She felt her eyes sliding closed. Trust. That was the word that came to mind. Unbidden, her parched lips opened for him, forming a tiny circle. Like a baby bird, she arched her neck.

"No more," he denied her silent request for a kiss. "Until we are in the room."

Request? Who was she kidding? She had thrown herself at him and been denied. Put in her place. Raylar was in charge here, and he had earned that right, by virtue of his superior willpower. Not to mention his inherent manhood, sexually explosive yet beautifully, powerfully contained, like the jungle cat on the prowl, in total lordship over its surroundings.

"Yes, Raylar." She wanted to call him something more. Something befitting their relationship—nebulous, yet hierarchical. Were she a mere obedient, a hundred percent submissive, it would be ever so much simpler. She would call him Lord, or Master.

"Raylar?"

"What is it?"

The bubble was setting down on a landing platform, on the lip of the saucer-shaped hotel. "Destination achieved," the computer told them. "Please enjoy your night and don't forget to use Dome Bubble, Incorporated in the future for all your transport needs."

"Never mind." She couldn't share her dilemma. He seemed suspicious enough about her nature already. She would have to muddle her way through. Continuing to fool him into thinking she was a fem, even if an awkward, uncertain one.

Hopefully he was chalking it all up to her virginity.

His brow crinkled as he studied her. She felt naked to her soul. Was he catching the blush, all the way to her cleavage? "Suit yourself," he said as the bubble top lifted automatically to reveal a busy landing area, with robot doormen scurrying to and fro to help the various guests from their vehicles.

The curved surface of the attached hotel glistened in the dim light of the night, rising up to the stars. They were still floating, halfway between the top of the dome and the ground, though motion could no longer be felt. Seria's stomach knotted a little looking up at all the tiny lights along the outer walls. They represented private rooms, one of which was reserved for her and Raylar.

To sleep in. Together.

She made no effort to move as he hopped out and came around to the passenger side. She doubted her legs would work no matter how hard she tried. As for the prospect of walking into the hotel, through the lobby past hundreds of people, in her present state, she would as soon try and negotiate a treaty with a batch of hungry Delorian bloodsuckers.

Fortunately, Raylar had no intention of overextending or exposing her. "A blanket, please," he ordered a hovering sphere-shaped arrival robot. "The lady is a bit overtired."

She had her wrap, of course, but to Raylar's primale mind, you could never protect a female too much.

"Certainly, Sir." A series of lights flashed on the display monitor and a door panel slid open. A folded blanket lay inside. It was one of a thousand or so simple items the machine could generate from its atomic memory bank.

"Thank you," said Raylar as though it were human. He proceeded to wrap Seria, covering her completely in the smooth, soft material—silver like her hair. Next he scooped her out of the seat, cradling her limp body.

It was instant heaven.

She pressed her cheek to his chest, relishing the sound of his heartbeat and the feel of his strong muscles. She could stay like this forever. Except there was so much else she wanted. Most of it she only knew by name or visual images. Before this night was over, she wanted it to be real.

By dome's dawn, she vowed, she would be Raylar's. And he would be hers.

Whatever that would mean exactly, she wasn't sure. A good part of her brain was quite aware that he was the fire and she was the moth. Fortunately or unfortunately, that part of her brain had been outvoted.

It was the other part that ruled now. The part connected to her body. Her inquisitive, starving, desirous body. A body that would never know peace—until it knew him.

Chapter Four

ຄ

Raylar carried Seria across the threshold into the hotel room, his mind whirling with activity. He had been a fool not to see it earlier. There was definitely something suspicious going on here. General Theron would never put him into a situation in violation of the Code without having some greater scheme in mind. This was no ordinary woman he was being asked to fly across the galaxy all by his lonesome.

He could not put his finger on what it was about her exactly, nor could he fathom what the General's motives might be in wanting the two of them together. Was he supposed to mate with her? If so, for what purpose? He was a warrior. It was all well and good the General had a happily-ever-after life with High Councilor Nyssa, but he could hardly expect that for Raylar.

Looking about the room, he decided on an optimum strategy. The décor was set to default—sterile, hyperspace-age white on the walls, floors and ceilings. The bed was disc-shaped, covered in a white artificial fur. His cock strained at the sight of it. The way Seria fit against him in his arms, the way he had fit inside her in the transportation bubble, he wanted her so badly it hurt. Not taking her right now on that bed was going to be one of the toughest things he had ever done in his life.

But this was not the time for sex-making. As a matter of fact, there would never be a good time to make sex with this woman. What he needed was information. Who was she, really, and why did Nyssa and Theron want so badly for him to be in her company in such tight quarters?

It occurred to him that he was likely going to have to interrogate her. Damn. How was he supposed to do that? Any form of physical discomfort or abuse was out of the question. He would have cut off his own right hand before allowing any harm to come to the mysterious little female.

Strange to feel such a bond to her. And yet he did not know her not at all, nor could he trust her to tell the truth of her own accord. It might be she was a victim here, like he was, but it was also possible she knew a hell of a lot more than she was letting on.

Raylar looked about for inspiration. The holograph on the wall, a nude goddess swinging a golden lariat representing the power of spinning Creation gave him an idea. "Décor arranger," he called out to the computer responsible for changing the room into whatever its guests desired. "Give me a Moorish sultan's bedroom. Equip it for slave-keeping and disciplining."

"Certainly," said the disembodied voice.

Seria trembled in his arms. Raylar felt again the contradictions in her. The fem part was there, the stiffening, the bodily rejection, but there was that other response, too — hot, almost welcoming.

"Does this meet your requirements?" The machine had transformed their surroundings. The bed was of intricate carved wood, four posts with a silk canopy. The walls were sandstone, painted with images of mounted, turbaned warriors fiercely wielding long, curved scimitars. The floor was pink marble, with cushions cast here and there along with several sturdy iron rings to which long chains could be attached. A rack of whips and long, thin instruments of discipline stood beside one of these.

Raylar noted the rings at the four corners of the bed, as well. A woman could be chained there, spread-eagled, conveniently secured for male penetration.

A woman like Seria. He thought of her, there, her eyes limpid pools of anticipation, her sexual heat so plainly evident in the heat of her skin, the motions of her breasts, the swollen nipples. Never had he known this kind of desire, this kind of raw, mindless need.

"This is good," he confirmed, attempting to keep his voice calm. "If you could do me one more favor, though."

"Of course, Sir."

Raylar was sometimes teased for his habit of treating computers and robots like they were people. He preferred to keep things simple. By acting courteously toward any voice or being, he need not ever make mental adjustments in his head, as to when to be polite or not. In his mind it would be all too easy to take the next step and treat people better or worse based on career or function. As far as he was concerned, all were equal, the more so for their particular differences.

This Seria was a real puzzle, though. A part of him wanted to accord her the fullest respect, but another part wanted to treat her…differently. Not disrespectfully, but with the inherent domination born of a primale.

In short, he was troubled by visions of her kneeling at his feet. And him enjoying the experience most thoroughly.

"I need a chain from the ceiling and shackles," he told the décor maker.

"You wish to secure the female?"

"Yes." The objective tone of the machine's question and his own reply sent a little charge down his spine. It was true and real. He was going to put Seria into bondage. Not for idle sex-making, but for purposes of information collection.

He had no choice, after all. There was deception afoot. His training was to trust nothing implicitly, not even the word of his highest superior. There was always the higher loyalty. To the Code. And behind this the implicit purpose of fighting for justice, and for the survival of the human race against the Narthians.

Raylar stood Seria on her feet. She was wobbly, unsteady. "What are you going to do?" she wanted to know.

"We need to get clear about some things. Lift your arms. Hands above your head."

She obeyed instantly, showing a grace and submissive beauty that nearly cracked open the seals of his tightly riveted heart. *This was no fem.* Raylar reached for her wrists, to secure them in the cuffs. With her heels on, the fit was perfect. Barefoot, however, she would be forced to stand on tiptoe.

"Have I done something wrong?" she asked.

He beheld her beauty. His now, until such time as he saw fit to release her. For a moment he confined himself to memorizing every detail, silently drinking it all in, her hands limp in the polysteel bonds, her breasts rising and falling lightly, the current state of bondage increasing the fullness of her cleavage. "So far? No. To keep it that way, however, you will need to cooperate."

She licked her lips, the action of her tongue quick, snakelike. "I will," she said, her voice husky.

Raylar frowned, his cock once again treated to a jolt of unsatisfied lust. Were she aware of the effects of her behavior in tantalizing him he would punish her quite soundly. As it was, he was quite convinced of her innocence.

Just another of the anomalies in the sexy, silver-haired woman.

"Don't make promises you aren't equipped to keep," he warned.

"I'll face the consequences, Raylar." Her eyes were trancelike. "After all, you're the sultan, right?"

"Forget the background, it's incidental."

Was it, though? Why had he chosen something with such strong connotations of female submission when he could simply have asked for the chains, the cuffs and been done with it?

"Yes, Raylar."

Blast her docility.

In a single motion, he tore down the front of her dress, baring her breasts. "You play with fire, woman, do you know that? Have you any idea what a primale can do? The effect he can have over a female? I could ruin you for any other man."

Seria didn't flinch. "I am in your chains." She met his bluster. "At your mercy."

He took hold of her nipple. "Primales have no mercy. Haven't you heard?"

Raylar did not relent until she was whimpering. To her credit, she did not beg him to stop. "Who are you?" he demanded, shredding the remains of her dress.

"I'm Seria." Her dress was at her feet. She was naked and her voice held no defiance. He had asked her name and she had told him.

"Don't toy with me." His hand moved between her legs. She had no clue to the kind of torture she was in for. "There's more to this. You're hiding something."

She gasped as he parted her sex lips, penetrating at will with his fingers. She gushed in reply, her hot opening more than ready for his attentions. "Raylar, I swear."

Raylar found her clitoris. Did she think she was dealing with some kind of amateur here? He was a Guardian, and a specially trained one at that. He knew everything about the human body and how to drive it to utter distraction. "Have you ever been held at the brink of orgasm, Seria? For five minutes? A half-hour? A whole night?"

She shook her head. The look on her face indicated she was not ready for so much as five seconds.

"You will tell me everything," he informed her. "You'll start at the beginning, and you'll go to the end. You'll leave nothing out. Every fact, every detail. Even the things you thought you forgot, the things you didn't even know you knew. Are we clear?"

Seria was shivering. "Y-yes."

"Step out of your shoes," he commanded.

She did so, planting her bare toes on the cold marble. As predicted, she could not touch the heels of her feet to the floor. Her calves flexed beautifully, naturally. She looked born to be this way. Bound according to his whim, her body at maximum display, for maximum pleasure.

"From this point forward," he told her, "you may consider yourself my slave. Until I say otherwise."

Where had that come from? Surely not from any tactical rationale? It wasn't even remotely true. She was neither slave nor technically even a prisoner.

"Yes, Master."

The words on her lips, spoken without hesitation nearly derailed him. Did she really see him that way? Did she have deep and abiding feelings? No, it couldn't be. She was speaking this way because he had her helpless. She would agree to anything, her body as vulnerable as it was.

"You do know something more about this mission," he said, removing his soaked fingers and putting them to her lips. "Don't you?"

"Yes, Master."

He pressed the glistening tips to her lips. She did not have to be told what to do. His cock pushed outward, nearly rending the material of his trousers as he felt her sweet, dabbing tongue. Slowly, methodically, she licked him clean, taking back her own inner moisture.

He pushed his fingers deeper, making her suck. She was a natural. He could only imagine how glorious it would feel to feed her his cock, letting it swell in her mouth to its natural proportions. Why did he feel like his cock was made for this? For this and everything else where Seria was concerned.

But that couldn't be the case. He was not born for any woman. Not with the job he held, not with what his eyes had seen. In truth, that part of him had already died, back on

Rensus Nine. He could no longer feel in his heart the deepest things. The things of life and love. He was a warrior now and nothing more.

Impulsively, he touched her clit, just to see the look on her face, the expression, half angel, and half fire-demon. She was hot, this one, in more ways than one. He was more than a little tempted to punish her for teasing him all night. "Let's start with your outfit tonight. Who picked it out?"

"Nyssa," she replied in a small, soft moan.

He wanted to make her come, but he had to hold back. "And the change in your hair? That was her idea, as well?"

"Yes...Master."

"Why? For what purpose?"

"To...to please you. To make you...interested."

Now they were getting somewhere. "And why would High Councilor Nyssa care if I was interested in you?"

Her thighs were slick with fresh emission. Beads of sweat formed on her forehead. Her tight, firm belly was undulating. He wanted to break the chains with his primale hands, bring her to the bed and lay her down. Slip inside her, sheathe his cock in her deep warmth, allow her to surrender herself. Completely.

"Please." She shook her head, more pitifully than defiantly. "Don't make me tell."

"I will make you," he retorted, without malice. "I absolutely will."

She gave a little cry of frustration as he took his hand away. Denying. Helplessly, she pushed out her pelvis into the air, begging. "Oh, don't stop."

Raylar bent to take one of her perfect nipples in his mouth. The sudden pressure broke her resistance. "I...I will tell you." She writhed in her bonds.

He bit down, just hard enough to push her along.

"They want us together. Nyssa said we were…made for each other."

Reluctantly, he released the little nub—rubbery, swollen and so very delicious. "What do you mean? Made for each other?"

"It's…complicated. I don't know how it all works. Supposedly we were engineered. Given compatible genes."

"Impossible."

"I thought so, too."

"If you are lying…" He looked at her sternly.

"I swear." She shook her head earnestly. "Raylar…Master…I'm telling you what I was told."

He ran a hand over her smooth, creamy breast, and across her taut, sweet belly. All this magnificent female flesh. Could it really be his?

"Have you ever been spanked, Seria?"

"N-no," she replied.

"Of course not. You're a fem." He spoke the word with slight irony. "Fems don't get spanked by males. Unless they want it, for sex-making. Obedients, on the other hand, are subject to discipline. On their lovely asses."

He paid attention to her breathing. The slight increase in her heart rate measurable with his extra senses. The extra micro-motions of her eyelids. The almost invisible twitching of her lips. She was hiding something, most definitely.

The tremors in her body as he rubbed her behind, only confirmed it.

Extending two fingers on his opposite hand, he poised them at her labia. "Impale yourself," he ordered.

Seria moved against him, her expression a mix of dread and need. She was hot and wet, her pussy incredibly tight and greedily grasping. If he were to move his fingers just so, she would come at once. But she had a long way to go to earn that privilege.

She managed to take him inside her to the second knuckle.

"More," he told her.

"I…I can't."

"Do you want a spanking?"

She looked at him, her smoldering eyes belying the expression of shock. The little vixen did want it. And badly.

"No, please." Struggling, she surrendered further to the invasion.

Still he was not satisfied. "All the way. Take them all the way, like a cock."

Seria hesitated for a second. All the time he needed to administer a swat, clean and crisp, to her shapely buttocks. She reacted like lightning had hit her, though she had nowhere to go but deeper into her temporary slavery.

"Look at me."

She was fully speared, at the utter mercy of his fingers. Her eyes dripped wonder and lust.

"Who are you?" he repeated.

"They told me…" she said huskily. "They said…I'm a hybrid. Master, I need to come."

"No. That will have to wait. Who told you that you were a hybrid? Nyssa? The General?"

"Yes. They said, I'm not…I'm not pure like everyone else."

"What the hell does that mean?" This was making less sense by the minute.

"I'm half…" she said, her brain largely preoccupied by what was happening to her sex. "Half one, half the other."

The truth hit Raylar like a sunrise on Mineus Two. Fast, explosive and world-changing. *Half one, half the other.* "You have obedient genetics mixed with your fem nature," he supplied.

She nodded her head. Raylar considered the matter. She was speaking of an utter impossibility, and yet it all made sense if you looked at the evidence. Her odd behavior and the inherent contradictions within her. Not to mention the conflicts she stirred in him. On the one hand, he wanted to steer clear of her like a Narthian Mother Nest, and on the other, he wanted her collared and chained, yielding to him. Absolutely.

"What you speak is tantamount to treason," he pointed out. "The Council could bring you up on charges for spreading such lies."

"That's how you know I am not lying. I'm telling you what they told me. The Council itself is behind all this. Nyssa is a hybrid, too. Fem and primale."

He clenched his teeth. Now there was a piece of news. So Theron didn't just have a fem wife to contend with, but one who was half primale.

"You mustn't tell," said Seria. "I would be in so much trouble."

"You are in trouble now," he reminded, moving his fingers just enough to make her squirm.

She suppressed a moan, halfway between pleasure and agony. "Yes, Master."

"Why would the Council make...mixed people?" he continued the interrogation. "I see no rationale. Society is perfect."

Seria thrashed her head. "Something about needing new types, to face new crises. New mating bonds, new...flexibility."

He thought of the Narthians, and what he had seen on Rensus Nine. If their enemy was evolving, shouldn't they be as well? Could it be their leaders had foreseen this need years ago?

"What about me?" he asked, seeking to poke holes in her story. "If what you say about us being made compatible is true, then shouldn't I be some kind of a mixture, too?"

"No, you are a hundred percent primale. You had to be that way to fulfill your function. You've just been given a predisposition to be attracted to me."

That was an understatement.

"If all this is true," he asked, "then why wasn't I told?"

"Nyssa said you wouldn't go along with it. You had to fall for me." Tears dotted her eyes. "It's too late now, though. Everything's ruined. We'll never be…we'll never be mated like we're supposed to."

He felt a little stab in his heart. So this was about matchmaking…

"You mean your little ruse failed," he retorted, covering over the pain.

"I didn't want to trick you," she said. "Honestly."

Raylar believed her. Still, he wondered how long she had been carrying secrets. "Have you always known who you are?"

"Not until today. I met Nyssa and she told me everything. She's my sister, you know. With chosen genetics, there are specific biological sources. Our father is Morax, the former head of the Guardians."

Raylar was momentarily taken aback. Morax was one of the finest generals of the last century. "You can't have finer genetics than that."

He looked at her with fresh eyes. The old General's daughter. Could such a thing really be possible?

"Our mothers are different. Nyssa's maternal genetics belong to Dekalia, the former High Councilor. My mother was an obedient, no longer living. I never knew her."

Raylar tried to comprehend that kind of loss. To be separated forever from a part of oneself, even a part one never knew existed. Was it anything like losing brothers in battle?

"I am sorry," he told her. His hand reached for her cheek, to wipe away the tear that was trickling down her face. He knew nothing of comforting females, but she seemed to derive comfort from his touch.

"Raylar," she whispered his name, as though it had never before been pronounced on human lips.

Indeed, it had never sounded that way before. Sweet, meaningful. Richly complicated, too, with everything rolled into it, from the title of Master he had had her use earlier, to many other things he could not yet begin to imagine.

He knew he *shouldn't* try and imagine it, either. What he ought to do was to unchain her, put her to bed and head straight to the General for reassignment. The last thing he could afford as a die-hard warrior was a romantic attachment. He had a fate, a destiny, far in space, and he would likely never return.

And even if he did, this woman needed more than he could give. The Council might know his genetics, but he knew the reality of the man he had grown into. He was no lover. No caretaker or potential mate.

Walking away, though, that was going to be hard. As hard as his cock.

Seria must have been reading the struggle in his heart. "Don't leave me," she implored. "Stay. Make sex with me."

That was the trouble, he thought grimly. There could easily be more here than sex. "That's not possible." He removed his fingers from her soft, yielding opening. "I'm sorry."

"It is possible," she defied. "If you want it to be."

"You are supposed to be half obedient. Obedients don't argue."

"The other half of me is fem," she reminded. "As if you haven't been enjoying that part of me, too."

He suppressed a smile. She was far too engaging for her own good.

"Teach me, Raylar." She was pushing herself, reaching and stretching. "You've already been the first inside me…finish what you started."

She felt good against him. Breasts and belly rubbing. Too good. "It's not that simple. There are implications when a primale takes a woman to bed. It's not bragging to say she is changed. So is the man—it is often difficult afterward to disengage."

"Are you saying you are too weak?" she challenged. "Is my poor little body too much for you?"

"Hardly." It was as close to a lie as he'd ever told. "It's you I'm worried about."

"I can handle myself."

Damn, if she wasn't egging him on. "You weren't handling yourself a little while ago," he reminded. "You were quite beside yourself as I recall."

"You have me chained up. Let me free, and see what I can do."

"It's almost worth it," he mused. "Just to see you try."

"You can make sex with me tonight," she tempted him, "and get it over with. I will be out of your system and then you won't have anything to worry about when we're in the spaceship together."

"That's female logic."

"The only kind there is…"

"More likely I would only want you again."

Her eyes twinkled. "So you're saying you can't handle it, after all?"

"I've never backed down from a challenge in my life."

"In that case, I'm waiting...Warrior."

His hands moved to the shackles above her head. Not bothering with the keys, he snapped the metal. "You may be sorry," he warned, scooping her into his arms.

She felt good there, natural and comfortable. Exciting, too, in ways he couldn't begin to describe. Now it was his turn to feel desire mixed with dread.

Someone would be sorry, all right, but it could as easily be him.

A lump formed in his throat as he laid her down on the plush, red silk of the conjured Sultan's bed. What a beauty she was. How incredibly irresistible. Not wishing to take his eyes off her for a second he tore off his uniform, baring his primale body.

Compared to Raylar's genetically perfect, exquisitely developed form, the finest statues paled. His was a chiseled male strength, unadulterated masculine delight, from his well-formed biceps to the smooth pectorals and muscle-ripped abdomen. Not an ounce of fat, not an ounce of waste, skin bronzed and squeaky clean, his cock rock-hard, his nipples tight, his jaw set with powerful need.

The air between them came alive. Desire and lust danced in the open space, and...memory.

Almost as if she were no stranger at all, but his oldest, most trusted friend.

Pushing the notion from his head, he pressed on with the challenge at hand. "Prepare to submit," he declared, "my little slave."

Seria grinned impishly, indicating that she was more than ready to give him a run for his money. "Whatever you say." She winked, head on the pillow, hair luxuriously spread, her body in irresistible repose. "*Master.*"

Raylar flipped her over, eliciting a squeal. It was time to get the upper hand. Literally.

* * * * *

Seria knew she had pushed things just a little too far. One just did not tease a primale about his dominance. Especially when one was a naked, desirable female, lying completely available in his bed.

"Raylar, what are you going to do?" she asked, though it was all too obvious why he had put her on her stomach, her bare ass exposed.

"The one thing a woman understands," he said. "At least an obedient one."

She wanted to remind him about the fifty percent deal, and how half of her would most definitely *not* respond to the punishment of a man's hand, but she didn't think that would help things any at this juncture. Instead, she aimed for a more general form of mercy. "I've never been spanked," she reminded him.

"That's about to change." He struck her firmly, sending a wave of fire through her behind and up her spine.

"Ow, that hurts," she complained.

He struck her again. Harder. "You have forgotten to call me Master," he reminded.

She was still twitching. She could feel a line of glistening moisture forming along the crack of her clean, hairless pussy. What a view he must be enjoying.

"This isn't fair," she attempted to squirm free, "Master. I didn't do anything to deserve this."

He pressed a hand to her lower back, holding her fast. "You don't need to have done anything. Primales behave as they will toward their women."

Waves of indignation rose, combined with soul-searing desire. "You said I wasn't yours. You didn't want me. I'm just…an innocent bystander."

"That's not so. I hold you partially responsible for all this," he informed her. "You knowingly deceived me. At no point did you resist the plans of your so-called sister, nor did you volunteer the truth to me."

It was true, and yet the whole thing seemed so unfair. How could she have gone against Nyssa—even if she'd wanted to? "I didn't mean to hurt you, Raylar. You have to believe me." She pleaded her case as best she could in her current predicament. "I just didn't know what else to do."

"That I do believe," he conceded, his firm voice resounding with just enough mercy to give her hope. "But the results of your actions are the same regardless of intent."

Seria felt a flash of temper. Would she ever get a break from this man? "So I'm guilty no matter what. Why even ask me questions, Raylar? Why not just beat me and get it over with?"

"Because," he slipped a finger between her pink pussy lips, still exposed, still engorged, "it is my will that you surrender to your punishment. Like a good obedient."

Seria moaned, the desire flooding her all over again. In a few seconds he managed to rekindle all the earlier heat and more.

"Had you not considered," he inquired, "the effects of your earlier appearance on me? Your body, scantily clad before my eyes? The scent of your cunningly applied perfume? Did you not realize what you would do to my primale blood?"

Seria squirmed, trying to avoid the truth.

In theory, yes, she knew what he meant. She had seen the hard-on to back it up, too. As for what it felt like to be him, she had no clue. As a diplomat, she should have immediately sought to reflect on the matter empathetically—instead she had played it differently. Dreading, and yet at the same time almost relishing, her position as femme fatale.

His finger snaked inside her, flicking over the surface of her engorged clitoris. Waves of deep pleasure surged through her, one after another, tight and hot. With each one, she generated more liquid, the essence of her female surrender, trickling from her gaping sex.

Stars, he knew how to play with her anatomy better than she did. "I-I didn't think about it."

"Really?" The finger disappeared. A second later her clumsy lie was met with the hot crack of his palm—hard, efficient and masculine. She trembled from the sudden humiliation of being dealt with like an errant pet. Not to mention the sting of the blow. "As thoughtful a woman as you are? I find that hard to believe."

"All right," she blurted, her toes curled in anticipation of what he might do to her next, "I did know. A little. I knew you were...aroused."

"How did you know I was aroused?" His finger was back between her legs, along with two more, working her, opening her up.

"Because I saw your...your cock," she confessed, wishing desperately as she said the word that he would put it inside her, finishing the work of her sexual conquest.

His smile was sly, infuriatingly masculine, as she looked back at him. She hated the way it accentuated his dimples so charmingly. "Drooling over it would be a more accurate description."

Arrogant bastard, she thought. Even if he was right, it was hardly the thing to point out to a woman. "So what if I was?" she shot back. "I saw you looking at me, too."

"My behavior is not at issue. Yours is."

"That's a fine double standard," she spat.

"I have one standard. The primale standard." Raylar pinched her behind, holding her sensitive ass flesh between thumb and forefinger. "We will now continue the questioning, and you will resume calling me Master."

She loved how he took control of things, how he steered her back on the path he wanted, over and over. Then again, she hated it, too. "Yes," she winced, "Master."

He released her ass cheek, only to spank it. Three times in succession, the strongest blows yet. Her skin continued to burn, even after he was done. "You were looking at my cock," he reiterated in conclusion.

"Yes, Master." Her breathing was erratic. Her ass twitched, her pussy twitched.

"You wanted to see it. You were curious."

"Yes, Master."

"You hoped I would be seduced," he further concluded, "just as Nyssa said I would be."

"I-I don't know, Master," she replied honestly. "I wanted it, but I was afraid, too."

"What did you want?" he demanded.

She couldn't spell it out. Not in so many words. "I wanted… I wanted…"

"Did you want this?"

Seria exhaled, wide-eyed. He was moving on top of her, covering her body from behind. She could feel the tip of his cock, at the entry to her sex. "Oh, Master…"

"I asked you a question." He took hold of her hair, tugging firmly so as to leave no doubt of who was boss. The pressure was just enough to excite her, enough to prick her dark lusts, but not enough to cause real pain.

"Yes, oh, yes, I wanted this, Master."

"Even if you had to deceive me?"

"Yes, Master," she hissed through gritted, pearl white teeth. "I wanted it that bad."

The response had been inevitable, given his sensual torture methods. Still, to hear it from her own lips cut her to the quick. He had her now, in every sense of the word.

"That was a mild spanking, Seria." His cock pierced her as he spoke. Just the head was penetrating, though already she felt full and overwhelmed. "It could easily have been much worse."

"Yes, Master." She wanted to feel more of him. She wanted him pressing himself inside her to the base, impacting her body with his own, forcing his front against her back.

The decision had been his, how much, how long to punish her. He was letting her know that, in no uncertain terms. It was a possession thing, a primale thing.

"You may thank me," he sank an inch deeper, "for your discipline."

"Thank you for spanking me, Master." Each word came charged off her lips, mini zings tensing her nipples and racing down to her belly.

"I'm going to fuck you like an obedient, Seria. You may thank me for that, too." He breathed the words, a searing wind, melting her very soul.

"Yesss… Thank you, Master, for fucking me." Just saying the words made her feel free and horny, which was ironic, because what it symbolized was her own possession and captivity. In truth she hadn't a clue what she was acknowledging. She'd never made sex at all, let alone with a primale.

The fact that he said fuck, though, and not the usual "make sex" meant something more animal was going to happen. And stars help her for wanting it as badly as she did. She could easily become addicted to this. Having the man swallow her whole, the scent of him thick in her nostrils, sweet man-scent—musk, lightly scented with the perspiration of his efforts. And his muscular flesh, touching, pressing, demanding. His thighs at the back of hers, his abdomen at the small of her back, his mouth closing in at her earlobe, within nibbling range.

"But I won't hurt you," he added, the tender vow melting her heart at once. "I would never hurt you. It must feel as good for you as it does for me. If there is pain, you must tell me and I will stop. Is that clear, Seria?"

"Yes, Master."

The tone of his voice was complicated. She could feel him tensing, measuring her perhaps. Maybe he was studying her body, making sure from her motions and her breathing that she was truly all right. She hoped he wouldn't ask the question outright. She was all right, she was ecstatic and out of her mind with lust, but she was half terrified at the same time.

"Seria..." he sighed, his voice tightening to a rasp as he pushed himself deeper, their bodies closing the gap, reaching the inevitable point of total union.

Seria nearly screamed out the question in her heart. It was scandalous, and a total violation of fem ethics. Was she good? she wanted to know. Did her cunt please him and would he deign to ejaculate inside her when clearly he could have any woman on the planet, obedient or fem?

"Oh, Raylar, yes!" She confined herself to encouraging him to take more from her, as much as he wished. "That's it...all the way, baby."

He made a deep groaning noise, primale to the core. His earlier words came back to her. He would never hurt her, ever. He would bring pleasure, equal or greater to his own.

Their bodies made contact at last and Raylar drew a sharp breath. They were linked now. Their sexes hand in glove. She tentatively clenched on him. Could she handle the heat, the fury he was likely to engender?

Of course not. She had but one hope. Mercy.

It was a quality she knew he had, as much as she knew anything about any male in the universe.

Raylar moved his mouth to her neck. At first he kissed and then he nibbled. Finally he bit down, just hard enough to make her feel possessed. At the same time his hands clenched on her waist. She was not going anywhere now. Not until he was through with her.

"Do you know what some primales are capable of?" he asked.

"No, Master."

"Multiple orgasm. One climax after another. Two, three, maybe four in a row. It's been a long time for me, Seria. I will come inside you many times before dawn."

Her fingernails clutched at the bedcovering. Her ass pushed against him. Blatantly begging, craving, advertising her desperation, her conquest. "Yes, Master."

"This will be the first."

She began to shudder, her body exploding against the relative cool of the sheets. She was there already. Without his even moving.

Raylar took hold of her hair. "No, woman. You may not come without permission."

His sudden act of forcefulness was itself a wild aphrodisiac. She moaned, her nipples threatening to explode, her pussy like a volcanic tunnel. "I-I can't help it," she whimpered.

Raylar whacked her ass with the palm of his hand. "Obey, girl."

Seria sniffled, humiliated, all the more so for how he kept heating her up further with everything he was doing. Still, she had to find a way to obey. She did not want to be a bad girl. Oh, stars, the very words were like a tickle to her clit. Her, a grown woman, having to act like a slave girl, having to please a strong man.

"Yes, Master."

Raylar withdrew his cock, leaving her empty.

"Master," she cried, fearing rejection. "What are you doing?"

"Making sure you understand that I mean business."

"I do," she promised. "I do understand. I swear."

"You will remain in this position until I say otherwise."

Seria felt his weight leaving the bed. "Yes, Master." It was all she could do to keep from saying something, to keep from getting up to argue. But she knew that would only make things worse.

This was a lesson she was being taught and she would have to endure it. Naked, facedown on a bed. She strained to hear where he was and what he might be doing. She prayed to the gods he wouldn't leave the room. She absolutely could not bear to be alone.

Thankfully, she could still hear him breathing. He was on the other side of the room. The slight hum of the objectifier told her he was making things. Things to use on her, no doubt. This would be a really good time to get up and run out of the room, but that was not going to happen.

She might as well have been glued in place. She was here for the duration. Waiting for sex. On Raylar's terms. Her entire body his plaything—her sex, her breasts and belly, her backside, even her mouth, open to his will.

Oh, gods, what was he making over there? He must be using the keypunch instead of the verbal controls. If she could only take a peek. Just one little look. She would feel so much better. Seconds ticked by and the wicked idea became reality. She stole her little glance, only to find him staring right back. Against the wall by the machine, arms crossed over his magnificent chest, his stiff cock pointed straight at her. Blast, it was almost as if he'd been waiting.

Too late, she jerked her head back around. *Damn it.*

"Blindfold," said Raylar, verbalizing his amended order. "Ball gag and butt plug."

That did not sound good. Not good at all. *What an idiot I am*, she thought. *Not only didn't I see anything, now I've let myself in for more punishment.*

"Raylar...Master, I can explain."

He towered over her, gag in hand. "I'm sure you would try, but I'm not interested. You will put your head back and open your mouth."

Seria obeyed. Raylar promptly popped the ball between her teeth and told her to bite down. She did so, tensely. He fastened the leather straps behind her head and neck, fixing it in place. Piteously, Seria whimpered, making a last-ditch appeal against the degrading bondage.

Raylar delivered a fresh spank. "Silence, wench."

He seemed rather pleased with himself, downright jovial. The bastard. She made a fresh noise, more indignant.

"Keep it up," he said, "and we'll get some nipple clamps, too."

Seria bit down hard on the plastic ball. She was not about to have anything on her nipples, thank you very much, let alone anything as nasty as clamps.

"This should take care of your being such a nosy little slave girl," said Raylar, putting the blindfold over her eyes.

Seria's world was instant darkness. He rested his hand on her back. "I'll be right here," he said. "All the way through."

She needed to hear that. How had he known?

The hand moved down her spine—gentle, teasing, but full of male energy. She tensed at every place he reached, micro-explosions going off until at last he reached her ass. Still warm from his spanks. "The butt plug will be inside you," he explained, "while I am taking your pussy. It's a form of double possession. Triple, if you count what I have done to your mouth. Count yourself fortunate I didn't order up a penis gag. You'd be biting on a rubber cock now instead of a ball."

Seria experienced a tiny zap of shame. A part of her wondered hotly what a penis gag would taste like—to have it thrust between her lips by Raylar's hand, fixed in place and left there as long as he wished.

"You should relax." He patted her round cheek. "It will go in easier."

Seria stiffened. But what if she didn't want a plug in her ass?

"I want you to feel the size first."

She felt something cold, plastic against her thigh. It must have been a good five inches long. Stars, she'd never take it all! Raylar continued to allow her to "feel" the device with her flesh. Slowly, he rolled it up her hip to her waist and then around to her belly. She gasped as he pressed it to her belly button.

"Don't fight it," was his advice. "Give in to all of it. You have obedient blood... I can see that clearly. Just respond naturally."

Seria's breathing became a mild form of undulation as one after another he taunted her nipples with the plug.

"You'll be lubricated," he said. "And then inserted."

She wished it would be her pussy—that portion of her anatomy was more than lubricated enough.

All at once, the plug was gone. She held her breath. It was time.

His fingers were cold and slick at her opening. He smeared the cold gel deep inside, readying her for invasion. For anal conquest.

At first she tried not to react. It was too shameful. Then, abruptly, as his fingers filled her, she found herself reacting, clenching unwittingly.

Taking advantage, he worked his way in and out. She tried to free herself, but it only resulted in her becoming more impaled, more hot and more aroused.

"Hold still," he ordered. "Submit."

Seria relaxed her body.

Raylar took prompt advantage, moving deeper inside her. She tensed involuntarily, earning a punishing smack.

"Submit," he repeated.

Her ass and ego both smarting, she surrendered once again. Were she being treated as a fem, he would be responsible for pleasing her and making her want to receive anal attentions.

As an obedient, her ass was property like the rest of her. Withholding from the Master meant punishment.

Raylar took his time exploring. Twice more he found her resistant, twice more she was rebuked with crisp spanks to her bared behind.

Eventually his fingers were withdrawn. She was left confused, throbbing and empty.

Moving swiftly, he removed her gag and blindfold. Seria squinted, adjusting her eyes.

"Are you ready for further anal training?" he asked, his voice dark and seductive.

She shivered at the very notion. Anal training. How could any man do this to a woman? Was she little more than a beast to be exploited?

In her heart she knew the answer.

Just like she knew that, for her, being treated this way was the biggest turn-on in the world.

"Please, Master, make sex with me," she cried. "In my ass, my pussy, however you want me."

He pulled her hair. Hard. "No one's making sex with you, you insolent woman. You are being trained, like the slave you are."

"Yes." She felt her will crumbling to his. "Oh, stars, yes, Master."

"Ask me to continue your training," he dictated.

"Please, Master," she complied, "continue my anal training."

A few more seconds elapsed, and then she felt the device, poised — hard and unyielding.

"Fuck me with it, Master," she groaned. "Take me in the ass."

"Yes," he encouraged, "that's it."

His voice encouraged her, making her want to do this for him. She actually did feel her muscles relaxing, though it was still a tight fit.

"If it hurts too much," he said, stepping for the moment out of his role as ravisher, "you must tell me and I'll stop."

"Yes, Master," she acknowledged. That was good thinking on his part. If she got too carried away, she might not tell him if it got to be too much. Thank the universe he was thinking clearly, because she certainly was in no position to do so at the moment.

Raylar pushed the plug deeper, creating in her a sensation of incredible, tingling fullness. Not pain, but a kind of edge she was slipping along, a razor blade that would lead straight to orgasm if she breathed too deeply.

"Damn," he sighed when he was done. "You look incredible like this."

Seria glowed, imagining him admiring his work—admiring her.

"Hell," he corrected himself, "you look incredible, period."

"Fuck me, Master" she rasped, unable to resist begging yet again. "Fuck me like you own me."

Raylar didn't punish her for the outburst. Instead he touched her last remaining opening. The one that had been waiting so desperately.

"So wet," he muttered. "So hot."

She looked back at him, with deep, moist, pleading eyes.

"Yes," he answered her unspoken request. "It's time. To do what I wanted to the minute I saw you. Seria, do you know how hard it was to hold back? Not to whisk you off to some alcove in the restaurant? So I could have you right then and there against the wall? But I knew it wouldn't be enough. Especially when I figured out you were a virgin. I knew then I had to have you in submission. In bondage. And so I will. And it will be good for you, I promise."

It was better than good.

Stars, he was so hard. Harder and bigger than she remembered on the transport bubble. She wanted him at full size, so he could maximize his pleasure, and hers, too.

Raylar wasted no time. His motions were studied and disciplined as he penetrated her, beginning with the tip and proceeding in the tiniest increments, each little movement setting off chills up and down her spine and igniting tiny firestorms within her.

It took him forever to impale her completely. She felt slain by the man, pegged and completely overwhelmed. And yet she was more alive than she had ever felt in her life.

And this was only the beginning...

No sooner had he sunk himself to the hilt than he pulled back for a second thrust. Harder, faster this time. *Yes. Yes. Yes. Finally...at last.* Her virgin body was being fully claimed at last. By the one man on this or any planet who had earned the right.

His cock was throbbing with each push. She could feel him burning, heating up her insides. In and out, in and out. Stuffing her, ever more of him, ever hungrier, ever more passionate. His breathing kept her focused. The butt plug continued with its own little reminders. She was a prisoner here...a slave for the night, albeit with her permission.

A primale's wench, filling the role of an obedient. And loving it. He was coming at her with incredible force now, bone-to-bone, lust-filled, their bodies seeking pure fusion, with all its promise of supernova. Raylar bore down on her, grasping for her breasts. Seria felt them explode into his hands, craving the crushing, hot grip. Sweaty, she arched her spine like an alley cat, seeking to maximize the contact. Their rhythm was that of wild beasts, with sheer grunting, melting and moaning.

Her heart soared. He wanted every bit of her, he'd said, and indeed there was nothing she could hold back. She was going over the edge and he would have to hold her tight or else she would dissolve entirely. His forward lunges were increasing in energy. What a perfect specimen he was, and such a perfect fit, too.

They fit together, that was it. Was all sex-making like this, or was there really something special about their genetics, just as Nyssa had said?

"I'm going to come," he declared, his voice like the growl of a lion. "Come with me. Let me hear it."

"Oh, stars, yes!" she cried, the very command causing her body to give itself over to the climax so long pent-up inside her. "Yes…yes!"

Raylar's cock expanded just as he released his semen. She could feel the heat of him, too. Enough to burn whole worlds. She could only imagine how long it had been for him. His semen came in tight, hot blasts. She felt the fullness even as she was overcome with a hurricane of fulfilled desire, swirling waves of orgasm perfectly counterpoint to his.

Again and again he plumbed her, reaching depths no man would ever find again. And she was letting him. Allowing this complete and total possession of her being. Just as he had promised, he gave what he took, ensuring her pleasure. On and on it went, until she lost track of the number of spurts inside her, and the number of her own explosions, invisible and body-shaking.

At last he was done. Unable to hold herself up any longer, Seria collapsed onto the bed, vanquished. She could sleep a hundred years, but it was obvious he had other plans.

"An excellent beginning, wouldn't you say?" His hand moved over the curve of her ass to grasp the plug and slowly, teasingly remove it. He then turned her over onto her back, moved her legs up and out and just as slowly pushed it back into her.

She focused on his handsome face, and his strong, unshakable presence. He was more beautiful every time she saw him.

She might offer a response to his question, but at the moment, she was unable to say anything at all. The best she could manage was a dreamy half-smile, filled with wonder. His own expression was subtle. There was moisture in his eyes.

She caught herself caring again, wondering what he thought and how he felt. Did a man like this know loneliness? If so, she would not want him to feel that ever again, not as long as she was alive.

Strange thoughts for a fem. She was supposed to be happy with her freedom, craving an endless variety of self-sufficient, pleasure-loving mems. But she was only half-fem, wasn't she? In the end, she had this other part of her, newly discovered, which needed its satisfaction as well. Would she ever learn to strike a balance? And even if she did, would Raylar come to accept both parts of her, even when they contradicted each other?

An excellent beginning he'd said. But where were they going? Did he know the answer to that himself? She could only hope that he did, because she was along for the ride. To the very end.

Chapter Five

`

ॐ

Seria took stock of her situation. She was lying on her back, in the wake of their first effort at sex-making. Her ass was still filled with the plug, her pussy was thrumming, full of his endless emission, feeling him as if he was still there. Raylar, meanwhile, was poised above her. More god than man. His eyes lit with power, his body like a panther's, sinewed, lean and perfect, fully prepared for a fresh strike. The sight of his tireless cock made her swoon. Just moments ago he had come inside her and here he was, still hard as a rock and ready for more.

It was just like he'd said. There was to be one orgasm after another, sex according to his superhuman pace. Could she keep up with him? She was determined to, that was for sure. She might die trying, but it would be a worthy cause.

"Wrists crossed," he ordered, setting things in motion, "over your head."

Seria complied, her muscles deliciously weak, her pussy freshly oozing in response to still more delicious and wicked control. What a dominant he was, putting her into further submission, as if she weren't helpless enough already. The new position accented her breasts, not to mention how it emphasized his mastery over her.

With a single hand, he grasped her wrists, pinning her. "Resist me," he said.

Seria swallowed. She might well have been ordered to hold back a sunset on an undomed world. "I...I can't, Master."

His lips thinned, indicating his level of seriousness. "Resist me," he repeated, this time leaving no room for refusal.

"Yes, Master," she replied, the words spilling forth slavishly.

His blue eyes were bright and razor-sharp in anticipation. She could see how her obedience pleased him. What a complicated creature he was. She saw the killer in him and also the lover. She would not want to be an enemy of his—that was for certain. As for being his lover, she could only hope she would meet his expectations.

Resist…

She made an effort, puny and futile. Quickly she realized what it was he wanted. Her squirming body, so much weaker than his, glistening in sweat, entertaining him with its contortions, and arousing him with the knowledge of just how enslaved she was.

"You cannot free yourself," he observed after a time.

"No, Master," she replied, sensing that this, too, was part of the ritual.

"You are mine," he concluded.

Her voice was a hot whisper. "Yours…"

But what did that mean? For how long? And how deeply? Was it only about the sex or was he claiming her as his mate, forever? To be treasured and cherished, stripped and spanked and loved and pleasured at his whim, bound and unbound, controlled utterly, and yet free beyond the dreams of any fem…

"Arch your back," Raylar commanded.

Seria complied, offering her breasts in the process—swollen, needy and gently tremoring.

"More."

The contact made her shiver all over. Her sex clenched at the empty air. Her nether cavity, occupied by the plug, did some clenching of its own.

She wanted his cock, more than she had wanted anything in her life.

"Your lips," he said. "Open them for a kiss."

He made her wait like that for what felt like an eternity. Parched, like petals ready to blow away, totally ineffective guardians for her mouth, so vulnerable and thirsty.

"Close your eyes, Seria."

She did so, still waiting for his kiss. It came from out of the blackness, with overwhelming gentleness, a brand upon her skin, conforming to every tiny little crevice and line. She could not help but mold herself, moving and pressing, encouraging him to go as far as a man could go.

His tongue took possession of her mouth, moving with the confidence and symbolic power of a cock. If a mouth could orgasm from the sweet, exciting motions of a man's invasion, hers would.

It was a foretaste of another round of sex-making, and her sex reacted accordingly, erupting with its fragrant need. She heard his indrawn breath—her response had not gone unnoticed by the man.

Without releasing her mouth, he moved a single hand down her torso. The electricity in his fingertips made her whimper. Her every muscle tensed, the nerve endings on high alert, and yet throughout her body she felt this magical slackening, which she could attribute only to his power over her.

His hand settled at her mound. He applied a tiny bit of pressure, compelling her to spread. His first touch was along the ridge of her moist lips, and then to her erect little bud of a clitoris. He had her splayed, completely exposed.

Releasing her lips, he spoke a simple word, fiercely whispered. "Come."

Seria cried out. He had caught her off guard, leaving her no choice but to erupt on his hand. She was a mess of writhing, overheated feminine passion, the liquid gushing from her, her body undulating, seeking relief with every possible contact. It was a mindless act of subjugation to his will.

The orgasm seemed to last for hours. He had his finger directly on her clitoris, ensuring maximum release. It was like having her body taken over, lifted aloft to the heavens and then plunged into a deep, cool sea. It felt like heaven. If only this man wasn't so capable of putting her through hell, too.

Seria felt shame as soon as the last wave subsided. She had responded as little more than a trained pet. Her body's deepest mysteries reduced to a reflex action, elicited on command. So why did that make it feel even sexier and hotter? Why was she relishing having him see her like this, knowing that her climax only made his cock harder?

Seria cried out, biting her lip. He let her ride the rapids and over the edge. Plunging down, and then back up, soaring under his protection. There were no words for how it made her feel. She wanted it to last forever, and yet she was afraid. If she became dependent on such experiences, if she came to need this man too much, she would surely have her heart broken.

"Lick." He placed his fingers to her lips.

Seria cleaned her own cum from his hand. She could see this turned him on. The servility of the act, the proof it entailed of his supremacy over her. There was nothing she would not do for him. No order she would not obey.

"Open your legs," he said. "Wide."

"Yes, Master." Seria did her best to accommodate. There was symbolism in this, too, for he could easily enter her without saying a word. After all, she was not likely to resist him. But he wanted this extra step, the assurance of her slavery.

Raylar pushed his cock into her slick, pink opening even as she attempted to widen her thighs even farther. Sighing expectantly, she wrapped her legs around his backside. She wanted him closer, in her as deep as he could be. "Can I take your full size this time, Master?"

He shook his head. "No. Not yet."

"Please, Master?"

"You aren't ready."

"But I want to try."

"You're a stubborn one, aren't you?"

"That's what you like about me." She smiled.

Raylar grumbled. "You asked for it."

At once she felt him growing within her. Longer and thicker. And hotter, too. Her canal sought to accommodate him. She suspected he was trying to get her to back down, but she was determined not to give in. "Is that the best you can do, Primale?"

His eyes lit up—she had definitely ignited something in him this time. It was like his cock was going to explode inside her, and not just the semen from the tip of it, but the entire thing. Gods help her if he moved an inch or tried to fuck her like this.

"Had enough yet?"

"No, Master."

Was she crazy? Of course she'd had enough. What was she trying to prove here?

He narrowed his gaze. It drove her crazy when he did that. It was like he was reading right into her soul. "Stop looking at me like that."

She had forgotten the "Master" part, but that was the least of her worries at this point. Her first concern was being split wide open.

Whether out of mercy or just for the sake of further torture down the line, Raylar reduced his size for the moment and bent to lick at her breasts. The motion was light and soft, though in her heightened state of arousal it was prickling, almost painful.

She was on the verge of a fresh orgasm.

"You are not given permission to come," he informed her, gauging perfectly her body's inflamed state.

Seria held herself back, barely. "I hate you," she blurted.

He smiled in reply, his eyebrow slightly raised. Would she escape punishment for her outburst or would he deliver a fresh round of stings?

"I am not responsible for this set of circumstances," he reminded. "You are."

"Don't try to pin this all on me!" she exclaimed. "You're the one getting your jollies here."

"And you are not receiving the least bit of enjoyment?" he quipped dryly.

Seria had no good answer to that one, though she was sure there must be some defense she could muster.

"Should I take your silence as an admission of surrender?" he wanted to know.

Seria clamped her teeth tightly, determined not to give him the satisfaction. Raylar responded by expanding a little further, just enough to make her ready to throw in the towel.

"All right, I give up," she cried, her body screaming out for sexual mercy.

"Wise choice."

Seria was sorely tempted to stick out her tongue, but she knew that would only get her in worse trouble. She would have her chance to get even, but this was not it.

"It really isn't a good idea to play with a primale's affections, you know." His hips lifted. His pelvis rose and then fell. The slight up and down motion of his cock left her a writhing mass of need.

"I-I didn't mean to…"

"You should take this lesson to heart." Raylar withdrew his cock to the halfway point. The shaft was glorious and glistening, the veins sticking out, thick and purple. "A primale takes what he wants. Had I been any other primale, one not committed to lifelong service in the Guardians, you would have found yourself in a state of considerably greater subjugation at the moment."

Seria could not imagine how anyone could do more to her body than he already had. Of course she was glad she wasn't being dominated in even more strict ways...wasn't she?

"A woman like you is going to need to be very careful," he counseled. "You will need protection. From yourself most of all."

"But not protection from you," she breathed, seeking to draw him back inside her more deeply.

"No. I've already told you where I stand."

"Yes, you have your ethics or whatever. But you are fucking me now, aren't you?"

He frowned a little. "That isn't the point. I am talking about your future."

"With your cock in me?" she challenged. "That doesn't sound real objective to me."

"Don't twist things," he warned. "Don't read in what isn't there."

She pulled at him, grasping his strong shoulders, his pecs, his delicious crotch. "What should I think, then? What should I make of this? Why aren't you just screwing me and getting it over with?"

"I should put the gag back in your mouth."

"If that's the only way you can control me."

"You aren't calling me Master—yet again."

"You aren't acting like one."

He slammed home, hard, pinning her beneath him. "What about now?"

"Yes," she gasped.

"Yes, what?"

Seria couldn't breathe—not without taking him inside her soul, not without melting down, completely and utterly. "Yes…you are acting like a Master."

"I'm not a mem, Seria."

"No…no you aren't."

Talk about stating the obvious.

"Mems make sex, primales possess."

"Let me be your possession, Raylar." She could scarcely believe the scandalous words she was whispering in his ear. "Let me come for you."

His teeth grazed her neck, once, twice, nibbling. "They shouldn't have put us together."

"It's too late, Raylar…Master. You've stripped my defenses. You have me."

"This is one night," he reminded. "The dawn will come."

"To hell with dawn. What we have…is now."

Raylar began to establish his rhythm. "It will be harder this time," he said. "Bigger. More semen, too."

"I want it, oh stars, I do."

His eyes burned fiercely, the color of a blue star deep in space. "Beg for it," he hissed. "Beg for your orgasm."

"Please, let your slave come. Master, let your woman climax."

Seria's declaration was all that Raylar needed. Arching his neck, crying out with passion, he plunged to the hilt. "Now," he roared. "Come…now."

Seria felt her body splintering underneath him. Raylar was driving into her sex and into each one of her nerve endings. He had her split open, and at the same time wrapped tightly in the coils of his own unleashed power.

His second orgasm was indeed far greater than the first. From what she understood of mems, they grew tired easily, but Raylar only seemed to pick up steam. His body was hot and hard against her, she felt his every muscle, sensed the release of his tension, and also the tension yet unreleased. There was more inside him, more that needed to come out than could be contained in these fresh spurts, prodigious as they might be.

She sought to take it all in. She was so slick and wet. She was made for this, for giving him pleasure and getting it back. Sinking her teeth into his shoulder, she released her own sigh of delight. Countless orgasms racked her body, one after another, until she thought she would explode from the ecstasy, die from it. And still, he was surging, in and out, his pure male energy translating into yet more releases for her.

Her body begged mercy. But she didn't want it to stop, either.

It could go on a hundred years, or maybe it already had. She thought she was in love with him, then again, she was real sure she'd never be able to handle this kind of sex-making again. The evening whirled through her mind, all the events between them, every word and touch and gesture, translated into this one shared primal release—bodies bucking, sweating on the hotel bed. Their little Eden reserved until daylight.

Finally, there was nothing left but their heartbeats. The frenzy past, they collapsed together, entwined. A perfect silence, all the questions unasked, at least for now. All too soon the complications would arise, much greater than before. But for now, they were simply a man and a woman who had just made phenomenal sex.

Correction. One man who had possessed a woman for sex and who was not done with her for the night. Not by a long shot.

"What next, baby?" she heard herself ask, the shy virgin gone and transformed into the wanton sex goddess.

Raylar gave a small laugh. "You're determined to go toe to toe, aren't you?"

"It's not your toes I'm interested in." She reached boldly for his cock.

"Easy, angel." He grabbed her wrist.

"You aren't tired, are you?" she teased.

"Actually I'm just getting started."

"Me, too," she bluffed.

"Liar."

"Just try me. I'm ready for anything."

He met her head-on with a kiss. A few seconds of his lips on hers and she was a puddle of liquid. Okay, so maybe she wasn't ready for *anything*.

She wasn't about to back down, though—not after coming this far. Kissing him back, she gave him a moment's surprise, her mouth showing some strength of its own. A moment later he locked her tight in his embrace, however, indicating it was all over but the count.

Seria sighed, praying the night would never end.

At the same time, she feared the dawn, not knowing what it would bring. Would it mark a terrible end or some new beginning, perhaps equally dread and uncertain?

The answer lay in their beating hearts and in the ticking seconds.

Not to mention in the intricate secrets of their genetic codes, which they had only just begun to unravel. Would their lives intertwine into one, or fly apart in a fiery explosion?

Chapter Six

∞

Raylar came to, the scent of Seria deep in his nostrils. She was breathing softly against him, sleeping the deep sleep of a fem. Her body was soft and naked and inviting. His cock hardened at the feel of her thigh against his. He wanted her again.

Gently he extracted the plug from her ass and moved her aside, lifting her head from his chest and onto the pillow. How had this happened? He had actually managed to slip into unconsciousness. Only once or twice had this ever happened to him before. As a primale, he ought to have maintained alertness, keeping his brain engaged even as his body rested. Instead, he had gone into dreamland, like some foolish mem.

It was her fault. The woman, Seria. She had managed to have some kind of bewitching effect on him. Look at her, though. You couldn't blame his body for succumbing. She was so incredibly breathtaking, her small body lying there in repose, so perfectly curved, her skin so smooth and pale, just made to be touched. And those lips—he could not get enough of their flavor.

But that was precisely the problem. Every time he looked at her he wanted to possess her. To sample her charms—hell, to devour them outright. How many times had they performed together? He had lost count of his orgasms at ten. She must have had double or triple that number.

Could it really be true, what she'd told him about her nature? Could there be the DNA of an obedient mixed in with her freewheeling fem self?

Her responsiveness was certainly incredible. Her body seemed made for loving. Lush, alert and vibrant. Incredibly sensitive to his countervailing male energy. Such was the very hallmark of a female obedient. But she was not entirely submissive. At times, there seemed a delicate, subtle balance to her, at other times she seemed at war with herself. The combination was volatile, challenging, but for Raylar, at least last night, it had been well worth the reward.

Seria was like a wild horse, waiting to be ridden. Promising loyalty, devotion and love to just the right person. Regardless of her real genetics, she would never find a mem to satisfy her, that was for sure. No primale was likely to take her either. Most of those he knew were a rather humorless lot. They expected military-like precision from their mates.

They did not want to be challenged or surprised, and they certainly did not want to ever be left in a state of near speechless awe as a result of sex-making, which is exactly what Raylar was feeling at the moment.

A kind of dark panic gripped him as he thought of the rest of what Seria had told him. Not only was she specially designed, so was he. And together they were supposed to form a unit. There was a conspiracy to bring them together, devised at the highest levels, by Nyssa, who was supposed to be Seria's sister, and by Theron, his commanding officer. It certainly would explain why a combat officer such as himself was being sent on such an obscure mission. But Raylar could not wrap his mind around the totality. He was a Guardian, born to fight. Why would any geneticists care if he had a mate at all, much less one made to order?

One thing was certain, whatever the long-term future of Seria, it must not include him. The same went for the short-term. He must not be sent into space with her. And he would tell General Theron this at once. It would be a huge mistake, one that might put both their lives in danger.

It was a question of safety. He could not be trusted to remain objective enough to protect her as a soldier should. He was a lover now and that was very different. There was also the question of free will. Whatever genes he bore, he had the right to choose his destiny.

At least in an ideal world.

Raylar dressed quietly so as not to disturb the slumbering Seria. He would go out into the corridor and speak with General Theron using his pocket holo-ball. Naturally, he dressed in his full uniform. Hopefully the General would release him from his assignment and send a replacement quickly, so that he could leave before Seria woke up. In that event, he could leave her some kind of note, but really, what could he say? Better to just leave things as they were. She would wake up, find him gone and move on with her life. No hard feelings. Or at least fewer hard feelings than if he allowed this situation to go on any longer than it already had.

One night was already like a lifetime with Seria. They had clicked so completely in sex-making, and in their conversations between, and in their dancing, and in the communication contained in their every little touch. Being with her just felt so natural and comfortable. Indeed, he could scarcely remember what it was like before he'd known her. Such a strange reaction for him to have. And in such a short period of time, too. She was hardly the first woman he had been with. He had known many intelligent, desirable females.

It begged the question of what was different about her, and about them together. Liking none of the answers, he dropped the internal dialogue. With that, Raylar tapped the release button on the wall, waiting for the door to slide open with its standard whooshing sound. A moment later it closed behind him, leaving him in the corridor.

Pulling a small, round object from his pocket, he tossed it into the air. It stayed aloft, at eye level.

"Guardian Command Headquarters," he addressed the small hovering holo-ball, no bigger than a marble.

"Certainly, Sir," hummed the machine, immediately configuring the needed coordinates.

If only the rest of life could be handled so simply and with so little conflict.

"Objective obtained," the holo-ball announced.

Raylar watched as the empty space in front of him was filled with a small pyramid-shaped tower, representing the actual Guardian building in the center of the city. It was a sight he never grew tired of beholding. The star and rocket emblem of the Guardians was emblazoned in gold on the side of the black onyx structure, a thousand stories high.

At the very top, the building glowed silver, indicating that the commander was present in his office. Raylar's pulse quickened just a little as he thought about confronting Theron. The General might not be happy. It had to be done, though. For Seria's own good.

Not to mention the good of his heart—which had suddenly found itself under siege from a most unlikely source. "Put me through to General Theron, please," he declared.

A moment later he saw the General's face, as robust and vibrant as in real life.

"Raylar, my boy, what is it?" he asked, a definite trace of a twinkle in his eye. "Don't tell me the little lady's too much for you to handle already?"

Raylar drew a deep breath, wondering just how deep he would have to go into the details of last night's extraordinary sex-making, not to mention the nature of her bizarre allegations against General Theron himself. "As a matter of fact, Sir…"

* * * * *

Seria floated gently on the edge of wakefulness. Warmth dawned in her bones as she remembered. Melting at a man's touch, capturing his heart and being captured in return, her body his ultimate fantasy, to be played on, again and again. A quiet orgasmic "Yes" as he locked the chains of possession on her. The chains of forever…

Lazily, her eyes popping open, Seria reached across the bed, feeling for some bit of wonderful, confirming male flesh. Had she really accomplished her mating mission, or was it all a dream. "Raylar?" she mumbled, still half asleep. There was no answer and after a few moments, she realized she was alone.

"Raylar?" she repeated, sitting up and gathering the sheet about her naked breasts.

Her nipples were tender against the fabric. Between her legs, she tingled. The air was filled with the scent of man, the smell of conquest. She'd been taken, all right, loved to the point of puffy lips and tousled hair and a still twinging pussy.

Stars and comets. Where had Raylar gone off to? He was supposed to be watching over her. Besides, they were lovers now. And that was supposed to mean something, wasn't it? She ought to be able to wake up with her head on his chest, or better still, feel herself stirred to consciousness by his wanting, a glorious morning erection poking her thighs.

Open, my love...

Yes, Master...

Seria slipped from the bed and lowered her feet onto the floor, which was cool and smooth and surprisingly erotic. Her entire body ached deliciously, every portion of her being echoing the events of last night. Raylar had stretched her, helped her body to move in all kinds of amazing ways. And he'd been insatiable. None of her girlfriends had ever spoken of their mem lovers being like that. Raylar was like a glorious beast, a gorgeous, sexily dangerous cat.

Had he really been a mem, of course, it would be no big deal if he just up and left this morning. That was what mems did and fems didn't mind. But he wasn't a mem. And she wasn't fem. Not purely, anyhow.

Blast it, where could he be? She was not going to get upset here, no matter what.

She would not feel alone, she would not feel empty inside, and she would not...panic...like some silly obedient without a Master.

Damn it, where is he?

Seria resisted the impulse to call Nyssa. Raylar was supposed to be here with her and she didn't want to get him in trouble. He'd be back in a moment, she was sure of it. In the meantime, why not treat herself to some time in the sanitizing cylinder? With some extra high-powered beams, the soft and sensuous ones that always went straight to her core.

She never had been one to masturbate very much, but when she did, it was always in the cylinder. Where she could be most alone and free. And naked. She programmed the chamber for a full cycle at maximum intensity. Standing beneath the circular pulsing lights, she inhaled happily. At once she was bathed in soft hues, shades of pink and green and blue. This was a luxury model, all right. Small sonar ticklers activated at the sides of the cylinder giving her the sensation of a mild breeze on her bare skin.

Closing her eyes, she imagined herself at the bottom of a waterfall, on some primitive planet. Her hair, long and loose, her body bronzed from the sun, well used to nudity as a member of some primitive tribe. Stretching her arms overhead she felt the full swell of her breasts. As a diplomat, she hid her femininity, but with Raylar around, she wanted to advertise it.

The imaginary waterfall continued to pour over her skin, even as the beams purified her body and worked away all the microscopic bits of dirt. She thought of strong warriors, bare-chested savages, watching her from the banks of the stream, enjoying the view. These were the sorts of males who took as they wished from a woman, demanding that she succumb to the depths of her feminine being. They would be like primales, only without the restraints of their own overly refined society.

Raylar was like that. She could see him, with that band of warriors. His rippling muscles, his piercing eyes, his narrow waist, the swell of his cock, the obvious power in his stance. None of the other men would dare to challenge him.

"I want her," he would say, pointing to the nymph in the river.

Seria ran her hands slowly down the front of her body, her eyes closed to foment the fantasy. Her nipples were hard, as they would be for him. One look from Raylar, one word from his lips and she would be helpless. So wet and open. So ready.

Seria cupped both breasts, imagining the primitive Raylar coming to her, wading through the water, his cock rock-hard, sticking out proudly, lifting the material of the tiny bit of cloth he wore at his waist.

He was coming for her, wading through the water. She was prey, small and pretty. She would be in his hands. At his mercy. He seized her arms, gripping them like hypersteel. She was drawn into the kiss, her lips instantly opened as his tongue plunged.

He took her mouth. Plundered it. She moaned, all too aware of what he was conveying. He would do the same with his cock. To her sex. He kissed her until he had his fill and then he pulled her still tighter, scooping her up and onto him, using her ass cheeks for leverage.

He impaled her instantly. Her pussy shoved full of cock. One breast swallowed by his mouth. He nibbled at the tender flesh, making her cry out with the need to come. Already. He pumped her, slow and sure, with the confidence and arrogance of one who owns his females.

She locked her ankles behind his muscular, powerful ass. He thrust all the way in, obliterating her with cock, overwhelming her with it. He was ready to come, his semen about to fill her, she could feel it…

Seria's fantasy came to an abrupt halt. She opened her eyes to see the flesh and blood Raylar standing there, right outside the transparent wall of the cylinder. Fully dressed in his uniform. Frowning. Looking so incredibly handsome, with that crease in his brow and those little lines beside his lips.

"Raylar…" She should probably be angry but all she felt was relief…mixed with lingering emptiness. "Where did you go? I was…"

"I had to speak to the General." He cut her off, precluding any show of emotion on her part. "It's not important. We need to be leaving for the spaceport. I need to use the beams as well before we go so you'll have to get out."

"Oh." So he wouldn't be coming in with her. For that matter, he wouldn't be saying so much as a good morning to her. It was no longer anger she was flirting with but tears. This was it, then. No continuation of their role as lovers, just an abrupt shift back to their professional roles.

Did she say abrupt? How about flat-out rude?

"I will be right out," she assured him, keeping her voice steady. "If you'd just give me another few moments of privacy first…if it's not too inconvenient?"

Raylar seemed uncomprehending. Was he really that oblivious to her feelings after last night? What was wrong with him? Could this possibly be the same man who had so completely possessed her, conveying her to the stars without benefit of a rocket ship?

Nyssa had to be mistaken. There was no way this man could have been designed to be her lifemate.

"As you wish," he acknowledged at last, not a trace of emotion in his voice.

Suddenly, she felt her nakedness again. "Stop looking at me," she demanded.

"I'm not," he said gruffly, though she'd been feeling his eyes, burning hotter than the beams.

Seria watched him turn about, trying her best not to get worked up at the sight of his fine buttocks in motion as he exited the sanitizing chamber. If he could turn off his passions at the flip of a switch, so could she.

Talk about a bizarre turn of events.

Maybe this was her fault. Maybe she just brought out the worst in males on account of her bizarre split genetics. All the more reason to hurry out to deep space where she could live sex-free, dealing with entirely different species from her own. Looking down, she realized she was glistening, moist, the fluids still trickling down her thighs.

Wonderful. Raylar must surely have known she was in here masturbating.

This has nothing to do with you, she wanted to shout. But that would only give him satisfaction.

Speaking of which, wasn't that an erection she had seen in his pants a moment ago? And why had he come in here in the first place, knowing she was naked? Strange, coming from a man who was acting like everything was all business again. Could it be there was a chink in his armor? Or maybe a full-blown hole to be exploited.

Time would tell. The deeper question, though, had to do with whether this was a battle she wanted to fight in the first place. Raylar was like a lion, sated now, returned to sleep. If she should awaken him again, they might both regret the results.

* * * * *

Raylar would give anything to be back on the Front right now. Taking on a Narthian nest single-handedly, wading through thick, viscous fluids, the stench unbearable as he fired his weapon again and again into the mass of pulpy larvae guarding the queen's chamber.

Or maybe hacking through flesh-eating webs, his skin on fire, hotter than the sun.

Anything would be better than this.

Standing outside a sanitizing chamber, his cock hard as a rock, needing so badly to make sex with Seria that it made him want to scream. And all the while knowing she was the one woman in the universe he could not afford to touch.

Not if he wanted to keep his sanity. His independence. His unique sense of integrity and duty.

And unique it was, because apparently no one else cared that he had broken the Code by having intercourse with Seria and that he was likely to again. Certainly General Theron did not.

Not only had his superior failed to relieve Raylar of his predicament, he had actually seemed amused by it.

"You're both healthy young people, my boy," Theron had told him. "You can't expect to fight nature like you do the Narthians. My advice to you is to lighten up. There's nothing here you can't handle. And don't worry about updating me constantly. It's strictly a 'don't ask, don't tell' situation from here on. Understood?"

"Yes, Sir," Raylar had replied glumly. What else was he supposed to say to his commanding officer? That he was afraid of forming an emotional bond that he wanted nothing to do with? That he feared becoming entangled hopelessly with a woman who wasn't appropriate for his sub-gender? That he doubted he could keep from making sex with her for five minutes let alone the six days the trip would take? That this tiny, feminine creature was threatening to blow his carefully laid-out life plan wide open?

Not that he wanted to be unfair to Seria by implying something was wrong with her or that she was in any way trying to hurt him. She was amazing—an incredible blend of personality traits. She was a unique individual. He just didn't want a unique individual to love, or any other individual, either. He wanted to be alone. He wanted to be a soldier. To fight Narthians. To the death.

But soldiers followed orders, and frequently the toughest ones to follow were those that kept a man out of danger rather than in it. And for the time being his assignment was routine, boring old escort duty. For Seria. Beautiful, intoxicating Seria.

The woman he had led on last night.

He didn't want to hurt her in any way, just let her down easy. Was there a good way to do this? Probably not. Women were complicated. Strong—but sensitive. Even the densest Narthian queen's nest paled in comparison to the complexity of the average female psyche.

Perhaps it was time to pray.

Would the god of war hear him? Or should it be the goddess of love? No—the love goddess was definitely biased. It would have to be war. Strength was what he needed. And the power to resist. From here to their destination. Which just happened to be on the other side of the galaxy.

That was a long way at this rate.

Especially if he was going to keep on acting like such an idiot. Barging in on her in the sanitization chamber was the worst thing he could have done. It was boorish. Unprofessional. And dangerous. What was he thinking, setting himself up for a fresh look at Seria's naked body? They were damn lucky he had not followed his natural impulses and taken her right there under the beams. She had looked incredible under the colored lights, her body so incredibly lush, her curves perfectly inviting, her lips full, and her eyes bright with desire.

There was nowhere a man would not journey to hunt down a female like this. No limit to the lengths he would go. And that was just from looking at her. He had gone deeper, felt the pulse of her soul, homed in on the intelligence of her mind, the fineness of her wit.

Why exactly had he gone in there? To prove that he could handle the sight of her, maybe? To make it clear to both of them there would be no more physical attraction between them, that he could see her naked and feel nothing more than he might in the presence of another male? That the space journey ahead was going to bring no opportunities for romance? That the tight quarters of deep space would pose no challenge to his iron will, none at all?

All he'd accomplished was to get worked up and frustrated.

Not to mention how he'd shaken up poor Seria. Surprising her like that. Right in her face, but not with any sort of intimacy. A woman needed a little debriefing after sex-making. Even he knew that. She needed to know there was some continuity, she needed to see where the relationship stood, wherever that might be.

Well, he'd certainly made it clear, hadn't he?

A cold slap in the face. That's what he'd delivered.

Just one more reason why he was not suited to have a mate. That was so clear to him. Why in blazes did no one else seem to see it?

Sighing, he looked down at his hard cock. He was going to have to deal with that erection. Willpower wouldn't do it. He would need to masturbate under the beams.

Under no circumstances would he imagine Seria. With her sweet belly and full breasts, her silky soft hair, her sweet scent and passionate lips. He'd think of something else, something safe and remote.

"Yeah, right," he snorted. Like that was going to be possible.

Change of plans, he thought. No masturbating. No feeling anything remotely sexual until Seria was safely delivered.

* * * * *

Seria yielded the sanitizing room to Raylar. She kept her nose slightly uptilted as she brushed past him, indicating that she, too, was to be all business from here on. He made no acknowledgement of her as he moved past. She attempted to do the same, though it was difficult the way her pulse was racing. She couldn't help it. Just having him near her affected the way she breathed, and how she thought, and how she felt as a woman.

It was so much more than the sex-making. His presence alone, everything about him made her ache and hunger and whirl. She craved every part of him—his voice, his lips, the way he walked and talked. Even when he was being stubborn and seemingly indifferent.

Wasn't he even going to offer to talk about last night? Didn't it mean anything to him that he had made love to her? That he had been her first? She'd be damned if she'd bring up the topic, though.

As far as she was concerned, it was a closed holobook. She could not care less about the man anymore, so long as he did his job getting her to her new assignment. And that was something which could not happen a moment too soon.

She wouldn't say goodbye to him, either. She'd just walk off the ship, say a curt thank you and disappear. Back to her humdrum life of predictability and duty. In the meantime, she would work out her frustrations in the sanitizing cylinder. There she could masturbate to her heart's content.

Once she made sure to lock the door, that is.

* * * * *

Raylar's cock ached under the beams. He was feeling hot, confused. Seria was right outside the door of the sanitizing chamber and he couldn't touch her or talk to her. Not if he wanted to keep his mind together. It was the right thing to do, cutting her off emotionally. But what about his erection? There was no getting rid of it and he couldn't possibly walk around hard all the time. Seria was bound to notice. She had already spotted his state of arousal this morning. There was no mistaking those pretty little eyes of hers, furtively darting up and down, stealthily observing. She probably thought he hadn't noticed.

That was one of the adorable things about her. She was so very disingenuous. On the outside, that is. Underneath, she was like a volcano. The most passionate woman he'd ever touched. No one had ever kept up with his desires before. She was more sexually charged than any of the pleasure women on Tarsus Minor. And they were bred for such things.

She didn't know this about herself, of course. She was much too gracious and modest. And a bit naïve, too. The gods help any male who ever took advantage of that and hurt her. Raylar would not hold himself responsible for his actions. He would hunt such a man down. And kill him.

This was not a matter of choice. It was his primale blood. He had been with Seria, intimately. Her soul, her scent, her being were mixed with his. Though he would never touch her again, though he would force himself to walk away, he would never be able to forget.

Groaning, he wrapped his fingers around his erection. He needed to come. Images competed as he imagined himself making sex with anyone but Seria. There were all sorts of women he'd had or dreamed of having. Sex sirens across the galaxy. None of them had staying power, though. They barely registered.

Grinding his teeth in frustration, he gave in to the inevitable reality of Seria.

What was the use, after trying any number of times to fight off her memory—the smell and feel of her, the way she moved beneath him and on top of him, the way she moaned in his bonds, the way she looked at him in awe as he took her, showing her the wonders of sex-making?

There was no escaping the impact of their union. On him, and on her, too, judging by the pain and longing he'd seen in her eyes as she left the sanitizing chamber.

Too bad for her…

She had been a virgin. She deserved so much more than him. It ought to have been some mem taking her the first time, showing her the wondrous journey of her body's magic. Primales lacked the finesse, the subtlety.

They were far too focused of consuming beauty, on mercilessly bringing forth the power of the female. He clenched his fingers tightly, forming a fist. His cock throbbed, the veins pulsing. He let himself expand to full size.

He was in her. Deep in Seria's hot, wet sex. He was fucking her in his mind. In his heart. His fingers moved up and down, the muscles battling those of his cock. Flesh pressed against cock.

Another groan, pure primale. He clenched his buttocks and pushed forward, fucking Seria again, having her. Demanding she take him inside her, demanding she look into his eyes and see her own destiny.

To be his woman.

His one and only.

You will never be touched by another, Seria.

By the Code, where did that come from?

Raylar pushed the thought from his mind and concentrated on the sex dream, so vivid in his wakeful state. It was like Seria was right there in the cylinder with him, her body up against the wall, no pain, only explosive, body-grinding surrender. She could take it. She wanted it. The full power of a man. A real man. In and out, in and out. Her ass cheeks flattened against the wall, her breasts flattened against his chest. Their bellies tight together, lean female flesh against corded masculine muscle.

So real, he could almost hear her hiss the words into his ear as she greedily nibbled at the lobe... *Take me, yes, let me feel your heat...*

Raylar put his free hand against the wall, fingers spread to brace himself. His semen blasted against the smooth, beam-heated surface. Spurt after spurt of milky white, sticking in gobs to the wall. Ten full pumps, each depositing a fresh layer to cover the old, his cock reverberating as his balls emptied themselves, his whole body tensing from the effort. Every muscle strained, from the sinews of his neck all the way down to his calves.

Son of a bitch.

It had been the most powerful masturbatory release of his life.

And it had been focused entirely on one female. The wrong female. The woman he had allowed to get far too close to him already. Damn it, he had gone so far as to have her call him Master. That was over the line. Was it enough to just step back now, or did he owe her something more?

Raylar considered the results of his ejaculation that was plastered across the wall. Incredible. And his cock was still hard. Hard enough to fuck. Hard enough to be sucked. Hard enough that he could march outside this room, grab Seria and throw her down on the bed.

So much for getting her out of his system.

Sighing heavily, he wiped away the evidence and finished his cleaning.

It was going to be a long space flight, all right. The longest of his career.

* * * * *

Waiting for Raylar to emerge from his suspiciously long time under the cleansing beams, Seria sweated out the crucial question of wardrobe. What exactly was appropriate for an interstellar space flight cramped in a small ship with a man who had seduced, used and spurned her in less than a day?

The dressing machine was patiently waiting for her command, the red light on the display indicating the need for human input. She ought to pick something practical. Pants. A jacket. Something suitable for space travel. Something unsexy, something to discourage Raylar and make it clear she had no interest in attracting him. Maybe a nice old-fashioned burlap sack. Or a suit of space armor.

She tried several different options. Including a baggy utility jumper and an oversize woolen habit favored by nuns of the religious orders of Sithios Ten. Each was more ridiculous than the last.

She settled on a midnight blue vylar top and slacks with the golden emblem of the diplomatic corps embossed on the right breast. The material was a bit too clingy and formfitting, but it was regulation and at least she wouldn't have to worry about a skirt.

The idea of having a hem made her more than a little queasy. Hems could be much too easily flipped up, baring the behind for spanking or other forms of naughtiness.

She opted for short hair, in her standard auburn color. Borderline mousy is what Nyssa had called it. Nyssa wouldn't like this outfit at all, but then her sister wasn't the one about to be locked in a hyper-light mini-spacecraft with a sex-crazed primale.

Even now she could feel him inside her. His cock plunging and thrusting. Just a little bit of touching and rubbing and she would be in orgasm all over again.

The test for how well she had done in underplaying the sexiness of her look was going to come soon enough. As soon as Raylar came out of the sanitizing chamber, freshly cleaned and back in his uniform. She felt so damn horny, thinking of him in the cylinder, naked, the sanitizing rays beaming down on his fine body, all those muscles flexing as he made sure every bit of his healthy, bronzed skin made contact. She wanted so badly to go in there, to join him in that tiny space, to push her body against him and beg for his touch.

She would do anything to get it, including dropping directly to her knees to suck that magnificent cock of his. Thick and long, covered in purple veins, splendidly erect, born to fill a woman's glorious sex. Created to make a female moan and scream and come. Just as it had done to her all night long. It pained her to think she might never see that shaft again or feel the indescribable heat he had kindled deep in her flesh.

Stars, but the situation was confusing. She was supposed to be seducing him. Making him want her forever. But he was giving her the brush-off, reminding her distinctly of her responsibility as a diplomat. And he was right. She couldn't deny it. She did have a duty to be professional and asexual.

It was a duty in complete conflict though, with the imperative her newfound sister Nyssa had laid upon her.

She was supposed to make Raylar want to mate with her. Forever. Never mind what she might want for herself. How could she want a man like that? A man who sent such mixed signals? Which set of behaviors represented the real Raylar? Those from last night, passionate and compelling, or the countervailing ones from this morning, off-putting and frustrating and aloof?

Either way, it was hardly fair. He was playing with her emotions, whether he realized it or not.

The man needed to be brought up short, frankly. If he thought he could gaze freely at her body, he had another think coming. She would dress and act the part of aloof fem.

Even if it did make her hot and weak-kneed thinking about how he had come into the sanitizing room, showing no regard for her modesty. His will had been paramount. His desire had superseded hers.

Talk about a dangerous and slippery slope. Suppose he had come in there looking for sex? Suppose he had commanded her to service him? The fucker had caught her with her hands between her legs. What if he'd told her to keep masturbating? What if he'd told her to push her fingers in and out, making the liquid drip down her thighs? What if he'd ordered her to taste herself, right in front of him? What if he'd made her talk about it, telling how horny she was? What if he'd made her confess that all that was for him? What if he had made her tell him what she really wanted, what she needed, more than the air she was breathing?

I need to be fucked, Raylar…Master…

That word, there it was, reborn from the ashes of last night's fires. Like a flaming ghost on her lips. So very potent and charged. And dangerous. Quickly, Seria made a vow to herself. She could never call him that again. It had been a mistake the first time and the next time…well, there couldn't be a next time.

She told herself it was all up to her. She controlled the situation and it didn't matter what he did. The truth was a little trickier, though. Assuming Raylar remained aloof as he was now, showing no interest in her as an object of sex-making, there'd be no problem. But what if that changed back again, the pendulum swinging once more?

If he were to give her one of those looks. If he were to call her his little slave girl, what would happen?

She wouldn't stand a chance, that's what would happen.

"Seria?"

She nearly jumped out of her skin at the sound of his voice. Raylar was standing right in front of her. Fresh and clean in his uniform. The Guardian emblem emblazoned on his chest, the line of medals—tiny blue and green star-shaped jewels—representing his various exploits in combat.

He had killed many Narthians. And seen many of his own fall in the process.

A defeat haunts him…a loss that no human could have prevented. He refuses to see his own heroism, how many he saved…

That's what Nyssa had told her. Would Raylar ever share these things with her? Would she ever dare to ask him?

"You startled me."

His lips curled downward. His thoughts, as usual, impossible to read. "We should be leaving. It's best to reach hyper-launch point before noon."

"You really are incredible, you know that?" The question came from Seria's lips before she had a chance to censor it.

"I beg your pardon?"

"You…you're just…" Damn it, what the hell could she say without revealing way too much of her own feelings. "Oh, never mind."

Raylar regarded her. "For a diplomat you are decidedly inarticulate at times."

Seria's eyes narrowed. "And you're pretty much of an asshole…for a Guardian."

"You're entitled to your opinion."

"And you're entitled to be an asshole, right?"

He remained placid, infuriatingly so. "We need to be—"

"Leaving, I know," she interrupted. "Our precious schedule must be maintained."

Seria stormed out of the room ahead of him, determined to give him a good look at her posterior. It was one ass he would never have again.

Chapter Seven

ဢ

Raylar eyed the spaceship warily. It was a simple Z-wing with a ball-shaped living compartment. Two chambers, one for sleeping and one for eating. Plus the sanitizing area and the cockpit. The construction gave new definition to cramped.

"There must be some mistake here," he said to the spaceport officer, a portly man in red coveralls. "This vessel is much too small."

"The requisition is clear." He checked his autopad. "Orders came straight from the top."

Raylar scowled. He should have figured. As much as Nyssa and Theron were trying to push the two of them together, why not send them across space in this glorified transport bubble?

"The ship will do fine," Seria supplied icily. "So long as you stay on your half."

"That's just it. We won't have halves. We'll barely have eighths compared to what full-grown adults are supposed to get."

"That's life, isn't it, Raylar. People don't get what they're supposed to. They get disappointed. Other people lead them on...and then fuck them over."

It didn't take a skilled diplomat to realize Seria was venting about this morning.

"Look, Seria, if you're trying to drop some kind of hint here about you and me—"

"There is no you and me." She cut him off, returning a dose of his medicine. "All I want to do is get on this ship and get going. Just like you said."

The spaceport agent looked warily back and forth between them. "Sir," he said to Raylar. "If you would initial this requisition?"

Raylar scribbled on the pad with a light pen. The man snatched it back and beat a hasty retreat, no doubt fearing more fireworks.

"Watch your step." Raylar held out his hand to help her climb the stairs. "It's a tricky climb."

"I'm not a child." She refused the help. "And I'd really appreciate it if you stopped pretending like you gave a flying fuck about me, while you're at it."

Raylar sighed. It was obviously payback time, and he had a feeling Seria was going to deliver with interest. His passenger safely aboard, he made the final outside checks on the ship. For its size, it was a good, sleek model. Silver hypersteel, reinforced with the latest in shielding technology, a little something called intel-mesh, a kind of renewable polymer which was capable of regenerating itself in the event of attack.

Of course this was unlikely in the lanes they were traveling. It was a straight shot to the interstellar launch ring at the edge of the system, where they would pick up the hyperspace link. This would push them into a nice, quiet wormhole. At the other side of that, they would travel through just one well-defended star system before reaching their goal.

Seria was fortunate in her new posting. The Narthians had not yet penetrated that region of the galaxy. Though the situation could change in a few solar passings.

Raylar read the fuel indicators. A full reservoir of hydrogen augment and a complete charge on the tachyon drive. Double the energy needed for the journey. A proverbial piece of cake, that's what this mission ought to be.

Except that I'm falling in love with my passenger.

Raylar looked about, startled. Had he just said that aloud? No, it was only a voice in his head. A foolish one which needed suppressing, and fast.

"We'll take off in two minutes," he called out to one of the launch technicians.

"Very good, Guardian." The thin man in yellow coveralls saluted.

Raylar retracted the automatic stairs and sealed the door behind him. They were locked in together now. For the long haul. He found Seria already strapped in the passenger seat of the cockpit. The way the belts crisscrossed her breasts and cinched her waist reminded him of bondage. A strap for each wrist to the armrests and she would be totally helpless.

Great...just what he needed to be thinking about right now.

Beads of sweat were forming on his forehead. The computer was already sequencing the countdown from launch command. They were under a minute and counting. He took his place beside Seria. Close—too close. With primale speed, he checked the interior gauges, his fingers flying over the complicated controls arrayed in front of him.

"Hold on tight," he told Seria, as if she could do anything else.

The engines hummed to life. The floor of the ship shook slightly as the thrusters lifted them from the landing pad. Retracting the spider leg landing gear on each side and grasping the control stick, Raylar engineered their ascent, higher and higher, up to the roof of the open spaceport.

In under a minute they were outside the City Dome. That delicate, yet impermeable layer protecting so many millions of humans and robots from the elements of Earth's atmosphere. It was a stunning sight from outside. Lights reflected off the beveled surface. The sun's rays were shining on it, making it sparkle like a huge diamond.

"It's so beautiful," exclaimed Seria, momentarily forgetting her anger.

No, he thought, *you're beautiful*.

"You're right. I never get tired of seeing it," he concurred. "Each time it looks brand new."

She looked at him, so piercingly that it made him ache.

"What?" he asked.

"Nothing." She looked away quickly, though he sensed she'd been trying to peer into his soul.

That's a mistake, he thought, *for both of us*. *"There are things no man should look at, Seria – let alone a woman."*

"What are you talking about?" she asked him.

Raylar startled. Had he been talking out loud? "It's nothing," he replied, throwing her own denial back on her.

Her lovely mouth formed into a pout. "I know more than you think I do. I know what you hide from me."

"I'm not hiding anything," he declared a little too vehemently.

"No? What about your last mission? You're still blaming yourself, aren't you? Still punishing yourself, denying any happiness you might feel."

Raylar was genuinely stunned. "How could you know about that?"

"It doesn't matter how I found out," she said. "I know and that's what's important. And if you'll allow me, I might be able to help. I could at least listen."

His temples began to throb. The very idea of unleashing that kind of hell on this woman, so kind and gentle and undeserving, tore him apart.

"Don't go there, Seria," he warned, his tone measured but intense. "I know that you must be a brave woman, taking on a posting all by yourself on the edge of known space, but there are things you could never handle."

"That's a convenient excuse, isn't it," she challenged, "for not sharing your feelings with me."

Raylar was wishing badly that he could express himself in a less confrontational way. But what could he do? He knew one thing, and that was combat.

"My feelings are beside the point, Seria. I have a responsibility to get you to your assignment safely and that is all." He tried not to sound cold, but it had to be said, for both their sakes.

"Yes, your precious duty," she said acidly.

"Exactly," he ignored her sarcasm. "Now in the interest of...smooth operations, I propose we do things in shifts. I'll eat while you sleep or else sit up here. This thing flies itself, but I enjoy piloting manually. I think if we are careful we will be able to avoid having much contact with each other. What do you think?"

She was glaring at him, her lip quivering. He had hurt her with his casual distancing, but she would thank him in the long run. Sex-making had to be avoided at all costs. Neither of them could afford to have a mate and that was what would occur between them, given their biological combination of primale and half-obedient.

"I think the same thing I did before," she declared, "only more so. You are an asshole."

Raylar let it roll off him, like the soldier he was. "Spoken like a true diplomat," he quipped, unable to avoid a bit of sarcasm of his own.

Seria flipped her middle finger and began to unbuckle.

"Where are you going?" he demanded.

"Away from you," she spat. "That's your plan, isn't it?"

"You will remain buckled in until we are in deep space. That's an order."

Seeing the heat in her eyes made him want her all over again. He was sure she would be exquisite in bed right now, with all that fire and anger.

What a pleasure it would be to tame her afresh, make her moan and squeal in spite of herself.

"What are you going to do, spank me?"

"I will lock you up," he said. "As I would any crew member or passenger who is a danger to him- or her-self."

"You would like that." She folded her arms over her chest.

"And you wouldn't?"

"Not in the least."

"Good, because I do not wish to be led on," he informed her.

"In your dreams," she snorted.

Indeed, yes…he would long for her, in dreams and in his every waking moment. He could not, however, afford to tell her that, under any circumstance.

Raylar turned his attention fully to the controls, seeking a few moments' respite.

They rose through the atmosphere in silence, the blue-white of the sky giving way to the phantom black of space. In place of a single big yellow star, there were now many tiny cold dots, distant and infinitely quiet.

Raylar looked across at Seria. She had closed her eyes. She looked so lovely, so damnably unapproachable. "I know you are faking sleep," he said.

"Go to hell," she snapped, eyes still tightly shut.

"You will have to watch your language with me," he said. "And your tone."

His heart was pounding. Why was he badgering her like this? What possible difference could it make? It was like a part of him didn't want to let go of her.

"Just leave me alone," she said.

"It's just that this will be a long trip. Sixteen hours, cold space time to the hyper-link and then six days of total interstellar grayness. The wormholes...can play tricks on people's minds."

"Thanks for the tip," she said with maximum disdain.

"You don't have much respect for authority, do you?"

Raylar wanted to take her over his knee. Either that or hold her in his arms so he could kiss her over and over and tell her...

Tell her what?

That was the problem, wasn't it? There was nothing he could say. Nothing he could do either, other than making sex again with her, which was easy as breathing. Beyond that, they were completely incompatible. Sure, they could converse a little, dance and laugh. But they couldn't really *relate*.

Whatever the hell that meant.

"Sure I respect authority," she said. "Just not yours."

This remark hit him right in the primale ego. "For someone's who's supposed to be half obedient you sure don't bring much comfort to a man," he struck back.

"Good." She smiled cruelly. "I hope I never bring you a moment of peace or comfort as long as I live."

Raylar felt the firestorm within. A wall of melting ice. Unspeakable liquid pain. A deep, open wound. His fingers trembled ever so slightly as he returned his eyes to the instrument panel.

Quite simply, he did not trust himself to say another word.

"What's the matter?" she taunted. "Am I causing too much stress for the big, bad warrior?"

Stress was right. And conflict, too. He wanted her. He needed her—or at least he needed something she had. At the same time, he couldn't afford her. She was too much. She was a danger, a risk to everything he had. She made him let go, she made him look too deep, and she made him question things.

Why had General Theron put him in this predicament? Was Seria right about the mating thing, or was this really just some kind of test to see what he was made of? Did he have to show he could resist the temptation of Seria before he would be allowed to fight the Narthians again?

A new layer of resentment began to kindle as he considered this possibility. What if Seria was keeping him from his real duty? He knew he shouldn't blame her, but she was the only available target.

This wasn't good. He should not be feeling these things. He should not be thinking about the woman so much, period. He should not be so...consumed. With an effort of supreme will, he pushed it all down. Down deep with the rest of the untouchable stuff. The things he didn't have time for. Not in this lifetime.

He must shut her out. Completely.

"I'm talking to you, damn it. I won't be ignored, Raylar." She was unfastening her seat belt.

"Don't do it, woman."

"Stop me, then."

He was trying to execute an acceleration maneuver. With one hand on the board he grabbed for Seria with the other. She was on him, grabbing at his uniform. She kissed him, hard.

"Am I getting through yet?"

Raylar held her at bay and finished the maneuver. This achieved, he pushed back his seat and swung her over his lap. He slapped her wriggling posterior hard.

"You will not disobey me again," he said.

Seria whimpered, a disciplined female.

"Are we clear?"

"Yes," she pouted.

He felt the heat of her through her pants. He could smell her. She was as excited as he was. "That will be all." He let her up before he got himself in trouble. "I want you to go and lie down for a while. The ship is stable enough."

Seria climbed off his lap. Her face was filled with a passion bordering on hatred. Without warning she reared back and slapped him across the cheek.

Raylar absorbed the mild sting, feeling it more in his heart than anywhere else. "I suppose you think I deserved that."

"No, what you deserve," she said, "is nothing."

With that she turned and walked out, her freshly spanked posterior wiggling indignantly.

Raylar clenched his fists, resisting the impulse to follow her. She needed to be put in her place. Taught a lesson. She needed a good stern whipping. A hard fucking.

But wasn't that what she wanted? To keep him engaged, to involve him in her ridiculous mating plan?

Correction — Theron and Nyssa's plan.

Raylar muttered a curse. Once again, he was fighting to keep control over his emotions. This is only a job, he told himself. And she is only a woman. One among many. It was a lie, of course, and he did not believe it for an instant.

Raylar decided to put himself into primale meditational mode for a bit. Dividing his mind, he put part of it to the task of monitoring the ship's instruments. The other part, his higher consciousness, he lowered to a quasi-dream state, one unique to primales. It was a combat technique, one that allowed them to push themselves far beyond normal human limits in times of extreme stress.

He had nearly succeeded when he picked up a perplexing sound with his supersensitive hearing. It was the beating of a human heart, the pace faster than normal.

It was accompanied by breathing, tight and heavy, on the verge of panting. The sounds were coming from the sleep chamber.

His pulse raced as he realized what it was. Seria, pleasuring herself. His cock swelled in his pants as he pictured her, lying there under the covers, her hand pressed between her thighs. Was she naked? Was she touching her breasts? Was her small pink tongue peeking out from between her lips? Were her eyes heavy-lidded with desire, closed and lost in fantasy?

What was she thinking, the little beauty with the exquisite body, the marvelous creature he so yearned to hold and protect and possess? Did she think of him or some other male? Was she trying to drive him mad with primale jealousy? Hadn't he made it clear enough that he wanted nothing to do with her sexually?

This was too much. Having to be on the ship with her was bad enough, but having to put up with such blatant sexual enticement was more than any man should have to bear, even a disciplined primale such as himself.

Putting the ship back on autopilot, he rose from his seat, determination burning in his gut.

It was time to set his lovely passenger straight.

Once and for all.

* * * * *

Seria had never been so angry in her life. How dare he put his hand to her bottom like that—again. Had he not just made it abundantly clear he was through with her physically?

How could he reject her like that and then inflame her all over again? He was a cruel man, insensitive to the core. She stripped off her clothes, seeking to reject any reminder of his touch.

Her bottom tingled where he had spanked her. She put her palm against her skin, shuddering. She had been disciplined. The fem part of her sought to maintain outrage, but the obedient part craved to yield—on her knees, begging Raylar's forgiveness. Begging him to take pleasure with her wretched body. Her open mouth, submissive and ready to receive his cock. Her legs parted for penetration.

She had disobeyed...she must be put in her place.

Her hand strayed to her breast, caressing. Her nipples were full and hard. They ached from the cold emptiness of the room, the dire emptiness in her heart and between her legs.

It wasn't fair, any of this. Why had Nyssa and Theron sent her out here like this, to face her destiny with Raylar all alone? Why should the responsibility be all on her shoulders, to make or break this union between them? Here it was supposed to be fate, and yet she had been appointed official catalyst to the fireworks. Wasn't Raylar the primale, the dominant? He should have been the one to whom the secret was revealed.

He should have been ordered to seduce her. To overpower her with his romantic dominance. Leaving her no choice but to accept.

This is how it is, Seria. You were not born free. You were born with my mark stamped on you. You were born to submit, and you will do so...now.

The words made her pussy pour forth. How trapped she felt. Raylar had made her wet from the first moment she'd seen the holo. So why did she have to keep acting like she had a choice? Her genetic engineers were cruel, she decided, and so were Theron and Nyssa for putting them together. Maybe it would be better if Raylar never knew how much she had been affected by the union. It was personal for her now, in a way that cut to the very core of her being.

I shall never tell him, she vowed, *though I'll burn alone for the rest of my life. Nor will I accept his touch ever again. Even if he begs me. I am through with him,* she told herself, even as her body beckoned, desperate to quench the fires. *Never again will I prostrate myself...*

Seria's legs parted before the invasion of her own hand. Her knees went weak. She clenched the muscles of her pussy, greedily taking in her fingers.

The orgasm came at once, quick and dirty. Enveloping and strangely shaming. She could not help herself and she was not supposed to.

Seria felt a chill down her spine, hot and tickling as she remembered Nyssa's words concerning her devious plans. *You will be put together in an environment where sex-making will occur. Tight, steamy quarters.*

That's what this ship was, an incubator for sex.

Sex with the man who most aroused her in the universe. The one who was supposed to be her lifemate. The one her body had already called Master. The one with the magic touch and the magic cock, the one who had owned her once and who could again at his mere whim.

Seria collapsed onto the bed, crawled under the covers and lay on her back. No power in the universe could have kept her on her feet. She was steaming, the liquid oozing from the opening of her puffy lips.

"Yes," she moaned, ever so softly, spreading her legs wide, arching her back.

Touching…

I must hurry, she thought. *He must never catch me doing this again.*

* * * * *

Raylar stood at the hatch to the sleeping compartment. Seria was huddled under the sheet. Only her face was exposed, but it was clear enough what was going on. The small, subtle motions, so quintessentially feminine. The closed eyes, the look of bliss behind pink cheeks.

And the unmistakable scent in the air.

Seria was masturbating, all right. His fists clenched in a torrent of emotion. His already tormented cock thrust itself against the material of his space uniform, threatening to rend it.

By the Code, this had to stop. He had to nip this in the bud.

Raylar yanked back the covers. Seria gasped, apprehended. Her eyes revealed the depth and conflict of her emotions. She whispered his name, as though there could have been someone else on the ship.

"Raylar...what are you doing here?" she questioned.

"You know very well," he replied.

Raylar rolled her promptly to her belly, shielding himself from the temptations of her sweet, swollen breasts, the nipples tight and pink, formed to hard nubs. So, too, did it hide away her tremoring belly.

Unfortunately, there was still her quivering ass and the all-too-tempting slit, glistening with feminine fluids.

"You will not do that on this ship," he ordered. Pulling her hands together behind her back, he administered a punitive smack, right to the center of her ass cheeks.

Seria howled. "That hurts!"

He spanked her five more times, just as hard. "So does having to watch you play with yourself."

"So don't watch," she spat.

"That is not the point. You are deliberately inflaming my primale blood. Do you wish me to enslave you entirely? To reduce you to a pleasure toy for the entirety of this journey? I could do that, you know. I could fuck you hour after hour, day after day, until you moan for mercy, until your body begs for respite. But that would only be the beginning. I would keep on making you come, exploding against your will, like some kind of she-beast, a zithrian tigress, consumed with sex-making, endless mating. Some diplomat you would be then."

Raylar punished her with another trio of blows, thankful she could not see the strain on his face, the intense anguish his own words brought him.

The fact was, he did want to do those things to her and not just for the trip. He wanted the right, the complete access to her body—and her soul—forever.

How could he not? He was a primale and she was an obedient. They had made sex and like it or not, bonding was occurring.

"You don't know the first thing about what it takes to be a diplomat," she fought back, "or a lover, either."

Raylar's primale ego bristled over that last remark. "Don't talk back, Seria. I'm in command on this ship and you will either obey me or be put in irons."

"If that's what it takes for you to be in charge..."

"It doesn't, but apparently you won't be satisfied until you are. A woman like you should be crawling at a man's feet, not negotiating treaties."

"I'll never crawl to you!" She squirmed.

The challenge was more than he could take. Fingers flying, he opened his trousers.

"What are you doing?" she screamed. "You fucking bastard."

His cock slid home decisively between her pussy lips. She was open and wet and hot.

Raylar sank himself to the hilt, pressing his body down on top of hers. Seizing her hair, he fiercely hissed a single word into her ear. "Submit."

Her moan began in protest but quickly turned to acquiescence as Raylar expanded his cock, sending more blood to thicken the round, veined shaft.

Seria stopped struggling, her body recognizing the natural mastery of a primale. Her primale. Still, he knew her mind remained unconquered.

Which in some crazy fashion was how he liked her best.

"I hate you," she said, her cheek pressed to the pillow.

"Duly noted. You will however, follow my orders."

"Why should I?" she snapped. "When you don't follow them yourself?"

"What are you talking about?"

"Your cock in my pussy, Ace. That's hardly keeping out of each other's way."

Raylar frowned. "I warned you about leading me on." He attempted to cover his slip.

"Yeah, right."

"Clearly you leave me no alternative," he pronounced, attempting to sound as authoritative as possible under the circumstances."

Raylar turned his head toward the ship's objectifier on the wall. "Shackles. Full wrist and ankle. Female size," he ordered the silver, mirrorlike surface of the machine. "Make them old-fashioned steel."

The silver mirror flashed red and then green. Raylar reluctantly withdrew his cock and went to the wall and opened the drawer underneath. The shackles were gleaming, connected by thick chains. He lifted the metal in his hand. It was heavy. Substantial.

A strange, unspeakable bliss flowed through his being. A rush—deep and primale. He was about to put Seria in bondage. The symbolism was almost overpowering. The naked flesh of the female, constrained in steel. At his mercy.

His every primale instinct was to possess her once more, to stake his claim. Filling Seria with semen, with cock. Not fucking her was going to take every ounce of willpower. As it was, his cock was throbbing with life, wet and glistening with Seria's fluids.

He should have ordered the chains for himself. Except that there wasn't a set of shackles strong enough to hold him. At least not that the objectifier could make.

Seria had taken the opportunity to turn back over. Scooted against the bulkhead at the head of the bed, knees gathered to her chest, the sheet gathered about her, she made her last stand. "If you think you're putting those on me, you're crazy."

Raylar ached to thrust his tortured dick between her lips...silencing her protests once and for all. "It's for your own good. And mine, too."

Seria snorted an obscenity, indicating she did not believe him.

"A lady does not talk that way," he said.

"I'll talk however I fucking want to talk...you bastard."

"Lower the sheet, Seria." His heart was pounding. His pulse racing. "Get back on your belly. Wrists and ankles crossed behind you."

"I'm not your slave," she defied.

"You want me to treat you like one, though, don't you?"

Seria flushed. Her eyes darkened. "I want nothing of the sort," she demurred, just a second too late to hide her body's desires.

"Lower the sheet," he repeated, his voice a rasp. "You may not hide your nakedness."

She licked her lips. A quick darting motion. Her breasts were rising and falling. There was heat in the air, a pungent thickness between them. The feel of power in the air. And submission.

Seria's hands moved, weak and trancelike. The material slipped from her hands, the sheet dropped to her waist. Her hands fell limply with it to her sides, giving him an unencumbered view of her bosom.

"Arch your back."

160

She followed the command. It had nothing to do with ship's discipline anymore and they both knew it. This was about a woman displaying herself to a much stronger and more powerful male. A male who desired her. And intended to have her.

"Touch your nipples. Make them harder," said Raylar.

Seria obeyed. She pushed at the nubs, up and down and sideways, using her index fingers. He rubbed his cock as he watched. It was blatant on his part. What was there left to hide?

"Pinch."

Seria whimpered as she followed the new command. Far from moving him to pity, her predicament only made him want more power. More control.

"Harder. Both at once."

She sucked on her lower lip. The pain was erotic to behold. He knew it well, from previous experiences. With women unable to hide their responses from his augmented primale sensory apparatus.

He drew a deep breath as her nipples turned from pink to red. They were swelling visibly, enticing him to push her further.

"You disobeyed me," he reminded.

"Yes..." She nodded her head, acknowledging.

"What should I do about that?"

"P-punish me..."

"I already spanked you."

"Yes..." She was in a kind of mist. The liquid heat of a woman deep in sexual submission. "It...it hurt."

"So it did. Remove the sheet, Seria."

She cast it aside, exposing herself completely.

"On your knees. Thighs apart."

Her easy compliance only made him want more. It was a dangerous game they were playing. Was it too late to fight the pull of biology? If he were to take her now in his present state…

"Look at this," he demanded. "Look at my cock."

She did so, hunger and awe in her eyes as she beheld his erection, full and thick, proudly defying gravity. His balls were hurting, so full they felt on the verge of bursting.

"You do this to me. And don't take that as a compliment, it's not. You are putting me in a damn difficult position, do you know that? This is a mating hard-on, Seria. Mating hard-ons are for keeps—not like what we had last night. Take a primale's semen in your belly when he is in the fever and you are his. Never mind that pregnancy is no longer possible in our society. You will be his property, as surely as if you were in the days of the cavemen."

"I don't care," said Seria. "I don't care if you do that to me—"

Storms erupted inside him. The woman played with fire. She had no clue. "Enough, Seria."

"Why do you fight your own impulses? I thought you were primale—don't you take what you want?"

"We are men of discipline. We live by the Code."

"Did your Code tell you to display me like this?" she challenged. "Did your Code tell you to make chains to put on my body?"

Raylar's jaw set tightly. She was pushing him to his limits. "Fingers interlaced," he said curtly. "Behind your neck. Henceforth you will speak when spoken to."

Seria moved into position with the ease of an obedient. Behind her eyes, he could see it, though, a most distinctive, I told you so… *I told you that you want to own me.*

"Is this what you want, Seria? My masculine control over your life? You want to eat and drink as you're told? To provide sexual service at my whim? To wear clothes of my choosing, or none at all if it pleases me? You want to submit to my authority—in bed and out of it? Daily spankings, restraints...the whip?"

Seria stayed in place. "I want what you want..."

"Eyes down," he commanded, unable to bear the soft intensity of her stare, the sweet seduction of her words.

Seria broke the silence that followed. "Raylar?" she whispered. "Master?"

His cock expanded a full inch in her direction. "What is it?"

"Suppose you came in my mouth instead? Would I still be...branded?"

"Woman," he growled, "why do you persist in this?"

The answer was no, probably not.

Still, the risks of being so close to her, naked and in heat like she was would be very high indeed. He was in the grip of primale fever, after all. If he were to plunge his cock between her legs at this stage, there would be no turning back. Indeed, it would be seriously unlikely that another man's touch would ever mean a thing to her. Not after such an experience.

"Don't deny yourself. Possess my mouth..." Her voice was an erotic rasp. The wench had chosen the words carefully, no doubt.

Possess my mouth...

What male wouldn't want between those sweet lips? To plunder them of any last vestiges of innocence, to render her into the flaming, fatal beauty she was intended to be.

"Possess me...Master."

He nearly succumbed. More than anything he wanted to give in—to yield himself to her passions, to entrust his raw manhood to her feminine designs. But he had as yet one scrap of will. Pushing aside the anticipated sensations, the glorious fulfillment that would come from the act of fellatio, Raylar wielded the chains.

Swift as lightning, causing her no discomfort, he locked her wrists behind her. Lowering her forward, gently onto the bed, her cheek on the silk coverings, he took hold of her trim ankles. He secured each one and then pulled the chain taut.

He employed a common hog-tie, wrists to ankles. Seria gasped in frustration. Stunned no doubt from the swiftness of his action.

"Raylar, why won't you let me?" she exclaimed.

"You don't understand now. You will later. You'll thank me for it, believe me." Raylar wasn't so sure, but it was the only thing he could think to say.

"Fuck you," came her reply. "You hear me?"

He was at the doorway. "I'm sorry, Seria. It's the only way. Try to get some sleep."

"You can't leave me like this." She squirmed.

Raylar sought, unsuccessfully, to stuff his cock back into his pants. "I can and I will. And if you do not calm yourself, I will gag you as well."

Seria released a sound of protest. She probably intended it to be something formidable, but to Raylar it came across as hopelessly adorable and strangely soothing to his animal desires. "Sleep," he urged, "little one."

"I'm not your anything," she cried as he closed the hatch behind him.

Raylar attempted unsuccessfully to extinguish the smile on his face. It was about as easy to eliminate as this accursed hard-on. Heading straight for the ship's stores—in the back beside the engine compartment—he did something he had never done before on a space journey.

He broke open the emergency bottle of brandy. Every ship carried one, by Guardian regulations. Ordinarily drinking on duty was prohibited, but Guardians were known to face situations that required extreme measures. This was one of those situations if ever he'd run across it.

Not bothering with a glass, he opened the ancient brown bottle with the gold label and hoisted it directly to his mouth. The hundred-year-old alcohol burned hot and smooth, opening a pathway right to his belly. If only he could open a path that clear in his head. Taking the bottle to the kitchen, he collapsed in one of the two chairs. He set the bottle on the table.

He had a sneaking suspicion he was going to be finishing it before all was said and done. Whatever it took to calm his passions. And to forget. Seria. And himself, too. At least that part of him that was betraying his own ideals.

No matter what happened, he would not go back there. He would not touch that chained woman. He would not kiss her, or love her, or possess her.

Oh, hell. He swallowed deep from the bottle. Talk about a lost cause. Two minutes and it felt like a lifetime. He couldn't leave her in there. Alone. Chained. He told himself he was doing this for her safety and protection.

The fact that he was feeling desperate and sick from being alone and apart from her meant nothing. Nothing at all. He was a Guardian. And he could not afford to be dependent like this on a female.

He'd unchain her quickly, and then leave the cabin again.

One more brace of the brandy and he was off. On the most dangerous mission of his life.

* * * * *

Seria was in bondage.

She pronounced the word in her mind, wrapping her head around the reality. A man had done this to her. Raylar, to be precise. This was his will and not hers.

The chains, the enforced nudity. The near sexual possession. All of it was his doing.

Her body couldn't help but respond, her nipples ached to be touched or pinched or bitten. Her pussy, dripped profusely onto the bed, her belly was so hot with need that she was unable to stop shifting, trying to get off in her state of total confinement.

What he had done to her...

The way he had gone inside her, eliminating her petty resistance. Nothing had prepared her for that feeling of total possession. His action in one fell swoop had stilled and calmed her, framing her reality even as it inflamed her body.

With that single act of penetration, Raylar had taken her in the deepest meaning of the word...

What would have happened if he had ejaculated inside her?

With a mating erection? The kind that released the semen of marking and branding. He had said, without boasting, that she would have been his. Forever.

A close call, indeed.

And where was her head? She had urged him on, as angry as she was at him.

But that was her mission, wasn't it? To allow herself to become his mate.

His sex slave.

Shivers passed up and down her spine. She pulled in futility at her bonds. She couldn't play with herself now, she couldn't touch or satisfy. Her body was off-limits. Her pleasure...and her pain were up to him.

Was he teaching her a lesson or what? What did he intend in the long run? He was fighting his mastery over her, that was clear.

She wished she could make it better for him.

She wished she could comfort him.

She wished she could scratch her nose properly. And have another orgasm.

Seria startled as she heard the door slide open.

Raylar was back.

Visions filled her tormented mind—being turned over, his hand taking its fill of her flesh, exploiting her bondage. He would work her to exquisite simmering, make her curse and beg and cry, all in the same breath, force her to shatter into a million pieces before finally putting her out of her misery. Unchain her, put her on her back, legs apart, enter her, pin her arms over her head, move in and out, perfect his rhythm for that one perfect release.

The release of possession. And enslavement.

His...by right of his semen. His by right of primale conquest.

Raylar sat on the bed beside her. "I'm releasing you," he announced, abruptly ending her fantasies. "We must act as though this never happened."

She could smell the brandy on his breath. He'd been drinking. Why in the blazes had he done a thing like that?

"Act as though it never happened?" she exclaimed. "That's easy for you to say. You're not the victim here."

Raylar sighed heavily. "I'm sorry, Seria. For all of it. I wasn't...thinking clearly."

He undid the chains, freeing her limbs. "What do you want?" she demanded, sitting up and rubbing her wrists. "Why won't you tell me what you want?"

"I want to do my duty. To take you to Alphus Six and never see you again."

She moved to slap him. He made no effort to stop her. "If you think you can hurt me," he said dryly, "trust me, I've seen more than you could dream of in your worst nightmares."

"But you won't tell me. Why won't you tell me?"

"I don't want to make things worse. We have our separate lives...why complicate it?"

"Get out." Tears stung her eyes. She couldn't bear to see him like that, sitting there so placid, looking at her like none of this even mattered.

"As you wish." He stood up, straight and tall. "We will continue with our original plan. Taking shifts, keeping out of each other's way the rest of the trip."

"I was already doing that," she pointed out rightfully. "You're the one who barged in here and forced yourself on me."

"You were behaving in a sexual manner, Seria and I responded by instinct. We both made a mistake."

Seria's mouth hung open. She couldn't think of anything nasty enough to say.

If only she were the stronger one. She'd make him feel submissive for a change—chain up his fine body and force him to accept a place of subservience. Naked and helpless. For hours she would tease and torment that cock of his, until he begged for release. And then she would torture him some more just for good measure.

"I am going to get something to eat," he said, changing the subject. "Are you hungry? I can prepare something and leave it for you."

"Why should I eat anything, Raylar, I'm a mistake. You probably wish I didn't even exist."

"I never said that."

"You might as well have."

"This is getting us nowhere, Seria. I am leaving."

"Good."

He nodded, oblivious as always to her feelings. "In that case, I'll leave you alone."

She made no reply. Less than a minute after he was gone, she was crying, weeping uncontrollably into her pillow. It wasn't fair. None of this was fair.

* * * * *

Raylar heard her sobbing. Blast it, what was wrong with her? Why were women so sensitive? He debated leaving her be, but the Guardian inside him couldn't let her suffer like that.

Or was it some other impulse calling him back? Something personal...

It was true he felt things for Seria in particular that no other woman had ever triggered in him. It was like she had become the template, the very model for femininity in his mind. Compared to her, every other member of the gender paled to insignificance.

He had never meant to cause her pain. And yet it seemed like the more he tried to fix things with her, the worse he made it. Wasn't he doing what she wanted? Respecting her privacy? Damn it, he was just a complete imbecile around her. He couldn't make firm decisions. He kept changing his mind, second-guessing himself.

Was there any way out?

She seemed to pay no notice as he came back into the sleep chamber. She was facedown, her beautiful head pressed into the pillow. Her fists were clenched in futility. She was the very picture of feminine frustration.

Never had he seen a more incredible sight on any of the worlds he'd visited.

Paralysis almost overcame him. Did he dare to touch her, to interfere in her sorrow? His own breathing felt like intrusion. At last he bent down, lightly resting his fingertips on one creamy shoulder. Seria stiffened in reaction. She didn't want him there...she didn't want him.

"Seria." He said her name, feeling so very lost. "Don't cry...please?"

Seria rolled onto her back, reaching. "Raylar...make love to me."

Her body beckoned. He craved it in a way he had never known. It was like a part of him, half even. Would they have to make the connection—male to female—in order to soothe the anguish?

Raylar's clothes tore away in his hands, his primale strength making a mockery of the material. Her eyes lit with need as she watched his flesh come into view. He would touch her everywhere, he would rub their bodies together creating heat and fire and liquid magic.

Her arms were outstretched, she had one leg up, the knee bent enticingly. She was pure invitation, back gracefully arched, her pussy lips peeking out like petals clothing her wondrous sex beneath.

His eyes riveted, his mind and heart focused like a laser, he crawled on top of her, his every motion designed to bring them together.

They fit. That was the only proper word to describe it. One single movement put them into instant harmony.

Make love, she had said, *not sex*.

Raylar clung to her.

Inside her. Trembling. His cock aching, stretching, finding its home deep, deep in Seria's sopping wet, though incredibly tight, pussy. Their flesh was fused. Neither spoke. They just clung. To each other. Two bodies. Alone. Deep in space. No right or wrong, no tomorrow. Just the now.

He let her cry against him. He was holding on for dear life, himself. This made no sense. It was a great, great mistake, all right. This was not the sort of universe for lovers. Least of all when you were a soldier, pledged to fight the likes of the Narthians.

Raylar wanted to come. More than once. He wanted to fill Seria with his semen. Mating semen. Not to give birth, that was impossible, but just to feel that bliss which others spoke of. The moment of primale truth. When one's mate has been identified. And claimed.

"Yes, Raylar," she read his mind, "I need it…"

"I can't." He shook his head, the anguish pouring into his voice.

"You can." She pressed her belly to his, arching her back, offering herself. "I'm yours…Master."

The way she said it, with such confidence…

"You don't know what you are saying, Seria."

"I do," she breathed. "I'm…nothing…without you."

Raylar groaned. He could not hold back. "Seria…"

"Let it go," she urged, clutching his shoulders. "Let it all go."

Raylar felt the release surging up from his toes, shooting like lightning to his cock. A single zap, expending him, like a switch flipped, a dam released, a star collapsing. The semen just poured out, spurt after spurt. He wasn't even moving, just holding tight to Seria, listening to her sighs and her endless sweet whispers of "Yes".

"Can't stop," he told her as the orgasm went on.

"Don't stop," she said. "Keep going. Come on my belly. My breasts."

Raylar withdrew, sending a white warm spray across Seria's torso. She cupped her breasts, smiling ecstatically as he bathed them in his cum.

"My face…my mouth," she exclaimed, extending her tongue.

The target proved irresistible. Pumping his cock, taking aim, he squirted over Seria's perfect face, covering her cheeks and landing a dab right in the middle of her tongue. He went for her hair next, then back to her breasts.

She was shuddering, moaning, and rubbing his cum all over herself.

Suddenly, he had to have her from behind.

"Get on all fours," he said huskily.

Seria put herself into position. She was woozy, but more than eager to obey. Raylar's first orgasm had nearly subsided, but he was still rock-hard, well on the way to a second one.

Seria grunted as he slammed himself home, filling her. Adrenaline surging through his system, he clamped his teeth down on Seria's neck. Not hard enough to break the skin, but just enough to make her feel possessed. He felt her spasm in reply. Her pussy contracting against his cock, rapid-fire.

She was coming.

He replied by pulsing his cock, adding to the heat of her pleasure. She gripped the bed, crying out with soft, feminine mewls. Finally, he pushed her, belly down, squashing her breasts. One hand pressed to her back, he pulled his cock out halfway. Seria was screaming, but not from pain.

"Say it," he hissed.

"Master…fuck me!"

Raylar descended, hard. Immediately, he withdrew and pounded her again. She cried out for more, prompting him to seize hold of her hair. "Submit…"

Her pussy opened for him, every fiber of her being moving into deep surrender mode. She was relaxed, her body was open. She was his.

He took her. With lightning thrusts. Powerful, primale thrusts. She was no longer able to control the orgasms. He made them happen, in his time, by his will. In and out. Tireless. He could do this for hours if he liked.

Or…he could come now.

"Beg." He slapped her ass.

"Come inside me, Master. Fill me…again."

Raylar cried out, a lion's roar of an orgasm. Seria took it all, shaking and writhing beneath him. They were at the center of a storm, a swirl of fire, invisible, but melting hot. He was scarcely aware of where he left off and she began.

At a certain point, he flipped them over, holding her above him. Like a rag doll, he teased her on the end of his dick, rubbing the tip of it against her engorged clitoris. She cried one minute, laughed the next.

Finally, he let her sit, allowing her to slide down the length of his cock, taking it inside her. All the way.

"Move," he commanded.

Seria planted her feet on the bed alongside his hips straddling him. Lifting herself, she exposed his cock, almost emptying her pussy, but not completely. A twinkle in her eye, keeping him waiting as long as she dared, she lowered herself, sheathing him fully in her sweet sex.

She repeated the motion several times, greatly adding to his pleasure in the process.

"Hold your breasts for me," he said, enjoying the fine sight of her, moving so wickedly.

She did as she was told, clenching her swollen globes. Her belly undulated as she lifted herself, again and again, only to descend once more, her pussy filled to capacity.

"Come for me," he ordered, needing to see her in the throes of possession. "Now."

Her face slipped into angelic ecstasy. The helplessness suited her well it seemed, at least in the bedroom. Closing her eyes, she leaned back, allowing the sensations to wash over her. He was in charge of her body and she was willing to accept it. He could feel himself in her, and not just in her pussy. He was in her head, too. Not to mention every muscle and nerve ending.

Once the orgasm subsided, he flipped them over, pinning her wrists over her head. Slow and deep, he had her again. With each downward motion she came for him. With every upward one, she whimpered for more. Twice more he orgasmed like that, until at last she was exhausted.

Not that she didn't want to go on.

"Don't stop, Raylar." She was slurring the words, barely able to stay conscious.

"Sleep," he soothed, brushing the hair from her face. "You need sleep."

She was shaking her head, attempting to give him some sort of argument even as she conked out, her conscious mind giving in to the inevitable human need for rest. He was smiling down on her, feeling such satisfaction and appreciation.

For all of her. The incredible sexiness. And her brain and courage, too.

Such a very dangerous combination.

He should leave. Right now, getting as far away from her as this tiny ship would allow. Escaping all the way to the bottom of that brandy bottle if he had to.

Raylar was just getting to his feet when she called for him, from somewhere deep in a dream it seemed. "Don't go." She reached for him. "Don't leave me."

"Seria," he protested.

She had hold of his arm. Wrapping her arms, she rested her head against it. "Um hmm…" she murmured, a smile of satisfaction on her face.

Raylar felt the stab of anguish in his heart. He desired nothing more than to give in to his mating urges. Lying down with her, allowing her to snuggle her head on his chest. Cuddling, comforting and protecting until the fever hit them again.

The beginning of a lifetime's pleasure. A lifetime's adventure.

But that was not his fate. He could never leave a female behind to weep over his absence, to mourn his death in battle. Especially not a woman as talented as this who needed to be living her own life of service to humanity.

There was irony in this, really.

Now that the two of them had shared bonding sex, they could not partake of the flesh of others. Which meant they would have to be celibate.

Good. He had had enough of sex-making as it was. It was energy better put into his work.

Seria would find the same. She would be stronger for this. She would rise to great heights in her career.

He would be proud of her.

Yes, this was really a stroke of fortune.

So why did he feel so miserable?

His lips were quite dry as he touched his fingers to them, preparing to transfer a kiss to her cheek. One last gesture of affection to her in her sleep. Her skin was warm and soft and inviting.

Desperately, he fought his urges. The die was cast.

No longer would he treat her as lover, as Dominant or Master.

No longer would he touch her, hear her sigh or enjoy their mutual ecstasy.

He retracted his hand, as if from fire.

Rising, he turned on his heel, squared his shoulders, and left her. Peaceful in her dreams.

His thoughts turned to the brandy, wondering what he would do when it ran out.

Chapter Eight

෨

Seria stared blankly out of the view port. They were just one day into hyperspace—one day out of six—and already she was feeling the weight of the oppressive grayness. Hyperspace was creepy as far as Seria was concerned. There was something unnatural about it. Oh, she knew the physics well enough, about the wormholes that wound their way through the curvatures of space and time allowing shortcuts that saved months or even years over conventional space travel, but there was no getting around how it made her feel.

Like maybe people really didn't belong out there.

At least not lonely, hopeless people without any sense of their future. Desperate people. Like her. And Raylar, too, whether he knew it or not. Maybe he fooled himself, but not her. She could hear the roughness in his breathing. And she could see the pain in his eyes, the way his brow crinkled and his lips pressed and twitched as he put himself in those meditative states of his.

Did he know she was spying on him when he did that? She felt a little guilty, but it was the only time she could get close to him. With his stupid separation policy that didn't even let her be in the same chamber with him. Why was he so afraid of her? Big, tough Guardian that he was.

Did he think he was protecting her? He had done nothing so far but leave her with a terrible empty place in her heart. Such a cruel twist. Bonding with her so passionately and then ending things with brutal, efficiency, abandoning her in bed without saying a word.

And he didn't seem affected in the least.

176

If anything he'd seemed pleased with himself as he had explained to her where things stood.

An opportunity for celibacy he had called it, a mutual agreement to ensure they would both be able to devote themselves fully to their careers.

Oh, goodie.

She had half a mind to pull the rug out from under his efficient, equanimous self. Then again, she knew better. How he was hurting underneath. Everything had come out already. There was no faking the way he had made love to her, the way he had touched her cheek just before he'd left, when he'd thought she was still asleep.

There was no mistaking the tenderness, the vulnerability behind the usual suit of armor.

But there was no getting through to him again it seemed.

So much for his being her natural-born partner and mate, she thought glumly. How could the geneticists have bungled things so badly? Environment must indeed count for more than DNA in determining a person's adult nature. Maybe in theory he was to be her hero and protector, but in real life, he was just another Guardian, doing an assignment he obviously resented the hell out of.

"One hundred hours, ten minutes hyperspace time left," Raylar announced crisply, popping his head out of the cockpit.

Something in her snapped. "You really hate me that much, don't you? You actually have to count the minutes you're stuck with me."

He frowned. "That isn't it, Seria. I just thought you'd be interested."

"Well, stop thinking," she exclaimed, letting it all out. "And stop with your little updates. Letting me know how wonderful and fine things are. Maybe they aren't fine. Maybe it's not just about the numbers on your precious dials and displays."

Raylar stared, assessing.

"Don't look at me like that. I'm fine. There's nothing wrong with me. I don't have any stupid space madness. I'm just…fed up."

"I didn't say anything about space madness."

"If anyone's acting strangely," she persisted, not really sure where her thoughts were coming from or where they were going, "it's you."

"Me?" He blinked. "What's strange about my behavior?"

"You're cut off from your emotions, for one thing."

"I was not aware of that." He shook his head.

"No, I suppose not," she shot back. "I guess fucking isn't an emotional thing for you. Just love 'em and leave 'em, right?"

Raylar pursed his lips. "You are referring to our sex-making activities?"

"No, Raylar," she replied acidly. "I meant the big chess tournament we've been having."

"I don't think sarcasm is going to help us, Seria."

"Why not? Nothing else has."

"We need to regard the matter with some maturity. And objectivity."

"Sex isn't objective. It's passion," she countered. "And cutting another person off without so much as an explanation is just plain cruel."

"What is there to explain? We succumbed to biological attraction. Bonding occurred, leaving us the possibility of mating or mutual celibacy. Clearly the latter is in our best interest."

Fury and boundless frustration bubbled inside her. Did he have to be so damn arrogant about everything?

"How do you know what's in my best interest or not?" She was on her feet, a mere six inches from his face.

"I am aware of a diplomat's responsibility." He stood his ground. "And I know the Guardian's Code. My responsibility is to get you to your destination and proceed to my next mission while you get on with your assignment."

"You don't know a fucking thing about responsibility, Raylar!" The strength of her reaction was surprising even her.

"Seria, you have no cause to say such a thing."

"I do...I do, Raylar."

"You are overwrought," he decided. "You need rest."

"Fuck you—you don't know what I need. Stop acting like you do."

He took hold of her upper arms. "Seria, it's the effect of hyperspace. It can feel like you're drowning the first time out. Trust me, I've been there."

"Oh, no," she laughed, without humor, "you haven't been here, not where I am."

"I have. Trust me."

She wanted to shake him up, like she was shaken up. She wanted him as insecure and unsure as she felt. And there was only one way to do that. By daring to open her heart, tearing it if need be.

"You want to walk in my shoes? Try waking up one day and finding out your whole life has been a lie. That you are really some kind of half-breed freak and that you have a sister who's head of the Council and that you're supposed to marry some impossible pigheaded Guardian so he can become some all-wise general and save the human race."

A dark cloud passed over his face. He was struggling to keep control. "I told you, Seria, no more. You are letting the madness talk. I am not going to be a general, and we are not going to marry."

"Ask Nyssa if you don't believe me. Or your precious General Theron, who you know damn well has been setting you up this whole time."

"I am going to have to give you a dose of calming serum, Seria. For your own good."

"Go ahead, it won't change the truth."

"The truth, Seria?" Raylar seemed as close to genuine emotion as she'd ever seen. Was she breaking through his shell at last? "You have no clue…"

"Really? Then why don't you go ahead and enlighten me, Raylar?"

"Truth is duty. You have yours and I have mine."

"My duty is to Nyssa and Theron. And so is yours. And they put us together on this mission for only one reason. To mate. You will obey your General and have me."

"I'm going to get the serum," he decided.

"Coward," she hissed. "Why can't you be a man and just deal with things?"

"What things?" he demanded.

"Sex for one. You want it, I want it. Why do we deny ourselves? And don't say it's because of the bonding business. We can make love all we want now and still walk away at the end of this trip. Unless you're afraid of becoming attached."

"I am afraid of nothing."

"Prove it."

"Very well." Raylar responded with a searing kiss. Hot and punishing. She felt the pent-up desire, the frustration he must have been enduring. So she wasn't the only one suffering for lack of making sex these past hours.

He took his fill from her lips, stealing her very breath. By the time he released her, what felt like a full interval later, her nipples were hot beads and her crotch a pool of liquid need. He let a single hand linger on her hip, his large, capable fingers pressing the firm flesh, a powerful reminder of what he could do to her.

"You really want me to deal with things?" he challenged, his voice a low rasp.

Seria could feel the primale energy, emanating from his body. "Yes," she whispered, knowing how much she was in over her head.

"So be it. But you must be prepared to go to my core. You must call upon your obedient side. In ways you never have before."

Seria nodded. Her only hope was to follow her instincts.

His gaze was fierce, unlike any she had seen in him before. And yet she felt no fear, only wanting.

"This will change nothing." He confirmed her earlier words. "When you are delivered to your destination, we will part ways...forever."

"For pity's sake, Raylar, stop talking, and just do it."

"Undress me," he ordered.

With trembling fingers, she moved to unclasp his uniform. All the way to his waist. He stood stone still. Observing, evaluating. There was no mistaking his calm and absolute control. She was on trial now. She must prove herself...by pleasing him.

Parting the halves of the material, she put her palms on his magnificent chest. Such a beautiful man, a living statue, a human god. Reverently, she touched him, enjoying the slight sigh he released in reply. Unable to resist, she moved her mouth to kiss the tip of each nipple. They were hard. Blood-filled.

In a moment she found herself licking his smooth skin. Dabbing her tongue across the well-developed pectorals and down his ribbed abdomen. And lower...

The words rang in her head as she pressed her lips again and again, dampening his skin. *Prove it...Prove you're half obedient.*

There was only one place to go, only one action to take. With all the ease in the world, Seria lowered herself to her knees in front of him. Raylar offered no assistance at this point.

It was up to her to open the fastenings and take out his stiff and ready cock.

She felt her pulse race at the sight of it. Stars, how she had missed it...missed him, too. She wanted it all. Every kind of sex-making, her every opening filled, her body pushed to its very limits. But first, one small taste...

Raylar took her head in his hands, preventing her from applying her lips to the tip of his cock. "Obedients do not initiate in sex-making. They follow orders."

Seria licked her lips, dry as any desert. "Tell me." She looked up at him. "Tell me what to do."

His lips angled into something of a smile. Was he mocking her? Lording it over her, or was it some other primale emotion, too deep to read?

"Tell me what you want, Seria."

She swallowed hard. He wanted her pride it seemed, more than her lips. "I want to...please you."

He shook his head. "You'll have to be more specific. You talk like a diplomat, not an obedient."

"I want to suck you," she said blatantly. "I want to suck your cock."

"Are you telling me, or asking me?"

Seria hesitated. It was different now than in their earlier encounters. This was not a matter of her initiating submissive behavior out of a sense of playful irony. This was the real thing. "I'm...asking," she said.

Raylar gave no quarter. "Obedients don't ask for sex. They beg."

Seria's belly clenched hot and tight. Floodgates opened between her legs. Far from gaining strength to resist, she felt herself falling deeper and deeper. He had her right where he wanted her.

But did he know any better than she where this was leading?

Seria looked up at him, blinking moist eyes. "Please," she whispered, putting the power and the responsibility squarely in his hands. "May I suck you?"

"You will do so as an obedient." It was as much a warning as a pronouncement.

"I understand."

"No," he shook his head, "you do not."

Neither do you, she was tempted to say. Because in as much as she was risking getting deep into his world, he was also risking being trapped in hers. For as much as she risked falling for a man who would accept only submissiveness, he risked falling for a woman who was not fully submissive and never would be.

Or was it too late? Were they already in love, just each of them too stubborn to admit it? There were signs of that, but she was hardly objective. All this genetic destiny stuff was playing with her head. Cloying, kind of like this horrible hyperspace, enveloping and sucking the life from her.

"You will take off your clothes," he told her.

She sought to rise, but he put his hand on her shoulder. "You will stay on your knees."

The fem part of her thought him an arrogant bastard for that, but the obedient side clamored to obey, to bare her skin in as servile a manner as possible.

Seria peeled her spacesuit down over her shoulders and down to her waist. Her naked breasts popped free, cool and tingly in the cabin air. Her nipples craved attention, as did the rest of her. Squirming, she removed her clothes, baring her legs and kicking off her slipper-like shoes.

"Is this acceptable?" she asked. "Master?"

"Kiss it," he ordered. "The tip only."

Seria planted her lips, delicately as rose petals, upon the end of Raylar's cock.

"I am going to come in your mouth," he said. "You will swallow my semen. Kiss along the underside." He returned her attention to his cock. "Find the vein, run your tongue along it."

Seria had been reminded of her place. She was there to please. Like a contract girl or some other sort of pleasure wench. She was also there to obey. As she started to put her tongue to Raylar, she was nearly panting. How could he have such an effect on her? Stirring her passion so deeply, but also making her dream of him and yearn for him in other ways.

If only he knew how she worried for him. How she sensed his pain and wanted to ease it. And how she longed to draw out of him the joy and laughter she knew was there, below his somber, self-punishing exterior.

It wasn't your fault, she wanted to shout at him. *You didn't kill your men in that battle. You saved as many as you could. No one would ever deny that, not even the Narthians.*

Raylar's cock swelled under her soft kisses. The feel of him was silken smooth. "Mmm," he groaned, guiding her head to the right place. "Rub your cheek on it next, like so."

Seria clenched her pussy, her libido surging as he laid his cock against her face. Slowly, he began to slide it lengthwise. He smelled strong and pungent, like a man should. Its proximity drove her wild. She wanted to devour it whole, the silky exterior flesh encasing a center harder than any space metal.

"Yes," he praised. "Yes, my pet."

The wickedly demeaning praise made Seria's blood surge with newfound need. "Master," she exclaimed. "Fuck my mouth…please come inside it."

"Things will happen in my time," he declared, taking her by the hair.

"Yes, Master."

"You will lick me first, slave. You will worship every inch of me. Then, when you've earned the right, you will receive the whole of me."

Seria immediately went to work on his throbbing, blood-filled shaft. She lapped eagerly, covering it with her glistening saliva. Every last inch, just as he had commanded. His cock seemed ready to explode and yet she knew he would hold back, using every opportunity to lord his power over her.

"You missed a spot." Raylar's voice contained more than a hint of irony now as he pointed to his balls.

That was more than a spot he had in mind...

"Do a good job, woman," he encouraged, "and we will see about fucking your mouth."

"Yes, Master," she said, reveling in the erotic power of his wickedly demeaning words.

Slavishly, she tended to them, one by one, licking them clean of any sweat. They tasted slightly salty, but not unpleasant. Stars, but they were full. She could only imagine how much semen he had stored up, even in one day.

Raylar ran his hands through her hair. His sighs were those of a purely satisfied male. Feeling bold, she made a play for him, capturing the tip of his cock between her lips.

"Insolent little thing," he rasped, feigning displeasure.

Seria took her cue to gobble more of him down, sucking his cock to the back of her throat. He felt so natural there, such a perfect fit.

Humming lightly, vibrating her lips, she sought to maximize his pleasure. Raylar rewarded her with a deep moan.

"Seria." He said her name with a warmth and devotion that made her heart swell.

At a moment like this she could almost believe things might yet work out between them.

If only a mating relationship could be as simple and straightforward as an act of sexual pleasuring.

"Seria…" he repeated her name like music, his hands bracing her shoulders.

He sounded as if he wanted to say more, or was she imagining things?

She looked up at him, her eyes a study in patience and openness. She was not afraid of him, not afraid of whatever might happen should nature take its course between them.

Let him come in her mouth. In her pussy. In her ass. Let him do as he wished, use her as he wished.

She offered him encouraging noises, pressing and suctioning with her tongue to get him to spill his thick, warm semen in her mouth.

Remembering a particularly arousing position he had put her in earlier, Seria put her hands behind her neck, arching her back in total submission.

If she could just swallow his come, she was sure she could change things between them. He would want her, he would be bound to her, finally…

Raylar seemed to sense the tension, the need she had to draw him into her world.

"No," he said, putting his hands on either side of her head, "I won't make it this easy."

"I don't understand, Master."

"Slaves don't need to understand." He snapped his fingers, a different man, one less willing to be swayed by her displays of will. "On your hands and knees," he commanded. "Crawl."

* * * * *

Raylar had his slave stop in the doorway to the sleeping chamber.

He made her wait there, on all fours, small and naked and submissive as he ordered a simple, nearly harmless flogger from the objectifier. He had no wish to hurt Seria in the least. In fact, he would die before he ever harmed a hair on her head. But he was not above a little sexual torture. For education's sake.

Seria had challenged him to treat her as a true obedient, and that meant thwarting her will completely.

She had wished him to come in her mouth, she had desired to take command of his body in that way. He could not allow such a thing.

He must teach her a lesson. Make her realize she could not handle being a true submissive.

The objectifier yielded him a beauty of an instrument. Genuine black leather, about a foot and a half long, braided, with a flat, soft end. The device could not break skin, but it could leave tiny red marks, and it could sting, too. Not to mention tease.

Was he making a mistake going back on his no-sex plan? Probably, but he was still, at base, only human.

At least he was not going to fuck her anymore. That just couldn't be. Things were confusing enough as it was. Ever since this ship had taken off, it was like Seria had gone inside his head and he could not get her out. He was obsessed with watching her, listening to her. Even when he tried to ignore her, she was there.

Mostly he wanted in her head. To guess where she'd been in her life and where she was going. Above all he wanted to understand what made a woman like her accept a life in the Diplomatic Corps. She would make an outstanding celibate diplomat, but she would be making a huge sacrifice.

A woman like Seria was far too passionate to live without love. And not just the pale, pathetic variety offered by mems, either. She needed the full devotion of a primale, who would worship the very ground she walked on even as he dictated the limits and confines she needed so very much in her own life.

She couldn't be caged, though. She was like a bird. And she needed to fly. Her man would have to dominate her in a very careful way, so as not to squash her spirit. And he would have to let her fly when she needed.

Not that it mattered. By making love with her as he had, he had spoiled her for any man but him—the one male in the universe she was guaranteed never to have.

They did have the present, however...

And right now, it was her passion he wanted more than anything in the universe. The deepest yielding of her nature. And he would bring it out with the flogger.

Standing in front of her, he tapped her shoulder with the whip. "Rise," he ordered. "To your feet."

She did so, timid, her body alert and charged. He smiled at her, enjoying the rising and falling of her breasts, the goose bumps up and down her arms.

"It's time," he said. "Put out your hands."

Seria obeyed, glassy-eyed.

Gathering her wrists, he wound fiber he had gotten from the objectifier around them and attached it to a protruding pressure nodule in the doorframe over her head. He raised her to tiptoes, leaving her in a perfect state of helplessness.

She was such a darling, the way she kept looking at the flogger in his hands. Such innocence mixed with obvious desire. "You want it," he observed.

She shook her head no, frantic to disguise her lust.

Raylar dipped his fingers into her delta, removing a sample of contrary evidence. "You want it," he repeated, holding his glistening fingers up to her face. "Say it." He took her chin between the thumb and forefinger of his other hand.

"I...want it," she breathed, red-faced.

He gave her his fingers to lick. She cleaned the evidence of her own arousal, all the while producing more, in the form of a thick fragrance that filled the air.

"You want it," he said again. "And you need it."

Seria sucked in her lower lip. He was sliding the flogger down her side, from under her arm to her waist.

"Tell me how much you need it."

"I need it," she said hoarsely, her body writhing ever so slowly in anticipation of the unknown. "Oh, stars, I need it."

Raylar flicked the tip of the flogger across one engorged nipple. She cried out. It was shock, not pain. He did the same to the other, making her moan. "When a female obedient has been naughty," he observed, "she can be made to fetch the flogger on her hands and knees, naked, carrying the flogger between her teeth."

Seria clenched her teeth. He slapped her belly with the flogger, watching the smooth, tight flesh jiggle ever so slightly.

What a woman she was, so incredibly delicious and desirable. He would never tire of making sex with her, though he be with her a hundred years. Just as he would never tire of looking at or touching her. The way she responded to him, too, was so amazing. As if he were discovering some new itch on her body with each contact and scratching it all at the same time.

It was time to watch her dance. At least as much as a tethered woman could dance.

His first pass of the flogger barely grazed her sex. But it made her cry out nonetheless. Very soon she would be screaming and begging, the receptors for pleasure and pain confusing themselves in her brain.

Raylar moved the flogger to her hip. He gave her a taste. A crisp smack. Enough to make her body go rigid for a moment. In its wake he watched the pink spot rise to the surface of her skin.

She was now officially a whipped female.

He lashed her again harder. "There are some primales, you know, who are able to be aroused only by the sight of a woman in heavy submission. They keep their mates collared and even shackled. I suppose I am a bit more liberal. Don't you think?" Raylar swatted her breast, enough to make her jolt.

"Y-yes," she winced.

He laughed. "Liar. You'd as soon spit nails at me. But your body still responds. Suppose we play a little game," he decided. "The object is to make you come. How would you like that?"

She nodded eagerly.

Raylar laughed, giving her a nice, soft caress with his hand. Beginning at her belly, employing the tips of his fingers, he moved them downward, across her pelvis, circling about her sex until finally he grazed her labia, light as a feather.

"Oh, Master…" Seria leaned her head back, enjoying the feel of his fingers along the crease of her pussy, almost but not quite penetrating.

"There's only one catch," he said. "I'm going to do it by whipping your pussy."

Seria struggled against her bonds. "Raylar, please, no."

"I will, Seria, and I'll make you beg for it in the process." He tapped her thigh, emphasizing his next point. "Open your legs."

Seria struggled to widen her thighs, given her current position on tiptoes.

"Wider," he commanded, forcing her still further into painful vulnerability.

Seria was breathing hard already, a fine sheen of sweat on her body. "Look at me," he commanded, slipping the flogger into place.

She struggled to maintain eye contact as he masturbated her with the whip. Just a few more seconds and they would begin. He needed her to be close to release first. Good and hungry for it.

He waited until she was on the brink before cutting her off.

"Raylar. Master," she cried predictably, "don't stop."

He showed her the braided leather. "If it comes back, it does so on my terms, slave."

"Yes, anything."

"You'll take pain." A statement, not a question.

"Yes, Master."

Raylar raised his arm, taking careful aim. Seria released a loud cry as he landed the flattened end right over her mound. Before she could mentally sort out what was going on, he bent to kiss her poor, captive lips. She moaned, opening beautifully for him. He worked her with his tongue, plying the soft, velvet insides of her mouth.

"The whip," he said when he'd slain her sufficiently. "Beg for it."

Seria hung, coated in sweat, utterly defeated. But completely sexually charged, too. She had no choice now, no way out but further down, into the dark depths of submission to Raylar's will.

"Whip me, Master. Whip my pussy," she croaked. "Make me come."

He delivered a series of strokes, building her to the very edge of climax. He stopped one short. It was time for another kiss. Soft and sweet. Lingering. And infinitely cruel.

"No, no, Master," she kept saying.

"What's wrong, angel?"

"I'm on fire," she confessed. "Please, let me come? Please, use your whip on me?"

Raylar grabbed one of her breasts, feeling the silky flesh compress in his hands. "So fucking beautiful," he hissed. He stopped short of saying the next thing on his mind.

It wasn't lust consuming him, but something else. Something much deeper and more pervasive.

"Raylar…" She pushed her body into his, willing him to go further.

He slapped her pussy with the whip, enjoying the fresh round of tremors up and down her spine.

All the way this time, no turning back.

"Yes," she began to call out in a steady chant. Her eyes were glazed over—she was at the brink and nothing would hold her back now.

A few more carefully placed strikes with the black leather…

"Come," he commanded at the fourth blow. "Come now, my angel."

Seria cried out, as if he were inside her, filling her to the depths. The sight of her transfixed Raylar. Her incredible eyes, her lips murmuring, her chest rising and falling. She was like some kind of drug, intoxicating, addicting.

He wanted her. Wanted her happy, wanted her ecstatic. Above all he wanted her near him. Close enough to touch. Always.

To hold and possess.

And love.

Damn. Had he said that aloud? She didn't seem to be reacting. Good. He'd be sure not to reveal himself. For one thing, he didn't know what he was talking about. He could not love Seria. He could not love any woman. He was a soldier. His heart, whatever heart he'd had, had been left back on Rensus Nine, with the bodies of his fallen comrades.

"Raylar…"

She was calling him. He blinked. Had he drifted off? Thinking of the war?

"Take me down," she urged, the fever of her climax passed. "Make love to me. Right now."

He couldn't help but smile at her. The small, chained woman dictating to him what would happen next. "I'm supposed to be in charge," he reminded.

"So prove it," she challenged. "In bed."

His smile broadened to an out-and-out grin. Untying the binding fiber, he scooped her up into his arms. Her body was warm and soft. Fragrant and very female. She felt so very natural against him. The way she snuggled, the way she sighed.

Damn it, why were his eyes tearing up?

He laid her on the ship's bed. The bed he'd been avoiding since their last coupling. They were in hyperspace now. Nothing around them but emptiness. Gray sponginess, unfit for human habitation. Men and women went mad out here, if they weren't careful. All this loneliness was the perfect breeding ground for ghosts.

Raylar fell on top of her, filling her sex in one smooth motion. His arms wrapped around her. He would not be able to let go of her again, not until they reached their destination. "This...is temporary," he reminded them both.

"After this, it's celibacy," she confirmed. "For both of us."

He sealed the deal with a kiss to her lips. The last lips he would ever touch. The last woman he would ever know. Would she give him a small holo-disk, he wondered, to take into battle with him? Or maybe some other memento of their time together?

Better not, he thought. Better to make a clean break of things for both of them. A burdensome past would only slow them down, bogging them in the perpetual sadness of that which could never be. At least not in this universe.

Raylar moved in and out of Seria's tight, hot pussy, relishing every inch of her. He must give it his all now, creating and destroying in one fell swoop their unborn love. For indeed, a relationship this fiery was by definition made to be all or nothing.

A shooting star in the heavens.

"That's it," she urged, sensing he was close. "Come, come for me."

Raylar obeyed her, yielding to his deepest feelings. It was a bittersweet climax, a torrent that carried him into a place of dark forgetfulness. Pleasure, all too soon ended. Clinging limbs, desperately holding to what time could not promise.

Hyperspace romances, it was said, were always doomed to failure. Theron and Nyssa should have thought of that, Raylar mused, *when they set about trying to make a love connection between the two of us.*

Just goes to show you, the biggest brains in the cosmos don't necessarily know anything more about love than the rest of us. It all comes down to a throw of the dice. The vagaries of fate.

And above all, the tides of war.

Raylar clamped his eyes tightly shut.

"Don't let go," she was saying, or was he saying that himself?

Funny how the mind plays tricks this far out…

He just needed to get her safely to Alphus Six. That's all that mattered. After that, they would go their separate ways. Her to a prosperous life and him to his duty, back to the battlefield.

With any luck he would die quickly, taking as many of the enemy with him as he could. Nothing else mattered now. He had no home, and no prospect of happiness. Everything he might have been lay here, with Seria.

He whispered her name, even as his cock grew hard again under her touch. The words stuck in his throat. So very close to being released and yet so very impossible to say.

I love you, you gorgeous little half-ling…more than life itself.

Chapter Nine

80

Raylar came up behind Seria at the viewing port. She had been watching the rust-colored surface of the planet, glowing gold under the influence of the rising pink sun. It was Alphus Six. Her destination.

The place where they would part ways forever.

After a whirlwind time in the wormhole, filled with wonder and sex-making and magic. He had taught her so much, about her own body, and about his. He had taught her to open up, to share, to come and scream with abandon. And to give in to dark desires, while soaring to unimaginable heights.

Like all good things, however, it had reached its natural end. The ship would land, and it would all be history, memory, etched in their life blood. In joy and sorrow.

"I managed to whip up a batch of this." Raylar offered her one of two polysteel cups in his hands.

"Thank you." She forced a smile, taking the cran-beer.

"You drank that," he reminded, "the first night."

She felt a lump in her throat. What a sweet thing to do for their goodbye. "Yes," she quipped. "And way too much of it at that."

"Yes," he agreed. "You know, you are very easy when you drink."

She punched him on the arm, having little impact on his iron biceps. "I am not."

"You're right. You're easy all the time."

"Only for you," she quipped.

He smiled, bittersweet. "Yeah."

Was that emotion under there? Could it be he was learning to let out his feelings, to trust just a little? If only they had more time.

In a different universe, she thought, maybe it would have worked out differently.

"You know," Raylar cleared his throat, studying his cup. "I've been thinking, and I may have an answer for you."

"To what?"

"The question you asked our first night. You know, the game about things from our childhood?"

"Oh…I'd nearly forgotten," she exclaimed eagerly. "What did you come up with?"

"Promise you won't laugh?"

"Diplomat's honor." She held up her palm.

"I used to make shadow puppets on my wall. I made a lion, I called it Leo. I've never told anyone that."

"I'm honored you picked me, Raylar," she said somberly. "I will treasure your secret…and Leo's forever."

"Thanks. Now I want to ask a new question, Seria."

She finished her cran-beer for fortitude. "Go for it."

"If you could change one thing in your life, Seria, what would it be?"

"I should have guessed," she shook her head, "that you'd go straight for the jugular as always."

Raylar smiled slyly. "I've been studying up on question games. You know how I am."

"Yeah…I know how you are." She took a deep breath. "The truth is, I don't know what I could change, without changing myself in the process. Everything I am now is a product of where I've been. I wear my pains and scars with all my other memories. It's there for anyone to study, if they want. I guess that's why I'm a diplomat. I think we all have to be that way with each other. No matter where we come from. How about you, Raylar, what would you change?"

"I think you know the answer to that."

"The battle," she said flatly. "Where you lost so many men."

"There should have been a way out. I just didn't see it."

"You know there's nothing I can say…"

"I know. And thanks for not trying."

"I respect you too much, Raylar."

What she could do was take him in her arms…damn him for not letting her. And damn her for not being strong enough.

"We're hitting reentry," he said. "We should prepare for landing."

She offered no argument. It was as good an ending to things as any.

* * * * *

"Well, I guess this is it," Raylar announced.

"Yeah." Seria nodded. "I guess so."

They were standing outside the spaceship, parked on the circular, silver landing platform, each postponing the inevitable. For his part, Raylar was fighting the urge to take her in his arms for a goodbye hug. The trouble was, he didn't know if he could let go again. No matter how much he knew he should.

"Would you like to come in the embassy?" she asked hastily. "For a drink? Something to eat?"

"Thanks," he smiled awkwardly, "but I really should get going. I have to get back to my base."

"Yeah…and I should get inside and meet the ambassador," she agreed.

"Okay, then…so this is it."

Damn it, man, you're repeating yourself like a blithering idiot. Just say goodbye and get on the ship.

It was Seria who made the move. Lifting herself on tiptoes, she delivered a peck to his cheek. "So long, Raylar. And thank you."

Just like that, she took off running toward the small group of gray and blue domes constituting the Earth embassy on Alphus Six.

He watched her, hair flying, her delicious little behind swaying after her. He would miss that behind and all the rest of her more than he could ever say. For what felt like the millionth time since meeting Seria, Raylar felt the hot welling of tears behind his eyes.

He held them off long enough to smile as she waved a last goodbye from the doors to the main dome. Extending an arm, he waved back. One final acknowledgement, one last contact with the woman who had touched him in ways he could not explain.

His hands were shaking just a little as he made the final launch check and climbed back aboard the small cruiser. Fuck, it was going to be lonely in there now. Way too goddamn big and empty, despite its narrow confines.

Concentrating on the takeoff, he double and triple verified the instruments. Twice he calculated the wormhole differential, using mental arithmetic. He also played the variations of a hundred of his favorite chess games.

None of it was enough to hold him together. He had barely gotten the ship off the ground when the dam broke. Not tears but a seething fit of rage. His scream was bloodcurdling.

At the last second, he had the presence of mind to put on the autopilot.

He clenched his fists, reaching for something to smash. There was nothing on hand but parts of the ship. To destroy them would be to end his life. Overwhelmed, he buried his head in his hands, unleashing sobs as dry as a desert.

Thoughts whirled in his brain, the same old laughing ghosts. The usual party of self-torture. But then something new happened. He thought he felt hands on his shoulders. The hands of his fallen comrades. The men who had died under his command.

Had they come back from the dead to forgive ĥim?

No. There was no point to that, not in the place where they lived now.

Theirs was a different purpose. A living purpose.

They were trying to get his attention...pointing to something out the front view screen.

Raylar looked up. He was in space by now. Everything was black, speckled with silver stars. There was nothing out there he could see. But the ghostly hands were pointing, persistently, to one little area.

A stinking little patch of darkness right above Alphus Six...

Suddenly his heart seized up. Little as the area was, there should have been stars. The only way an area could go dark like that was if a wormhole were opening up.

Grabbing the controls, he put the ship in full reverse. He only prayed he would get back there in time, before the wormhole opened completely.

Because unless he was very mistaken, it was not a Guardian ship that was going to emerge, but a Narthian one.

And that would spell doom for the inhabitants of Alphus Six.

Including Seria.

* * * * *

Seria sat waiting for the Earth ambassador in the antechamber to the main conference room. Ambassador Trelor had been occupied in a meeting since her arrival. To an uninformed observer, it might have seemed that the man was at a table talking to a couple of petri dishes full of fungus, but actually he was communing with the Grand High Vizier of the planet's dominant intelligent species, which was in fact, fungus-based.

The conversation was made possible with a special machine that translated fungi speech into human and vice versa. The ambassador had seemed quite animated when Seria had poked her head in the door a few minutes ago, though she thought the proceedings frightfully tedious.

Maybe it was because she was still so distracted, thinking about her time with Raylar. Things felt so damn out of kilter. It had ended way too abruptly, for one thing. True, they had agreed that after the trip was over they would go separate ways. But it hadn't been a reality at that point, and now that it was real, it hurt like hell.

Oh, sure, she still knew it was right, for the sake of both their careers, but that didn't mean she wouldn't mourn the loss.

If she had one real regret it was not telling him to be careful. In his next battle, wherever that might be. Living without him was bad enough. But if she were to ever find out he had been killed, she could not bear to live.

Just then, the door to the conference room opened, Seria stood, relieved. At last she could get down to work. "Ambassador Trelor," she said. "I am so pleased to—"

Trelor was wobbling in the doorway. The irises of his eyes were rolled up into his head. He had his mouth open, but nothing was coming out but a sickening, crackling sound, like a death rattle.

Something was wrong with his chest, too, under his long, gray tunic. All at once the material tore open, revealing a single black tendril-like arm with prickly red thorns.

By the gods…it was piercing him like a skewer.

Seria screamed. The sound was immediately drowned out by a rattling hiss. Straight into the air went the ambassador's body as the owner of the black arm emerged from the shadows behind.

The bug stood eight feet tall, like a spider, with half a dozen mouths, filthy and dripping green fluids. The fluids were like acid, and as they touched the floor a horrible smell was emitted.

Seria didn't wait to see the Narthian eat the ambassador alive. She was already turning, running for her life. She made it through the door into the corridor. To the left, she saw two more bugs approaching rapidly, crawling on their black legs. They had a dozen apiece, maybe more, and every one of them was covered in the horrible thorns.

Each of the legs made a chilling, clicking sound on the floor as the creatures made their approach. Dozens of legs, terribly ugly and horrible.

The creatures hissed as they advanced, spitting green acid out of their mouths. All those mouths. With teeth ringing the insides. And completely inhuman eyes covering the tops of their hairy heads.

Seria went right, praying the way would be clear. She didn't know this building. She had no idea how many of the Narthians there were. Dear god, how had they gotten in? She hadn't heard a thing.

Her pounding heart squeezed off an invisible and impossible plea.

Please, Raylar, save me...

Seria felt a surge of heat to her right. Something was on her arm, dissolving her uniform. They were shooting the acid at her! From out of their mouths.

She stumbled, trying to remove her singed clothing. The acid was going to burn her alive. Just in time, she got it all off. She couldn't stop, though. She couldn't let them catch her. Seria picked herself up, stark naked, and ran on. The corridor was coming to a T junction.

She had always heard that Narthian attack bugs were limited in intelligence. They might not think to split up. Maybe they would both go the wrong way. She darted around the corner. It was lined with small rooms, the doors white and windowless. She picked one midway down.

Leaving the light off and locking the door behind her, Seria hid under a table in the corner. She gathered her knees to her chest, not daring to make a sound, even though her arm hurt so much.

Tears poured down her cheeks. She had never felt so alone, so scared, so doomed in all her life. It was all her worst fears brought to life, all the things people had warned her about, why she should not go into space and be a diplomat.

But here she was, and fuck all of them.

The only thing worth thinking of now was Raylar, and how she'd felt inside the first time she'd seen his holo. All weak and giddy and alive. That feeling had been reinforced when he'd taken her in his arms and danced her across the floor. And again, when he'd kissed her and loved her, showing her all the pleasures of the universe.

She held herself tightly as the images played in her mind and heart. Counting seconds and heartbeats.

This is it, she thought. *My destiny…*

Filling her mind with images of Raylar, she did her best to tune out the sounds just outside the door. Scratching. Clicking. And hissing.

* * * * *

Raylar's mind had moved into a place both unspeakable and dark. There was no space now for doubt, no room for hesitation. Only killing. It was said a Narthian could smell fear on a man and it was true in his experience. They were primitive, simple beings, but ruthless and much to be respected.

To overcome them, a man must have a singularity of purpose that overrides all else.

He must have no fear, least of all of death.

And he must have rage within him. A seething will to fight. To protect, to hold something much more dear than his own existence.

In Raylar's case, he had Seria.

Slipping the knife into his belt, Raylar pulled the laser rifle from the rack on the wall of the ship. He had never been calmer in his life. Never more certain.

Never more dangerous.

Every Narthian in that attack ship would die. That was his pledge. His bond.

He had set the cruiser down on the far side of the dome. The Narthian ship was a Class-One Patrol. Lost from a Nest Fleet, most likely. There would be four, maybe five bugs on board, soldier drones. Not as bad as nesters, but bad enough.

Raylar wasn't sure how he knew Seria was still alive, but he did. She wouldn't die like that, not now. It wasn't her destiny. Besides, if she were already dead, he would know it in his gut. He would be keeled over. Ripped apart by fear and guilt and self-blame. But he wasn't. He was mad as hell. And he was going to blast every one of those motherfuckers straight to hell where they belonged.

He found the first of the bugs waiting in the ship. The dumb fuck. Raylar popped open the hatch and fired a single blast. Closing it back up, he let the laser do its thing, bouncing off the walls until the bug was nice and fried.

A couple more shots destroyed the ship's external propulsion drive, making sure the rest would stay here permanently. Not that they were going to have to worry about going home again.

Eschewing the front door of the main dome—never a good mode of entry when you had bugs around—Raylar went in through the ventilation system above the ceiling. Sure enough, two of them were chowing down on some embassy technicians in the lobby.

Seria was nowhere to be seen.

Raylar used his knife on one of the bugs, tossing it down, right smack in the eye. Eye number fourteen, that is. It was a good choice—that being the eye which collected light on the normal color spectrum.

The fucking thing started screeching, running around like crazy, spewing its green vomit all over the other bug, which was minding its own business, trying to clean bones from between its teeth.

Pretty soon, they were going at each other. Raylar jumped down about two feet away.

"Boo," he said, opening fire.

They went down hard and fast in a fury of red laser lightning.

Not bad for pyrotechnics, but he had to keep moving. There were one or two left and they were probably hot on Seria's trail.

Luckily, they left a trail of their own. He followed the green acid down the corridor. His stomach hardened like a rock as he saw the familiar uniform lying on the floor, half-eaten away.

It was Seria's.

Had the bugs gotten her? There was no sign of blood, and it was strange for just her clothes to be left. Generally, the Narthians did not undress their victims.

Raylar pressed on, until the corridor came to a T juncture. He scanned in both directions, looking for signs of life, Narthian or human. There, to the right, a hundred meters down, he saw them. Two bugs, large and nasty, sniffing under one of the doors lining the corridor. Seria was in there, he felt it. Taking aim with the laser, he pulled the trigger.

The rifle made a popping noise, followed by a shower of sparks.

The gun had jammed up on him. He was going to need a new weapon.

Raylar spotted the heavy hypersteel tubing, just overhead, by the air ducts. Jumping, he reached with both hands, tearing out a large section. With primale strength he snapped the tube in half. He now had two sections about six feet long.

Getting a good running start, he headed straight for the pair of bugs.

One of them was squirting acid to dissolve the door of the room. Raylar cried out, getting his attention. As soon as the Narthian made eye contact—with half its eyes, anyway— Raylar let loose one of the pipes.

A flying projectile, a death javelin, zero to sixty in under a heartbeat.

He hit the bug in the belly, driving it backwards and onto its back. Still alive, it spun in circles, flailing its legs to right itself. The second bug, alerted by now, turned its attention to the attacker. Drawing a full breath, it prepared to unleash its venom.

"Not today, you cockroach from hell!" Raylar leaped right over the mouths and landed on the bug's back. Now it, too, was spinning around, trying to dislodge its unwanted passenger. Raylar held tight, using one of the thick hairs as a handle. He bided his time, waiting for the insect to slow down so he could get the right angle for his attack.

Twice the bug nearly flipped him, but Raylar held on.

He stabbed straight into one of the vulnerable side air pockets with the improvised spear. Three times more he struck at it, until it collapsed right on top of the other one. Raylar hopped down. It was time to finish off the one flopping on its back, but first he needed to make sure it was the last one.

Grabbing the brain box, a tiny nodule on the underside of one of the legs, he cracked it open on the floor. A series of white gems fell out. Raylar dropped to his knees and put his palms down on top of them. They were memory crystals. Raylar's hands burned for a moment, as he absorbed the information from within. They contained not only the original orders this bug had ingested back in the nest, but also the data he was supposed to bring back home.

All Raylar wanted to know was how many were left.

Originally, there were five. Which meant this was the last one. Not only that, but the ship was a lone vessel, lost in the wormhole, just as he'd suspected. Breathing a sigh of relief, Raylar finished the job, killing the final bug with another stab wound.

Only one thing remained now. To let Seria know she was safe.

Raylar didn't bother with the door button. He knocked it down, with a single kick of his foot. "Seria?" he called.

She didn't answer. But he could hear her breathing, in the corner, under the table.

"Seria, it's me, Raylar. It's all right. The bugs are all gone. I'm going to turn the light on, okay?"

"N-no light," she whispered.

Raylar left the light off. "Seria, it's okay," he soothed. "You can come out."

She started to crawl from under the table. He went to her, lifting her into his arms. She was nude and trembling. "Baby, I've got you," he rasped. "I've got you and I'm not letting go."

"I knew it." She squeezed him tightly, her bare breasts against his chest. "I knew you'd come back."

"I don't know how I ever left you," he croaked. "I swear, by the Code, I love you, Seria, more than my life, more than anything."

"Oh, Raylar, I love you, too." She put her lips up to his, craving a kiss. They went at each other, all the pent-up tension released in a single explosion.

The intensity was fierce. Seria was panting, pressing her naked body against him. Her hands were all over him. "Raylar, make love to me, please? Right here..."

Their hands worked in the dark, both of them taking off his uniform, stained with sweat and bug blood. She gasped at the feel of his cock. "Oh, baby." She tried to impale herself, crawling up his body.

He grabbed her right thigh and left hip, helping her pussy to sheathe his throbbing cock. Half lifting, half pushing, he put her on the edge of the table. She grasped the edge of it and leaned back.

"Ohmigod, Raylar, fuck me..."

He took control of her waist and began pistoning, hard and deep and fast into her dripping wet pussy. Her nipples were hot and sweet as he took them, one after another between his teeth. She screamed out at the mild pain, pounding his back, locking her ankles around his pumping ass cheeks.

"F-fuck me..." she hissed. "Make me...come."

Raylar exploded his semen into her, inducing her own cries of victory. The orgasm was simultaneous, world-shattering, and totally mind-blowing. Planets detonating, years of guilt and sadness shaken off, life restored.

By the time they'd both subsided, relaxed and peaceful in each other's arms, there was no question of what lay ahead.

"I can see," he teased, gently stroking her hair as she sat on the edge of the table, his cock still inside her, "that I am going to have to keep a closer eye on you. How long did I leave you before you created a diplomatic incident?"

"I wasn't counting the time," she replied. "But if you're looking to report me to the ambassador, I'm afraid he's been...um...eaten."

"I'm sorry for that. Did you have to see it?"

"Yeah." Seria shivered. "I hardly even knew him, but seeing that expression on his face was so horrible. I can't imagine what it was like for you, losing men you were close to."

Raylar shook his head. "It's okay now. Really."

Her smile lit his world. "I'm glad, Raylar."

Raylar kissed her again, happier than he'd ever thought he could be in his life. "Do you know what this means?" he said. "I have actually found a lifemate...who makes me a stronger soldier."

"It's not luck," she pointed out. "It's genetics."

Raylar shrugged. "Either way, it's a pretty good deal, don't you think?"

"I suppose," she teased. "As long as you throw in some cran-beer from time to time."

"Sure." He swatted her behind. "And some of these for good measure."

"Ooo," she wriggled enticingly, "now that *is* an offer I can't refuse."

AZAR'S PRIZE

ॐ

Chapter One

∞

Look in the galactic dictionary under death wishes, and you would find the name of Theryssa, first female officer of the Star Guardians...

At this very moment Theryssa was floating weightless off the starboard bow of her class one solo cruiser, two parsecs from nowhere, deep into pirate space, happily ripping out the nav-com beacons and hyper-drive relays, without which she had no chance of ever getting home.

Why was she doing such a damn-fool, idiotic, black-hole-for-brains thing? Incredibly enough, it was a top secret mission—one she had devised for herself and sold her superiors on. Certainly, it had seemed a good idea at the time...sort of.

A lot of people said Theryssa was only doing this to prove that she was fit to be in the Guardian Corps, and not there merely because of the special entrée given her by her parents, who happened to be the two most important people in the galaxy. Others thought she was just plain reckless and unstable.

What kind of normal person, after all, would be willing to set herself up as bait to be captured by a sex-crazed pirate king so they could spy on him and see if he was in bed with the Narthians?

Bed being a highly charged word in this context, given how much time this particular pirate king was said to enjoy spending in them with his captured females. Azar Xenelion was his name, and supposedly he was irresistible to the female sex. According to space lore, a woman need be brought to him chained or tied only one time—that being the first. After that, she would return to him willingly, begging his touch.

Theryssa knew that was ridiculous, not to mention an insult to female dignity. She would just as soon believe that little yarn as she would some of the other tales about the man, such as the time he purportedly eluded an entire Guardian escort flotilla, capturing an armored freighter loaded with fifteen cosmic tons of priceless velocite gems.

What was not an exaggeration, unfortunately, were the many accounts of how incredibly ravishing he was. His holoid images made her wet each and every time. Her favorite one showed the man bare chested, with his razor-sharp energy sword and scabbard, the leather belt swung over his muscular shoulder. He was beautiful and sexy and manly in a raw and primal way. Not like the genetic perfection of the primales, among whom Theryssa's father was one of the finest.

It was hard to pinpoint the appeal. Perhaps it was just the idea that this Azar was so alien to her own carefully planned world. That his body had grown strong purely through labor and war, that his skin was bronzed by the sun, his biceps and triceps and rock-hard abdomen forged in the wilds. Not to mention the scandalously earthy method of his birth—out of the womb of a mother, from the planted seed of a father. No genetic planning, no seeding laboratory. No test tubes, no endless statistics.

Even his age was hard to pinpoint. In some of the holoids, he looked to be in his early thirties, while in others he seemed closer to her father's age. If that was the case, he was certainly maintaining his raw vitality.

Or was savage the better word, what with that long, tawny hair hanging down his back, the fierce blue eyes, quick as a jaguar's? And that mind—cunning as anything the geneticists could devise and yet free of all the restraints that could possibly be put upon it by society.

Azar Xenelion. Free in thought. Dangerously so, choosing an outlaw's life, living off the wealth of the liners and freighters unfortunate enough to cross his path. His prey, he called them, and their contents, booty.

The women were booty, too. Fems, obedients, aliens, no distinction was made. He took as he wished, making the women want him in every way possible before casting them aside for new ones. An abhorrent philosophy, yes, but still there was a magnetism to the man that even Theryssa, a female with three quarters primale blood, raised by the most powerful two members of the government, could not deny it.

Some said it was even worse than that, that the reason he attacked Guardian ships had to do with his desire to destroy the genetic system itself, creating a world of natural birth. The very thought made the skin crawl.

Living with Azar's images burned into her brain was not proving easy. So far it had been touch and go. She could have sworn the bastard was grinning at her from the other side of those holoids when she'd sat in her quarters on the edge of her seat, her coveralls hastily pulled open, her hand shoved down between her legs, absorbing the wet heat, her fingers simulating the action of a cock. His cock. Thrusting. Thrusting. Thrusting.

She had come harder than she had in months, maybe ever, soaking the plastiseal seat and leaving herself open and vulnerable in a way that defied description. It was crazy. All she had done was masturbate to his image and yet she'd felt like she had been physically and mentally had by the man. Possessed in the fullest sense of the word.

Twice that night she had buried the holoids as deep as she could in her backup system. If she could have destroyed them outright, she would have. As it was, she had pulled them back up on her personal monitor both times, again achieving mind-blowing orgasms.

She even went so far as to fabricate a dildo from the objectifier, one that she thought would appropriately simulate the shaft of a man that size—six foot five, two hundred plus pounds of sheer muscle, broad shoulders, tapered waist, rock-hard thighs.

Oh my fucking stars. She was sure her screams were audible all the way to the next galaxy. She shoved that thing so far inside herself, so deep that she was actually shivering and panting and grunting, hot and cold, filled to the point of explosion and totally fucking needy and empty all at the same time.

She shouted fuck a million times, and every other swear word on top of it. Colors poured into her brain that she had never seen, and sensations in her breasts and belly that she had only ever associated with the intoxication of bubble juice. In short, she went supernova, suns imploding inside suns, collapsing down to the tiniest little pleasure points, and then expanding all over again, rushing to fill the void at hyper-light speed.

Her pussy had a life all its own, contracting and bearing down on the dildo like they shared some secret language. The liquid just kept flowing and her clit, so very full and swollen just hung there, like a laser trigger, locked on constant feed.

Nonstop firing. Blast. Blast. Blast. Eye-dousing pinks and purples and reds.

Then she got really wacky and ordered her auto-grid host to sim the holos up a bit, showing the pirate in various fun poses. Sans clothing of course. She had to stop herself from putting her own holos in the mix, simulating sex acts. What was next—scribbling their initials in her notepad like a first term adolescent?

She put up a sex blocker against him—part of her Guardian training—and tried to figure what was wrong with her. Was it all that silly talk about his being so sexually invincible? Was she just more nervous about the mission than she was willing to admit to herself?

She knew better, of course, than to complain to her parents. As far as her mother was concerned, she was getting everything she deserved after pushing so hard to be the first female cadet in the all-male Guardian service.

She would never forget her response when she'd first told Mom she wanted to join up.

"You ought to be taking this time to explore," Nyssa, the current Head of the High Council, had counseled. "You're only twenty-three. You should be sowing your oats, making sex and music like I did at your age. You'll have responsibilities soon enough."

Pointing out that she was not her mother's clone and that she might wish to lead her life differently would have been pointless. It was times like this that Theryssa found it hardest to be one of the precious few persons in the world whose genes had come from two specific people rather than an abstract, engineered mix.

The program was experimental and highly secret. Her own parents were two of the first. While her real origins could not be made known to the general public, she did manage to grow up with both of her progenitors as opposed to being raised in a cluster with many other children. Having a biological mother and father to live with, and who saw one as reflections of themselves, Theryssa learned, could be a real drag.

Her father was initially a lot more helpful. As Commander of the Guardians, General Theron had smoothed the way for her groundbreaking entry into the Service, not only with its primale members, but with Mom, who in Dad's opinion was a far more fearsome adversary.

Once she had joined up, however, he'd become like a second drill sergeant. Worse really, because he could interrupt her any time day or night, even if she was on leave. As far as he was concerned, the tougher the assignment she took on, the better.

His daughter was, after all, the best of the best, destined for great things.

Shooting comets, how many times had she heard that lecture? Since she was a little child, four or five solars old they had been telling her the story of how they had been engineered themselves, just so they could come together and support each other and so their DNA could be used to make a new, stronger kind of human being...of which Theryssa was the first.

That story became the template for everything. The time she'd played tag with her robo-dog in the house when she was six and broke one of her mother's prize holo-acting trophies, she was betraying her destiny. The time she only got a ninety-nine instead of a hundred on her interdimensional geometry final when she was fifteen because she had stayed out too late kissing a boy the night before—that had been betraying her legacy, too.

Did they have any idea how hard it was to live with that kind of pressure? Didn't they see that Theryssa was just a person, trying to live out her life like anybody else? Besides, from everything she had grown up seeing of her parents exploits, battling the Narthians and fighting back the anti-geneticists led by Malthusalus, they were the real heroes, not her.

Theryssa did have an aunt, her mother's younger half sister Seria, and her husband Raylar. Raylar was second in command of the Guardians and would take her father's place once he retired. He was a good man, though a bit stiff at times. Aunt Seria was a lot easier to talk to and pretty sympathetic when it came to sharing her frustrations with her parents.

Seria had a legacy of her own thrust upon her, as the chosen mate of Raylar. Since she hadn't been engineered to serve in a leadership position, she tended to be a little more laid-back about things. Seria shared the same father as Nyssa, the dynamic Marax. Her mother, however, was a very beautiful obedient who had died a long time ago.

Theryssa had been a little girl when Seria's identity was revealed to her. Theryssa had bonded with her right away. In some ways she was like a big sister. Although half obedient by blood, she was pretty bold and independent in her own right. She still worked part-time in the Diplomatic Corps.

The bulk of her time was spent with their son, her cousin Saymar. Saymar was barely ten, though he already fancied himself a great warrior. Theryssa wondered how in the world he was going to have the patience to wait for his own turn at leading the Guardians after the eventual retirement of his father Raylar, who had yet to assume command himself.

Theryssa would have been perfectly happy with a normal, unremarkable military career, albeit as the first of her gender to serve in the Corp of Star Guardians, responsible for defending the humanoid planets against all barbarian or Narthian bug invasions. But destiny has a funny way of catching up to a person. Case in point, Theryssa's current mission. It didn't take a robo-surgeon to figure out this was no ordinary assignment. She was about to go seriously undercover, unarmed into pirate hands, with no hope of backup.

In the back of her mind, Theryssa had to know that she might never get home again—most especially if she succeeded in passing along the information about the Narthians, thereby engendering the pirate's eternal wrath. Still, it was too good an opportunity to pass up. For a decade Guardian Command had been after Xenelion and now, through Theryssa, fresh from the Academy, they had a chance to infiltrate his operation and link him to the Narthian Bug Hordes in one fell swoop.

All because Theryssa was a woman. Talk about ironies.

She was a little surprised they had let her do it, to be honest. Her superiors had balked at first. And while no one ever said so, Theryssa's father, and therefore her mother, must surely have had to sign off on the idea.

Theryssa wasn't sure whether to feel good or bad about them letting her do this. At one level it meant they really did trust her as much as they were always saying they did, which was cool. But they had been so damn calm when they said goodbye. What was up with that? Were they just being callous, all disciplined and command-like, or did they have some kind of ace up their sleeves that was going to keep her safe? Some secret bit of knowledge that changed the equation she thought she was dealing with?

Would the possibility surprise her? Not really. After all, that was how her grandparents, Nyssa's mother and father, the former Head of the Council and Commander of the Guardians had always worked things. With bigger purposes, as they put it.

Or as Theryssa preferred to think of it, playing things the sneaky way.

Speaking of being sneaky, she had to work fast to finish sabotaging her ship and get back inside. She had to be careful, of course, to make it look natural, like meteor damage, or space shrapnel. Never mind that any halfway competent star pilot would never allow himself to be hit by a flying rock in the middle of a million mile wide void—Theryssa was just going to have to play dumb on that one.

Tee, hee. Look at me, the bimbo woman astronaut.

They'd probably buy it, too, the way all chauvinists do when offered a chance to reinforce their stupid ideas about male supremacy. What these pirates would never know, assuming Theryssa played her role as helpless captive right, was that she was not just another reasonably pretty face. She was a trained expert in self-defense, with lethally registered skills. She also had those primale genes, a hundred percent on her father's side and half on her mother's. That meant she had a fair share of her Dad's augmented powers, including super hearing, ultra-range sight and a strength factor that ought to make her able to knock any dozen or so of these pirate morons back to whatever Dark Age they'd skulked out of.

She would need the super senses pretty quickly to tell when they were coming up on her ship, too. Without her nav-com beacons, she was blind as a Corian bat fish out here.

They couldn't come a moment too soon at this point. As much as Theryssa didn't look forward to being plucked up as "booty", she was far more afraid of *not* being found. Sure, Guardian Command would institute a search if she failed to turn up in some shape or form within the next Solar, but they would have only an approximate idea of where to look for her. She had gone off the holo-trackers some time ago, so as not to scare the pirates away. This meant no visual tracking or any spacecraft to come to her rescue.

If anyone else found her, they would never believe she was a Guardian. Not flying as she was, incognito, wearing an interstellar delivery uniform, her craft marked with the logo of an outfit which transported one of a kind items for people rich enough not to have to create simulations using their objectifiers.

Theryssa would tell them she was lost, drifted off course. She sighed thinking of how she would be making a moron of herself, complete with batting eyelashes and looks of awe. What an acting job, complete with painful, bimbo-like slowness as she pretended to realize that her rescuers were not knights in shining space armor, but interstellar ne'er-do-wells. *Please don't hurt me with your mean old swords, Mr. Pirates, sirs.* Back inside the ship at last, Theryssa occupied herself playing a game of groak against the ship's computer. She noted the time. A minute since she checked last.

This waiting was killing her. Whatever destiny she faced on that pirate ship, whoever this Azar Xenelion turned out to be in real life, it was going to be a hell of a lot better than dealing with her own imagination out here in space. Any

Guardian would tell you, battle came as a relief after a long flight in the deep black reaches. Out there the ghosts got real. Especially when you fly solo.

Voices, not necessarily good ones, can drown out a person's rational thoughts. Questions floating past your front grill, again and again, the answers never satisfying. Would she really be able to finesse this just right? A Guardian, a trained warrior pretending to be a damsel in distress? Being that she was the first female in the Service, it wasn't as though Theryssa's colleagues or even her superiors could offer much practical assistance.

Her father had given her a long speech, recounting his role in the defeat of the Narthian Bug Nest on Tubos Minor and told her to remember the Guardian Code. That was all well and good, except her father did not have female hormones. He had no clue what it was like to fight that kind of primal urge. It was different being a woman, when you had the kind of biology that made you want to have the enemy inside you, making love to you, showing you what your body could do under the influence of a finely wielded cock. Part of her wanted to attack, but another part just wanted to get close enough to surrender, so she could feel what it was like to be the pirate's prisoner. Or even worse, his toy.

Oh, to be played with by the likes of Azar Xenelion.

Theryssa wasn't the only woman to feel it. Her mother had taken one look at the holo of Azar and turned stonily silent.

"What now, woman?" Theron had demanded of his wife. She had sighed at her husband's naïveté and left the room. Nyssa knew full well what her daughter was dealing with, and Theryssa was sure she didn't envy her. But she had asked for this, hadn't she? And she was about to get it in spades.

As if it hadn't been bad enough so far. Five days in deep space, resisting every urge to masturbate, trying to stay cold and hard and professional. All the while rehearsing her role as the proverbial fluffy female, easy pickings for sexual predation.

She checked the clock again. Another minute had ticked off. Wonderful.

Hurry up, damn you, Azar. Get here and enslave me, already.

* * * * *

Azar studied the small cruiser through the starscope of his pirate ship, his eye pressed to the lens. The cruiser at the other end continued its slow, aimless drift in space. Thus had it been for the last half hour, seemingly alone, and crippled. The damage to the engines was evident and quite severe. It looked to have taken a random meteor hit. A one in a million chance, but not entirely impossible out here in the space lanes between Earth and Beta Prime. The Navigation and communication lines looked torn up, too. Presumably, the courier ship was unable to call for help.

A sitting duck. Likely laden with some sort of treasure. Ancient gold artifacts, perhaps, or antique artwork. Maybe even a first edition of a real book, with paper and ink.

What a lucky day to be a pirate. How entirely fortunate.

A little too fortunate, as far as Azar was concerned. Opting for caution, he held their observational position at a safe distance, the pirate ship's invisibility shields still engaged.

"Captain, what are we waiting for?" demanded Oleron, his bearded, increasingly insubordinate second-in-command. "There is prey right in front of us. Why do we not seize it?"

This was Oleron's problem—he had allowed his own short-sighted egoism to blind him to all other considerations. In order to score quick points by appearing bolder than his superior, he was surrendering the true judgment needed to lead. "If it is prey, Oleron, then it will wait...while we ascertain fully the nature of the situation."

221

"What is to understand? I see booty—all the men do. Too long have we waited, and too often turned away when we could have fattened ourselves and lined our coffers."

There were others on the bridge, listening, watching.

"A fat predator does not make for an effective predator, Oleron. You must think of the long term."

"A pirate has no fear, *Captain*."

Azar turned from the scope to confront his accuser. "Nor does a fool, Oleron. Are you sure you can gauge the difference? Besides, we are not blind killers. We have objectives. We are at war, or have you forgotten?"

Oleron scowled, his eyes darting back and forth. The others were grinning, chuckling. Knowing himself beaten, for the moment, he backed down. "I know nothing, sir but what I am ordered to do."

There was no missing the sarcasm, the intended challenge to his rule...and the cause, which was to defeat the Galactic Council and its cruel program of genetic mating. A program which had cost the life of the only woman he'd ever loved.

"In that case, you will de-cloak the ship and apply the magnobeams," he commanded, dropping the matter for the present. "Bring the cruiser into the lower bay. I will await its arrival there."

"Sir," Oleron saluted, the tiniest bit of grudge showing through.

Azar gave him a month, maybe less until he tried a mutiny. He had seen any number of men like this over the years, spineless and greedy. It ought to be child's play to defeat him, and yet as Azar rode down in the elevator he felt, for the first time in his life, an overwhelming fatigue, bordering on exhaustion.

He'd been at this so many years now, having single-handedly organized the galaxy's worst outcasts into a fighting force capable of matching even the Guardians and using it with ruthless efficiency time and again.

In exchange for their loyalty he gave the men plunder, and a cause. They were standing for free and natural humanity, for the right to mate with the person of one's choice, and to have babies in the natural way. Imperfect, unpredictable babies who could marry as they wished.

Not genetic slaves whose lives were fixed from before they were old enough to speak.

Few of his pirate crew cared for politics, it was true, but they were better men for believing in something larger than themselves.

As for the secret he was forced to keep about his own nature—that he was not in reality a natural-born rogue like them, but a product of the Council's elite technology—this had caused him to lose many a night's sleep and had aged him prematurely.

But he had no choice. If the men knew they would run from him in terror.

Or was he only justifying himself, manipulating those around him to maintain his own private vendetta against the Council?

Could it be time to come clean?

He had been wondering about this almost nonstop since receiving a secret communiqué from the Guardian High Command two days ago. It was an urgent request for a meeting, to discuss peace.

This alone would have brought only his contempt, but there was with it a personal transmission, from General Theron himself.

A handwritten letter of apology.

This would have meaning to no other living person except himself. It concerned an event of long ago...*the event*. And he was not as yet decided as to how to respond.

In the meantime, there was the cruiser.

Why exactly had Azar agreed to take it onboard, anyway? Something was wrong with the situation, his gut told him that. Anything that came too easily always was. There were no Guardian ships in range, so he had decided to take the chance. Still, he sensed no good would come of this.

As a precaution, he ordered extra men with heavy lasers, to the bay. If anything untoward was in that cruiser, it would be vaporized to the next universe. He took up position at the front of the storming party.

Azar waited until the crippled ship was fully inside and resting on the deck, the bay door closed behind it. Raising his hand, he gave the count. On three they moved in fast and hard, surrounding the ship and blasting the outer hatch. They had the pilot down on the ground before he or they could draw another breath.

"Don't shoot, oh, please," came the high-pitched voice belonging to the small body—far too curvaceous to belong to a man. "I beg you, please don't kill me!"

Azar felt the blood drain from his face. Correction. They had the pilot down before *she* could draw another breath.

By the Holy Raiders of the Arc Nebula, the pilot was female. No wonder his gut had been ringing the alarm bells. The last thing he needed with a possible mutiny on his hands was a woman for the men to fight over.

"Captain," cried Koros, a toothless, crusty veteran of a hundred campaigns. "We got ourselves a wench."

"Let's strip her down," said the stalwart Robo-Leg Jim, his cock suddenly as stiff under his breeches as his artificial limb. "And give it to her good."

By the gods, his crew was degenerating badly. His leadership must surely be lacking of late.

"No," Azar boomed. "We'll have none of that. Have you men forgotten what we stand for? This is no willing space prostitute here. Since when do we abuse females?"

"Perhaps, Captain," said Oleron. "If you allowed them to enjoy female companionship as you do, they would not be so…impatient."

Azar turned on him. "Do you presume to question me?"

"No, sir." He bowed, avoiding a fight.

Azar regarded him, even as his mind tried to recollect recent history. Oleron had a point, mean-spirited as he was. Azar had been neglecting his men's needs in favor of his own. He'd been trying to keep them focused on work, even as he sought women for himself to maintain his flagging spirits. He would have to address this.

"Are you the Captain, sir?" The young woman addressed Azar. She had risen to her knees. She wore a tight uniform, with a zipper down the front, the emblem of her company incised just above her left breast. She was about five foot five, with long black hair and piercing eyes.

For a moment, Azar could not speak. She was that beautiful, that breathtaking.

Hands down, in fact, she was the loveliest creature he had ever laid his weary, jaded eyes upon. "I am Azar Xenelion," he confirmed. "Captain of this ship. By the laws of interstellar piracy, I declare your vehicle and all its contents to be forfeit."

The lovely, raven-haired angel shook her hair over her left shoulder and crossed her arms over her breasts, the very picture of feminine helplessness, and yet at the same time possessing of a playful, even bold nature. Such a strange contradiction.

She made him feel energized.

"Sir, I appeal to you…do not let these men take my clothes…or my…my honor. If I must be used, let it be by you alone."

The blood surged to his cock, as if on cue. What man in his right mind could refuse such an offer? A captured angel, offering herself for the price of protection. Conveniently on her knees, eyes seductively moist. How simple to ball that luxurious mane of hair in his fist, to put her immediately to his pleasure, making her swallow his throbbing, erect cock inch by inch while his men watched, licking their own lips, hoping against hope for their own turn with the beauty.

Oh, to be an ordinary pirate, with no code or ethics.

What fun he would have.

On second thought, such a woman could not be shared, even visually. It would dishonor her high nature. Besides, she would probably find a way to fight back, making him sorry he'd ever tried to shame her.

He suppressed a smile. Again, she was making him feel light on his feet. How long had it been since he'd stood in one place and breathed deeply, happy to be alive?

How many starry nights had he gazed upon, how many fallen comrades, how many bottles of rum in a hundred space variations, how many soft lips, whispering his name in awe, master and captain in more languages than he could count.

But none of those planets were Earth, and none of those women were truly his.

Not like Solania.

Azar pursed his lips as that feeling came rushing back. The one he'd had watching the ship out there a little while ago, drifting, and dangling. Like shark bait.

This was all too perfect…too easy.

"Search the cruiser," he ordered Robo-Leg Jim, circumventing Oleron for the moment. "And have the wench brought to my quarters."

"Yes, sir," said the obviously disappointed Jim.

It was on his way out that Azar heard the whispering. He had his needle sword to the man's throat in the span of a heartbeat. "Would you care to repeat that in a volume more suitable for a man than an old woman?"

Oleron's forehead beaded with sweat. "It was nothing, sir."

Azar knocked the man swiftly off his feet.

The stunned Oleron clutched at his stomach. "What was that for, Captain?"

"That," said Azar. "Was my own version of *nothing*. Next time it will be far worse."

Azar's heart thudded in his chest as he left the bay. He had made a mistake allowing Oleron to live. Mercy, given to the wrong people, inevitably came back to haunt one. Sometimes fatally. For some reason, though, he could not kill the man in the woman's presence. It wasn't that he thought she couldn't handle it—he was sure she could. Under her damsel exterior, she was feisty as his beloved, lost Solania had been. Maybe more so.

More than ever he felt an overwhelming drive to be with the dark-haired woman captive, to speak with her, to learn her name. She represented danger of a very different kind, one that at the moment he far preferred. To die at the hands of an Oleron, or in the face of nameless Guardian laser guns was tragic at best, but to die in the arms of a green-eyed angel, with an oval face like a goddess, a noble brow and the body of a virgin sea nymph, that would render an existence like his meaningful, as miserable as it might have been heretofore.

Besides, there was a mystery to be solved. And Azar loved puzzles. The beautiful young woman had a story, an identity, and depending on what his men found on that ship, it was quite possible that her true identity would end up having as little to do with interstellar package delivery as Oleron had to do with being a real man.

The trick now was to make them sweat a little. The woman, Oleron, all of them. Let him be the one with the answers, keeping them all off balance. To that end, he made himself briefly incognito, taking a detour into the ship's kitchen.

"Rum," he told the robo-chef on duty. "Natural, not synth."

The machine floated by anti-grav to a metal cupboard to fetch the bottle.

"Skip the glass." Azar put out his hand. Experts had studies from here to the next system that it was impossible to taste the difference. But experts couldn't quantify the really important things in life. Like loyalty and trust. And desire for a woman.

"To life," he toasted the machine.

The rum went down like fire and molasses, like sweet memories, mixed with an unknown future. He took another drink. Images conjured, waking dreams, from the tips of his toes upward, through the heart, to the head where they could be interpreted. He was seeing the woman in the bright yellow flight suit with the green trim and the logo over her breast, the slick, glossy material hugging her every curve, the shiny metal of the zipper inviting a downward tug, inevitable and complete.

Did female space pilots wear underwear? Something practical, made of clingy, see through absorbex, or would she be more daring, perhaps even donning some wispy, silky things, wickedly old-fashioned, a bra and pair of panties, black or red, barely covering her full breasts and sweet ass?

As captain he had the right to see her underwear and any other part of her. Including her naked body. And it hardly ended there. He could see that body writhing underneath him, her legs splayed open as he pumped her warm, slippery pussy full with rock-hard cock. He could also see how she looked with stripes, the red marks of the crop or cane lining her soft flesh, inviting his touch, his conquest. Or perchance in bondage, hands behind her back, drawing emphasis to her outthrust breasts. Ankles, chained apart, too wide to cover her desire, the dripping moistness, the swell of labia, the glimpses of still pinker flesh, begging further examination. That look in her eyes as she realized what he already knew, that everything would be done to her according to his will, male to female. Just as every man desires, looking at every beautiful woman, to take and chain and own her.

Galaxy Shipping Pilot W45-76, according to her uniform. How much more he would learn reading her nude. Absorbing and studying, playing and teasing, holding him hostage to sex, hour after hour, taking such unfair advantage of her gender, reducing her to naught but a silent whimper, to yearning, reaching flesh, which will do anything, take anything, if only to be granted the smallest of male attentions.

Such a lovely little jewel this one would be to dangle from his chain. It was not about the number of women, or even the act of conquest itself, so much as it was the thrill of unfolding the nature of each new flower. At the moment he was loving a female, there could be none before or after her. She was center of the universe. And he was its challenger, its explorer.

The ultimate pirate.

Azar knew of the stories of his prowess that circulated. His exploits with the fair gender. They had become a bit exaggerated, as were the other tales—those of his exploits against his enemies.

If it was a matter of mere flattery, Azar wouldn't be concerned. Unfortunately, his image had been converted by Earth media into that of a mere self-serving plunderer and not a freedom fighter.

More than anything lately, he felt like a dinosaur, fighting for a forgotten cause, feeling a thousand years old and completely misunderstood.

Would this young, voluptuous new female be the one to give him back his youth? Not if he played her game. The easy surrender she offered in the bay was false. A trap more than likely. But set to what end? This was no mere damsel throwing over her virtue. She had spoken her lines a little too boldly, moved with a little too much assurance. Not quite, but almost to the point of mocking.

The one thing he did not smell on her fine, exciting little person was fear. A star courier, especially female, ought to have been terrified half to death. This one had a kind of deadly calm. An anticipation almost to the point of eagerness.

There was only one sort of human being who reacted in such a way, and they were neither star couriers nor female.

He pushed this possibility aside for the moment, for it made no sense. Another drink, and then he would see what he would see.

"Captain," Robo-Leg Jim stood in the servo doorway of the old gray metal ship, the Sabre, Azar's only real love, his only real home for ten years.

"What is it, Jim?"

"We have taken the cruiser apart, down to the rivets."

"That was fast work," he approved. "What did you find?"

The pirate signaled two of the others to bring in the items. Azar identified them one by one. An antique suit of clothes, called a tuxedo, a genuine box of cigars from New Cuba with a personal note from his Highness, King Fidel the Eighth, and the piece de resistance, an ancient Egyptian figurine, probably from the days of the pharaohs.

The cruiser's manifest confirmed the diminutive but priceless cargo. Nothing else had been found, not one shred of suspicious evidence linking it to the Guardians or the Council.

Too perfect. Too easy.

"The female is in my quarters?" he confirmed.

"Aye, Captain."

"She is secured?"

"Chained tight, sir. Not going anywhere in a hurry."

Azar's balls tightened and his cock thickened as he pictured the beautiful female, helpless in bondage. It was so very difficult to think of her in terms other than purely sexual. "I must attend to her interrogation. I am not to be disturbed, except for emergencies."

"Aye, aye, Captain."

The pirates stepped aside as their leader strode past, his leather boots tromping down the corridor, his long mane of bound hair hanging down his back. He was a man on a mission now, and the gods help any who stood in his way. He would not rest, nor would he divert his attention one iota from his stated goal. The woman would speak the truth.

And she would speak it quickly, no matter what means he must apply. Unless he missed his guess, there was something afoot here that threatened not only his own peace but that of the entire brotherhood of pirates.

He could not put his finger on it, but something about the courier was very, very wrong. Her overwhelming beauty and sexual magnetism was a clue. He would find other ones, he suspected, in short order.

Then again, there was virtue in taking his time.

Especially as the means he intended to use were highly erotic in nature. Methods that would, as a pleasant happenstance, result in him enjoying the woman not only as a mental conquest but a sexual one as well.

Chapter Two

ഇ

Theryssa's hands were shackled behind her back. The pirates had put her on her knees, on the captain's bed, an ancient four-poster carved out of a very rare living gem material found on Zanhus Two.

A collar of old-fashioned steel circled Theryssa's neck. It was attached to a metal chain, which they had secured into one of the four identical metal rings attached to the posts.

They were enjoying themselves immensely, though her pirate captors had no clue, of course, that she could break this steel with her bare hands. So, too, could she have disposed of all three of them on the way down here from the cargo bay without even breaking a sweat.

What a bunch of arrogant fools they were, thinking her just a poor defenseless woman. Especially the baldheaded one, whose name she had learned was Oleron. He was as dumb as he was crass. His hints about his rising power among the crew were hardly subtle.

Nor was his promise to one day become far more intimately acquainted with Theryssa's charms.

"What goes around comes around," he told her, though she had no clue what the man was talking about. Frankly, he was damn lucky he hadn't actually laid a hand on her, or she would not have been responsible for her actions.

The thing she had to bear in mind was that this Oleron was of no more importance than an ant crawling across the blanket of an old-time picnic. He was annoying, but in the end, he didn't matter in the least.

Her job was to figure out what Azar was up to. And that meant letting herself be chained to the bed like a common wench, a lot of horny grinning males drooling over the sight of her.

"Please," she begged, laying it on thick, "don't hurt me."

They left her alone in the captain's cabin, happily snickering. Never realizing that she was already well on her way to getting what she needed. So far, in fact, she was collecting intelligence faster than a spy droid operating full throttle in a nest of Calossian gun runners. Less than an hour in pirate custody and she had already gained a working knowledge of their engine and weapon's systems as well as a good sense of their fighting capability.

Scanning ship computer schematics with her hypersensitive brain waves and monitoring internal communication systems was the easy part, though. The hard part remained. Namely the collection of intelligence for the Council. Information about Azar's connections to the Narthians and to other pirate groups.

One thing she had picked up on so far was some surprising hostility among the crew. Not all the men supported Azar. Their body language, the motions of the eyes of certain members in the captain's presence spoke volumes.

And that did not begin to approach the blatant dissension she had witnessed in the little incident between Azar and one of his lieutenant's in the hallway, the one called Oleron.

The underling Oleron had been seething under his breath, and Azar had called him to task. Azar had made a fool of the man, dominating him thoroughly. Theryssa had to confess to feeling a slight tightening in her belly when she'd watched him draw his sword and upend the baldheaded man.

Were Theryssa a man, she would mark the incident well as a warning of Azar's power. As a woman it signified something else.

Azar was a pirate's pirate. He took what he wanted, including women, and he was first because none dared oppose him.

In this environment, Azar was like her father. The undisputed boss, and so far he looked more than up for the job. Plenty of times Theryssa had rolled her eyes seeing how her mother bragged on Theron and doted on him. But now she could see how a woman would get caught up in a man's aura and she began to wonder if she wasn't a little jealous of the fact that her mother had a husband—a hero and protector. Just like Aunt Seria had Uncle Raylar, another man whom Theryssa followed as a child, seeking his constant approval as she had with her father.

She had to admit, seeing Azar's holoid and living with his stunning male beauty for so long had done little to prepare her for the real thing. Unlike with most holoids, he was actually more vivid in person. More charismatic, too. She could see the attraction women must feel in his presence, hell, she could feel it herself.

Try as she might, she was like a moon being drawn into orbit. Those eyes, so deep and compelling, that rock solid form. And that cock, outlined beneath his skintight britches. Wild, half hard, promising a woman pure bliss at hyper-light speeds.

It was said that women loved by him were ruined for others. The Princess Galina of Menos One, having been held hostage by Azar for a fortnight, had begged to remain behind as the man's slave rather than resume her ransomed place on the throne of her home planet.

Had Azar lain with her on this very bed? Certainly it was equipped to keep a woman subdued, what with the iron rings in the posts. A female could be chained any number of ways, including spread-eagle on her back.

Theryssa felt a tingle down her spine as she looked at the rack of floggers on the wall. They were made of quaint leather, of varying lengths and styles. Beside them were hooks on which hung chains and shackles. Was it all for show or was she getting some insight into the man's sexual tastes?

She could only imagine if she were an ordinary woman, really trapped here, looking at all these things, and awaiting their owner to come back to his cabin. Were she not imbued with primale blood, were she not a Guardian, she would be at this moment, little more than a possession at the sexual mercy of a potential sadist.

What a relief that wasn't the case.

Strange, though, how a part of her felt a little twinge of regret...at not being able to experience such emotions, or face such erotic dangers. Given her genetics, three quarters primale and one quarter fem, she shouldn't be feeling things like that.

According to her Aunt Seria, however, there was more to life than genetics.

"You might be seventy-five percent primale by blood, Theryssa, but you are also a hundred percent female. And sooner or later, hormones are going to trump DNA."

"When will that be?" she had asked her Aunt.

"When you find your lifemate." The beautiful Seria had smiled.

Sometimes she envied her aunt and her mother for the love they had in their lives, though Theryssa did not want a lifemate of her own. Relationships were too complex. She wasn't all that interested in sex-making partners, either. Most men bored her. And those who weren't boring tended to be too self-absorbed and shallow. The really good ones were off limits, having devoted themselves fully to careers, especially in the Guardian Corps.

She had to laugh when her father gave her lectures. He thought she was still a virgin and she didn't do anything to correct him on that score.

Damn it, why did the man keep floggers in here? The place was intimidating enough with the animal skin rugs on the floor and the snarling animal heads on the walls. The latter being interspersed with an assortment of spears and other deadly sharp weapons. What really got her, though, was the painting on the wall opposite the rack of floggers.

It depicted a woman, incredibly graceful and beautiful. She was on her knees, naked, save for a tight, jeweled necklace, almost a collar. Her back was arched and her thighs were wide apart. She had her head back, mouth open, tipped up, her tongue stretched just far enough to catch one of the drops of rain falling in the forest around her.

Her pussy was totally exposed, the lips glistening wet. She had placed her hands behind her head, fingers interlaced. Thus was she rendered completely helpless.

Theryssa had never seen an image so scandalous and at the same time, so erotic. The tension in her body, the expression on her face made it clear she was in subjugation. A slave. And yet she seemed so completely at one with nature. So very free.

She felt her mind drifting as she sought to fill in the details. Who was the man who had put her in that position? To whom was she kneeling, so much in another's power that she dared not break position to seek shelter from the rain?

Who was the man she called Master? Was this a painting of a real woman? Someone Azar knew? Galina, even? What if it were she in that position? What if she were forced to abase herself, exposing her sexual heat to a male…to Azar.

What a sight she would make. The rain dripping from her hair, beading on her breasts, plinking off her swollen nipples, running in tiny streams down her belly and between her legs. Her own fragrant scent mixed in the air with the smells of the forest, wet earth under her knees, wet moss and leaves…and a wet, throbbing pussy.

Open for Master. Hot and ready to be stuffed full of hard cock. Or maybe he would take her mouth, conveniently opened, lips already parted.

Would he ask her what she wanted, what she needed? Would he make her say the words she feared most?

Fuck me, Master. Throw me down on the forest floor. Fuck me in the dirt and the leaves. Fuck me in the rain. Take me like an animal. Hard and nasty. Make me come, again and again, make me scream out so the whole forest can hear me and every creature in it...

Azar, pinning her down, underneath his rippling muscles, letting her feel everything a woman should. The delicious surrender that even a fem could enjoy at the hands of any ordinary mem.

Or, what if he could take her further? Let her experience what an obedient feels when she becomes the absolute sexual possession of her primale? Indeed, what if she could feel the orgasm of an obedient—that release which was said to be the most profound of sexual pleasures in the world?

A pleasure that began with the meeting of eyes...the matching of wills. That eternal male-female exchange which in this case ended up with one of them wearing a collar of brilliant jewels, obeying, like a pretty, beloved pet.

Yes, my Master, come to me...and tell me what to do...

"I see you are enjoying my artwork."

Theryssa started at the sound of Azar's voice. The blood rushed to her face as she realized she had been rubbing her thighs together staring at the picture...daydreaming as she knelt, shackled on the pirate's bed.

Quickly she hopped off onto the floor, stretching the chain on her neck as far as it would go. "I demand you unchain me immediately."

Azar smiled at her, turning her insides a few hundred degrees hotter. He was regarding her with the amusement of a predator, a big cat, in the company of a small, fluffy rabbit. "I see you've lost some of your initial fear."

Theryssa frowned. He was referring to her sudden show of spunk. It was in sharp contrast to her earlier performance as the ultimate helpless, ditzy damsel.

Stars, this was going to be a hard line to walk. Not being too tough or too weak, all the while holding her temper in check so as not to bust out of her chains and give the pirate a sound thrashing.

Something felt very wrong about that last idea, that of beating up her handsome, alpha male captive. Would he really be that easily overcome? She didn't see why he wouldn't be, being that he was an ordinary man and she was imbued with primale power.

It was a pity, in a way. If ever someone looked like a primale, it was him. In fact, she had never felt this attraction to any primale, not even the strongest among the Guardians.

Theryssa ground her teeth.

There she went again…playing with mental fire. It was suicide to wish for this man to be stronger than her. Not to mention a complete betrayal of her mission. She was to collect her information and escape scot-free.

Strange how she hadn't considered taking *him* prisoner and forcing him to reveal the information. Her superiors hadn't suggested that either. She wondered why.

"I just want to go home," she said, making what she hoped was a reasonable statement coming from the mouth of a captured female courier held by deadly pirates. "Please…won't you just let me go?"

Azar moved to the wall with the rack of floggers on it. Her stomach tightened. Was he going to pull one down? What would she do it he sought to apply the leather to her skin? She couldn't allow herself to be flogged like a common slave.

No, it wasn't a flogger he wanted, but one of the knives. It was a long, jagged one, with a two-sided blade. For a moment she thought he might attack her. Her muscles flexed in readiness to break the shackles.

She would have snapped them like twigs, had he threatened her even one iota.

"You see this instrument?" He held the knife up in front of her, maintaining a safe distance of several feet.

Theryssa relaxed her guard, but only a little. "It would be pretty hard not to see it."

Damn it, she'd used sarcasm. Definitely not in character for a damsel in distress.

The remark earned her a second smile from her handsome captor. He was definitely analyzing her, testing and probing. She would have to be more careful. This was not a stupid man. Far from it.

"You're right, the question was rhetorical," he acknowledged. "As for the knife, this is the blade which I once used to defeat an entire squad of Zanamian Assassins, eight in all, armed to the teeth. Their commander tossed it to me as a joke, prior to what was supposed to be my execution."

"Oh, my," she said. Was he trying to scare her? How was she supposed to answer? He was expecting her to say something. Revealing that she was turned on by the thought of him fighting so valiantly and that she wanted him to throw her down on the bed and ravish her would probably not be in order. "It's such a...big knife," she observed.

"Yes, it is," he agreed. "Does it frighten you?"

She suppressed a smile of her own. The poor man was so clueless, really. She could disarm him and shatter that precious weapon of his in seconds if she wished.

Still, this didn't stop her from fantasizing about him battling Zanamians to the death. Was he bare chested at the time, she wondered?

"I-I can't lie…yes, it terrifies me," she replied.

Blast it, why hadn't she thought to say that in the first place? It would have fit in perfectly with her role.

The pirate pursed his lips. "Funny, you don't seem frightened," he noted, innocently enough.

"I'm hiding it deep inside."

Oh, fuck, this must be sounding so corny.

"Really? That's a new one on me," said Azar. "Generally women are pretty vocal, at least in my experience. Being chained up, no escape, my knife so close to them, tends to make them pretty expressive, hysterical even."

"I don't want to make you angry by saying the wrong thing," she offered.

"It's not a matter of saying the right or wrong thing." He shrugged. "I suppose it's just a matter of my expectations."

"Your…expectations?"

"Yes, I will admit I have never thought of it in those terms, but I suppose I have some expectation as to how a woman will act when confronted with a knife, by a murderous pirate such as myself."

Damn it, was he playing with her?

"Well it is my first time," she pointed out. "Having a knife pointed at me and all…"

"Granted," he nodded. "I can see where that might leave you at a loss. Might I ask you a question, though?"

Theryssa frowned. He was being way too polite and charming for her liking. "Yes?"

"Are you expecting to be ravished?"

Theryssa felt instant heat between her legs. Was he reading her mind?

If only she wasn't on a spy mission. If only this man wasn't a sworn enemy, she would be able to strip the clothes from his body, bare those fine muscles, and kiss and lick every inch of that bronzed skin of his.

A natural man. Born of a woman. Not a test tube. He was like an animal in the forest. Raw and completely…sexual.

"I am at your mercy. I know that."

Actually, it might be great fun to have him at her mercy, too. She would chain him down, mount his magnificent cock and ride him until he came, spurting helplessly into her hot, tight sex.

The pirate ravished by the woman with super genetics. Now there was a twist on the old kidnapping plot. How would he react? Something about him was so different than she'd expected. He was dressed like a pirate, doing a damn good job as one…but there was more to him.

Why did she feel like he was play acting as much as she? She'd love to ask. She'd love to drag the truth out of him.

Except she couldn't reveal herself. She had to keep her powers under wraps. For as long as necessary to get the information she needed. And if that meant playing along with the man's sex games, then that's what she would have to do.

Up to and including pretending to be overpowered.

And pretending to like it, as well.

Somewhere in the back of her mind, though, she could see Seria smiling indulgently, reminding her of the damn twenty-five percent fem that might make her enjoy it for real.

"You seem quite agreeable." Azar moved toward her, seemingly oblivious to her internal chaos as he touched a finger to her cheek. He was so much larger than she, seemingly so much stronger. "Are you telling me you will not fight me…no matter what I choose to do to you?"

His finger sent waves of raw energy, like hyper-drive fuel, coursing through her veins. She opened her mouth, which was suddenly quite dry. "How…could I?" she said, her voice a hot whisper. "As strong as you are?"

"Fighting is an instinct. You are offering me reason." Azar brushed her hair behind her shoulders, arranging it as if she were already his woman, to do with as he chose.

The tenderness, the heat of his eyes on her made her melt. If he were to ravish her now, she would not need to fake surrender.

"I will release you from the chains." Azar slipped the knife into his belt and reached for a key in a small pouch beside it. "If you promise to be good."

She suppressed a sudden urge to tell him to shove it.

Her eyes darted to the jeweled handle. She could, if she wished, take it from him and hold him hostage, even dispatch him. That is, if she could stop her body from trembling.

"You hesitate. Is it that you're afraid you can't be good or do you like being chained?"

"Neither," she snapped, unable to stay in character.

He smiled, looking much more the pirate. "What are you? Obedient or fem? Surely you're not obedient."

Try primale, asshole, as you're about to find out. "I'm fem."

His hand moved to caress her arm. It was an itch and a scratch all in one. "That's too bad."

"Why's that?" she whispered.

"The things I'm going to do," he rasped, "are better suited to an obedient."

Her mind surged with the implications.

He's going to take me…use me.

"Do you know yet who I am?" he asked casually.

Her heart pounded. "No," she lied.

"I am Azar."

"Oh."

"You know me?"

"Everyone knows you."

"What about me," he queried, "do people say?"

She swallowed. How much of her real knowledge should she give? "They say you enslave women. Steal ships."

"So they do."

She recoiled slightly — very out of character — as he reached for the steel collar at her neck.

"Don't be afraid little one," he rasped.

I'm not your fucking "little one", she wanted to shout. *I'm a trained warrior, and I'll see you rot on a prison planet for the rest of your life before I'm done with you.*

On the other hand, there was something almost endearing in it...

She couldn't succumb, though. He would have her eating out of his hand, like Galina, begging to be used and abused.

"There, much better," he approved, removing the collar. "Now I can see your lovely neck."

Theryssa felt her cheeks pinkening. Suddenly her neck felt quite naked.

"Let's see about those wrist shackles, too, shall we? Turn about, little one."

He had said it again. Like he had the fucking right to give her pet names. Quickly, she turned her back before he could see the expression on her face.

"You do realize," he undid her cuffs, "there is no hope of escape from this ship. Even if you managed to get out of my quarters."

So you say, buckaroo.

"I understand."

"You should call me Sir," he suggested. "From here on out."

"I understand," she let the charged word off the end of her tongue. "Sir."

Azar whirled her about, catching her completely off guard with a kiss. His lips were red-hot, searing against hers. Her initial resistance gave way to openness, complete and total.

He had her. The fucker had her.

His tongue was in her mouth. Probing, playing with her, like she was any captured maiden he was about to possess. Desperately, she fought to keep her wits about her, even as her nipples pushed against him, hard as pebbles.

His body was so firm. She could feel every muscle. His cock was rising, too, against her delta, pressing between her damp, needy thighs. She could feel her arms lifting, her own hands, wanting to hold him.

How she had dreamed of this moment, masturbating over his image, picturing his cock, hard and exposed, sliding inside her, conquering her sex, making her his lover, his object of plunder.

Stars, she wanted him to be a primale, strong enough to just take her.

But that would destroy everything.

At last he broke the kiss. He seemed perfectly calm and in control, unlike her—she was on the verge of panting.

"Tell me your name," he said.

"Theryssa," she breathed. "I'm Theryssa."

"Theryssa." He weighed the sound on his tongue. "That is a beautiful name. It suits you. Such a pity it was chosen at random. By computer."

But it wasn't, she thought. My name is a combination of my parents', as I am a combination of their love.

"Your name," she said, "it's natural, like you."

His eyes showed pain. She didn't understand why. The fact that he was born of a woman's womb was one of the main things that made him so fearsome, strange and formidable.

"This isn't about me," he dismissed. "You're the prisoner, Theryssa. You're the one who will answer...or face punishment."

Her pussy sizzled. "Yes, Sir. And I thank you, for the compliment. No one...no one's made my name sound so good."

"You are unique," he told her.

Theryssa was lost in his eyes. So very deep and complicated. Was this man good or evil?

"Indeed," he continued, "I do not recall ever running across a courier with such a beautiful name. Or face."

She gasped inwardly as he caressed her cheeks with the tips of his fingers. She was completely helpless as he moved to her mouth, running them across her lips. Light and wet and teasing.

Electric surges shot down her belly. Spasms gripped her pussy.

He was staring at her intently. But what was he thinking? She could imagine all kinds of things. Not least of which was taking his fingers inside her mouth and licking and sucking them.

"You should know, Theryssa, I will interrogate you. Thoroughly and without mercy."

Theryssa arched her back. She wanted him to touch her breasts. To rip off her uniform and bare her swollen globes, not to mention the rest of her. She wanted to be naked. She wanted...everything.

"I'll tell you whatever you want to know," she assured him.

"Yes, little one, you will."

The way he said it, it was like he was inside her already, enjoying her body, making it sing.

Slowly, agonizingly, he moved his damp fingertips down to her chin. He tipped it back ever-so slightly, so he could touch her neck. With thumb and forefinger, he took her pulse. "Your heart is racing. Are you nervous about something…or just scared and aroused?"

"I'm…scared."

He angled her head backward a little more, so she could no longer see what he was doing.

"And aroused," he repeated, brushing his finger over a single nipple, all too evident against her tight uniform.

"Yes…"

"But not nervous…"

"Why would I be nervous?"

He touched her other nipple, making her moan softly. "Perhaps you are concealing something."

"You only have to ask me…"

"I want you out of your uniform, Theryssa. Release yourself from it."

"Yes…Sir." She gave the voice command, initiating the opening sequence in the tiny computer brain concealed in the emblem on her breast. At once the courier's uniform divided into two halves, right down the middle of her chest. Simultaneously, seams opened on her sleeves and down each leg. The built-in boots did their own separating routine.

Theryssa had only to lift each foot and take a step forward. She was naked now, entirely exposed to the pirate's viewing pleasure.

"Stand for me," he said. "Over there."

Azar indicated a place in the center of the cabin. She walked on tingling bare feet. The thick, white fur was luxurious against her skin. Theryssa fought an overwhelming desire to lie down upon it, feel the surface of it against the rest of her body.

Hands at her sides, goose bumps on her skin, Theryssa put herself in position, under inspection by the sexiest, most devilish man she had ever encountered.

"You stand like a soldier," he said, his tone neutral.

Theryssa considered her posture. Damn it, he was right. Instinctively, she had stood straight and tall, almost at attention. A captured damsel would display a good deal more modesty.

Quickly, she cupped her hands over her pussy, her lips puffy and moist against her equally damp palms. She hunched her shoulders, too, trying to look a little more overwhelmed.

Azar stood there watching.

Damn it, could he make her feel any more self-conscious? She clenched her toes, digging them into the fur. By the second he was gaining more control over the situation...and over her.

"You covered your sex," he observed. "But I can still see your breasts."

She moved to rectify the situation, quickly realizing that left her dripping wet pussy exposed. She moved to cover her mound, only to leave her breasts vulnerable. "I can't do both!" she protested.

"No," he agreed, "you can't. Reason tells a woman that. But instinct...that makes her want to try nonetheless."

Theryssa was losing her patience. Cat and mouse had never been her game and she was not about to start now. If indeed he saw through her disguise, better to find out so she could devise some new strategy. "I'm sorry I'm not meeting your expectations for a hysterical kidnap victim. I'm doing the best I can."

The pirate was nonplussed. "Tell me, Theryssa, are you a virgin?"

"No," she stiffened. "I am not."

"You have made sex with many men, or only a few?"

"Enough," she replied curtly.

"You would consider yourself a good lover, then? You know how to please a man?"

"I haven't heard any complaints, if that's what you mean."

He nodded. "I didn't think so. And tell me, do you like being a fem?"

"It's all right." She shrugged. "It's all I know."

"Indeed. You've never had the chance to explore any other part of yourself."

"I know who I am." She was tiring of the game. She wished he'd step up the pace.

"You won't ever submit to a single man as husband," he mused. "No fem ever will."

"We all serve our function."

"For who? The corrupt Council? The power elite?"

Theryssa had to hold her temper. This was her family he was talking about. "The Council serves humanity."

"How, exactly?" He snorted.

"For one thing, they keep us all from being Narthian bug food."

"Maybe death is preferable to some, than living a life dictated by another."

"That's easy to say when you live out here all on your own, doing whatever the hell you want. Some of us humans take responsibility for the race."

She watched him pull the knife from his belt. Here it comes, she thought. Badass pirate show time.

"Theryssa, if there is something you want to tell me, about your real identity, this would be the time to do it."

"I don't know what you're talking about. I'm a courier."

"Really? So there's nothing special about you?"

"Nope."

"In that case, I think I'll let the crew use you for a while. Fems like superficial sex, right?"

"You know it," she gave it right back.

"You will be taken, Theryssa, by a hundred horny men. They will come in every orifice, unless you seek my protection."

"I think you're bluffing. I don't think you like to share."

He weighed the knife in his hand. "You may beg me nonetheless," he said, not bothering to look up at her, "to not share you with my crew. You may beg me. On your knees."

"Go to hell."

The invective slipped out before Theryssa could catch herself. Meanwhile, Azar was making his move...

The events of the next few seconds took place so quickly she was not able to sort them out until afterward, when she was holding the dagger, having snatched it out of midair at lightning speed.

"You son of a bitch," she screamed. "You were going to kill me."

Azar's arms were folded across his massive chest. "It is as I thought," he said, revealing that he had thrown the knife directly at her head as a test. "You have primale genetics."

Theryssa's heart slammed in her chest. What a fool she was. She could have dodged the blade or thrown herself to the floor, maybe allowing it to graze her. But, what could she say at this point?

Damn it, what had given her away in the first place? He must have been pretty sure of himself to risk her life like that, or did he care so little for her existence?

"Never mind that—what if you'd been wrong?" she demanded.

Azar stood his ground. "But I wasn't."

"You could have been...and I'd be dead. Not that you give a damn." A part of her was angry at this. Another part was a little sad. She had hoped for something more from him. But why? He was a ruthless pirate.

"That's a moot point, Theryssa. What you need to focus on right now is telling me the truth."

"Why should I? The cat's out of the bag. We both know there's nothing you can do to control me. As a matter of fact," she glared, "I think you're the one who'd better start taking the orders."

Azar continued to be unfazed. A fact that was more than a little unnerving. She could tear him limb from limb. Didn't that bother him just a little? Or was there more here than met the eye on his part as well as hers?

"You gave yourself away the minute I walked in," he said, as if she'd asked him for an explanation. "The way you held yourself in those chains made it obvious. You could break free any time you wanted."

"Bully for you. Remind me to send you a galactic detective's license when I get home."

Actually, his accomplishment in guessing her identity seemed to rank more in the category of super-sleuth-works-small-miracle than rudimentary observation. He was hiding something here, too, but what?

Theryssa ordered her uniform back on her body. The material slid back up her skin, like a banana being peeled in reverse. Instantly, she felt her confidence rise.

"Speaking of which," she informed him. "Since we both know what I'm capable of now, I would like you to take *your* clothes off and put your hands on your head. It's time I did a little interrogating of my own."

Azar shook his head. "I'm sorry, that's not going to happen. Guidance computer," he addressed the empty space above his head. "Initiate self-destruct sequence alpha. Ten second countdown."

"Acknowledging captain's voice print," chimed the melodic voice of the machine. "Sequence initiated. Ten, nine…"

"What the fuck are you doing?" Theryssa demanded.

"I am destroying this ship, Theryssa, and everyone onboard."

Great Supernova – is the man completely insane?

"You wouldn't dare go through with that." She attempted to maintain her calm. "You'd die, too. And your whole crew."

"We all die sooner or later." He shrugged. "A pirate lives every day as his last."

"Seven," said the computer, as if to rub it in how nightmarishly real this was. "Six…"

"You would really die before surrendering to me?" Theryssa asked, feeling a whole new layer of awe for this man. Not to mention blind terror.

"Yes, Theryssa, I would."

"Four," the computer confirmed, ticking off yet another second of existence.

"What do you want?" Theryssa blurted, unable to resist the call of her survival instincts.

"Your submission," he said simply. "In no uncertain terms. You will yield to me from now on as any ordinary woman."

"Never," she hissed, desperate to call his bluff.

"Three, two…"

Azar folded his arms. "Well?"

He isn't bluffing…

"Done!" She exclaimed.

"One…"

"Swear it upon your honor."

"I swear!" she cried. "Now stop it, damn you!"

"Abort destruct sequence."

"Zero…"

Theryssa shut her eyes. Fuck. There went her mission.

"Destruct aborted."

She opened her eyes again. The ship was still here. As was she. And Azar, too.

Her momentary thrill at being alive evaporated as she considered the implications of what she had agreed to.

Yielding to a pirate captain…as an ordinary woman.

Azar's hands moved imperiously to his hips. There was no mistaking his readiness to enjoy his prize. "Get on your knees," he dictated. "You will present yourself to me. Naked."

Theryssa's belly clenched. She had never felt so hot and weak in her life. As the clothes fell away, so did her lifelong protection.

Thanks to her promise—which she could no more break than she could turn against her people and work for the Narthians.

For all intents and purposes, she was a normal female…not to the world but to this one man. The worst possible one to be helpless before, too. Because, unlike any other in the world, this man seemed to understand her weaknesses.

Weaknesses that had to do with lust…and maybe more.

Her heart thumped in her chest as her clothes fell away. She was nude again, but it was different than before. More real and profound. More excitingly dangerous.

This time she felt genuinely stripped. Exposed.

More naked than she had ever been in her life…

She took a deep breath, her head swirling as she tried to sort things out.

So much for the supposedly foolproof plan they had sent her in here with. All hope was not lost, however. She was pledged to obey, but not necessarily to tell the truth. Her mission would go on. She would remain undercover, continuing to collect data on Azar. She would, however, need a new cover story. Her guise as Theryssa, innocent female courier caught in the wrong place at the wrong time, had been unmasked, but she could come up with something else.

The problem was she wasn't sure what more he might know already. She was the first of her kind — how had he even known to look for such a possibility as a woman with three quarters primale genetics, in effect the very first primefemale?

What if he had spies working close to the Council?

A chill went down her spine as she considered that he might have known all along that she was a Guardian and who her parents were. In effect, he might have lured her into a trap.

In that case, she was going to have to fight her way out of here or else end up being a hostage. She couldn't imagine her father or mother caving in to any demands for her release, but she could never take that chance.

She would do anything to avoid that. Anything at all.

"I'm waiting, Theryssa."

The sound of his voice jarred her back to reality. She was naked, in front of her gorgeous and dangerous captor, whose breeches were currently being stretched by a mammoth erection. He had given her orders, the first she was to follow as the man's submissive.

She went down in slow motion, her body trembling. At last, her knees touched the thick fur. It tickled her skin, making her senses come alive. She could smell tobacco in Azar's cabin, and rum on the shelf. She could smell the leather of his boots, as well — so very close to where she knelt for him in subjugation.

He took several steps forward, and now she could detect the musk on Azar's skin. Mixed with raw testosterone. His boots pressed the fur as he moved. Closer and closer. She could almost hear his breathing, the raw desire, and behind that the hum of the ship's engine.

The raw power vibrated through the metal floor beneath the furs, and reverberated through her unclothed body.

His approach seemed to take forever. Each step stretching to interminable lengths. No doubt this was part of his strategy — to make her needy, jittery. Horny.

He stopped a foot away. She licked her dry lips at the sight of his leather-covered shaft. Larger than life. Almost close enough to taste.

"Knees apart," he directed.

Theryssa hesitated. Nothing was holding her down here. Except her damn honor. Sometimes she really hated being her father's daughter.

Maybe she could break her oath. After all, the man was a pirate. A real cutthroat. A man who could not begin to understand the meaning of integrity.

Azar did not take kindly to her delay. Reaching down, he seized the back of her hair in his fist, balling it painfully. "I gave you an order, young lady."

Theryssa cried out, her eyes watering. It was the shock more than anything else. The man was daring to treat her as if she really *was* some ordinary wench — an obedient, even.

Funny, he was so sure she wouldn't rebel. Didn't he realize her power? He seemed pretty familiar with it, so why put himself at risk like this?

"You're hurting me."

"That is the price of disobedience. Keep it up and I will take the flogger to you."

Theryssa slid her knees apart on the fur, complying with his earlier order.

"Wider," he said, not letting go.

Theryssa opened her thighs as wide as they would go. Her pussy was going wild. She would take any kind of attention now, the rougher the better.

He released her hair. "That's better."

"No it's not," she shot back. "It's inhumane. Don't you ever do that again. And don't call me young lady anymore, either. It's insulting."

"You are younger than me. And you're a lady…"

"I'm a woman, damn you."

"You're a female," he compromised. "In the keeping of a male." Azar ran his hand over the top of her head, lightly caressing her earlobe for emphasis. She tried to jerk away, but he snapped the fingers of his other hand, keeping her in place.

"Never seek to deny me your body, little one. You are mine to touch as I please."

Theryssa shivered. What he was doing to the tender flesh of her ear was having direct consequences in other parts of her body. Consequences which were distinctly detectable in the sweet scent emanating from her forcibly displayed sex.

"This isn't fair, Azar."

Azar laughed. She loved the deep, rich sound of it, like coffee from the far reaches of the rim forests of Fralos Ten. "It isn't designed to be a fair arrangement, angel. It's designed to maximize my enjoyment of you, as a captured commodity."

Theryssa did her best to fight back the gyrations, her pelvis pushing forward against the air, only to retract in favor of thrusting breasts. It was bad enough he had to tease her body, did he have to call her sweet little names, too?

"I'm not your commodity," she insisted.

"And yet your body is responding exactly as I wish it to."

"I'm going along with this because I have to. That's the only reason."

"Is that so?" His amusement was obvious. "In that case, I'm sure you'll want to resist me as much as I'll let you. Every step of the way."

"Damn straight." She gritted her teeth as he touched the back of her neck, sending icy hot spikes up and down her spine. "I'll obey you, but I will let you know how much I hate it. And if you leave a loophole, I promise I will take it."

"I consider myself warned." Azar took her hands, lifting her back to her feet. "Undress me," he ordered.

Theryssa could barely stand. As he let go of her fingers, she nearly fell to his feet. He was like a magnet of maleness, a singular powerful mass, drawing every ounce of strength from her.

She dared not take a single breath, lest he see even more clearly the state of her body. Swollen nipples, puffy red lips— above *and* below. Tight, contracted belly, quick little half-breaths, each of which only served to make her breasts feel a little more swollen, a little more achy and needful of his squeezing hands, his biting teeth and warm mouth.

Theryssa sucked in her lower lip, feeling the blood inside coursing against her teeth. She would never be able to do this. Not without losing her mind. There was no telling what she might say. What she might do.

Agonizing seconds passed between them.

Azar measured her defiance. "Are you planning on being a bad girl, Theryssa, or a good girl?"

Hearing him call her a girl did things to her. It was a scandalous thing to say, more demeaning than "young lady", and she knew from the light in his eyes that he was playing with her, waiting for a reaction.

Frankly, Theryssa felt a bit of both. A bad girl and a good girl. Mostly she wanted to be on the floor, where he could pound her into submission with his cock. She reached for the front of his vest. It was made of an animal hide, the front of it held together with rawhide lacing. Feeling just a little galvanized by his latest prod at her feminine independence, she opted to tease him.

"What if I am a bad girl?" she wanted to know, determined to beat him at his own game. "Will I go over your knee?"

"Is that what you want, Theryssa?"

"What do you care what I want? I'm your slave, right?"

"A Master can be generous with his slave. I've possessed hundreds of women and I have bestowed kindness on them all."

Theryssa didn't like the idea of other women for some reason. Was he trying to rub it in her face? As if she cared. "I'm not going to compete to be the highest notch in your belt, I hope you know."

"You already are," he floored her.

Stunned, Theryssa tugged the lace in the key spot. Like a snake, it slithered free from the holes, causing the two halves of the shirt to part ways. She had to catch her breath as his chest came into view. The awesome abs, the incredible pecs. And such a tight waist. You could not design a better male in any laboratory. Primale genetics were a joke compared to this.

At least on the outside.

What a bizarre thought, that with her small female body, she could bring this man to his knees. For real.

And yet he wanted to be kind to her...

"No. I just figured it was part of your whole macho trip."

Azar claimed her ass, grasping it easily, possessively, with a single hand. "Have you ever been spanked, Theryssa?"

"No." She attempted an expression of disgust, though what she felt was far different. "You know corporal punishment isn't allowed on Earth."

"Obedients are spanked."

257

"That's their business."

"Actually, it's their mates' business. Tell me…primefemale. Are you mated? We heard a few of you were being made. It was a matter of time until one came this way."

"I'm single," she said, attempting to end the conversation.

"Indeed. You aren't alone, though. You have some purpose in being here. And we will find it out, won't we?"

All too painfully she was aware that he could draw her against him now, her bare pussy against his leather breeches, her breasts against his smooth, hairless chest.

And that did not begin to cover the emotions roused by his sudden play for dominance. Taking a physical hit from a male in a wrestling ring or martial arts contest was one thing, but humbly accepting smacks to one's naked behind as a prelude to sex-making was quite another.

Theryssa had to draw a line here. Without breaking her promise, she had to let him know there were limits. The question was how to get that message across.

"Being spanked is an experience," he shifted his grip. Azar was drawing her closer, his index finger creeping lower, within dangerous proximity of her labia. "Some women find it quite arousing. Obedients can't live without it."

"I can't imagine why." She stiffened, trying hard not to breathe. Oh, stars…he was grabbing her ass. She tried to squirm free, keeping the conversation casual.

"It's the loss of power, I suppose. The feeling of sexual surrender."

She moved to brush his hand off her ass, an attempt to get her way without exercising primale force.

Azar's grip was steel. For a minute she wondered if she *could* get loose.

His gaze narrowed. "What are you doing, Theryssa?"

"I'm…" Oh, fuck, she was cheating, that's what she was doing.

"You weren't trying to take my hand away?"

She swallowed, unable to lie. "Yes…"

He clenched her behind. Hard. "Whose ass is this, girl?"

There was only one answer. "Yours."

His hand lifted and fell, smacking her efficiently, masterfully. "I touch this ass when I want, how I want."

"Yes, Sir," she breathed.

He pulled her closer. She didn't resist.

"Whose pussy?"

She gritted her teeth, knowing what was coming next. "Y-yours."

"And if I want to touch it?"

"You may."

"Any time? In any way?"

"Yes…"

"Beg for it, Theryssa."

"Please," she tremored, feeling the mounting heat of anticipation. "Touch my pussy."

He gave her another spank, hot and degrading. "Whose pussy?"

"Yours, Sir," she responded quickly. "Please touch your pussy."

"You're quite wet," he observed.

She couldn't help moving against him. "Yes, Sir."

"Stand still," he chided.

Theryssa whimpered, all her dominance and power lost. She couldn't strong-arm him if her life depended on it now. He'd played the gender card. Appealing to the obedient in her, not to mention the one hundred percent that was female.

Theryssa tried her best not to move as he slid his fingers to the second knuckle.

"You're not only wet, you're close to orgasm," he said.

Theryssa tried one last attempt to regain her dignity. He wanted her helpless and begging and she was determined to deny him the satisfaction. "What do you expect?" She smiled bravely. "It's a mechanical reaction."

Azar caressed her clit with his knuckle. "I think you're splitting hairs. A reaction is a reaction. Your body is telling its own story."

Fuck, he was right—damn her female hormones.

"But…it's not real." She stifled a moan.

"It seems real enough to me."

"You're not really in control," she protested, trying not to sound too terribly shrill or desperate. "I'm letting you. Because…of my promise."

"Ah, yes. I'd nearly forgotten. Your super powers." The fucker sounded like he was mocking her. "The ones that would let you resist me to the bitter end."

"The ones that would let me lay you out flat on your arrogant, ignorant ass, more like," she hissed.

Azar lifted his hand and spanked her again. Nothing erotic this time, just pain. Theryssa squealed. Hardly a proper reaction from a Guardian under torture.

"Are you out of your mind?" she cried.

Azar punished her again. "Hold still," he ordered, precluding her attempted escape.

Theryssa put her hand on her buttocks. Hot and throbbing. He had really done it. The son of a bitch was treating her like an obedient. "That hurt you sadistic fuck."

Azar took possession of her nipple. "You will not swear at me."

Theryssa sought to hang tough, but he pinched her harder and harder. "All right," she whimpered, "I won't."

He didn't let go. "Was that kind of language allowed growing up in your common house?"

"Yes...no."

"Which is it? Did you even have a common house? Bet they kept you in the test tube until you were full grown."

"I have parents," she spat. "They loved and cared for me."

"How sweet." He let go of her nipple. "Take off my pants, spoiled primale girl, raised by her parents."

"I wasn't spoiled."

He pushed her to her knees, making her feel really overpowered. Impossible.

"Did you have little test tube brothers and sisters?"

"Only me." She opened his breeches.

"Bet you were daddy's little girl."

If you only knew who he is, she wanted so badly to say.

"Daddy's little girl," he repeated. "A pirate's slave."

He wore no undergarments. His cock sprung out fully erect, long and thick, uncircumcised. A prominent vein was pulsing underneath. His balls were full and tight.

"How about mommy? She an obedient?"

"She's a mix, like me."

"A freak, you mean."

"Don't say that." She covered her ears.

"Freak!" he roared. "Freak."

Theryssa didn't mean to cry. The stress of the mission, the captivity, dealing with this strange, paradoxical man. "I...I thought you might be human, but you're a monster."

He lifted her by the hair. "You will not cry."

His face was in anguish, twisted. As if realizing what he'd done, he grabbed her and held her tightly. Tighter than she had ever been held in her life.

At once she felt protected and secure, but she was also overcome with need.

"Theryssa," he said softly, "I'm sorry."

She began to rub her nipples against his chest and press her crotch to his, begging penetration. The only thing on her mind, in her world was quenching the submissive fire he'd ignited. "Use me, Azar...Sir."

"Not like this," he kissed her neck, inhaling her scent. Bend down," he commanded. "And take hold of your ankles."

She was momentarily confused. He helped her, turning her about and putting her into position. Facing away from him. Her hindquarters exposed. To the air. To punishment. To him.

Theryssa gasped as she felt him pressing her crack—the tip of his rock-hard cock pulsed to enter her desperate lips. He was going to fuck her...at last.

Oh, god, Azar...yes...take me.

She did not dare speak the words aloud, on account of how much power it would give him. He was insufferable enough as it was.

"I want you, Theryssa," he croaked. "You can't imagine."

His fingers splayed on her back, sending shivers up and down her spine. She clenched and released her toes, every breath like a knife stab of waiting. "Azar, oh, stars, don't make me wait."

His cock was right there, aligning itself. Any second now...

Azar thrust his cock deep and hard, a slide down her canal, filling her totally and beyond redemption. The heat threatened to melt her insides, but still she wanted more. She squeezed him with her super muscles. He matched her. His hands clamped at Theryssa's slender waist, assuring her complete impalement. She groaned as his massive shaft retreated momentarily and then pushed back, deep into her. She was so open and wet and ready, accepting every last inch of him.

Her body exploded on the third thrust.

It was like she had never been fucked before, like this man was the first, his cock blazing a trail for all the rest to follow.

The first of the orgasms came from down deep in her toes. It had been building from the moment she had laid eyes on his image, reaching its crescendo here, with all their charged dialogue and his arrogant claiming of her body.

No man could do this to her, and yet this one was.

And she was taking it...coming and coming and coming. Even as he smacked his balls against her tender, spanked ass cheeks, pushing her to greater and greater limits.

"Mine," he growled. "My pussy...to fuck...and own."

"Yes...own it, own me," she said, lost in the heat of the moment, unable to see beyond to the very real impossibilities of the High Councilor's daughter submitting to a pirate on a permanent basis.

"My good little girl, my good little slave."

Theryssa screamed out, a fresh orgasm overtaking her, this one coming through every nerve ending, opening her thoroughly to the man's predations. Deliciously wicked and scandalous, demeaning and enrapturing all at once. Like a flame igniting her entire being, burning her right down to the ground.

"Yes, my Theryssa," Azar rasped as he reached around to grasp hold of her breasts. "My reborn angel."

What did he mean? Theryssa wondered, her fleshy globes pulsing and aching in his viselike grip. What exactly did he want from her and who did he want her to be? How far was this game going to go?

If indeed it was a game at all.

Theryssa felt a fresh spasm as Azar readied himself to come. By the goddess, he was swelling up, and getting hotter, too. If she didn't know better, she'd almost think he was more than a normal male…

But no, that was impossible. This man was a pirate, raised on an outlaw planet. There was no way he could have any artificial genetics at all, let alone the DNA of a primale.

She was imagining things, she had to be.

Azar leaned back, releasing a mighty roar. His semen came in hot bursts, thick shooting streams filling her canal. On and on, until she felt like she might explode. So hot…not like the mems.

Once again she thought of the times, brief though they were when she had lain with primales. Fellow students at the Guardian Academy. Her father would have had her hide if he'd ever found out. Aunt Seria had smirked, warning her to never tell a soul.

She hadn't told anyone, nor had she ever thought about it again until now. It was just that this experience was feeling so familiar.

What if it was true? What if…

No. She couldn't let her mind play tricks on her like that. She had been in space a long time, that was all. She was still a little susceptible to space madness.

In fact, she might be dreaming this whole thing. Yes, that was it. She was only imagining Azar fucking her from behind. In a few moments, she would come to, safely in her little space ship, still on her way to meet him.

She would have a good laugh over the whole thing. And then she would turn around and head straight back home.

Unfortunately, this particular Azar refused to vanish into the mist of fantasy. Withdrawing his cock from her twitching, burning sex, Azar ordered her to attend to him.

"Lick me clean," he said.

Theryssa's jaw dropped at the sight of him. Dripping as it was with his come and hers, the man's erection had not flagged in the least. If anything, he was harder than before.

There were only two ways that was possible. One, the man was some kind of android, which seemed highly unlikely, or two…he really was a primale.

And if that was true, she would have an entirely different possibility on her hands. Namely that she was not a prisoner in name only, but in reality.

There was only one way to find out. Theryssa was going to have to test him, just as he had tested her.

Chapter Three

ဆာ

One look at Theryssa's eyes told Azar of the woman's suspicions. He had been careless, giving her far too many reasons to suspect he was more than he appeared to be on the surface. At more than one point, he had nearly shown his primale powers, kissing the very breath from her body in their initial embrace. He had been unable to sufficiently control his cock, either. He had wanted her so badly there was no way he could have kept himself from swelling beyond normal proportions.

Too, he had filled her with far too much semen, and at a much higher temperature than any normal man should be capable of.

And now he was standing there, after such a titanic ejaculation, still as hard as ever. As though he had not come at all. How could she not suspect something was going on?

Quickly, he willed his erection down.

Theryssa watched it decline to half mast, though her body was still on high alert. Given the tension in her limbs, he was fairly certain she was going to try something foolish.

Would she openly break her promise to obey him? He doubted that highly. But she had already warned that she would take advantage of loopholes.

In short, Azar expected an escape attempt in the near future.

He would have to handle the situation with extreme care. He must let Theryssa think she still had the advantage as the only primale in the room, and yet he must also make sure she did not actually leave the cabin. For her safety as much as anything. Strong as she appeared to be, he could not take the chance on Oleron and the others overcoming her.

He simply would not allow harm to come to her. Whether she realized it or not, he was actually guarding her with fierce intensity. Nothing he was doing would bring harm to her. Even the little test with the knife had posed no threat, for had she been unable to deflect it, he would have used his own augmented reflexes to save her from the blow, either deflecting the blade or moving her at lightning speed out of the way.

Whether she knew it or not, he would die before he let harm come to her. No woman had been able to do this to him. Not since Solania. He'd suppressed the primale protection desire with every female after her. He'd forced himself to be as a mem, sleeping with anyone he wished.

It wasn't easy, but it was possible.

He wasn't a slave of Council genetics. He could be as he chose. Just as he had fallen in love with Solania in the first place—a fem, the most beautiful woman he had ever seen.

The first time he's seen her dancing, she had taken his breath away. By law he should never have pursued her, never talked to her. Instead he had made sex with her that night and within two weeks had made plans to marry.

The Council had other ideas. They had sent Theron, a junior Guardian then, to warn her away. She had become despondent and gone for an air-car ride to clear her head. She had taken it off autopilot. No one could ever be sure how the accident had happened. She had hit the dome full speed.

His fallen angel.

By the gods of vengeance, he had called Theryssa his reborn angel…in the middle of sex-making with her.

What was happening to his life? First the call for peace from the Council and the letter from Theron, attempting to explain about Solania and now this…the dark haired beauty come to him like a ghost.

He needed to get control of himself. Her life was not important, only the information she could provide as to who had sent her and why.

Because where information lay, there was always power, in one form or another. That's what women were for. They were power. Directly and indirectly.

The fact that he had never made better sex with a woman in his life, not even with Solania herself, did not matter. Nor did it make the least bit of difference how his heart raced in her presence and how her eyes and smile and indeed her every feature, intrigued and captured him beyond measure.

Never before had he been this intoxicated by a woman. Making sex with her, far from sating his curiosity, had merely whetted his appetite for more. What would she be like the second time and the third and beyond?

What if he were to become completely entangled in her dark-haired beauty, in the magic of those green eyes, and the grace of those lithe limbs? He was thirsty for her and hungry. And not just for her fair form. He wanted to know the inner woman, too. What made her tick and what her hopes were, and her dreams.

Dangerous indeed was this unexpected package snatched from the depths of space. His instincts had been right. But it was too late to cast her back out. She was his to deal with. For the long haul. Until he could determine her identity and find some way to get her home safely. Wherever home was.

In the meantime, he must continue on in the role he knew best, that of plundering pirate. It was one he had played for well on two decades. Ever since Solania's death. That terrible point of delineation marking his self-exile from everything he had ever known.

"You were given an order," he reminded Theryssa.

She looked at him, conflict evident in her eyes. "You don't really expect me to…"

"You will lick my cock clean," he confirmed. "And you will do so to my satisfaction or I will display you naked for the pleasure of my crew."

Theryssa tossed her dark curls. "No one else can look at me naked. That's not the deal."

He couldn't help but smile. For all her obvious courage and strength, she was so very female. "Want me to keep you for myself, do you?"

"Don't flatter yourself. I'm just sticking to the deal."

"The deal is obedience, young lady. If you choose not to honor your responsibility, I can and will punish you as I see fit."

Theryssa frowned. "Real men don't need to humiliate women to get off."

He watched her approach, in spite of her protests. "Does it humiliate you to give a man pleasure?"

She stood face to face with him, defiant. "Make no mistake, Azar," she squared her jaw, "there isn't a thing you could ever do to me in this lifetime to take away my pride."

Her eyes were shining like emerald fire. What a marvelous creature she was. Any man would be honored to have her at his side, in battle, or in peacetime for that matter. Did she have any love interests, he wondered. It would be difficult for her. She wasn't a fem, which meant no mem would dare touch her. She wasn't an obedient, either, which meant most primales would avoid her like the plague.

Were there any more like her? What game was the Council playing at this time? When he had served as a Guardian, back in the days of Marax's command, he had been aware of certain experiments. Plans to create hybrids on a mass scale.

Not all of the Council members had approved. Chief among the opposition was Malthusalus. The debate had reached a point of open conflict and Malthusalus had fled, fearing arrest. He and others had begun a campaign of subversion, designed to return society to its old ways. Azar, known then as Azariel, was sympathetic to Malthusalus' ends, though he could not condone acts of terrorism.

Even after the death of Solania, he could not join up with the infamous rebel. Instead, Azar had tendered his resignation from the Guardians and headed for the Outer Starfields, well beyond the influence of either the Council or Malthusalus' agents. Concealing his primale powers, he had signed on with a crew of space pirates, and over time, came to be king among them.

He used his forces to attack the Guardian ships, which he considered fair targets, but he was no friend to Malthusalus, and certainly not to the Narthians.

"I have no wish to take your pride," he told her. "Or anything else that you do not give freely."

"I shall give nothing," she said.

He smiled, enjoying her thoroughly. "Then I shall have nothing. Except a bath, my sweet, with your tongue."

Daggers shot from her eyes. His cock swelled with thick, hot need. This proud beauty was all his...and in a matter of seconds, she would be servicing him.

And why not indulge himself a little? He was still in control here and he could stop things whenever he wanted.

His pulse raced as she lowered herself to her knees, her lips even with the tip of his shaft. "Take your time, love. We're in no rush."

"If I were you," she advised, her hot breath on his balls, "I would give me specific orders not to bite your cock off, otherwise I won't be held responsible for my actions."

Azar laughed—a deep roll from his belly. "Have you any idea," he queried, "just how charming you are?"

"No. Do you have any idea what a pig you are?"

Azar caressed the top of her head, doing the one thing he knew would infuriate her most. "That's enough, little one. Time to tend to your work."

Theryssa made a noise, indicating her anger. Any further protests, however, she kept to herself. Instead, she extended her tongue and tentatively touched the tip of his cock.

Azar ran his fingers through her thick hair. "Yes, baby, that's it."

"Don't call me that." Theryssa slid her tongue underneath, running the top of it along the thickly protruding vein. Azar released a low groan. He could see this cleaning exercise was quickly going to turn into something else entirely.

"I mean it in the best way, I assure you. Put your hands behind your back, Theryssa. Clasp them."

The new position accentuated her breasts as well as emphasizing the helpless servitude of her position. She was shackled now by something better than steel—his will.

Her eyes were closed. She was working tenderly up his shaft. What was she feeling? Was she as immersed in their connection as he was? He made a mental note to return the favor. Later it would be her facing the pleasures and tortures his tongue on her sex.

"Oh, Theryssa," he rasped, "you sweet, mysterious thing. I want to shove my cock in you so far. I want to make sex with you...for a hundred years without stopping."

Theryssa's pace quickened, as did her ardor. She had managed to reach the base of him and now she was working back to the tip, along the side. As she reached the tip again, she took care of the small drop of pre-come, dabbing it with the end of her tongue.

Was that a trace of a smile he saw on her face?

She did his cock head next, her tongue making luxurious swabbing motions. When she had managed to cover every inch, Azar took hold of the sides of her head and guided her underneath. One by one, she took his fully loaded balls into her mouth. Her sucking motion was sweet and gentle, natural and perfect. No captured female had ever done it better.

Had she received some kind of training? What was the Council trying to do, develop a race of super-powered pleasure women?

"That's enough." He tugged her head back very gently, almost like a dream, his fingers interwoven in her hair. He hardly needed to guide her as she sought his cock again, this time with her mouth opened into a sweet, accepting oval.

The opening was cock-shaped, and he went between her lips, as if in a dream, when you feel like you've come home to the very source of pleasure in the universe.

Theryssa's jaws were slack. She was surprisingly relaxed. He sighed his affirmation, as he slipped into the pocket of her cheeks, sheathing himself. He wanted to be completely immersed, but he knew her mouth could not take all of him. Finding the back of her throat, he pulled quickly forward again, so as not to overwhelm her.

She showed no signs of gagging. In fact, she was trying to suction him back in again—harder, faster.

With both hands, she covered the exposed part of him, forming an extension of the tunnel made by her mouth. He reminded her that she was supposed to have her hands behind her back, but he wasn't much disturbed by her willfulness, especially as it was designed to increase his pleasure.

Theryssa made a slurping noise. She was a hungry, eager little thing. By the gods, if the male members of the Council had known the possibilities of feminine primale power in the area of fellatio, they would have made millions of women like this.

Azar gripped her shoulders, steadying himself. It was very tempting to ejaculate this way—into her sweet mouth. He wasn't going to, though, not until he was sure just how much experience she had actually had with primales.

Obviously she wasn't a virgin and she didn't seem totally freaked-out by his super-powered cock, but Azar was considered to be extra potent, even by primale standards.

In his younger days, it had often taken two, even three pleasure women to satisfy him over the period of a single night. He had not wanted Solania to mate with him for that reason. He had feared what might be unleashed should he become fully bonded with a woman. Such a level of possessiveness and sexual demand might be more than a woman could handle.

Solania had been a brave woman, however, and very stubborn, too. She had refused to take no for an answer. She had pleaded and begged, tirelessly working to make Azar see that she was the one female made for him.

I cannot live without you, she'd said, *so why should I ever fear what might happen with you?*

There was no way to argue with such logic.

Ten times he had ejaculated inside her, all the while bringing her to countless orgasms, both clitoral and vaginal.

They enjoyed one another in every conceivable position, their bodies covered in sweat, limbs intertwined, hearts slamming in unison, blood pulsing—two systems made one. He scarcely knew where she ended and he began. Time and space disappeared. There was only his sweet, curly-haired redhead, with her small, perky breasts, pale white skin and rounded, eminently spankable ass cheeks.

When the loving was done, she came to him on all fours, a collar and leash in her teeth. Laying it beside him where he reclined on the bed, she begged him to collar her, put her under his discipline.

"Do you know what this means?" *He brushed the hair back from her forehead to gaze into her pretty brown eyes.*

"It means you will be my Master," *she said.*

Tears in his eyes, he affixed the leather around her slender throat, the chain leash hanging between her breasts.

"Beat me," she whispered when he was done, her finger touching the collar in awe and astonishment.

His cock popped to full erection. Half crawling, half scrambling, she made it onto his lap. He had her mount him sideways, so he could spank her while he was inside her.

Solania screamed, orgasming with each spank. Her pussy clenched him tightly, the helpless spasms driving him onward to more and more punishment. Twice he came inside her that way, until her ass was red and twitching between blows.

"Clean me," he ordered her.

Eagerly, Solania fell to the task, the words "Yes, Master" . pouring hotly and submissively from her lips.

Azar steeled himself against the power of the memories. Something about Theryssa was making him feel it all again, like it had just happened. What was going on here? If he was supposed to be in charge, why did he feel like he was losing control by the minute?

And this was with Theryssa on her knees in front of him, his erection deep in her mouth, silencing her willful tongue. How much worse would it be in a more equal position?

Time to find out.

Consider it another round of testing. The seasoned pirate primale and former Guardian against the up-and-coming superwoman. No holds barred.

And may the better person win.

* * * * *

Theryssa was only sucking Azar's cock under duress. She wasn't really enjoying it. And she was going to tell him that, at the first available opportunity. The fact that he tasted so wickedly pungent, so totally male and salty sweet meant nothing. As did the fact that she was stuffing him down her throat, trying to inhale him like a greedy little eager-to-please obedient, her pussy on fire and demanding a fresh injection.

If anything, she was being ironic, sarcastic even, showing him how totally opposite such behavior was to her true nature.

In truth, she hated his pulsing heat, the way he was playing her, sliding in and out, controlling how much she got of him at any given moment. If he thought to break her, he had another think coming. She was a free woman, a Guardian, with a fine lineage, and she would never beg a man for anything sexual, least of all a pirate.

Hate was a bad emotion, though. It was the flipside of another — the totally wrong one to have here. She decided to refocus on feeling neutral. This was a mechanical act and she was going through the motions. Just like they practiced going through Narthian bug torture.

Granted, Azar was no bug. He was more like a god dropped from the depths of space into her lap.

His hands were at the side of her head. He had her hair insolently twisted in his fingers. No man had ever dared to treat her this way, using her precisely as he wished, for his own pleasure. Even the primales she had known treated her with kid gloves. For while it was not generally known who her parents were, it was clear she was someone special.

The first female in the Corps. That distinction came with a certain aura. To top it off, she was primale herself, which meant she fought for control in every encounter. Her primale lovers, though few in number, tended to direct her to the weaker brand of males, the mems. These were more than happy to bed the beautiful Theryssa, though they promptly found themselves in over their heads.

Most ran like hell, though a few enjoyed it. Theryssa, however, was profoundly frustrated to find herself taking on the dominant role. Having a man on his knees in her presence was not a particularly great turn–on. Although her rage at the moment made her more than a little anxious to turn the tables on Azar.

The question was, could she actually manage the feat? When the time came to make her move, would he fold to her primale strength, or would he reveal himself as what she suspected him to be—some kind of rogue primale himself.

She was pretty much convinced of the fact. No natural-born male should be able to keep up an erection like this. Nor should he have been able to shoot her full of what felt like a gallon of sticky, hot cum inside her. The way he was keeping hold of her head, too, gave her this uncanny feeling of a whole lot of latent power.

Plus there were the intangibles. The way he stood here, expecting her to pleasure him, as though it was his right, as though she had no hope of real resistance.

Theryssa was fighting strong emotions in the process. The idea that she might be a real prisoner right now…a slave, even…was making her pussy drip. He had told her he wanted her again. And he sounded like he wasn't going to let anything stand in the way.

She remembered the time when she was eighteen and she had inadvertently discovered her friend Urella pleasuring a mem in the back of a dimly lit orbiting dance club. Urella was a fem and not an obedient, but it was clear enough she was able to give in to some pretty deep female surrender urges as she had taken her lover's cock all the way to the back of her throat. The mem had been pumping her like mad, his fingers wound around her long blue hair, manipulating her mouth like a pussy.

Urella's face had been lit with pure bliss. Her jaw had been slack and her hand had been between her legs, underneath her short skirt. She'd been making herself come, even as the mem had worked her.

His eyes had been closed and his teeth gritted, and Theryssa remembered being so jealous because at that moment he had been so completely into Urella and she into him.

A few moments after the tall blond mem had ejaculated inside Urella's mouth, they'd switched positions, so he could eat out her pussy. It was at this point that Urella had looked out and seen Theryssa.

Theryssa had run off, all the way home. She'd never spoken of the incident again, and when Urella had pressed her to talk, she'd stopped seeing her.

Theryssa had always been that way. Stubborn like her father. Her mother knew this, and had given up dealing with both of them years ago.

Azar stopped Theryssa's rhythmic motions, breaking her reverie. Removing himself from her mouth, he helped her back to her feet. "Tell me," he said. "What you want now."

"From you? Nothing," she lied, squeezing together her throbbing, engorged pussy lips.

"Your nipples are hard," Azar noted. "I assume that's just another mechanical reaction?"

"Yep. I'm cold," she replied, tightlipped.

"But you're sweating."

"Must be space flu."

His lips angled into a rakish smile, one part gorgeous, two parts infuriating. "Got that flu in your pussy, too?"

"Fuck you."

"Pinch your nipple, Theryssa."

The order took her aback. "What for?"

"I don't have to explain my orders, young lady. But if you must know, it's punishment. For being disrespectful."

Theryssa wanted so badly to say something even worse. Instead, she said, "No."

"If you don't, Theryssa, I will."

Theryssa took hold of one of her aching little buds, figuring she would get off easier that way. "There? Are you satisfied?"

"No, I'm not. Do it harder."

Theryssa applied a little more pressure.

"More."

"That's enough," she said, wincing.

"Pinch it for real, Theryssa, or I will put you in chains for the night."

The blood left her nipple. She brought a whimper to her own lips. "Azar, please."

"You may apologize."

"I'm sorry." Theryssa's pussy flooded afresh. The man was being so strong with her, so firm and…masculine. He was tolerating nothing, just as if she were his obedient, mated and fully submitted.

"You may let go," said Azar.

The release of her nipple brought a fresh wave of pain, hot and pulsing and sexual.

"You may thank me for disciplining you."

"Thank you," Theryssa whispered, her eyes fixed intently on his feet.

"Is your pussy wet?" he wanted to know.

"Yes."

"Show me."

Theryssa moaned softly. Under his command, her fingers moved to her own opening. She tremored, collecting the required evidence.

"Taste it."

Hot and helpless, weak as a kitten, Theryssa sucked her fingertips.

"What do you taste?"

"M-myself," she said, stuttering for the first time in her life.

"Speak up."

"I taste myself," she declared, his stern tone making her startle.

"You taste your come?"

"Yes…I taste my come." The word made her feel invaded, taken by the man. Far from wanting to fight, however, her body was craving more. Like the moth that hovered dangerously close to the burning power of the fire.

"What do you want?" Azar repeated his earlier question.

The lesson was not lost—of Azar's power in the situation. And her lack of it. "I want to make sex," she said, giving him a better answer this time around.

Or at least what she thought was a better answer.

"You speak in Council euphemisms, Theryssa. I want to hear you spell it out, in plain English."

"I want to fuck," she corrected.

Azar remained unsatisfied. "Do you wish to fuck, or be fucked? There is a difference."

Theryssa swallowed hard. Damn straight there was a difference. Fucking meant equality, *being* fucked was something else altogether. "I guess you're looking for me to tell you how I want you to fuck me…"

"Do you?" He was standing half a breath away, his eyes intense upon her—cool and clear, like a predatory cat. He was acting as though he had all the time in the world and not a bit of desperation to contend with.

She, on the other hand, was a mass of need, her confidence evaporating, her will melting in the heat of her passion. "Azar," she pleaded, "don't make me…"

"I'm not making you do anything, little one. If you have no desire to continue our time together, I can put you in irons, or remove you to a cell. The choice is yours."

"Azar, you know I'm aroused…" She put her palm against his chest, barely grazing his smooth skin—a velvet covering to rock-hard muscle.

He grasped her wrist. His grip was like steel. Could she break it? Her head was swimming. Of course she could. She was just getting a little delirious.

Azar held her arm over her head. "It doesn't matter what I know or don't know. I asked you a question, and I want the answer."

Theryssa felt as if she might faint. If he were to let go, she would slip to the floor, weak as anything. What was going on here?

"Yes," she whispered, her chest rising and falling under the man's imperious gaze.

"Yes, what, Theryssa? I do not want to play games with you."

"Yes, I want to be fucked. By you."

Azar released her. "Describe it. Tell me, exactly."

Her mouth was dry as a desert planet. Why was he doing this? "I-I just want you to fuck me with your cock."

"More," he demanded.

"I want your cock in my pussy," she supplied. "I want…I need it inside me.

"Touch yourself. Tell me how badly you need it."

"Yes, Azar…" She moaned softly as her finger tips traveled down her tingling flesh, over her undulating belly to the delta of her thighs. "Oh, god, yes." She flicked the tip of her swollen clitoris. "I need it very badly. I need it fast and hard."

Azar reached for her nipple and gave it a punitive tweak. "You're not talking about my cock. Tell me how you want my cock."

Her moan turned to a half-groan, peppered with pain. "I want...your cock." She arched her back, thrusting her breasts out masochistically. "I want it...pummeling me. So hard and fast. Filling me...driving me into the ground. I want it to own me and brand me and mark me..."

Azar showed no mercy. Grabbing the other nipple with his free hand he pressed her even farther. "Make yourself come, Theryssa, and tell me how badly you want it."

"I'll do anything," she cried, her fingers racing up and down her slit. "I'll crawl for you, Azar...I'll beg."

In the back of her mind somewhere, she thought of Galina. The princess who had turned slave. Was this the same road that other women had traveled with Azar?

"That's it, little one," he encouraged, manipulating her pinched nipples. "Give it to me. Give it all to me."

The things you will never take, but which I will freely give...like my pride. Isn't that what you mean?

Theryssa shook her head, attempting to resist. Azar broke her with a kiss. Hot and hard and punishing. As she yielded her mouth to his plundering tongue, she found herself giving way below. Whimpering, sweat pouring down her forehead, she took the only option left, riding the overwhelming outpouring of sex, fingers stuffed obediently in her pussy.

Never before had she experienced a climax as a complete and utter act of subjugation to another's will. It was his command, and therefore his fingers inside her. The fact that he was not orgasming, but merely manipulating her at his leisure, only re-enforced the feeling of being controlled.

And then there were his fingers playing with her nipples, squeezing and releasing, tantalizing, raising her high and bringing her low, mixing the pain and pleasure into an indescribable soaring.

There was no mistaking it as his own recipe, a unique blend against which Theryssa stood not a chance of keeping her freedom. Up, over the mountaintops, through the atmosphere and into space. Out to the nearest star for an explosion, a supernova blast—enough searing heat to melt matter.

Never had she masturbated like this. Never had she breathed like this.

When it was done, she could not bear to be released. Sucking on her lip, nearly to the point of drawing blood, she fell against him, shivering. It was not a matter of craving release now, but one of holding herself in one piece. Body and soul, she felt like she was falling apart. Drifting away on a cloud.

She needed his touch to be reminded she was real. And she needed his cock to be sure she was still capable of feeling anything.

"Touch it," he whispered, his breath hot in her ear, his teeth lightly nibbling at the lobe.

Theryssa did not need to be told what it was he was requiring her to touch. She drew a sharp breath, holding it. Her fingers moved in slow motion, down to Azar's cock.

Oh, god, he was throbbing. And so big and hard. Much bigger than before. She retracted her fingers, as though electrocuted.

"Touch it," he repeated.

Theryssa returned her fingertips to where they belonged. Tentatively, luxuriating in the feel of him, she ran them up the length, all the way to the base.

"Wrap your fingers tight."

She did so, marveling at his thickness. The vein underneath pulsed, responding to the pressure. Azar remained impassive, a study in utter self-discipline.

"Tell me what you want," he said, his voice bearing only the slightest edge, husky and sexy as hell.

It was their third go-round with this particular question and this time she was more than ready to give him a down and dirty answer. "I want to be fucked, Azar. I need you to fuck me like an animal. I need you to make me scream, and fuck me into submission."

Azar ran his fingers through her hair, tilting back her head. "I am going to take you harder than I have ever taken a woman, Theryssa."

"Yes…I want that," she croaked. "I need it."

"On the rug," he said. "I am going to have you on the rug."

"Yes…" It was perfect. He would subdue her and fill her and possess her. Exactly as he pleased. Not on any civilized bed, but on the surface of an animal fur, as soft as it was barbaric. "On the rug…"

His eyes never left hers as he made his move. One hand behind her back, supporting her as he lowered her to the floor. With the other, he was already staking his claim, running his capable, strong fingers up and down her torso, sending rivulets of pleasure up and down her spine.

Theryssa was on the verge of another orgasm.

She cried out softly as her buttocks touched the thick, absorbing surface of the white animal fur. Azar had set her down perfectly, with the grace of a dream. But there was no mistaking the ferocity of his intent.

"Mine," he loomed above her, his hand moving between her thighs.

Theryssa felt the spasms deep inside. Foreshadows of climaxes to come. "Yours," she replied, opening her legs. The statement was acknowledgement and surrender and foreplay all at once. As admissions went, it did more to turn her insides to jelly, head to toe, than all the touches of all the men before her in her life.

She had but one purpose now, one goal.

Azar's cock.

"Please…"

He possessed her in a single motion, using his hand to guide himself home. Either his erection had shrunk back down or she was much more open and ready this time, because it was an instant, easy fit. She had expected a much tighter fit, given how large he had appeared earlier.

Once again she was reminded of the power of primales to change the size of their erections at will, in the same way mems could direct their chests to puff out or recess into concavity.

Was that what was really going on with Azar? Could he really be a superman in disguise? The evidence seemed to be mounting.

That was as far as her thought processes were allowed to go. Azar had her occupied with other things.

Gathering both her hands into one of his, he pinned her wrists over her head. "You will not come without permission," he dictated.

Theryssa arched her spine, attempting to free herself. He pushed her back down. Was she trying her hardest? Was he? It was all so hazy. Which one of them held the real superiority?

For the moment, Azar did, at least as far as the sex went. Her body had its needs, its cravings, and those were leading her directly into submission. The fact was, having her wrists held down was exciting, all the more so for how it would have made her furious any other time.

So was having her body so intimately controlled. This man had dared to take away her most fundamental right—that of orgasming as she saw fit.

She would have to get permission…

The idea scandalized and thrilled her.

"I want to come now," she declared, deciding to test his power.

"Permission denied."

Bastard. Would he really try to stop her? Assuming such a thing was really possible if she wanted to badly enough. And what would he do if she disobeyed?

"What must I do to get permission?" she asked.

Azar shifted position, managing to sink his cock even deeper inside her pulsing sex. "You must tell me who sent you. And what you are here for."

She shook her head bravely, hiding her uncertainty. "I'll never do that. It's not in me to betray those I love."

"Then I will climax alone."

"You wouldn't be that mean."

Azar shifted again, this time withdrawing almost to the halfway point. "I'm a pirate," he reminded, clearly toying with her. "It's in my blood."

Theryssa felt the immediate emptiness. Damn it, she needed that cock in her and he knew it. "There's more to you than being a pirate," she attempted to distract herself from her desperation. "I can feel it."

"You're a woman," he dismissed. "You feel too much."

"I'm my father's daughter, too," she said. "Remember, you told me that?"

"Daddy teach you to disrespect your elders?"

"No. Just outlaws."

"Some people are driven to do what they do."

"Funny, I never heard a pirate apologize for plundering."

"And I never knew of a Guardian who squealed while getting a simple spanking."

"Screw you," she reddened.

Azar bent his head, taking a single ripe nipple between his teeth. He bit it. Just hard enough. Theryssa cried out, though she dared not writhe in her current state. Holding herself absolutely still, she took what he had to give.

Pleasuring and tormenting.

"Azar," she sighed his name, totally breathless as he let the nipple go.

"You will surrender to me. Completely. You will not hold back."

"Yes, Azar."

Stars, did he intend to interrogate her during sex?

"Do not move," he commanded. "Relax your body, completely."

He was compelling another level of subjugation, depriving her of even the pretense of resistance. Never had it been clearer to her in her life what it meant—the difference between fucking and being fucked.

Slowly, almost painfully, Azar lowered himself, filling her once again. "Look into my eyes," he said. "Do not look away."

She had to watch him dominating her.

"You haven't a clue, Theryssa, what I've been through in my life. I lost everything that mattered to me. All I have is my fight...and it's your fight, too, and the fight of everyone who wants to be free."

Her eyes watered. "But we are free. Why can't you see that. My par—the government is good," she corrected the near slip.

"It's not real life. You love who you're programmed to love." He settled himself to the hilt. Angling his body slightly, he left room for his hand. For the tips of his fingers to press her clit.

Theryssa leapt under his calculated touch. "But people have choices…"

"Wrong, Theryssa. Love the wrong person, the wrong classification and see what happens."

"Things are changing. There are new mixtures, not everybody is the same old type. Look at me."

Turning them both sideways, he exposed her ass. "I said, lie still."

She yelped as he smacked her exposed cheeks, three times in succession.

"You may thank me," he said.

"For what?"

"For disciplining you."

"Thank you," she muttered, her ass hot and stinging, her pride smarting.

"Are you ready to be a good girl, my horny little Council spy?" He wanted to know.

"I'm not—" She cut off the words. He knew full well how she felt about him calling her a girl. And she certainly wasn't a horny little spy. But that was the point, wasn't it—making something sexual out of pushing her buttons. It was all part of the power game between them.

If you could properly call something so deep a game.

"I'm waiting, Theryssa." He had her twisted on her side, fully impaled, front to front, her wrists still held, his left hand poised to strike her ass again. "Tell me you want to be a good girl, a good lay, a good agent for your masters back home."

She twitched in anticipation. She wanted it. And she didn't. She was anxious to avoid pain…but she needed his strong touch.

"Azar…" It was all so confusing. If only they were just making plain, normal sex. "No."

Azar leaned in closer. His breath burned her earlobe with a tiny, devastating whisper. "Tell me you don't want this."

He was giving her an out. A chance to reject the whole thing. Would he really let her go? She ought to call his bluff. But the thought of being left alone right now, of having him leave her without finishing was worse than anything else she could imagine.

Seconds ticked by, her hollow breathing comprising her only answer. What was she supposed to say with his cock in her willing pussy, her body thrilling to his raw, commanding power?

Azar nibbled at her neck, his hand caressing her sore ass at will. "I'll take that as a sign you want to go on."

Theryssa closed her eyes. She was moving for him, responding under him. Cooperatively. Erotically.

The question came again, penetrating, pouring over her needy flesh. "Are you ready to be a good girl, Theryssa? A good, horny little spy?"

"Yes, damn you," she said, a hissed confession in broken stabs of breath. "I am ready…to be a good girl…a horny spy."

He delivered a smack to her undefended behind. "I hope so."

Theryssa pushed against him, craving.

Azar rolled her flat onto her back once more, compelling eye contact. "I will not allow you to hold back from me, Theryssa." Azar's cock swelled on cue. She also felt the added heat burning deep in her pussy. Like a fire, consuming her, which only he could put out. "I will accept nothing less than your full submission." He clasped her buttock.

"Would you know it if you saw it?" she wondered.

"We will find out, won't we?"

"What do you mean?" She asked warily.

Azar pulled out completely, leaving her bereft of his formidable, glistening shaft. "I mean that it is time to see what you are made of."

She didn't like the sound of that very much. Warily, she watched as he lay down beside her, his miracle cock pointing straight into the air, strong as ever. He put his hands behind his neck, looking quite relaxed.

"You may mount me," he said.

Theryssa's stomach turned somersaults as she looked at his erection, thick and ready. How was she supposed to get on top of it without a stepladder?

Okay, maybe it wasn't that bad. But it was bad enough.

"You have until the count of ten, Theryssa, to take my cock inside you."

Ten...as in the self-destruct sequence, she thought glumly.

Gingerly, she straddled him. Such a fine and perfect body. She could spend the better part of a solar year just worshipping every inch of him, kissing, nibbling, licking and pleasuring his fine body.

Her pussy was dripping wet. Parting pink, swollen lips, she put herself into position. The right angle, the right placement.

"Stop."

Theryssa was squatting over him, the tip of his shaft just separating her labia. Only by her extraordinary physical training was she able to hold the position.

"You will make me come," he said, "without coming yourself."

Fuck. What a bastard.

"Is there a problem, Theryssa?"

Waiting like this was sheer hell. She wanted to stuff him inside her, she wanted to scream and tear at her hair until she exploded into a million pieces. "No...*Sir*," she denied him the satisfaction of knowing he was getting to her.

"Good," he nodded, "because as you probably guessed, I have a large crew. And I would insist on each man using you at least twice."

"Good, I'd enjoy it, they probably don't talk the whole time like you do," she snapped. He smirked with pleasure. She would really like to have him tied up right now, to give him a dose of his own medicine.

"You may resume, Theryssa. And if I may point out, you were the one talking just now, not me."

Theryssa gritted her teeth. In vain, she tried to will her pussy to be numb. Unfortunately, her primale genetics did not give her the same sexual control as the males. If anything, it made her more sensitive.

Inch by inch she descended, whimpering in sexual agony. "I...need...to...come," she said haltingly.

Azar ignored her. "You have the most perfect body," he noted, taking hold of her breasts. "Your designers knew what they were doing."

She was barely half impaled, but out of her mind already. "Azar, please..."

"Are there any more like you?" He manipulated the soft flesh. "Or are you one of a kind?"

Theryssa was shivering, tears in her eyes. "Azar...I'm pleading with you..."

He remained unmoved. Just as he'd said, her begging would come in his time, in his way. Such would be his complete and utter victory over her.

"You may pleasure me," he said, "with your pussy."

Theryssa sobbed. She lifted herself, only to collapse back down.

"Move," he ordered, slapping her hip.

She attempted to rise, her hands braced on his chest. Each millimeter was molten agony as she sought against all odds to hold herself back from climax. "Come, damn you," she screamed. "Don't make me wait!"

Azar was a rock. "I seem to be having trouble," he teased. "You'll have to go faster."

"Please, I'll do anything, Azar…I'll…I'll be your slave."

By the gods, what was she saying? She sounded like Galina. There was no way he could hold her to a promise like this. It was entirely under duress, in the heat of sexual torment.

His answer pushed her over the edge.

"You already are, Theryssa."

"Fucckkkkk," she screamed, convulsing. "Fuck, fuck, fuck."

Azar grabbed her hips, lifting her bodily. As though she was little more than a rag doll, he swung her up to his face and deposited her pussy on his lips.

By the very genes of creation, he was going to use his tongue on her.

I've died, she thought. *I've been sucked out of my ship into deep space and gone to horny woman heaven.*

Or is it hell…

Chapter Four

ဇာ

Cunnilingus as torture?

Few would think of it as such, but actually, Azar had chosen a particularly cruel form of punishment for his prisoner. If she was going to insist on orgasming without his permission, than she would find herself inundated with them.

Her pussy was sweet like nectar. Her lips opened to him, as if they had been made for his probing tongue. Moving the rough surface across her clitoris, he pushed her immediately into a fresh orgasm.

It was only the beginning of the treatment he intended to impose. Pleasant at first, she would soon find the tables turning.

Before it was over she would be begging him again—this time to stop.

"Oh, god!" She thrashed. "Oh, Azar…god!"

His hands held her hips. She was not going anywhere. Tickling her with long strokes, he wore her last defenses. The last bastions of her pride.

"Fuckkkkk…" She was crying out again, shouting out to whoever might listen.

No one would, of course.

"It's so…" The words escaped her. Reduced to grunts, she ground her pelvis into his face, bathing him in fresh liquid— pungent and totally female.

He allowed her satisfaction, rolling his tongue into a miniature cock. Over and over she hissed her affirmations. Her body was beyond tense, like a coil, winding and unwinding itself.

"Fuck...fuck me...Azar."

Azar doubled the speed of his tongue and then doubled it again. Theryssa went stiff—the shooting waves of pleasure going like quicksilver straight to the core of her being.

The next two orgasms were more properly endured than experienced. It was like trying to hold onto a bronco. Each time he took her aloft, shooting her high into the stratosphere. He could feel the raw sex surging through her body, straining her every nerve, exploding every sensitive ending.

She was being battered with pleasure.

The trap was nearly set...

Theryssa was unable to keep from grinding and writhing, desperate to draw him deeper inside her pussy. For a brief few minutes he slowed the pace, letting her catch up, until he had allowed her to think she was regaining control, her fingers clutching his head, her voice urging him on, as if he was there only to do her bidding.

Instead of the other way around.

"More...more...more," she urged, sliding her pelvis up and down. "I...I...need more."

Such sweet motion. Such a beautifully sexual creature. The most amazing he had ever known.

It would be interesting to break her.

His tongue moved in for the kill. Speeds so fast, her clitoris had no time whatsoever to recover. Her liquid dripped over his face. One, two, three orgasms in under a minute.

And still he went on.

Theryssa cried out. She was not really in danger. She would not really be hurt. But she would learn her place in the scheme of things.

"Azar..." She clutched his head. "No...please...I can't..."

He paused for only a second, just long enough to utter a single word. "Beg."

"P-please...no more..."

Abruptly, Azar stopped, lifting her pussy just out of range of his dastardly tongue.

Theryssa's relief was short-lived, as he knew it would be.

Unfortunately for her, she had been left midway to climax number whatever-it-was.

Just like that, her world fell apart. Like an addict, cut off from her supply. "Don't stop, not like this. Azar, oh fuck...don't..." Theryssa was shuddering, shattering. Trying to come with all her might.

He let her thrash a while, like a fish thrown onto dry land. Each time she seemed to be receding from the brink, he ran his tongue quickly over the rim of her sex lips, sending her into a fresh frenzy.

At no time, however, would he put her out of her misery. Eventually, he seated her on his thighs, just behind his cock. She could see it, but not touch it.

"Play with your nipples," he ordered, doubling her agony.

Her face was a study of womanly passion, pink-faced agony brought on by thorough and sadistic male control.

"What do you want, Theryssa?"

And so it was coming full circle, back to the original question he'd posed. The first time she'd been snide, the second she'd admitted her sexual needs. This time, he hoped she would see the deeper lesson.

"I want...I want to be a good girl."

Azar smiled in deep satisfaction. "On all fours," he commanded. "Head down."

She moved into position, her breasts hanging sweetly, her ass sticking out invitingly. He was so very ready to fuck her. But first...the collar.

* * * * *

Theryssa dug into the fur with her fingernails and her toenails, too. A battle was going on inside her, between her reason and her lust. Her reason, which had been asleep up to now was awakening and asking some hard questions.

What had she done? Why had she told Azar she wanted to be a good girl? She wasn't his girl, his slave or anything at all to him. She was a Guardian, an officer working for the Council.

To the extent that she was acting like a horny little damsel in distress, it was supposed to be just that. Acting. Playing the part of the seduced wench—breathless and in heat so as to lull Azar into a false sense of security.

She was supposed to make him lose his cool, so she could take advantage of him.

The trouble was, she really did want to be fucked. Hot and hard and dirty, in all the wicked ways she could think of. On her hands and knees. Pounded with Azar's cock until he had taken every bit of pleasure from her that he wished. Yes, she wanted to be a wench for him. She wanted to satisfy him so much with her body that he never turned to another woman again.

God, did she even know what she was saying? This was worse than letting her lust rule her. This was giving in to the false delusions of her heart. She hardly knew this man and what she did know should tell her to avoid an emotional entanglement like the plague. So why was she thinking in terms of not only fucking him, but keeping him?

He was a cutthroat, for heaven's sake.

She couldn't get over the idea that there was more to him, though. He wasn't just an interstellar brigand with no care for anything but his own purse. There was something he was trying to hide. Almost as though he had a different identity altogether. And there was more to this mission, too. Her folks were up to something, she was becoming more sure of this as the hours passed.

Call it instinct, or just experience from watching Theron and Nyssa at work.

But what *was* really going on? This was some kind of dangerous game here, just on the surface, let alone any secret elements. A pirate was sexually dominating her, after all, and she enjoyed it.

Azar was dominating her…the blue-eyed rogue she had dreamt of and fantasized over all this time. A dream come to life, with his sexy ways and strong loving.

Azar. The only man who had ever rocked her world, launched her to the stars, and set free her soul, all the while commanding her onto hands and knees.

Too bad this dream had so much potential for nightmare.

Her heart pounded as she waited for him. On all fours. As he had ordered. What was coming next? Chains? Other pirates to satisfy sexually? He had her, didn't he? Trembling and naked, spasming inside, like his cock was in there, having its way with her.

He was walking over to the wall. Fiddling with something on the rack. Her body tensed in all its aching vulnerability. Was he getting a flogger to use on her?

Hadn't she been a good enough girl? Wasn't she pleasing him?

Theryssa clamped her thighs tightly, trying to hide her arousal. She was dripping, desperately in need. It was getting too hard to fight. The feelings of being Azar's girl. His nude booty. And everyone knew it, too. The crew had chained her in here, totally aware that this would happen, confident that she would end up a slave, like all the others.

They probably knew, too, that Azar would eventually spurn her, just like those others. That had to be the case, or else there would have been someone in this cabin already, before she got here.

Lifting her head, she stole a peek to see what he was doing.

"Head down," he growled.

Theryssa lowered her eyes instantly. Would she be punished for that? Her nipples throbbed as she thought about the pinching. Or would it be her ass again?

Perhaps if she were able to appease him...with her soft body, her proffered breasts, her pussy. Images filled her mind, of slave girls crawling on their bellies to the feet of their Masters.

"Sit up," Azar commanded.

Theryssa started at his sudden presence. Back on her heels she went. The first thing she saw was the collar. Thin leather, studded with jewels. Like the kind used on pets in ancient times. There was a leash with it, made of metal chain.

"I am going to put this on you," he stated the obvious. "And then I am going to fuck you. Like a tamed animal. I want you to give me your permission to do this."

"Why do you need my permission?" she asked. "When I am already bound to obey?"

"I do not need your permission, I want it. They are not the same thing."

Theryssa shook her hair back over her shoulders. She was not sure why he suddenly wanted her approval, but refusing him was unthinkable. "I give you permission, Azar. To collar me. And fuck me."

"Do you know why I punished you before?"

"Because I came, instead of making you come."

"Yes. As a result, I delayed my own pleasure to tend to your discipline."

"How sporting of you."

"You really are insufferable, aren't you?"

"I've been told that, yes."

"That is what makes you so special?"

"Well that makes you the first guy to say that."

"Oh?"

"The rest think I'm a pain in the ass."

"They were boys. Or idiots."

"They were Guardians."

"There is not always a difference."

"You talk like you know."

"Tell me I'm wrong."

"Only if you promise immunity from punishment."

"How about I use you instead," he suggested, "like the owned wench you are?"

"So long as you know it's only for play. A person cannot really be owned." Her heart was beating like a rabbit's. Was she trying to defy him? Egg him on? Or just confirm what she already feared…that this little undercover assignment was headed somewhere she could not possibly imagine.

"If the collar fits…" Azar wrapped the leather about her throat. His fingers were masterful, but not harsh. How many females had he done this to? Had they all been so willing?

She held her breath as he fastened the tiny clasp and padlock. As far as security went, it was laughable. She could break it between two fingers. But the symbolism was quite real. Locked collars were for slaves. And for all intents and purposes, given her promise to obey the man, that's what she was.

Azar paused to admire her. "You look right this way."

Theryssa flushed hotly at the remark, the redness passing from her cheeks all the way to her breasts. Azar took the leash in his fingers. "Open."

Theryssa parted her jaws, then bit down on the cold, smooth metal chain.

"Even better," he approved.

Her eyes flashed, communicating indignation.

Azar laughed, patting her head. "Fury makes you even more gorgeous. I could only imagine you in a little cage, with your own water dish."

Theryssa's mind turned instantly to rebellion. "Fuck you, asshole," she spat out the metal.

She was already on her feet when he stopped her, using his favorite technique.

"Down," he commanded, controlling her with the twist of a single nipple.

Anguish surging through her veins, her poor nub screaming for mercy, Theryssa submitted on bended knees. "Swear to god, I'm gonna figure out why you're so strong."

"Enough fooling around," he said. "It's time to give us both what we need. Get on your hands and knees, Theryssa. Before I explode."

What a complicated man. Trying to degrade her one minute, treating her like some kind of partner the next.

Of course she was pretty complicated, too. Actually being caged was something that would happen over her dead body. But talking about it...and having Azar threaten it, that was arousing to no end.

"So you like putting women in cages, do you?" She tried to keep the dirty talk going.

"Only if they ask me," he teased.

"What about love?" she asked impulsively. "Have you ever been in love?"

He plunged a finger deep inside her, instantly reconfiguring her priorities. "None of your business…spy."

"Please, Azar, I really want to know."

He played with her, making her pant. She pushed her ass up against his hand, seeking pleasure even as she listened to his answer.

"There was a young lady, once."

"Was she…like me?"

He inserted one finger into her anus, using the others to work her pussy. "There were similarities."

Theryssa moaned, broken. "What…happened?"

"She's gone, that's the end of it."

So were his fingers. She cried out. "Azar, Sir, please, don't…leave me like this."

"I said no questions."

"I'm sorry. I'll take punishment. Please, spank my ass, then use me for your pleasure."

"You'll be punished all right, girl." He got a dildo and a butt plug. The dildo was a slick, cool material, smooth against her pussy walls, titillating but offering no relief. He pushed it far inside her, then told her not to move.

The butt plug was a hard little bastard of a thing. It made her feel dirty, invaded and horny as hell.

"Not one word," he said.

She stayed as quiet as she could. Like a statue. Except she was sweating and fighting off spasms every other second.

Her worst fear was that he would leave her.

Twice he came over from whatever he was doing on the other side of the room to swat her with something leather. His belt, probably.

She whimpered appropriately.

Did it go five minutes or was it an hour until he came by to check on her? She thought he was going to take out the anal plug, but it was the dildo he grasped.

"You'll take me with your ass filled," he said, refusing to take out the plug.

Her buttocks clenched on the anal invader. Her pussy screamed as he removed the dildo, so slowly, shredding her nerve endings, make her feel empty and hot and cold and confused all at once.

"No," she cried, "don't...take it."

"Would you like my dick instead?"

"Yesss..." He had her moaning, her sex spasming in anticipation.

She cried aloud as he touched her, grazing her clit.

"Ready?" he teased.

She shook her head frantically.

"Hold still," he commanded, slapping her ass.

Theryssa shivered as he pushed his cock into place, parting her sex lips. "You'll take it on my terms, girl, or not at all."

"Your...terms," she panted.

He pushed his thickly veined cock an inch or so between her puffy, waiting lips. He was hard and molten hot. She burned at the feel of him, lost to the sensations. She wanted more. She couldn't live without it.

His hands went to her hips, steadying her. She was the perfect target, a vessel for his plundering. He sheathed himself, pushing all the way to the hilt. She felt his pelvic bone and his heavy, full balls.

He enjoyed the position for a moment, readying himself. Then he began his motions, expert, more familiar than before.

She sensed he was learning her body, how to please and torment it.

Azar kept her on the razor's edge until she could stand it no more. Her body was quaking. She was dissolving.

One or two more thrusts, to cement his dominance and then he gave the word, the command. "*Now.*"

She came instantly, swallowing his cock whole. Azar kept ahead of her, moving faster and faster.

She couldn't keep track of the orgasms as he masterfully pistoned into her. His fist was in her hair, the pressure just right as he tugged, letting her know he was there, turned on out of his mind, fucking crazy for her, needing this more than air itself.

She was so full, so thoroughly possessed.

"Come," she cried. "Come in my pussy...your pussy."

Azar's breathing quickened. She relished the sound of it, knowing he was taking his ultimate pleasure in her. She could feel his cock hardening, getting ready to shoot itself deep up into her. He was beyond talking, he was all beast, a beautiful male animal using his female.

His growl was like a star lion, from the distant nebula of Tresos. His orgasm was so magnificent, a work of art, liquid wonder to fill her belly...and her soul.

"Yes," she cried a dozen times over. "Oh, fuck, yes."

Azar expelled the last of his come, but he wasn't done. Manipulating the butt plug to keep her at a fever pitch, he continued pumping—as though he had yet to come at all. His thrusts were at near hyper-speed. She had to use primale strength to keep from collapsing forward onto her belly. This was one worked up pirate.

Azar's second orgasm came like a blast of energy, instant, irradiating fluid heat, obliterating everything in its path. Theryssa couldn't help but climax with him. He was a force too powerful to resist. A sunstorm, a moonstorm and windstorm all wrapped into one.

I don't want to leave, she thought, I want to live here in this union, forever. The two of us in a perfect rhythm. Until all the troubles of the world disappear forever.

For the briefest few seconds, it all felt true. But then reality returned. With a vengeance.

She was on a mission, she reminded herself, and this man who was loving her so wonderfully was her enemy. It was her job to collect information and maybe even do battle with him. One day she might even have to kill him, should he indeed prove to be a Narthian ally.

Azar pulled out his cock. It was still hard, still filling her to capacity. The man was still unsated. Was there no end to his desire?

She awaited his next move as he rose to his feet, bidding her to do the same. What was on that devious mind of his this time? It didn't take him long to reveal his plans. In one motion, he lifted Theryssa into his arms. Her heart commenced racing again as he carried her to the bed. His body was so hard and smooth against her, so warm to the touch. How was she supposed to stay strong, a Guardian and warrior, when he kept putting her in the mood for sex-making?

"You will remain here," he laid her down on the fur covered surface. "Until you have permission to get up."

Theryssa sucked in her dry lower lip, thirsty. She was a prisoner in his bed. Naked. The implications did not escape her. Nor did the dark intensity of his gaze on her body. Instinctively, her hands went over her head, palm up on the pillow.

"Take me, again, Azar," she murmured. "I'm ready…I'm a…good…girl."

Azar unclipped the leash from her collar. She held her breath as his fingers worked, so close to her breasts. She could smell him, deep and pungent. His hard cock was so very close, and the rest of him, too—his body dotted with sweat, his muscles corded tightly with fresh lust. She was amazed at how familiar he was beginning to seem.

Her heart skipped a beat as she anticipated penetration. Instead, he straightened, his spine as fixed as that of any Guardian.

"Go to sleep," he said. "That's enough for now."

Theryssa's mouth hung open. She couldn't believe it. He was rejecting *her*? But what about that monster erection of his? "You can't be serious," she said.

"I am not in the habit of making jokes, Theryssa. Especially where it concerns issuing orders to one of my slaves."

Theryssa's pussy twinged in reply to her being called a slave. "I'm your prisoner," she corrected.

"I am making use of your body for my pleasure," he explained. "That makes you a slave."

"So why don't you do that now?"

"I don't want to."

"Bullshit. You're hard as a rock."

"I'm sorry," he shook his head. "I know you are in heat and you need to be ridden hard and long, but that's part of slavery. Your purpose is my pleasure, not your own. If it's any consolation, I will use you first thing in the morning."

Theryssa pulled her knees up to her chest and folded her arms over her breasts. *The nerve of the man.* "Screw you. I don't need a damn thing. I just felt sorry for you, that's all."

Azar moved quickly and efficiently, descending on her and rolling her to her stomach. His hand rained down like fire, peppering her behind with punitive blows.

Tears stinging her cheeks, she cried out her apology.

Azar poked a finger into her crack. Moisture oozed readily. "You are a hot and horny slave girl. Say it."

The sudden pressure to her clitoris mixed with the throbbing from her spanking. "I'm a hot...and horny slave girl," she exclaimed.

Azar rolled her to her back. "Can I trust you to keep your hands out of your pussy until morning or do I need to chain you up?"

Theryssa's cheeks brightened. Beneath her veneer of anger was shame and below that, a sea of lust, like magma bubbling from her core, unknown and threatening to engulf the whole of her. "You have no right," she blurted. "To stop me."

Azar seized her pussy, making clear with the movement of his fingers just how much he considered her to be his property. "Nothing enters here against my will. Not even your hand. Is that clear?"

Theryssa stiffened, a shock of pleasure passing through her. "Y-yes." Her teeth chattered.

He left her unsatisfied. "Go to sleep, Theryssa."

Trembling, she turned to her side. She dared not ask for a blanket. Presently, he shut the lights off and climbed in beside her.

She felt overwhelming relief at his presence. Enemy though he might be, and source of her unbelievable torment, she felt this strange need for him. Somehow, deep down, she knew she was safe here. And that he would never allow real harm to occur to her.

Too, she was afraid to be alone. All that time in space, indeed, for a lifetime before, she had never worried about anything. Did it have something to do with how full he had made her feel before, and how alive? It was almost as if by awakening in her that sense of belonging and connectivity, he had also made it possible for her to feel loneliness.

Hugging herself tightly, Theryssa willed her body into a state of lower consciousness. Her mind was racing and twisting and she needed to get a hold of it. There was only one way to focus at this point, and that was on devising an escape plan.

It was not her intent to actually get away. She merely needed to know if she could. That would tell her for sure if he was primale or not. It didn't have to be anything sophisticated. A simple act of trying to sneak out the door or trying to grab one of his weapons to immobilize him.

She would wait until he seemed more or less asleep and then she would make her move. With any luck, she would buy herself a little time to snoop around his cabin first to see what she could learn about his Narthian connection.

In the meantime, she would bide her time. Turning up her auditory powers, she tried to hear the sounds of any crew members nearby. There were two heartbeats in the corridor, and three more directly above them. The ones in the corridor were awake. Walking.

Idly, she set about matching each heartbeat to the other data she had collected, including voice prints. Before too long, she had a working map in her head, of who was where. The really obnoxious one, Oleron, was on the bridge.

No doubt pretending to be captain.

Theryssa turned to hear Azar's heartbeat. It was very strong. Lulling in a way. Damn, but she was exhausted. She watched him roll to his back. His chest looked so inviting.

Theryssa licked her lips. She wanted so badly to lay her head down. To pretend, just for a little while that they were a normal couple. Her, on leave, and him, fresh from wowing her folks, taking her on an interstellar cruise.

What a foolish little romantic she was. Since when did she like cruises?

Nevertheless, Theryssa did lay her head down, very gently. Just for a second, she thought. But the second dragged out to a minute and a minute into ten. She put her palm down, absorbing his strength. His warmth on her cheek, his chest rising and falling like clockwork to put some order back into her world.

For the first time since Theryssa was a little girl, her eyes grew truly heavy. It was that twenty-five percent of her that was mere fem. She had inherited this from her mother, who was no slouch herself.

Theryssa had always hated this weaker part of her nature, but her mother and Seria both had predicted one day she would come to cherish it. Rely on it even. Was this what she meant? Was it something she needed to have a relationship?

If so, it wasn't going to be now. Not with this man. Pirates didn't have relationships. They kept slaves. At least until they got tired of them.

Funny, though, at points she thought she could sense a bit of vulnerability in Azar. A look in his eyes from time to time. Even in his breathing, there was this undercurrent. Almost a tenderness.

She had to be imagining it.

Stars. Now she was yawning. What was the world coming to?

The next thing you know, she would be having actual sleep. With dreams. Real ones—the kind you couldn't control.

And it didn't take a robo-psychic to figure out who would be in those dreams, doing what to Theryssa's poor, innocent person.

Chapter Five

ஐ

Azar was surprised but pleased to see Theryssa settle so deeply into unconsciousness. Sleep was considered unnecessary for primales, but personally he had always felt it was an important part of the body's restoration process.

Having her lay her head on his chest had filled him with feelings of protectiveness. Superwoman though she might be, she had chosen him to watch over her. At least for this one night.

How good she felt against him. So natural. His hand on her back, fingers fanned, was a perfect fit. So were her breasts, squashed against him. Her little nipples were tight and hard.

And so was his cock. He wanted to do things to her, to touch and squeeze and have his way with her incredible body. Again. And then again after that.

Never had he dreamed of finding a woman who could keep up with him, who could take the sting of his hand and the force of his cock and come back wanting more with barely a breath in between.

Refusing her offer of sex—correction, her self-surrender for sexual possession—had been maddeningly difficult. He could easily have jumped on her and ridden her for hours.

But there was more to sexual play than the act itself. Especially when you were a primale like Azar. Half the thrill was in the conquest, and with a female like Theryssa, primale herself, you could hardly expect to achieve that conquest in one session.

He would be lying if he didn't admit to some amusement, even a little sadistic delight in seeing her so angry with him.

Her frustration turned him on, too. It was going to be worth it, though. She would be red-hot when he finally had her again — eager and desperate. And he would be feeling strong, like he was truly making her his own.

Azar told himself this would lead to nothing new or different for him. Once the objective was reached and he was bored with her, he would move on to someone new, just as he always did. Naturally, he would make sure to glean what intelligence he could first.

The whole process should last a few days at most. Then she would be gone, and he would forget soon enough. He always did. And she would be fine, too, going back to her life on Earth.

A life, by her own admission, without much male appreciation.

Azar's stomach tightened into a thick knot. He couldn't picture her alone. She needed to shine for a man. A man strong enough and compassionate enough to handle her complicated nature. A man who would be her partner.

And what about him? What did he deserve? A woman he could really sleep beside at night, like this one, and not just a fresh sex partner?

After sex-making, Solania had tried to stay awake like a primale, but she had always fallen asleep, much to her chagrin. Azar greedily enjoyed the times of total possession over her physical form, deep in the dead of night.

Azar stilled his breath for a moment. Theryssa was stirring. Keeping his eyes closed, maintaining himself in a primale trance, he observed her with his inner vision.

It was an ancient technique among primales, one which involved utilizing the subconscious mind, tapping it into the deeper recesses of sensation. The entire area around him was clear to him. He could even perceive through walls.

After a while he detected her eyes popping open—lovely, green and curious. She blinked several times, her eyebrows shifting rapidly. He knew that mind of hers was working overtime, he could almost guess her thoughts, reliving events up to now and calculating her current situation and future possibilities.

Good girl, he thought, admiring her ability to stay perfectly still, not panicking despite being caught up in such a potentially unnerving situation. She had been through quite a lot and yet she was cool, calm and collected.

He swelled with a strange pride.

Few people he had known, male and female alike possessed such qualities. The fine tension in her limbs indicated she intended to make a move. It was an interesting situation. She had promised to stay in bed. Would she openly defy him? Her other instances of disobedience had been rather unavoidable, having come in the heat of the moment. In truth, he had set her up to fail, just to see how she would handle punishment.

But now she would have to choose between keeping her word and taking her chance at freedom. Assuming freedom was what she really wanted.

The freedom to spy on him and learn what she needed to know.

Theryssa was already putting her plan into action, delicately lifting his arm off of her body. He remained motionless, giving no indication that he was fully aware of what was transpiring. She had no trouble wriggling free and in seconds flat she was padding around his cabin. A naked, prying little minx.

She went to his communication logs first. She would not find anything, at least not anything she was looking for. For a while she stooped over the log machine, reading the entries, her pert breasts hanging down, her tight ass wiggling very slightly as she shifted her eyes.

He fought back a smile as he noted the little habit she had of moving her lips as she read. Before too long he would have those lips back where they belonged. Caressing his burning shaft.

Theryssa frowned, indicating her frustration. Abandoning the log machine, she took out her displeasure on her collar. Quite impressively, she ripped it off with a single tug. No doubt she thought herself above being fettered, but as it just so happened, he had some special chains, made of a material so dense, even a full-grown, fully male, primale could not break them.

"You don't like your collar, Theryssa?"

Theryssa turned to face him. "It's not my style."

Azar was sitting up in bed, his cock poking straight out at her. "Maybe not, but you weren't given permission to remove it. Nor were you told you could get out of bed."

"Remind me to give myself a good spanking later," she quipped.

Azar inclined his head toward the door. "I assume you intend to escape?"

"It depends. You plan on trying to stop me?"

"I'll admit, I'd rather not see our time together end so quickly," he conceded.

"Of course not," she noted sardonically. "You were having a blast. Beating me, abusing me."

"Did I do anything you didn't ask for, Theryssa? Beg for, even?"

"That's not the point and you know it. You had me under duress."

"In that case, you know where the door is."

"And how far do you think a naked woman would get on a ship full of pirates?"

"You're not just any naked woman. You're a superwoman."

"Right now I'm just super pissed." She reached behind her for the Zeerian lance on the wall, part of his display of captured primitive weapons.

"Good choice," he approved as she leveled the long silver weapon—saw-toothed and tipped with long hooked bear claws.

"Thank you." She smiled grimly. "Now unless you would like to become intimately acquainted with it, I suggest you start marching to my tune for a change."

"You make a persuasive case."

"Get off the bed." she waved the lance.

Azar stood, quite interested to see what she would do with her presumed power.

"I will admit," she said, "you have me wondering how you knew about my primale blood. I have been racking my brain, and the more I think about it, the more I think maybe you're primale yourself."

"But of course that's impossible."

"It is," she agreed. "Then again it isn't. The only real way to know is to test you."

"Like I tested you? With a thrown knife, you mean?"

She licked her lips. She was looking right at his cock. "Actually, you've given me the idea to do something a little more interesting."

"Such as?"

"Such as me giving you some commands. Some submissive commands. If you really are primale, you'll break down at some point and show yourself."

He arched a brow. "That doesn't sound overly wise." He arched a brow. "You might provoke me too much."

"I can handle myself." She waved the lance. "Enough talking. I want you to put your hand on your cock. Start masturbating."

Azar wrapped his fingers around his thick erection. He was more than happy to show Theryssa his arousal. "Like this?"

His fingers pressed casually, but authoritatively. He moved them up and down, with purpose and command. There was no mistaking his intentions. This was his dick to play with, the way he wanted. Nothing submissive here.

Her breathing was a little shallow. Her eyes looked a little glazed. "Yeah…like that."

Azar allowed himself a small smirk. She would never hold up against him. Not in a head-to-head battle for sexual primacy.

It pleased him to look at her like a predatory cat, and use her image in front of his eyes for his pleasure. He was in control not her.

He made sure to shift his fingers a little as he moved them over the vein underneath. When the first drop of pre-come appeared at the tip, he gave her a wink.

"Pinch your nipple," she ordered, sounding peeved over her backfiring experiment. "Give yourself some pain."

Azar complied, sending surges of white-hot energy through the tip of his cock as he did so. "Is this what you had in mind?" he queried, his voice a raspy whisper, full of seeming innocence.

He let her see as he twisted the nipple, how it tightened, how inviting it looked.

"Harder. Make it hurt."

"Already does." He grinned. Azar sucked in his belly just a little, emphasizing the muscles all along his hairless torso, a direct contrast to the succulent nipples.

"Harder, then." She thrust out the spear, menacingly.

Azar did so, absorbing the sensation, and building on it. "You're going to be punished after this, Theryssa," he turned the tables. "You've been a very bad girl."

"Fuck you," she snarled. "And get down on your fucking knees."

Azar knelt, though the stance in no way diminished his power. "I'm going to use the flogger, Theryssa. I will chain your hands over your head and flog every part of your disobedient flesh."

She was doing her best to ignore him, though he could sense the confusion and torment in her body. "Shut up and keep jerking off, you bastard. I want you to come in your hand and show it to me."

"If I do, Theryssa, I am going to feed it to you."

Her mouth dropped open. "Like hell you will."

"Don't fight it," he pumped his cock in long, languid strokes, from the base all the way to the tip, the motions designed to drive her wild. "You went to bed as my slave, Theryssa. Do you think you woke up something different?"

She thrust the lance forward and down, to within an inch of his chest. "Does this look like the act of a slave?"

"One whose Master has been toying with her—yes."

"You're not toying with me, you pirate scum. I am in charge of myself."

"Put the lance down, Theryssa. And go back to bed."

She smiled, half devil, half angel. "Make me," her eyes burned hot.

Azar did not flinch, despite the repositioning of the weapon directly at the level of his crotch. "I won't ask you again. This is your last chance to obey."

"And this is your last chance to beg for mercy before I cut your balls off."

Azar did not give her a chance to carry through with her threat. Before she could draw her next breath he was on the offensive. Pivoting himself on one hip, he swept out with his left leg, upending Theryssa. She was tossed into the air along with the lance. By the time gravity kicked in, he was standing over her, pointing the blade at her throat.

She was breathing heavily, but she was mad, not beaten. Anticipating some super move of her own, Azar snapped the blade over his knee and collapsed on top of her, pinning her.

"Get the fuck off me." There was no acquiescence this time. Theryssa was bucking underneath him, using her full strength. She could probably have dislodged a full-grown bull or a work droid, but Azar held fast.

He let her exhaust herself without saying a word.

She glared at him at last. "You're a fucking primale. I knew it!"

"Guilty as charged."

Theryssa's eyes were speaking volumes. He could only imagine what was going through her mind.

"I'm your prisoner for real," she acknowledged. "I demand the rights of universal capture."

Azar had expected as much. Fortunately, he was a step ahead. "You have no rights, Theryssa. I have already claimed you as a slave."

"No fucking way," she squirmed.

"When and where I want," he reminded.

She was powerless to prevent him exploring, reclaiming. At last, Azar pushed her legs apart with his knee and entered her, his cock pushing to the hilt in her silky softness. "You exist for my pleasure," he said. "As evidenced by your constant wetness in my presence."

"You arrogant prick," she tired to push him off. "You don't have a clue."

Azar let her struggle, enjoying the feel of her breasts and belly rubbing against him. He decided to ejaculate, just as he was.

Theryssa exclaimed in total frustration, realizing that her rebellion was turning him on. Too late, she tried to keep still, denying him.

Azar sighed with satisfaction, releasing himself. Pure jets of come, nicely released, no sweat, no grunting. "Good girl," he approved. "That is how you please your Master."

Theryssa had hoped to push him off now, but Azar was staying put, at least for the immediate future. His hard-on undiminished, he laid down the law.

"I was quite serious about the flogger, Theryssa. You will be hung upright and marked. I have special chains, ones you will not be able to escape. That will be your punishment. And also your interrogation. You will tell me who you are and what you are doing on my ship."

"You can't violate intergalactic law," she warned. "If you insist on enslaving me, there will be a price to pay."

"The laws allow sentient beings to give themselves over in bondage," he reminded.

"But I haven't given over squat."

"Really? Would you care to testify to that in court?"

He waited for her to remember. The words she had uttered, about how she would do anything for release—even become his slave.

"There's no way you can count that," she snorted.

"Kiss me." He decided to end the debate for now.

Theryssa shut her mouth tightly. Vigorously, she shook her head no.

Azar lowered his face to her, taking her lower lip between his teeth. He bit down, just the tiniest taste of pain. Theryssa moaned in immediate surrender. It was amazing how her primale genetics seemed to work against her. The more pressure was put on her sexually, the hornier and more yielding she became.

Her eyes filled with desire and trepidation, she lifted her head, touching her lips to his. He made her do the work, molding her mouth and moving it in time to her rapid breathing. He kept his own lips perfectly still, measuring, biding his time.

Second by second, she grew hotter and needier. He denied her as she sought access to his mouth with her tongue. It wasn't enough for her now. It was too gentle, too pretty.

She tried to seduce him, wrapping her arms around his neck. Nothing worked for her, not even when she ground her full, perfect breasts against his chest.

He waited until she was completely overwrought, writhing like a snake. Pulling her by the back of the hair, he disengaged her. Cutting her off cold turkey.

"Move your pussy muscles," he ordered.

Theryssa clenched and unclenched. She was showing her primale genetics, exhibiting a control impossible in a normal female.

"Work it to climax."

Theryssa licked her lips. She was a study in concentration. Azar stifled a groan as she squeezed his cock. Such an incredible, pulsing tunnel—a perfect fit. It was so very tempting to come again, but he wanted her to climax alone, so he could fully appreciate the look on her face, the reactions of her body.

It was part of the ownership process. Just as being forced to reveal one's most intimate sexual responses on command was part of slavery. The control would be his. She would be the one to reveal herself, the one to dissolve into a puddle.

"Azar," she sighed. "Oh, god."

"That's it. Move that little pussy," he coached. "It's punishment after this—no orgasms for a long time."

She started to spasm as soon as he spoke the words. Being dominated appeared to suit her, even more so talking about it.

"You may thank me for the privilege of being able to come, slave girl."

"Thank you…thank you," she cried. "Oh, stars, Azar. It's so…"

She clutched at his upper arms, digging into his flesh with her fingers. She was looking into his eyes, trying to convey what it felt like. To let go and give up everything. To be completely under the spell of another person. A strong, uncompromising lover.

So strong, in fact, as to be able to hold himself back in the midst of a hurricane of desire.

Azar enjoyed the crashing waves vicariously. Theryssa was transparent, a living radiator of the bucking, writhing pleasure she was experiencing. It was like being inside her, with her. His eyes began to burn. She wasn't the only one who was grateful. It was a gift she shared, the most precious in the entire universe. A gift of trust…of truest passion.

Not only was she giving over her body, but her eyes, and the expressions on her face. Azar was mightily humbled. He felt as though he had never truly seen a woman in the bloom of lust before.

"Azar," she called to him, as a fresh wave overtook her. "Come inside me. Come with me…together."

Only the cruelest and most stone-hearted of men could refuse such a plaintive request. So sweet and eager, and eminently female. He knew enough about the female body and heart to know she was reaching deep, risking much by showing so much vulnerability.

If he were to reject her…

Damn it, why did Theryssa have to be so sincere, so goddamn open, and so goddamn courageous?

Compared to her, he was a coward. His prowess in battle meant nothing. Because he was incapable of reaching out to others.

"Theryssa," he said huskily. "We mustn't..."

She silenced him with a kiss, branding his lips with a bit of domination all her own. She was adept, he gave her that. Not to mention the most incredibly sexy creature in the universe.

Wrapping her in his arms, he gave her what she wanted. What they both needed, though he was not ready to admit it.

His thrusts were decisive, but also smooth and deep and gentle. His every fiber strained to listen to her body. He did not want to let her down. With everything that had gone on before, and regardless of what might follow, he was determined that this at least would fulfill her.

She was moaning lightly into his mouth, clinging to him with damp fingers, clutching greedily, wanting him everywhere at once. At one point, she rolled him onto his back and then over again. Back and forth they went, shifting positions, but always maintaining the essential contact.

His cock, cemented inside her, hand in glove, sealed with liquid passion. Theryssa sucked at his tongue and lips, rubbing her nipples against him. She pushed her pelvis, too, maximizing the contact between them.

As his climax approached, Azar grabbed hold of her ankles, lifting them in the air and wide apart. Spreading her open as far as he could, he managed another half inch of depth. Theryssa's body was racked with pleasure. Her eyes were half-closed, focused on some distant point. She had her teeth clenched and she was holding the backs of her thighs, trying to retract her legs even farther.

Azar controlled the pace. He wanted her positioned perfectly.

Once, twice more…

There. He had it. The supreme moment of release. Timed exactly to Theryssa's latest roiling crescendo. Shutting his eyes tightly, he let loose, expending his full stock of semen, holding back nothing. Every bit of him was unleashed, every nerve ending, every living cell. The drain, the opening and spilling was total and complete. Primale though he was, he would be tired after this and it would take some time to restore his energies.

But it was worth it. Feeling Theryssa's symbiotic spasms, absorbing her willing female heat. Unlocking with her the secrets of her sexual being.

"Hold me," she whispered.

He did so, falling into her, wanting nothing more than to lose himself in her heartbeat. There were answers here. Answers to questions he never knew existed.

Truth is painful, though, and so is pleasure when one is aware how short-lived it is destined to be. The fact was, he did not deserve this woman's affection. Whether love, or merely lust.

"What are you thinking?" she asked.

It was a dangerous sign. Women who wanted to know what was on a man's mind were way too involved for their own good.

"I'm thinking about your punishment." He sought to put her off.

"My flogging," she supplied, as though it truly were her own.

"Yes, and I am not backing down in administering it."

"Why should you? I have it coming."

Her attitude surprised him more than a little. "You accept my sentence?"

"I tried to escape. I disobeyed you. I invaded your privacy. I broke my word," she read the list of her own crimes.

"You owe me nothing. I am a pirate."

"All the more reason for me to have been more careful."

"Not to have been caught, you mean."

"Something like that."

Azar stroked her hair. "You could just tell me who you are right now, you know, and save a lot of trouble down the line."

"I can't do that." She shook her head. "I'm sorry."

"I expected as much." Azar disengaged, rising off the bed to his full height. "I must attend to some business. Can I trust you to stay in the bed until I return?"

"Probably not."

Azar nodded. "Your honesty is appreciated. In that case, I will shackle you."

He gave her a chance to use the sanitizing chamber first. Once she was back on the bed, her body squeaky clean and pink, her hair fluffy and silky once again, he brought a pair of handcuffs, made of the special, unbreakable metal. "Put out your hands," he instructed.

Theryssa did so, palms down. He clicked the cuffs shut. There was a chain attached, which he secured to one of the metal rings on the headboard.

"That should do it," he announced, covering her nakedness with a thin fur. "I'll be back in a while. Get some rest. You'll need it."

She called to him just as he reached the doorway. "Azar?"

"Yes?"

"After you flog me...what will happen?"

"We finish the interrogation and I'll see to it you get to a Guardian vessel or station."

"Oh."

Azar tried to read something into her tone, but it was exasperatingly neutral. How this woman managed to inflame his blood. He wanted to kiss her fiercely, all over her body. He wanted to read her mind. He wanted to know what no one else did. Her secrets, the things she did not even tell her closest friends.

"I would think you'd be happy to leave here," he said.

"I am," she said, though she didn't sound it.

Women, he thought.

He must have been smiling as he left his cabin, because Oleron, who was standing in the corridor, remarked upon it immediately.

"Been enjoying yourself, Captain?"

"That's not your affair," he told the man. "Have the sensors picked up any more traffic out there?"

Oleron licked his lips. Like a jackal, ready to tear at a wound. Azar cursed himself for revealing his obvious interest in Theryssa. Now she would be a target for Oleron.

"A couple of freighters. We didn't want to disturb you, so we let them go."

Azar stiffened. "I'll decide what's a disturbance next time. Is that clear?"

Oleron barely concealed his venom. "Certainly, *sir*."

"To the bridge," said Azar, pointing the way. "We have work to do."

And quickly, too, so he could get back to Theryssa. He told himself he was anxious merely to get on with punishment and interrogation. But the truth was, he was already feeling, in her absence, an odd hole in his chest. Invisible, but real nonetheless.

Things felt off-kilter. Confused.

Not a good sign, not a good sign at all for a pirate, a sworn rebel destined to die an unpleasant death. Theryssa was alone, too, he thought. In his quarters. Chained up. That image made him want to comfort her. And dominate her. And everything in between.

His stomach did a flip. Half hot, half cold.

I should never have picked up that ship. Not in a million years. It was too easy, way too fucking easy…

He was paying the price now, wasn't he? And this was just the beginning. Who knew where it would all end. For him, for her…for everyone aboard this ship and maybe far beyond.

Chapter Six

ඐ

Theryssa resisted as long as she could. She was nude under the black and white fur, her wrists encircled in gleaming metal. Her sex beckoning. Suddenly insatiable. Where had he gone? Her body wanted to know. Where was the man with the magic, conquering hands who made everything else disappear?

Azar had not specifically mentioned the subject of masturbation before he left, but he had certainly made his wishes—correction—his demands known on the subject.

No one touched her but him. And that included her.

The trouble was, it made her burn and twitch to think of a man owning her like that. Forbidding her to pleasure herself. Damn it, this was her pussy, not his.

And what was with these chains? They really were unbreakable. This wasn't Earth technology. Fuck it—was it Narthian? She couldn't bear to think of that now. If Azar really was a traitor to his people, to humanity…well, she didn't know what she would do.

Obviously she would have to try to kill him. But it would hurt. In her heart. She didn't love the man, certainly not. It was just that they had shared some pretty close, intense experiences.

He had taken her somewhere. A place in her own soul she had not known existed. All her life she had been hiding feelings—trying to be tough, trying to keep ahead of her overambitious parents. So many expectations.

With Azar she didn't feel like she had to be anything. Except herself. Theryssa. Whoever that was.

Stars, she had to pull herself together.

Wanting to surrender to a man sexually was dangerous. Feeling conflicted about escape, about her mission was suicidal. Too many emotions swirling in her head. She was worried about Azar. She didn't like how tired he seemed. Not in bed—god knows he was a tiger—but outside of it, the way he had looked when he was on his way back to deal with his crew.

She had seen that kind of fatigue in soldiers who had seen too much.

Unbidden, Theryssa's fingers touched her belly. She was on her side. *Why not play with yourself?* said the voice in her head. *It's not like you can get up and go anywhere.*

Perhaps if she tried not to think of Azar. Could she get him out of her mind? It wasn't like he was the only attractive man in the universe. She sighed inwardly as her fingertips reached her clitoris. Yes, this is what she needed. Some private time with her own body. A chance to wipe the slate clean.

There were plenty of other men to think about. With hard, smooth bodies and gorgeous cocks. Men she had seen naked, men she had made sex with. It was no big deal. Sex could be made with lots of people. Azar had come into her life and he would go away soon enough.

She would deal with him. As soon as she cleared her head. Plunging her fingers inside her slit, she sought to banish him.

The chain slid across her breasts as her hands shifted position. Cold metal on her nipples. Azar's metal. One more fucking reminder...

Theryssa rolled onto her back. She could still smell him on the furs. Fiercely confident and masculine. She could picture him, looming over her, that look in his eyes. The one that let her know he was a man who took whatever he wanted.

He was not a ruffian, though. As sure as he was of his power, he was even more certain of his prowess. Calmly, quietly, he knew how to take care of business, making a woman feel like she was the only female in the universe.

Theryssa played with her swollen clit. Unsuccessfully, she tried to duplicate his technique. The way he teased so gently one second, manipulating so masterfully the next. He really could make a woman beg for anything. She hated the idea of any other receiving that treatment. She would want to kill with her bare hands any other wench he tried to chain up.

How crazy was that? What sort of privilege and thrill was it to be held prisoner? Azar had left her here, nothing to think of but his return. And what was happening then?

A flogging, that's what.

The man actually intended to hang her by her wrists and apply leather to her skin. It wasn't a matter of the pain. Guardian training had equipped her for much worse in the way of torture.

It was the sexual side of it. She wasn't a slave, she was a prisoner.

And yet Azar awoke things in her. Not a desire to submit to all men—just to him. When he had collared her, it had been like making sex, like being penetrated in some wicked, secret way. The same thing happened each time he held her fast, pinning her down.

And when he had given her commands. Stars, that had made her skin tingle, head to toe. How was it Azar could make her want to be owned by him? Why did she want him for a Master...at least in bed?

Theryssa's breasts ached to be touched. But she could not reach them while her chained hands were between her legs. Her motion had been limited. By the very man she could not get out of her mind.

The harder she tried, the more her current circumstances reminded her.

She wasn't free.

Far from being enraged, she was thrilled. Excited beyond all imagination. She belonged…to a man.

Fuck…she was coming again. How many orgasms did that make in this bed? Sucking in her breath, clenching her pussy muscles, she held it tightly as long as she could, relishing every second as the climax ran through her body, like a series of cords snapping, energizing and enervating.

Eyes closed, her world dark as space, she tried to sink to a place below dreams. A place of peace. Where maybe there would be some answers to all her questions.

When the shock waves had passed, Theryssa put her fingers to her mouth, licking them clean. It was the one thing she could think that she would not do on her own, but which Azar might order her to do.

She tasted scandalous to herself. Her limbs felt transcendently weak.

I'm doing this, she told herself, for Azar.

My captor. My Master.

Shivers claimed her.

Lying there, wrapped in fur, she had never felt more at home in her life.

Or more terrified.

* * * * *

Azar's gaze through the viewfinder was unwavering. For the second time in as many days, he was studying the movements of a ship that was not what it appeared to be. Yesterday, he had hauled in a courier express, netting himself one small cache of treasure and one big, complicated headache of a female.

Today he was looking at a civilian transport cruiser. A basic two-seater tourist model used for interplanetary weekend jaunts.

"Looks like this is our lucky week," said Trelorne, the navigator. "Probably a couple of rich fools who missed their turnoff on the hyper-way."

"This far out? Not likely," said Azar. "No, they're pros. See how they've been compensating for stellar drift?"

"What the Captain means," piped in Oleron sarcastically, "is they might be dangerous. We had best evacuate the area before they attack."

Azar's hand moved to his dagger. Oleron's eyes darkened. Two of his henchmen moved in beside him on the crowded bridge.

"Have I offended you, Captain?" Oleron asked, clearly spoiling for a fight.

Azar could easily have cut down all three men where they stood. It wouldn't have been the first time he had put down a mutiny. He opted for a verbal retort instead. "That isn't possible, Oleron. You are far too insignificant to ever cause offense."

Oleron smiled sideways, relaxing. For the moment, the crisis was averted. Soon he would make his move, though, and Azar would have to respond.

Damn it, why was Azar waiting? He needed to stop thinking about the past, about that note from Theron. About Theryssa.

Oleron licked his lips. "What are we going to do," he pressed, "about the ship?"

"We will take the ship onboard," Azar decided. "You will recover it in the cargo bay. The rest of the ship will be sealed off. In case of a trap."

Oleron's already cruel features pinched in obvious displeasure. Azar had gotten the best of him once again.

Instead of showing up his captain, he had only endangered himself with his insistence on dealing with the mystery ship. "Yes, Captain. Where will you be? Back in your cabin?"

It was an obvious aspersion cast against his decision to remain exclusively with Theryssa since her arrival.

"That is not your concern, Oleron. Securing the passenger ship is."

Oleron nodded brusquely and left the bridge.

Azar found his thoughts drifting as he looked at the ship again on the viewer. With the mention of her name, he couldn't help but think of Theryssa. Was she resting properly in his absence? More than likely she was trying to escape. Perhaps he should have put a guard on the cabin. Not that any normal man would be able to stop her if she broke free.

His mind turned to what he would do when he was with her again. She would be flogged, of course, her golden skin deliciously pinkened by the many-stranded leather flogger he had especially in mind for the occasion.

Not much of a punishment, really. He wouldn't cause her much discomfort. But he would play with her mind, tease her just a little. At every available opportunity, he would make it clear that he saw her as a woman ripe for his exploitation.

He loved the look in her eyes when he talked to her about slavery. He loved how her body sang for him, how she purred in captivity. Such a proud and noble creature. He could never break her—just let her play with her inner demons.

Those that longed to know what it was like to crawl and beg. To be used for a man's total pleasure. To be desired beyond all reason, to be so much an object of lust as to be taken as a possession. A piece of property, never to be sold or traded.

The trouble was, Azar had never managed to hold onto anything in his life. Especially not a woman.

"Employ beams." He gave the order to bring the tiny ship onboard. "Maximum power."

Azar had a feeling deep in his gut. Something about that ship felt familiar. It had something to do with Theryssa. But what?

He shook his head, trying to clear it.

He was letting himself be consumed. Theryssa was in his quarters, and whoever was out there could not possibly have anything to do with her.

Not in a million light years.

* * * * *

"They've activated the beams," said Nyssa to her husband. "Shouldn't we shut down the main drive systems?"

"Not yet." Theron shook his head, sitting beside her in the cockpit of the small civilian cruiser. "Let's not alert them to how much we want to get caught."

"But we could overshoot their landing bay and end up halfway into the hull," she pointed out reasonably.

"We have time to compensate. Blast it, woman, must you keep arguing with me? I'm a trained star pilot."

"Who's been in dry dock for a decade," she shot him down.

"You're just itching to go over my knee, aren't you?" Theron grumbled.

Nyssa stole a quick glance at Theron's lap. His cock was deliciously outlined under his flight suit, as were his muscular, sculpted thighs, his powerful legs and trim waist.

And those hands...which still rocked her world and made her body dance after all these years of marriage. "No," she lied, trying to keep his mind on the track of their mission and off of anything sexual. "It's the farthest thing from my mind."

Theron raised an eyebrow. "You're a terrible liar," he crooned.

Nyssa tried to keep her eyes glued to the console. She knew that tone in his voice. She also knew how outrageous he could be when he wanted her. The fact that they were about to be brought onboard a ship full of potential pirates meant nothing to him. Admittedly, there were worse things than having a husband that much in lust after twenty plus years of marriage. But still…

"I can see you're aroused. Your nipples are rock hard," he persisted.

Damn it, why did the man have to be so fucking sexy. He was still a perfect specimen, all the more so for the slight gray in his hair and the tiny character lines around his eyes. He was aging splendidly.

And she wasn't doing so bad herself, at least if you went by how much trouble Theron still had keeping his hands off her.

"Has it occurred to you I might be cold?"

"You're wet, too."

"Fucking primale sense of smell," she muttered.

Theron grinned. "Busted."

"We're both going to be busted if those pirates catch us with our pants down," she declared, pointing to the looming cargo bay, its main doors open like the jaws of some kind of space shark.

"Pirates understand about a man needing a wench. They capture them all the time." He ran his hand over her cheek.

Nyssa pulled her head out of the way, trying to keep her sanity. "I'm not a wench, mister. I am the Head of the Council."

He moved his fingers to her breast. "You're my wench."

She tried to brush his hand away.

"Leave it."

Fuck. He was pulling rank. She might well be in charge of the Galactic Council, but when it came to sex-making, he called the shots. And why not? As a primale he knew instinctively what she needed. Especially when it came to submission.

"Theron, we can't…" Gone was her surety and authority. She was just a woman now, trying to bargain with a man notorious for doing precisely what he wanted.

In fact, her little shows of resistance tended to turn him on.

"Of course we can. You are my beautiful wife, and I will have you where and when…and how I want."

Nyssa sighed, so very full of love for this man. "Oh, Theron…"

"Clothes open," he gave the command for the seams on her suit to part.

Nyssa never failed to get a charge from that, the fact that every one of her outfits was coded to his verbal pattern such that his was the final word.

At any point in time, in other words, he could render her naked as he was doing now.

"Let's get these off," he patted her thigh, indicating she should lift her ass.

"Yes, Sir," she smiled, her anxieties melted away in the moment.

Theron helped her to strip the suit down over her legs. When she was bootless and completely naked he had her climb over the console between them and onto his lap.

His own suit was already open all the way down the sides, freeing up his cock. Inserting it inside her hot and open sex, she settled down on his lap, chest to chest.

"Fuck," she hissed. "I needed this…"

"You always need it," he teased. "You're insatiable."

"Me?" She pushed her palm against his massive pectoral. "You're the one who can't ever get enough."

"Stop being so goddamn sexy, then." He grasped her breasts, crushing them in just the right way.

"Oh, baby," she moaned. "I love you so much. I love being your woman...belonging to you."

"That's why I have to take you when you don't expect it. Keep you on edge. At any second, you need to be prepared."

She rocked her pelvis, pushing his massive erection against the walls of her throbbing pussy. "Have I ever been unprepared?" she retorted, alluding to the constant state of wetness she maintained in his presence.

It was true. Never once had he reached for her and found her dry. Not even on those occasions of total surprise. But that was part of the thrill, wasn't it? Knowing that her man might make use of her at any moment, day or night, that he might lay his hand on her, drawing her close to inspect her readiness, to whisper in her ear, perhaps. Telling her to go to bed and wait for him, or lift her skirt at once, so he could he take her. On the floor, or against the wall.

"You damn well better be wet," he growled playfully.

Nyssa wrapped her arms about his neck, relishing his masculinity. He would never, ever hurt a hair on her head, but she knew damn well from experience what it was to be punished by his hand—and the flogger, too.

It aroused them both, the rules between them, and the undercurrent of power. If she were found unprepared for sex she could be spanked. If she failed to please him, she could be spanked. Being too sassy, too, was grounds for a healthy peppering to her behind.

He gave her lots of leeway, of course. She was a fem and he had to treat her as such. She would never find her fulfillment through absolute conformity to a man's will. For any other primale, that would be a deal breaker. But Theron was not any other primale. He had been made for her — literally, genetically — and she for him.

She couldn't explain the science of how it worked, any more than she could define the emotion of love they shared. It was real and profound, that's what mattered. Sure, they had their disagreements sometimes, like any couple, but the bond they shared was unbreakable.

"You really are incorrigible," she lifted herself, partially exposing his glistening cock once more. "You know that, husband?"

"It's a characteristic I pride myself on." He took hold of her hips.

Nyssa gasped as he planted her back down, firmly.

"Were you given permission to move?" he chided.

"You didn't tell me not to."

"Keep it up, wife, and you will be spending the return trip in irons."

Nyssa's pussy spasmed. Just the mention of bondage was all it took. "You would never chain me that long," she teased. "You would miss the fucking too much."

"Who says I can't do both?"

Nyssa pictured herself spread-eagled on the bed, left shackled, to be used at his leisure. No doubt he would torment her, leaving her unsatisfied for hours at a time.

"You're in a mean frame of mind," she pouted.

"That I am. I might even give you to the pirates."

She nibbled at his earlobe. "Like that would ever happen. You can't even stand when other men look at me. Remember what happened with the Gibnian ambassador?"

Theron swelled his cock. Deliberately. "Damn straight I do. The bastard was drooling over you all through dinner."

"He has three mouths. He can't help but drool. As for looking at me, he has six sets of eyes. They can't all be staring at the wall."

"Never mind. You know what I'm saying."

"No, I don't, Theron. But it doesn't matter. We're going to be on that ship any minute. If we're going to come, you better make it quick."

"Who says I'm going to let you come?"

Nyssa's pulse raced. Nothing went deeper to her sexual core than when he took control of her orgasms. "Theron, you wouldn't leave me hanging?"

He certainly was capable of it. Possessing a will of iron, he could shut down his own sex drive and close up shop any time he wanted. He was also not above orgasming on his own and making her wait under threat of the paddle to her ass.

"I think I might do just that," he mused. "You'll be hornier for the return trip. More cooperative."

"Theron...please."

"My mind is made up."

Fuck. *Double* fuck.

"Just one orgasm, baby..." Nyssa wheedled, nuzzling his neck. "I swear, I'll be extra good on the way home. I could wear that little slave girl costume you like, with the bells? And I'll push all the buttons and cook for you. Whatever you tell me, I'll obey the first time."

"You're supposed to do that anyway, not that you ever do. Now get dressed, woman, before the pirates see you like this."

Nyssa whimpered as he removed her from his cock and set her back down in her own seat. She made one last desperate attempt to seduce him by putting her head in his lap, but he held her fast, his fist curled in her long, light auburn hair.

"You'll have lots of time to worship my erection later," he promised. "First we need to attend to some cosmic business."

"You really are impossible, you know that?"

"And you love every minute of it." He flashed a rakish grin.

She hid her pleasure at the sight of his smile. Why did the bastard have to be so gorgeous? Hustling back into her suit, she gave her prognostication for the much vaunted return trip. "You won't get a thing from me all the way back to Earth, you hear me?"

"That's fine. I'm sure the pirates can supply me with a slave girl or two."

"Yeah, well maybe they can supply you with a new cock, too, after I cut yours off." Her fingers flew over the panel in front of her. "And I'm shutting off the fucking drive system, too."

Theron put his thumb and forefinger, under her chin.

"What?" she demanded as he turned her head to face him.

"On the way back," he said, his voice smooth and cool and sexily matter-of-fact. "You'll be wearing nothing but your collar."

Her heart skipped a beat. "We don't even know if our mission will succeed. What if Theryssa ends up coming back with us once she finds out the truth?"

"She won't, Nyssa. Things are already settled, I guarantee it. It will be just us on the way back. You, me...and the collar."

Nyssa thought of the circle of steel—a delicate ring encrusted with pale-colored stones. She did not wear it often, but when she did its implications were as powerful as they were unmistakable.

The collar symbolized that place between them where they were anything but equal. When she donned it, she became a very different creature, one for whom everything, even clothing was at the whim of another.

It had reached the point over the years where simply touching the metal could make her orgasm. She could scarcely imagine what it would mean to wear it out here, in deepest space, where she would be in Theron's clutches, alone with no hope of distraction.

"Do we have an understanding, Nyssa?"

Her pussy was shamelessly liquefying. He could not have said anything more tantalizing and agonizing in her current state.

The collar. The fucking collar.

And all that came with it. The constant sexual charge, perpetual arousal. The groveling, the begging for her every little need. The delicious feeling of being a pet, stroked and petted...and owned.

And the sex...wall-to-wall fucking horny, wild, endless sex as she dealt with the out of control hormones of a man whose very blood was programmed to respond to a subjugated, totally defenseless woman.

"Yes," Nyssa replied, her voice reduced to a croak.

"Yes, what?"

"Yes...Master." The word exploded off her lips, sealing the bargain. It would happen all right, just as he said. She would take off her clothes and put the steel on her throat. Sealing the bond with a kiss. Deep and expressive. Changing everything, for as long as he wished to keep it on her body.

In the meantime there was reality...

"That's my Nyssa." Theron leaned forward, rendering a kiss to clear her head a little. "You gonna be okay?"

She nodded. The sex stuff had to go to the back of her brain.

It was time to carry out their mission.

To meet with a pirate captain, a self-styled king who had once been one of them. The very same Azar whom they must now convince to help the Council against the Narthians.

The stakes could not be underestimated.

It was a matter of survival for every man, woman and child. Beginning with their own child, their beloved Theryssa, whom they had sent out here with a mission of her own.

Not the one she'd been told about, but a quite different one. One she would have balked at mightily if they'd told her up front.

For as it turned out, they did not really need her to spy on Azar at all, but rather to seduce him. To become his lover, and hopefully his mate. This in turn would assure her happiness, and also secure his help for the Council.

It was a wild risk to take, especially where Theryssa was concerned. Their daughter might well never forgive them for tricking her like this. But Nyssa and Theron had seen no other way.

The odds were against them. But if anyone could believe in the possibilities of love to change the fate of worlds, it was her and Theron. They had witnessed firsthand how passion could overcome suspicion and doubt in the romance of Nyssa's sister Seria and her husband Raylar.

Seria's life had been on a one-way track to loneliness, and Raylar had been threatening to self-destruct. And now, together, they were an unstoppable force. The Council's best diplomat, working hand in hand with its best soldier.

They could point to their own story, as well. From initial sparks to open hatred, two unlikely lovers had formed a symbiotic union which allowed each to shine, giving of their best gifts—her as Council leader, and him as Commander in Chief of the Guardians.

Granted, in her and Nyssa's case, there was some genetic help along the way, but they had a feeling about Theryssa and the man once known as Azariel. Even before the crisis, when Theryssa was coming of age and they saw how the other males were threatened by her prowess, Theron had told her that his friend could understand their daughter best.

Nyssa trusted Theron's instinct, after all the two men had fought alongside each other in some of the worst battles of the last Narthian war, prior to Azariel's self-exile.

On one occasion, Azariel had saved Theron's life. A favor her husband had returned a few months later.

You didn't forget a bond like that. Not even if you ended up on opposite sides with someone years later. Or so Theron had laid it out for her. Nyssa trusted Theron implicitly, of course, and if he thought Azar was a good man and that he might click with Theryssa, that was good enough for her.

Besides, she had seen how Theryssa had reacted to Azar's holoids. It had been love at first sight. Just as with Seria and Raylar.

Those were a mother's hopes, though. Nyssa also had her fears to contend with. Not least of which was that her daughter's heart would be broken, or that she might even be faced with mortal danger.

To say that letting Theryssa go had been the most difficult decision of her life was an understatement. Nor had Nyssa's anguish lessened over the course of Theryssa's journey. Being able to monitor her condition via the retina transponder they had secretly placed in her retina had certainly helped, but Nyssa was not about to draw an easy breath again until she had her daughter safely back in her arms.

When Nyssa had first raised the idea of coming out here with Theron as he met with Azar to enlist the pirate's help and check on the status of things between he and Theryssa, Theron had gone through the roof.

"I will not put you at risk," Theron thundered. "It is out of the question."

Nyssa had waited for his bluster to subside and then said her piece. Short, sweet and to the point. "Theryssa is my daughter, too, Theron, and if you think for one minute I will sit by, half a galaxy away, while you go after her, you are sorely mistaken. I am getting on that ship with you, and there will be no more discussion. Ever."

It was one of the few times in their marriage that Theron had backed down without a fight. He had known she was right, he'd just been afraid for her. She loved that about him, how protective he was. And how he did what he could to keep her calm and peaceful, like playing sex games on the way to the pirate ship.

She gave Theron's hand a squeeze as their small ship eased through the doors of the much larger pirate vessel. This was it, the moment of decision. Up to this point, Nyssa hadn't really considered what might happen if they failed. Theoretically, they could be killed or held hostage.

Not that her husband was a man to be taken prisoner easily. He was a force to be reckoned with. The Guardian had yet to be commissioned who could beat him one-on-one, in fact. With the possible exception of his brother-in-law Raylar.

Their personal combat record was a source of much argument between them, much to the consternation of their wives. Boys will be boys, was Seria's analysis. Nyssa knew there was something deeper at stake.

For Theron, maintaining supremacy against his eventual successor was a sign of his own ongoing vitality. More than anything he feared that once he retired he would pass quickly into decrepitude.

As if that was ever possible. Theron's predecessor, his mentor Marax was still rim gliding on Cerus Minor, winning races against pups young enough to be his grandsons.

"Are we ready for this, babe?" Nyssa asked as they stood side by side at the exit portal.

"We were born ready." Theron winked.

Their ship was landing, still under the automatic control of the beams. Nyssa's stomach tightened a little at the sound of the metal doors closing behind them. There was no turning back now.

"Should we be armed?" Nyssa wondered.

Theron tapped the key pad, unlocking the portal and extending the ramp. "I already am."

She noted the solid figure of the man she loved. His hands were weapons enough, and the rest of him, too. Happily, proudly, she stood beside him to face their fate.

"Come out with your hands up," growled a particularly nasty looking pirate as the portal slid open.

Nyssa gauged him to be at least seven feet tall, with enough muscle to outfit an orbit ball team. There were five more, gathered around the base of the ramp, armed with beam weapons.

"Where is your Captain?" Theron ignored the giant of a man.

"You deal with me," snarled a bald man, pointing a silver laser rifle. "And you better not give me any trouble, or I'll melt you down right where you stand."

"Look at this, Oleron," said the giant to the bald man. "The troublemaker brought us a wench for sport."

Nyssa leaned instinctively against her husband.

Theron's body tensed ever-so slightly. "I'll ask one more time, politely. We are here to see Captain Azar."

The one called Oleron laughed out loud to the others, the sound echoing in the huge, empty bay. "You hear that, boys? He's only going to ask us once…politely."

"I'll be polite, too," the giant took a step up the ramp. "While I'm giving it to his woman."

Theron moved so fast Nyssa didn't even have time to think how fucking stupid and suicidal that bruiser was. It lasted less than five seconds. Theron simply grabbed him by the neck, hoisted him into the air and threw him a hundred feet against the far wall.

The other pirates were so shocked they just stood there for a moment, mouths hanging open. Finally one of them got the brilliant idea to shoot. Before he could pull the trigger, however, Theron reached forward and bent the barrel one hundred and eighty degrees.

"Captain Azar," Theron reiterated to Oleron, who had claimed to be in charge. "Tell him it's a ghost from Bralon."

Oleron's eyes were wide with terror. He and the others almost fell over themselves in their retreat, running backward, trying to keep their guns aimed at Theron.

"How did I do?" Theron asked once they were gone.

"Not bad," she conceded. "Maybe a little melodramatic."

He pulled her close for a kiss. "Are you mad I didn't let you stick up for yourself?"

"Nah," she grinned, "I like it when you act like a brute."

He held her tightly against him. She relished the sound of his heartbeat. There was no more calming, centering sound in the entire universe. As long as she had this heart to attune herself to, and these arms to hold her, everything would be all right.

For her. And for Theryssa, too.

There was only one variable left here. And that was Azar, the mysterious former Guardian turned pirate captain.

Should she be worried that he wasn't here to greet them? Maybe he was busy with Theryssa. Making sex. With any luck it was even more than that.

Chapter Seven

ℬ

"Falthar is dead," said Oleron, standing at the entrance to the bridge.

Azar sought to contain his glee. That was one less of Oleron's thugs he would have to deal with down the line. "I take it you encountered something a bit more hazardous than tourists?" Azar asked dryly.

Oleron did not appear to appreciate the humor. He never did, especially when he was the butt of it. "They want to see you," he said flatly. "One man and one woman."

"Two people?" Azar raised a brow. "It ought to have taken an army to bring down Falthar."

"The guy is an army," he said bitterly. "He's got to be some kind of cyborg."

Or a primale.

"What about the woman?" Azar inquired.

Oleron shrugged. "She's a looker. About forty. But don't say anything to her, or that cyborg thing will tear your fucking head off."

"Duly noted. Have them meet me in the war room. I will speak to them alone."

"You'll get no argument from me," Oleron declared. "If you want me, I'll be in the galley getting drunk."

"You'll tend to Falthar first. Dispose of his remains out of the main hatchway."

"It'll take a while to find all the pieces. He must have hit the bulkhead at light speed."

"What exactly did he say to this woman to get the man so angry?"

Oleron's grin was physically nauseating. "Nothing we don't say to the rest of our female guests."

Azar frowned, thinking of Theryssa. "You're dismissed, Oleron," he said curtly.

Oleron grumbled and left. A second later he popped his head back in. "I almost forgot—he had a message for you."

"Oh?"

"Yeah, something about him being a ghost from Bralon?"

Azar's blood chilled.

"You know him?" Oleron read his expression.

"Of course I do, you fool," hissed Azar. "Everyone in the galaxy does. Except for you and your idiotic cohorts."

Indeed, there was only one person such a description could fit. This man was indeed a ghost. At least he would have been had Azar not pushed him out of the way of a collapsing beam tower under Narthian fire.

Theron had come to see him.

But why? He was Commander in Chief of the entire Guardian force now. A sworn enemy. The man was as good as turning himself over as a hostage. For what purpose?

Had his old comrade gone mad? Bringing himself and his woman here?

By the gods, this wasn't just any woman, either. His mate was Nyssa, the Head of the Council.

"Who are they?" Oleron demanded. "What are you hiding?"

Azar struck him, the pent-up fury boiling over at last. A single backhand sent the man sprawling. "Silence, you imbecile. Speak to me like that again and I will have you drawn and quartered."

"Yes," the man groaned, licking the blood from the corner of his lip, "sir."

Azar stepped over him, his mind already racing ten steps ahead.

Theron had come here. To him.

Something was going on. Theron was not a madman, nor was he a fool. He had come, unarmed, bringing his mate. The highest official in the government.

His heart raced as he descended in the elevator, to the war room. It did not take a cyber genius to figure out his extraordinary new visitors bore some connection to his other guest, a person whose presence here was equally improbable.

Theryssa. The female with the genes of a primale. A creature who, by all rights, should not exist at all.

At this rate, he could only imagine who would be coming to see him tomorrow.

The Narthian Next Queen maybe, begging to make peace? Or how about Santa Claus, asking him to deliver toys throughout the galaxy in his pirate ship?

One day I'll laugh at this, he thought. *If I live that long.*

* * * * *

Theryssa stood on the mattress, pulling the chain with all her might. Gritting her teeth, she let loose a grunt of sheer anguish.

The novelty of the whole shackle and fur thing had most definitely worn off. Theryssa was bored. And pissed. And more than a little anxious about what was taking Azar so long. She should have pressed him for a specific amount of time. What if he was in trouble? Here she was stuck, chained up like a girl.

Which is what she was, technically, though that hardly represented the full fearsomeness of her woman's spirit. She was a warrior — her mother always said that. Dad had called her Wild Thing since before she could properly talk and say her name.

Fuck. Maybe she could twist the thing off her wrists.

It was such a joke. Confined in a bed. A sexual prisoner. A freaking slave, according to her captor.

What a little fool she had been, getting all wrapped up in his whole snake charmer routine. Now that he had been gone a while, things seemed a lot clearer.

At least as much as they could in a situation like this.

Azar was either a traitor or he wasn't. He was in bed with the Narthians or not. In either case, he was a pirate, who attacked Earth ships. Guardian ships flown by men who were her friends and brothers in arms. He also made slaves of women, although he seemed pretty sensitive with her.

When he wasn't making plans to whip her.

Damn. The twisting wasn't working either. Maybe she could use something else. Where had that lance ended up—the one she had attacked him with?

It was then she saw a tiny glimmer on the floor, near the end of the bed. Her heart skipped a beat. It looked like a key. Son of a bitch. Had the all-knowing, in control Azar actually screwed up and dropped the key to the shackles on his way out?

It sure as hell looked like it.

It was about time she got a break her way. The question was—could she reach it. Not with her hands, but she had feet and toes. She was pretty good with them, too, thanks to a lot of sessions of toe wrestling with her father, a game the two of them had invented when she was little.

How easy it was back then. When he would just play with her and talk and laugh. Once she had grown up, it all seemed to get so much harder.

Theryssa scooted down the bed, stretching her arms over her head. It took her a while to find the key again with her foot, since she was on her back, staring at the ceiling.

Finally, she felt the cold metal with her big toe. Now came the tricky part. Getting it between her toes without kicking it out of reach for good. Once she nearly lost it. A couple more times she came close, only to drop it halfway up.

Finally, she was able to lift it all the way over her head and drop it straight down.

She caught it with true sass, clamping it right between her teeth.

A second later she was free.

Now all she had to do was find her way out of the cabin, past a whole crew of horny pirates and make it to Azar. Then she could make her decision.

Either to kill him or kiss him.

Whichever of the two came into her mind first.

* * * * *

It was not his old compatriot who Azar noticed first. Of the two highly attractive, physically fit persons of early middle age standing in the war room waiting for him, it was definitely the female who caught and kept his attention.

"You…are Nyssa?" he asked, astonished.

Azar had seen holoids of the woman here and there, official pictures off the hologrid, and scenes from Council meetings. But nothing up close and personal. In real life there was no mistaking the resemblance.

She could be Theryssa in twenty years.

"I am." The woman nodded. "And you are Azar. King of Pirates."

Azar was at a loss for words. Was the Council cloning its best citizens now, creating new organisms from the exact same genetic material?

"Nyssa is Theryssa's mother." Theron inserted himself into the conversation. "That is the reason for the resemblance."

"Her...mother?" This was getting more incredible by the minute. "But natural genetics has been outlawed for centuries. You mean to say you carried her...*in your womb*?"

"Perish the thought." Nyssa shook her head. "I love my daughter to death, but I would never endure such a thing. Theryssa was made in a test tube, the healthy way. It just so happens that her genes, unlike the rest of the population, are an exclusive mix. Mine and—"

"Yours," Azar finished her sentence, looking directly at Theron. "Theryssa is your daughter. I should have guessed as much from her stubbornness."

Theron attempted unsuccessfully to hide his pride. "She does tend to take after me, it's true."

"But she has your beauty," Azar declared to Nyssa.

Nyssa smiled in definite appreciation. "Thank you," she said, "though there is no need to flatter an old lady."

"You are hardly old, Nyssa." This from Theron, who clearly adored his wife. "But see here, Azar," he riveted his eagle eyes, "now that the introductions are out of the way, I must insist that you guarantee the safety of my wife and my daughter from this point forward. Otherwise, I will not be held responsible for my actions."

"You have my word. On my life," said Azar. "As for the men you encountered, I shall deal with them. I promise you, they did not act on my orders."

"We believe you," said Nyssa speaking for them both. "And we trust you."

Azar marveled at the woman's grace and boldness. Theryssa had learned much from her mother, no doubt.

"Theryssa's name," Azar exclaimed, the pieces continuing to fall into place in his rapidly whirring brain. "That's a mix, too. Theron and Nyssa. Therr—yssa."

"I can see your powers of deduction remain as strong as ever," Theron quipped. "I imagine you will be able to guess the real reason why we sent her here, too."

"Not bloody likely. By the gods," he shook his head, still overwhelmed at seeing Theryssa's progenitors, "I can't believe my eyes. It's so clear. She is the perfect combination of a warrior and a politician. Tell me, is she truly unique, or are other couples being allowed to create natural children?"

"It's a very select group so far. Our daughter, as well as our nephew born of Nyssa's sister Seria and her husband. Of course Nyssa and I are natural, as well," Theron explained. "Although Theryssa is unique in being the first female born of a primale father and a half primale mother. That makes her quite extraordinary. She is the first female in the Guardians, as a matter of fact, though she is seldom linked to me or her mother."

"We have tried to protect our children's identities," said Nyssa. "Theryssa was raised by us, but only a few outside the family know who she really is. It's the same with Seria and Raylar's son."

"Which begs the question," Azar decided to get to the meat of the situation, "why tell me all this? For that matter, why choose my humble ship for this little family get-together of yours in the first place? Are there more coming? Should I expect a reunion?"

Nyssa's smile broadened. The room lit up, the same way it did when Theryssa smiled. "Not exactly. Could we sit down, though? I'm afraid it's a bit of a long story."

"Forgive me." Azar rushed to get a chair for this dazzling woman...the mother of the woman he had been sharing such incredible sex with.

The same woman Azar currently had chained on his bed.

How could he have forgotten such a thing, standing here, casually talking to the woman's parents? Looking at Theron, he had sudden visions of himself flying through the air like Falthar.

"If you'll forgive me, I need to tend to something." Azar bowed, offering Theryssa one of two simple metal seats. "I'll be right back."

Theron remained standing. "If you don't mind, I would like to get right to business."

"Theron," Nyssa scolded lightly, "stop being such a bear."

"It's all right, Nyssa," said Azar. "If Theron was too easygoing, I would start to worry."

Theron sat down, with Azar following suit. Unfortunately, Theryssa would have to wait just a little longer.

"I'd worry, too," agreed Nyssa, squeezing the powerful arm of her husband.

"The first thing I must ask you, Azar," Theron settled imperiously into his seat, "Is to confirm your receipt of my transmission. I assume so, since you haven't tried to blast us to atoms."

"I did receive it. As for letting you live, credit your lovely wife. I'd have shot you on sight if you'd come alone," he joked grimly.

"It's true," he acknowledged with a gallows smile. "We have been enemies, you and I, for a long time. Were we meeting under different circumstances, I would be sworn by my office to destroy you."

Azar nodded, seeking once and for all to lay to rest the memory of Solania. Whether it was indeed an accident or that she had killed herself after being told by Theron that she couldn't see Azar anymore, it wasn't Theron's fault. He had come under orders and he was not responsible for her subsequent actions. "That said, let's get down to business. The past…shall be left in the past. I accept your personal words to me and your invitation to dialogue."

Theron nodded. "In that case, let us propose to you a new beginning between us."

"What new beginning could there be, Theron?"

Nyssa eyed her husband, indicating a desire to take over their end of the conversation. "Azar, we sent to you the most precious thing to us in the entire universe. Our only child. Forgive us for not being up front about why. Forgive us, too, for sending her in disguise, and for keeping tabs on her while she's been with you."

"Keeping…tabs?"

Theron nodded. "Unbeknownst to her, we inserted a transponder into her retina. The procedure is a new one. It was done while she was asleep one night. A remote android, a ball little bigger than a man's hand administered it by microbeam. It's painless and is designed to dissolve in a few weeks. Thanks to it, we have been fully aware of everything happening to her since her arrival."

Azar swallowed. "Everything?"

Nyssa smiled knowingly. "Don't be embarrassed Azar. We are adults, we are aware of what sex-making is. Theryssa is grown, too, and we know that all that has transpired between you is consensual and fully natural."

Azar looked at Theron, blinking. "You saw…"

Theron was frowning heavily, fists clenched. Clearly he was far less comfortable with his daughter's sexuality than his wife.

"Let's not drag this out," he cut Azar off. "We did what we had to for Theryssa's security. This is a pirate ship for star's sake. You have my word, the receiver will be deactivated as soon as we get back on our ship. The point is, Theryssa came to you unmated, you interacted with her and now you will be her lifemate."

Azar's eyes widened. Was he hearing right? Theryssa was certainly sweet, but what, for nebula's sake, gave Theron the idea they were going to hook up for life after less than a day together.

Although now that he thought about it, he did feel intensely comfortable and at home with Theryssa…more so even than in his own skin.

"Theron, with all due respect…"

It was Nyssa's turn to interrupt him. "Azar, you needn't answer now. I know it's a lot to absorb. And we owe you an extra apology for spying on you in bed. We just needed to know she was safe at all times."

"It's lucky for you she was," Theron said. "I have had half the fleet on standby in the next star system."

Azar had had just about enough. "Well, you might as well use it on me, Theron, because I am not mating with anyone against my will. Ever."

"You have no choice," Theron pressed. "You possessed her…as a primale. She is your woman. You must protect her, and lay down your life for her if need be. Your genetics will allow nothing else."

Azar's blood pounded in his head. "I have been with many women…with all due respect, and never had that happen," Azar argued, as much against himself as Theron.

Theron was on his feet. "Do you dare to compare my daughter with a horde of pirate wenches?"

Azar, no physical slouch himself, met him eye to eye across the table. "I said no such thing, Theron. And if you think for one moment that I dishonored Theryssa in word or deed, then you will meet such wrath as you have never known."

"Both of you, that's enough!" Nyssa was standing, too, holding them back, one palm on each of their chests. "You are both acting like boys in a schoolyard."

Theron's breathing slowed and gradually his face resumed a less predatory expression. Azar extended his hand. "Forgive me...old friend."*

This sudden act of mercy surprised Azar as much as it did Theron. Truly, Azar would not have been capable of this a day ago. Something about Theryssa, her warm beauty, the hope she held in her arms was making him see the world differently.

"Theron," Nyssa prompted, her voice possessing more than a little authority, "take the man's hand."

Theron's handshake was firm, bordering on painful.

"Now, Theron," Nyssa instructed, "I want you to stop playing the warrior for a few minutes and tell Azar what you really feel."

Theron looked as though he would rather slit open a Narthian bug and eat its insides raw. "It was my idea," he confessed. "I thought that you were...right for my daughter. Our daughter. You're the only man, after all these years..."

Azar came around the table to embrace him. "We are brothers," he whispered, "we owe each other our lives."

And yet Azar could not marry Theryssa. All the more so for how much he loved and respected Theron, and now Nyssa.

"Theron, listen to me. We can settle everything between us. If you can forgive me for leaving the Guardians. If you can understand that I could not accept the death of Solania. If you will recognize my subsequent actions had to do with Council policy."

"I do. Things in those days were...not so clear. Malthusalus was a dire threat. He nearly killed Nyssa."

"I know, Theron, and I understand why you stayed a Guardian. And why you are one today. And why you kill pirates like me. We are outsiders, threats to your way of life. Which is why you must take Theryssa away from me. Forever."

"Is that what you really want?" Nyssa asked. "If this is about Council policy, you should know things are changing. Theryssa is only the beginning. We now see there is wisdom in letting people have more choices. We are actively seeking to vary the possibilities of humanity."

"The future is wide open," said Theron, "but we need good men like you to help us."

Azar's heart was aching. He did not want to abandon the human race, even more, he could not imagine never seeing or holding Theryssa again, never seeing what new adventure another hour with her might hold. And yet, he could not take the next step. "It's what's best for me personally," he insisted.

"Damn you, man," thundered Theron, "she opened herself to you. The transponder readings show passion deeper than anything ever seen on a woman, next to her mother."

"I'm sorry Theron, but you can't just manipulate people's hearts. We aren't pawns to be played with. That's the problem I had with the Council's way of doing things in the first place and now I wonder if you're really capable of change at all."

Theron's goodwill was threatening to go up in flames. It was typical of the men's relationship. Love and hate. "And your problem is an inability to accept authority," he pointed out accusingly.

"I have one authority, Theron, and that is my own conscience," Azar declared. "And I will thank you not to raise your voice. In case you haven't noticed, we are out of your jurisdiction."

"Well, it's going to be Narthian jurisdiction if you don't stop being so blasted selfish and start cooperating with your fellow human beings," Theron exclaimed.

"What are you talking about?" Azar demanded. "There are no Narthians within a dozen systems. They won't be back for generations."

Theron threw up his hands. "You see," he said to Nyssa, "the man knows everything. Far be it from us to try to enlighten him."

"Honey, you need to calm down," said Nyssa. "This is getting us nowhere. And Azar, you need to hear what Theron has to say. Just because the Narthians are not on our doorstep does not mean they aren't a threat. We have intelligence, credible information, that they are growing new nests. A super strong variety which we've faced only once before. And it didn't go well. If not for the bravery of my sister's husband Raylar, we would have lost an entire company. We had hoped that was an isolated strain, but we are seeing birth nest heat traces all along the rim area."

Azar turned to Theron, the wind momentarily taken from his sails.

"We give them six months, a year tops, before they hit us straight across the galaxy arm. From the Centon System all the way to Devalos," Theron elaborated. "In the meantime we have to build a larger fighting force."

"A fighting force of Guardians," Nyssa said. "And pirates."

"Pirates...under my command, I assume?" Azar guessed the rest of their plan.

"Yes," said Nyssa.

"And you want it kept in the family," said Azar to Theron. "You want me as your son-in-law before you will go back into battle with me. Is that the real reason I'm supposed to marry Theryssa?"

"Of course not," Theron snapped. "I already told you why I chose you. It's a matter of your character. At least the character I thought you had."

Azar laughed without humor. "You pick the strangest ways to flatter a man, Theron. With that approach, I wish you luck giving Theryssa away."

"Don't you take that tone with me, Azar. You will marry her, and that is final!"

Azar was about to retort when he was preempted by a new voice. Very female and very angry.

"What the hell is going on?" demanded the tousle-haired, freshly escaped Theryssa, her body deliciously clad in one of Azar's tunics. "Mom, Dad, what are you doing here?"

Nyssa ran to embrace her daughter, who was not very interested in a hug. "We came to check on you, baby."

"Like hell you did. I could hear you in the corridor. You're in here planning my life. Dad, you're trying to make me marry *Azar*?"

"This isn't the time to talk about this, Theryssa."

"What do you mean it isn't the time? When would be a good time? During the mating ceremony?"

"You know I don't like it when you raise your voice," said Theron.

"And I don't like it when you try to make me marry a man against my will."

"You're being melodramatic, Theryssa—"

"I'm being *what*? Dad, have you lost your mind? I feel like I have woken up in some bizarre nightmare, except it's my real life."

"Sweetie, it's not as bad as it seems," Nyssa attempted to calm her down.

"It's not? By all means, Mom, enlighten me. I'm all ears." Theryssa thrust her arms in the air, employing the very same gesture Theron had a few moments ago.

"We wanted you to get to know Azar," explained Theron, "and this seemed the most logical way."

She whirled on her father. "By sending me halfway across the galaxy to spy on him while posing as a courier? You couldn't have introduced us at a dinner party? 'Theryssa, this is our sworn enemy I've been trying to kill for twenty years. I hope you two will be very happy.' That has a real ring to it, doesn't it?"

"You are being sarcastic, young lady," her father disapproved. "But you are owed an explanation, nonetheless. There are things in my history that I've not been able to reveal up to this point, Theryssa. Azar and I were once allies. He was a Guardian too, a few years younger than me, not that it mattered. Much happened between us. He saved my life, and I returned the favor. We were as close as men can be. But then political circumstances intervened. An unfortunate...situation with a woman. We parted ways. Each of us acted in good faith, but there was nothing we could do to prevent our becoming adversaries. That was a very long time ago. Circumstances have changed and we must reunite to fight the Narthians. This new alliance allows me to renew my relationship with Azar and to express my long-standing hope that the two of you might somehow be mated. I always thought he would be the best man for you, Theryssa, and now there is nothing standing in the way."

Theryssa turned to Azar, a mixture of emotions on her face. "Azar...this is true? You served with my father?"

"We were comrades," Azar confirmed. "Your father was the finest soldier I ever served with, though he had a tendency to ignore orders. It was a habit that nearly cost his life on more than one occasion."

"I ignored orders?" Theron defended himself. "What about that little stunt of yours on Teranium?"

"How else was I supposed to save your miserable neck?"

Theron shook his head. "You see what I had to deal with," he said to Nyssa.

Azar smiled thinly. "We muddled through, somehow, didn't we? It's a wonder either of us made it."

Theryssa's eyes narrowed. "So you knew all about this?" she asked Azar. "You were in on my father's scheme?"

Azar shook his head. "I had no idea, Theryssa. I did not know who you were. Your parent's arrival here is as big a shock to me as it is to you."

There was so much more he wanted to say to her. But he couldn't form the thoughts clearly in his head. There were too many questions. For one thing, he had yet to figure out how she had managed to escape.

That metal in her cuffs was strong enough to hold a full-grown Mongro beast.

"Oh, I doubt that," Theryssa countered. "Shocked doesn't even begin to cover what I'm feeling."

"Baby, I'm so sorry." Nyssa stroked her hair. "You know the last thing in the world we would ever do is hurt you. We wanted you to be happy, that's all."

Theryssa shook her head. She looked at a total loss. He would give anything to be able to hold her in his arms right now.

"Mom...I know you mean well...but, damn, you guys are just...you're just not normal."

"You'll think about it," Theron predicted. "It will all make sense soon enough. To both of you."

"Dad, I'm sorry, but you can't just snap your fingers and make it all fall into place. I know you see it in your head, and you love me, but life just isn't like one of your strategy games."

"You liked my games just fine when you were younger. You even beat me once or twice."

Azar could picture the two of them, intently concentrating, on opposite sides of a holoscreen. He would give anything to have known her then, to have watched her grow up. Every second of her life was so very precious, just as was everything about her now. Just seeing her parents made him feel more alive, more a part of her. If only this could have happened differently. If only it were not about to come to an end. Abrupt and bitter.

"Theron," Azar interjected, making a valiant effort at defending the woman who had worn his chains and turned his world on its ear in a matter of hours, "Theryssa is right. Emotions cannot be manipulated. Nor can loyalties be manufactured. I cannot, in good conscience, join my forces with yours. Should the Narthians come, I will meet them as best I am able, fighting to my last breath. I do appreciate the offer, but I think it is best we part ways. As friends."

Theron's face showed no emotion. "Very well," he said stiffly. "Nyssa, Theryssa. We are leaving."

"I will see to it the three of you are escorted safely back to your ship," said Azar.

"You've been very kind," Nyssa said. "And we wish you the best."

Azar gave a small bow. Let this be done quickly, he prayed, while I still have the strength to let her go.

"Wait just a minute," demanded Theryssa. "I'm not just a suitcase here. No one is telling me to go anywhere."

Blast it. She was asserting that firebrand will of hers. He should have known she wouldn't be pushed around.

"Theryssa, you can't stay," said Theron curtly.

She gave it right back to him. "It's not your ship, Dad. You can't tell me to leave it."

"Theryssa, please don't talk to your father that way," Nyssa said.

Azar felt for Nyssa. He had a feeling the woman was used to running interference like this.

"This is what I get," Theron complained to his wife, "for loving my daughter."

"You have strange ways of showing it," said Theryssa.

"Theryssa, please..." Nyssa's voice sounded strained for the first time.

The sound of it touched off something in Azar. "Theryssa, your mother's right. This isn't doing you any good."

Theryssa's displeasure shifted with a vengeance. Azar might as well have had a magnet on his head. "Excuse me," she blasted him, "am I wrong, or is this none of your fucking business? Because I thought you made it pretty clear I don't mean a fucking thing to you."

"Theryssa, I never said that."

"No," she agreed, "you didn't say anything. Not even goodbye."

"Theron," said Nyssa, "I think we need to give them some time alone."

Theryssa wasted no time gainsaying that idea. "Over my dead body Mom. I have nothing to say to this...this man."

"Theryssa, I think your mother is right. I would like a chance to talk."

"Well I wouldn't, Azar," she shot him down. "And seeing as how you don't fucking own me, I guess you're out of luck."

"Theryssa, don't be unreasonable."

"I'll be whatever I want to be."

Azar clenched his fists. His every inclination was to seize her in his arms, to settle this matter sexually, resolving the tension in the only way he knew...by pinning her body down, hot and hard.

If only her parents weren't here.

"Theryssa, we really need to talk..." His voice had more punch this time. Not strident, but...potent.

Theryssa scowled, but offered no immediate reply. Was Azar imagining things or was she conflicted...a part of her wanting to be with him as much as he wanted to be with her?

Nyssa seized the opportunity for a graceful exit. "Azar, I think it would be best for Theron and me to go. If someone could take us back to the hangar bay?"

"I'll send for my best men to escort you," assured Azar.

"Mom, you're not going anywhere without me," Theryssa insisted, in a sudden about-face.

"You just said you weren't coming with us," Theron reminded, slight exasperation in his voice.

"Stop arguing with me, Dad. I'll just take my own ship, then."

"Are you sure?" asked Nyssa.

"Yes!"

"Theryssa," said her father. "Do not raise your voice to your mother."

"I am sorry," she said.

"It's all right, darling." Nyssa smiled. "We just want to be sure you're going to be okay. It's been so much already for you."

"I'm okay." She forced a smile. "Really."

"We will meet you back home, then," Nyssa kissed her daughter's forehead. "We love you very much."

Theron turned to Azar. "Do I have your permission to dispatch a military patrol to the area? To escort Theryssa back to Earth in her own ship?"

Azar nodded. "Of course. I insist upon it."

"I don't need babysitters," Theryssa snapped at both men.

"Why not?" Theron showed his thinning patience. "You're acting childish enough."

Nyssa touched his arm, silencing him.

Azar pressed the intercom button on the wall. "Squad One to the war room. On the double," he summoned the escorts.

"That won't be necessary. We will go on our own," said Theron, straightening himself to his full, proud height. "Theryssa, you may kiss me goodbye."

Theryssa had a most delicious look of defiance on her face, but she went to her father nonetheless.

"Someday you will understand," Theron whispered, hugging his daughter tightly.

Theryssa hugged her mother, too. This was followed by embraces by both of them with Azar. A moment later, the pair left.

His pulse quickened as the servo door slid shut, closing them in the gray, metal room. They were alone at last.

"I have nothing to say," Theryssa announced. "And I really have no intention of listening, either. So how about we make it easy on ourselves? You leave me alone and as soon as my folks are gone, I will head off on my own."

He shook his head. "I'm sorry, Theryssa, but we have unfinished business."

She glared. "What business?"

"There was the matter of your punishment," he reminded. "Which must now be compounded as a result of your attempted escape."

"You can't be serious? Not after what's happened."

"I've never been more serious in my life."

Her jaw gaped slightly, ovaling her pretty lips. "But…I'm not your prisoner," she reminded. "I never was. You heard what my parents said. This was all a trap. A bizarre matchmaking ploy."

"I am not interested in the motives of your parents, Theryssa. You came here of your own accord and you subsequently submitted to me. You cannot renege now. You are a grown woman, responsible for your own actions."

She took a step backward. "My father will destroy you if you harm a hair on my head."

"I do not intend to harm you, little one. Only punish you."

"Don't call me that!"

"You're wearing my tunic," Azar pointed out. "I would like it back."

Her eyes flashed. "I'm naked underneath, Azar."

"That's a good way for a slave to be."

"I'm not a slave," she insisted.

"Aren't you?"

Theryssa backed up again, then ran from the room as soon as her ass impacted the heavy metal table, the one used for planning battles. In short order, it would be used for a conquest of a different kind.

"If you touch me, I'll fight," she vowed.

"You can. But you will lose."

"Maybe, but I will take the fun out of your victory."

"Oh, I think it will be quite enjoyable for both of us." He smiled.

She tried to dart past as he approached, but he was too quick. Grabbing her arm, he pinned her between the table and his rock-hard torso.

Her breathing was hard. Her chest rose and fell furiously, her breasts pressed to his pectorals. "I'm warning you," she hissed. "Get the fuck off me."

"Not until I've straightened a few things out."

Like his cock, which was pointed directly at the apex of her thighs. Theryssa grunted, more out of desperation than actual power. Her attempted knee to his groin was easily anticipated and fended off with a turn of his hip.

"That's a bad girl, Theryssa." Azar did a little jackknifing of his own, managing to wedge her legs apart.

"I'm not...a girl..." she pushed at him in vain. "I'm a...woman...a pissed-off woman."

Azar savored the scent of her sex, freshly released into the air. "You're aroused."

"I hate you, Azar," she spat.

Azar ripped open the front of the shirt, baring her heaving breasts. "You don't hate me," he palmed her left breast, clutching it in his hand, "you hate how much you need this."

"You're hurting me," she said.

Her flesh felt so good in his hand, so alive, so captive. "Then tell me to stop."

He was taking the risk of losing her, but it had to be done. He had no interest in forcing her, really.

Theryssa clenched her teeth in rage, but she couldn't get the words out. She was as hooked on this as he.

"That's what I thought," he declared in triumph. "You don't want me to stop. You know what I'm going to do to you, Theryssa? As punishment for trying to escape?"

She shook her head, trying to look away from him, over his shoulder, anywhere she could find relief from his unflinching stare. "No, and I don't care."

"Oh, but I think you do care." He massaged her breast, applying just enough pressure. "I think you care a great deal."

Theryssa arched her back, moaning. "N-no." In spite of her protests, however, she was giving him better access to the swollen globe.

Azar smiled wickedly. He knew damn well she was in too deep, but he gave her another out. One more, just in case. "If you want me to stop, tell me now. You can go home with your parents. Just say the word."

Her head was back, her eyes closed. She sucked in her lip...saying nothing.

"Very well." Azar leaned forward now, whispering in her ear what her punishment would be.

Theryssa gasped. "No, I can't. I've never—"

"Of course you can." Azar took her nipple between his teeth, bending his head low to get it. Employing a subtle but devastating mix of suckling and biting, he brought her to a state of near hysteria.

Her body was writhing, slithering in place like a snake straight out of Eden. The nipple was beet red, hard and supple when he finally released it.

She whimpered, abandoned. "Please...don't stop."

"But I thought you didn't like where things were going?" he reminded her. "You just rejected your punishment, remember?"

"Azar, you're tormenting me," she sighed, her breath coming in broken stabs. "Don't do this."

"Tell me, then. Tell me you are prepared to accept what I am choosing for you."

"Not...not that. Anything else."

Azar repeated the treatment on her other nipple. He could feel the energy surging through her body. She was close to coming, just from the pleasure of his mouth on her breast and his knee on her vulva.

"Tell me." He surrendered the second nipple to the open air.

Theryssa was writhing. "I...accept."

"Accept what? Speak the words."

"Your cock...in my ass." She mouthed the sentence hotly from dry lips.

Azar gave her breasts a mild slap, enough to jolt her senses and fill her with even more unanswerable pleasure. "Is that how you ask for something, Theryssa? From your Master?"

"No, it's not..." Her teeth chattered. Her forehead was drenched with sweat.

So much pleasure in her bittersweet expression, her curling lips. So much scandal, too. For she was once again enjoying and wanting things that good young women of Earth, good Guardian's daughters, were not supposed to want.

"You're stalling, Theryssa." He readied himself to slap her again.

She tried to cover her breasts instinctively, but he spoke a command, harshly, firmly. "Arms down."

She dropped her hands to her sides. His cock swelled in response to her act of lightning fast obedience. His desire to be gentle with her overcame his desire to be firm. Instead of slapping, he offered a caress, as soft as it was insolent, to her left nipple.

Azar could feel her sex liquid soaking through his trousers on his thigh where he was holding her legs open.

He thought she would melt from the act of submission…being made to endure his touches like this, having no ability to protect herself.

"I need your discipline," she cried. "Oh, god, I can't help it. I need to be fucked by you, hard and strong…in my ass."

Azar laid his palm on her cheek. Hot and pink. "Do you know why it will be punishment for you to submit anally?" he inquired.

"Because of the degradation?" She licked her lips. He could feel her sinking into a trance, readying herself.

He stroked her forehead, brushing away strands of her long, silky, damp hair. It was time to bring her deeper still. "No, Theryssa," he countered. "As my slave, you can't be degraded. Shamed, yes, but I define that differently — as part of the power dynamics between us, the thrill we share when I push you beyond yourself. Care to guess again?"

"No." Her voice was a ghostly whisper, erotic and curling up toward the bulkhead ceiling of the room.

"It's a punishment to sink my cock deep into your ass, because your pussy will be deprived in the process. You will endure the feelings of invasion without the normal stimulation. And you will know, too, that this is happening by my will. Because I am displeased by your behavior."

"I don't have to please you," she squirmed.

"But it arouses you to talk about it. To think about it."

"I don't want to think!"

"Very well." Azar spun her by the hips, facing her away from him. "Down," he ordered. "Palms and breasts on the table top."

She shivered as her sensitive nipples touched the cold metal.

"Open," he slapped her ass, compelling her to widen her stance.

Theryssa treated him to a most delicious view of her pink labia, thick and moist. No doubt, she would dearly love to come, but at the moment, he had only one use for her dripping opening.

Namely as a source of lubrication for the tinier one.

"You're a beautiful woman," he pinched her perfect ass cheek cruelly. "A man could easily be overcome by you. Which is all the more reason to keep you on a short leash."

Theryssa jerked, though not entirely in pain. Azar tore at the opening to his breeches. He could not get his cock out fast enough.

"You don't have me on any kind of leash," she defied. "You don't have me at all."

"You will only worsen your punishment, little one, by backtalking me."

"Fuck you, you bastard."

She tried to rise, he kept her in place, a firm hand on her back, fingers splayed. "Rub your nipples on the table," he ordered, thankful that Theron had promised to deactivate the monitor for the retinal scanner in her eye, hoping that he had, "my horny little spy."

Before she could think of arguing, he went to work on her clitoris. As usual he was able to get her body to betray both her will and her pride.

"I...hate you," she moaned as he plucked at the center of her desire, arousing but not satisfying, touching in such a way as to leave her hungrier with each passing second.

"I am waiting." He focused her on his command.

Theryssa submitted, sliding her breasts, slippery with sweat, over the table. Just a few inches up and back and she was out of her mind. The smooth hardness, imposed as it was on soft flesh...

"Azar," she gritted her teeth, "I can't take much more."

"You're a Guardian. Strong and quick enough to get out of my chains," he pointed out.

"Damn you, I'm female, too."

"When it's convenient."

"This is hardly convenient!"

"It is for me," he mused. "Tell me, what would make it better? How about if we go straight to here."

"Here" was her pussy, which opened like butter to his fingers.

"Oh, stars, Azar," she groaned. "Do it, fuck me, put me out of my misery."

"But we have to tend to discipline, don't we?"

He had her right where he wanted.

"Yes," she replied miserably.

"Tell me your punishment."

"You know what it is, Azar...you came up with it."

"Tell me anyway."

"Anal...intercourse."

"My cock inside your ass," he restated the matter in plain terms. "Using you at will." She gasped as his finger gathered moisture from her pussy. "A little lubrication," he explained, applying the liquid to the tiny opening. "You would do well to relax, Theryssa."

She curled her toes. "Azar, I'm not sure it will fit."

"There's no need to be nervous," he soothed. "This is erotic punishment. This is the pain of psychological submission...knowing Master can have you as he wishes."

"Yes," she picked up on his words, "I'm your slave. You can take me...even in the ass."

"Whose ass?"

"Your ass," she cried. "You can fuck your slave in the ass because it's yours."

He continued to prepare her, making her hole wetter and wetter. "My Theryssa." He stroked her pussy.

"Oh, god," she responded to his presence, his words. "Oh fuck."

Had it been less than a day since he had first called her his? How much more meaning it carried now, knowing as he did the connection to her father, the one true friend he had ever had in his life.

"Azar, wait, tell me something first."

"What is it?"

"My father mentioned a woman...is she the one you once loved?"

"What did I tell you about asking questions?"

"I want to know. I deserve it."

"You're a slave being punished. Concentrate on that."

"Do you still love her?" she persisted.

His cock was at the puckered entrance. The head of it was slick and moist. "That was another life."

She groaned as he slid his cock inward an inch or so. "It's not fair." She shook her head.

"What isn't fair?" He took another inch, making her breathe faster still.

"Any of this…how we met…how we are now…we didn't have a chance to…"

"A chance to what?" he pressed. "Fall in love? It doesn't matter how people meet. It either happens or it doesn't."

"I know nothing about you…"

"You know what matters." His cock enjoyed the raw tightness. A place no man had been before. Virgin Theryssa. Unknown, and yet surprisingly familiar. Pulsing and spunky…deliciously, yieldingly defiant.

"So full," she sighed. "So…different."

"It's another kind of closeness," he said, using his primale powers to regulate the size of his cock, allowing careful, but satisfying penetration, farther, farther. "I have wanted this since I saw you. Wanted to possess you this way."

"And I…wanted to be yours. Though I wouldn't admit it. Azar, I looked at your holos."

"Did you?" The idea made him smile. "Tell me more."

She sighed, pushing her ass back. He moved in farther, then retracted. It was time to fuck her for real.

"They drove me crazy…I masturbated."

"You wicked little girl," he teased.

Azar plunged himself back in, widening her a little more. He was tuned in to every subtle motion in her body, being careful to push her only to the limits of ecstasy and not beyond.

"I had to put up a blocker against you."

"I had the same reaction," he admitted, "when I saw you in your little uniform, flame of black hair, bright-eyed, putting on that little damsel routine."

"Pretty bad acting."

"Charming, though."

"Oh, Azar…come inside me, will you? Come in my ass? Show me I'm your girl. Show me why it is I shouldn't want to escape."

"If you insist," he said. "But I warn you, the journey is deep."

"Deeper than your cock can go?"

"Yes," he replied. "Much."

Chapter Eight

ഔ

Theryssa should have her head examined.

Captured…naked and penetrated, ass full of cock, her pussy craving attention, dripping for it, her breasts squashed, helpless already…and she just asked for more?

"Use your tongue," he said. "On the top of the table."

"My…tongue?" Theryssa stiffened. Like the rest of this or any space ship, it was a clean, hygienic surface, but it was the symbolism more than anything. The idea of giving in to him, of behaving…like some kind of pet.

"Yes, lick it. And give in to the sensations. That is how you will feel your slavery to me. Your powerlessness to resist your own pleasure."

Tentatively, she opened her mouth. With her head sideways, she had to apply the side of her tongue. She did so, quickly retracting it. The taste was metallic, and deliciously wicked.

Azar told her to do it again, more lingeringly. Whimpering, Theryssa moved her head into position, just grazing the shiny metal surface with her pink tongue.

"Yes, Theryssa." His voice was a hypnotic rasp. "See how obedient you can be? See what a good little slave you are?"

Yes…Theryssa could see the point now. Hungrily, she lapped at the metal, again and again. Cold and hard, completely unyielding. She felt weak all over, her ass and pussy open and totally vulnerable in comparison. He could take her now, she was ready.

"Theryssa," he sighed in approval.

"Yes, Azar." She said his name as a plea, an encouragement, an utterance of awe, all wrapped up together.

"Theryssa," he said her name once more, sending spasms of joy through her body, "you are so incredible."

"But you don't know me," she reminded.

"I know what matters," he said, using the same words he'd used for himself.

The passion in his voice made her untouched pussy burn. "I want to take more of you. Make your cock bigger. I know you can. You're primale."

"It's your first time," he cautioned.

"I don't give a fuck," she defied. Adding, in afterthought, "I mean I don't give a fuck, Master. I'm three quarters primale—primefemale. I can take it."

Azar growled. "Tell me again why I let you stay?"

"You didn't. I'm here of my own volition. Oh, god, Azar, you're a perfect fit. Give me it all, I want it all."

He swelled his cock—thicker, longer, harder. "No woman has ever been able to bear this much."

"I'm not just any woman."

He reared back and slammed himself deep. "You talk too much...still."

"You love it and you know it."

"Only when it's what I want to hear...slave."

"You'd be bored to tears if I did that...Master."

She could swear that this marvelous, hard, veined cock of his was made for her and her alone. Theryssa thought of that cock being elsewhere. She thought of its history, even as she sought to take it deeper, inviting it inward to her center. She decided she didn't care for its history, for all the places it had been. And she did not care for its future.

At least if that future meant being inside any other female but her.

"Galaxy forbid boredom. Speaking of which, how is that pussy of mine?" Her pussy spasmed in response to his words of possession. "I'm burning up," she confessed.

Azar shifted positions somehow, putting a little pressure on her pelvis. She groaned, feeling suddenly better. And worse. She had no choice now but to move, rocking her hips from side to side.

It was her clitoris. He was using the edge of the table, the cold beveled metal for leverage. No direct contact, but something indirect, and therefore more teasing.

"Azar, tell me what it looks like," she said impulsively.

Azar laughed. She tensed just a little, knowing him well enough that he was about to shift once more, from doting lover, to his pirate persona.

"It looks like my little slave," he said, right on cue. "Bent over, submitting…taking her Master's cock."

The provocative words coursed through her, snapping at her sensibilities like a whip. "Yes," she hissed. "Master's cock in my ass."

"You attempted to escape me," he reminded her, pounding without mercy. "You were a bad girl."

"Yes…Master."

"There's no escape now, is there?" Another push and then another, until she felt she would split wide open, into pieces of herself—exploding, sizzling, lust-fried pieces.

"No…"

"I left you chained in my bed, Theryssa. That's where you belonged until I released you."

"Yes, Master."

"Take it, Theryssa. Take your punishment." Another push, decisive and domineering.

"Oh, god…oh, Master…it's so…tight."

"You're the most beautiful, captivating woman I've ever known, Theryssa. Every time I look at you, touch you, it's like I plunge into some unknown universe, one where I will never find the bottom, and yet I can't live without a second of the journey. You know what it does to me, to think of you…apart from me?"

"Oh, Azar," she cried, "what you do to me. I knew there was more to you, I saw in your eyes your history, your pain, the first time I beheld you."

"I want you chained, Theryssa." He pulled back, nearly to the tip. And then he descended again, reclaiming all the territory he'd won. And more. "I want you naked. In a collar. I want you in my bed. Begging. Dripping and open — helpless."

"I am helpless," she said. "You have me. I'm here…I'm yours. I shouldn't want it like this, but I do. I can't help it. I'm supposed to be a Guardian."

"You are," he insisted. "One of the bravest I've ever known. Coming here like you did…"

"You made it possible. You gave me courage, even though you were supposed to be my enemy."

"Mmm…" He grunted. "I'm going to come so fucking hard. I'm going to give you as much primale seed as I can muster."

"God, yes. Shoot it inside me. All the way, hot and thick." she acknowledged the genetic ability of all primales to control the amount and even the heat of their emissions.

"There's one thing more I want first, though. I want to hear you tell me…that you need to come."

Her insides twisted in reply. She squirmed, wanting to touch herself, him, everywhere at once. Sweat covered her, her nipples were on fire, her belly burned. It was agony. "Yes, Azar, I need to come. More than I've needed anything in my life."

"I know you do. But you can't, can you?"

"Not…without permission."

"Your body is mine," he affirmed. "It obeys my commands." And yet there was so much more. He sensed it. A spirit that would forever beg to play, to fight, to surrender and rise again. "In your eyes, I saw the burning fire. The unquenchable need. The wildness."

"Yes, Azar. You know me, like no one. I think you've always known me. Take me Azar. Oh, stars, tame me."

His fingers clenched in her hair, holding it tightly. Symbolically. Satisfyingly. "Surrender…"

His command opened her still further and he immediately exploited the opportunity—penetrating, expanding, until she could feel him, almost as if he were in her pussy, after all.

"Fuck…fuck me, Azar…Master…lover."

Azar's pace quickened. It was like magic. She couldn't explain how he was generating such speed, how she wasn't splitting asunder under the man's powerful assault. No doubt her own primale genetics helped, but her will must have had something to do with it.

"Almost…there," he said, his voice low and ragged.

She could feel the heat. Primale heat. So much blood pounding in his cock. So much pent-up energy. "Mmmmaster…"

One final thrust, in slow motion, the downward descent like the tripping of a trigger, the hammer slamming on metal, sparking old-fashioned gun powder.

The first spurt of Azar's semen shot deep into her anal canal, satisfying, rich and tantalizing. It was followed immediately by a second. And a third.

How many would it be in all? It was pretty much up to Azar, being that he was primale. And a fantastically virile primale at that.

"Oh, god, Theryssa, oh my fucking god." He was surging with power, his muscles driving him onward and forward.

"Give it to me," she turned from abject slave to demanding female. "Give it all to me."

Azar shot several more times and then pulled himself out. He wasn't done, though. Not quite yet. "I'm going to come on your ass," he said, breathing heavily.

He pushed a finger down on her clitoris.

"Please," she writhed, "may I...come?"

"Yes," he said fiercely, his warm thick jets already landing on her ass and back. "Do it. Come for me. Come now."

Theryssa did not need to be asked twice. The dam, held back by Azar's will, burst with a singular spectacular rush. She was twisting her torso, reaching around to find him. He took her hand in one of his, squeezing tightly. The semen sprayed wildly as he let go of his cock, concentrating on her finale.

He placed his finger—gently, firmly, decisively, lovingly—on her swollen, eager, overripe clitoris, urging, inviting, *commanding* her to give in to the deep rhythms of her body. Oh, how he knew her anatomy, how to set off the trip wire, releasing pulse after pulse. Theryssa felt the energy—microshocks through her entire system—even as the main eruption occurred in the vicinity of her pussy. Over and over she said his name as both of them completed their bliss.

At last, there was nothing of her left. Expended, she felt herself collapsing, fainting. But with a smile on her face.

Azar didn't let her slide down but scooped her into his arms. Immediately, she cuddled against the warmth and solidity of his chest. Superwoman though she might be, there was nothing like this feeling of being cradled, knowing that her weight was as light as a feather to this man.

"Azar...thank you."

"You'll thank me more later." He grinned mischievously. "Assuming you survive the flogging."

He was headed straight for the door, both of them sans clothes.

"Azar," she clung to him, "we can't go out there like this."

"Why not?"

"We're both nude!"

"It's my ship," he growled, "I'll go about it as I wish."

Theryssa made an appeal to his possessive nature. "You really want them seeing *me* naked?"

Azar frowned, considering the matter. "Good point." Setting her down on the edge of the table for a moment, he went to retrieve his tunic, the one he had been wearing, which was not torn. "We'll cover you up with this."

It was Theryssa's turn to grin. "I like that you don't want to share me...not even visually. I guess that means you won't be passing me around like a rum bottle the way you threatened, huh?"

"I wouldn't get too smug, woman. You may find yourself wishing I *would* share you."

"So I'm a woman, finally," she noted the change in nomenclature.

"It wasn't meant as a compliment...slave girl."

Theryssa couldn't help but laugh. How bizarre was that? And yet it made sense, given the special, magical bond between them. Like a dance, where each knew the limits of what was serious and what was play, each delivering precisely what the other needed.

"Of course not...Master."

Azar laced up his shirt, covering her nakedness. This time he put her over his shoulder, like a rolled rug, facedown, backwards.

"Azar," she screeched, "what are you doing?"

He slapped her conveniently placed behind, covered by the tunic which was long enough on her to be a dress. "I am taking you back to my cabin. To find the chains you managed to shed. I assure you that you will not shed them again."

"But people will see me!"

"You're not naked, Theryssa, I thought that was your chief complaint."

She sought to grab hold of the doorway as they walked out. "No, I won't be shamed like this."

"Let go." He stung her ass with a considerably harder spank.

She did so, her cheeks flushed, her pussy freshly moistened. "You are impossible," she declared. "Do you know that?"

"What is so incredible about a pirate carrying booty?"

"I'm not booty." She kicked.

"Keep struggling, little one, and you will be naked again. On a leash, dragged behind me."

Theryssa settled down.

Damn it, she was horny all over again. With his every jostling step, her insides only got more scrambled, more ready for more fucking. The elevator ride was even worse.

"Azar? I could go down on you," she tempted him.

"You can wait a little longer," he rubbed her upturned bottom.

Theryssa sighed in frustration. "No, I can't."

At last they got off the elevator. They were nearly home free.

Famous last words...

"Oleron." Azar acknowledged the man waiting for him outside his cabin door.

Theryssa held her breath. He was the last man they needed to be running into. To make things worse, she could see nothing, positioned as she was.

"Captain," replied the baldheaded pirate Theryssa hated on account of the threat he posed to Azar, "I was looking for you."

Azar's voice held little warmth. "You have something to report, Oleron?"

Theryssa could feel Azar's body on alert. Subtle, but very real.

"Yes. The Earth ship has left. With our two visitors." Oleron cleared his throat, probably in recognition of Azar's current state of nudity. "Am I to assume you will be keeping this one?"

"You are to assume nothing, Oleron."

"I never do, Captain. I prefer to gain my own experience. Take your new wench, for example. I would like to experience her. I assume she's a good lay? Judging by all the time you've spent with her."

"You will not talk about her that way, Oleron."

Oleron laughed under his breath, a kind of dark chuckle.

"I fail to see anything funny."

"I just never thought I would see the day, that's all," Oleron declared, "when the great Captain Azar would get himself wrapped around the finger of a common slut."

Azar tensed. It was a primale stance. Usually one that precipitated attack. Theryssa felt a complex wave of emotions. Part of her wanted to fight for herself, but another was flattered, even a bit overwhelmed that Azar would defend her honor this way.

"You will not speak of the woman in such terms, Oleron," Azar dictated. "In fact, you will not speak of her at all."

"He better not," Theryssa piped up. "Or he will find his words shoved right back down his throat. Along with my fist."

Azar smacked Theryssa's ass. "Silence, woman."

Theryssa drew a deep breath. She had been disciplined...in front of another man. Biting her lip, she held back a retort. Much as she might want to fight back, all she could think of was what Azar would do to her when they got inside his cabin.

Wicked, sexual things. Things she feared. Things she craved.

Oleron laughed again. "I see you've begun training her."

"She obeys me," said Azar, "and no one else."

Theryssa could kiss him. And kneel to him. And punch him, too.

It was complicated, this submission thing, this...

Theryssa stopped short. She had almost said this love thing.

How messed up was that? she mused. After all the men who had wined and dined her, making spectacular offers, this was the one sweeping her off her feet, literally. And he was doing so by ravishing her step by step, putting her into a place of complete sexual slavery.

She was supposed to be dominant, the daughter of Theron. So why did she want nothing more in the world right now than to be brought inside Azar's quarters, tossed down on the bed and told to strip in anticipation of his will? His chains. His cock. His punishing hand. His flogger.

"She'll obey me, too," Oleron defied. "Once I've taught her the meaning of fear."

"This woman will never fear you," Azar vowed. "Nor will any other."

"What is that supposed to mean?"

"It means that I must now attend to something I should have a long time ago." He set Theryssa down on bare feet. "Go in my cabin," he commanded her. "Clean yourself in the sanitizing chamber. Then choose one of the floggers from the wall. Place it between your teeth and wait for me on the bed, on your hands and knees."

She glanced quickly at Oleron, who was sneering. Her breathing was quick. Strangely, she did not feel degraded. It was just as Azar had predicted. She felt the definite sense of submission to her man, but in front of this other, she felt only pride.

There was no dishonor in serving the pleasure of the right man. She saw that now. For a man like Azar would honor her pleasure, too.

"Yes," she replied, catching Oleron's expression out of the corner of her eye, "Master."

Azar pressed the button to his cabin door, allowing Theryssa to go inside. "And now for you," he said to Oleron.

Oleron drew his sword. "I don't want to have to kill you where you stand, Azar. But I will."

"Be careful," she raised herself to tip toes to kiss his cheek. "Please?"

He smiled at her, giving a slight wink. Theryssa did not know what chance he was taking, really. Was Oleron a primale, too? He didn't seem to be, but he might contain some superior genetic material. And what about the other pirates who seemed to be allied to him?

As the door slid closed, Theryssa heard the sound of a man screaming. A second later, she heard the sword fall to the floor. The suspense was too much. She had to know. Desperately, she pushed the button. Let Azar be upset with her, she just wanted to know if he was all right.

Oh, stars, if he'd been hurt or killed, she would never forgive herself. In a single instant, she came face to face with the most terrifying reality of her life. She was in love. With Azar Xenelion, King of Pirates. Against all odds, in a matter of mere hours, it had happened.

Was it just power of suggestion, the influence of her very persuasive parents? She might have dismissed it as such, were her heart not stopped at this very moment, its further beating hinged completely on Azar's existence.

The servo door whirred open. She held her breath. Oleron lay dead on the floor, a single stab wound through his heart, his sword beside him, broken into two pieces.

But where was Azar? There was no trace of him. Emotions flooded her. She had half expected to see his body out there. The other half of her expected to see him alive.

She was wrong on both scores.

Clearly he had gone off to take care of Oleron's allies.

He would be back soon. And he would expect her to be waiting. As ordered.

Touching herself briefly, sucking in her lower lip, she enjoyed a small jolt of pleasure.

I must prepare myself, she thought. I must clean my body. I must choose a flogger. I must be in bed. On my hands and knees. The leather handle between my teeth.

Waiting...for my Master.

Theryssa pressed the door button, sealing herself inside Azar's cabin. There was come on her fingertips. She licked it off, savoring, moaning, and removing the evidence.

But what about the button panel? That had come on it, too. Pressing her belly to the wall, she thrust out her tongue, licking the round surface clean. Her nipples were rubbing, squashed.

Oh, god, she needed sex.

Come back soon, Azar. Come back safe and sound.

And hard.

Yes, they would fuck. But they would have to talk, too. About each other's feelings. He was not indifferent to her, she knew that much. But how deep did it go? And could he get to it...while he had the chance to be with her?

One way or the other, the subject must be broached. And she would have to take the lead. For in as much as he was meant to be the Master of their sex-making, she was going to have to be mistress of their dawning relationship.

If indeed they had one outside of bed at all.

Chapter Nine

ร่ว

Azar struck terror into the hearts of his crew as he moved among them, stalking the corridors of the ship, searching for his enemies. He was like some animal predator—keen, intelligent and efficiently deadly, eyes intent on vengeance.

Like rats, they sought to scatter. They did not need to know about his being a primale, in the midst of attack rage to be convinced of the need to flee for their lives. It was enough to see the man, fists clenched, stark naked, his powerful body bathed in the blood of the dead Oleron as he hunted.

Weaponless, save for a pair of tightly clenched fists.

It was certainly a surprise, to say the least.

Azar himself had not expected to be put into such a state. Any more than Oleron could have known what he was unleashing, threatening the safety of Theryssa.

Apparently Theryssa meant something to Azar. Something deeper than mere sexual attraction. This was classic mate protection behavior, exhibited by primales in defense of their pair-bond.

No one could hope to stand against such an expression of power, not even another primale. It was said such a reaction was a sure sign that a primale had found his mate, the woman he was to spend his life with.

Once such a woman was found, he would never be able to touch or desire another. His monogamy would be unbreakable. Absolute. And so would his possessiveness.

Such absoluteness would overwhelm any fem, which is why there were the obedients, the women genetically designed to find bliss in submission to a super-strong, super-devoted...and super-domineering primale.

Azar had fought these feelings before, with Solania. He had been too afraid. Too young and unsure. His hesitancy had cost her life. For when the hour of challenge had come, when Malthusalus had stepped into the picture to prey on her vulnerability, he had not been there to protect her.

Nor had he fought the Council afterward, to secure her life.

Had he admitted his love, had he not been the stupidest and most stubborn primale in history, he would have brought down the whole of the Guardian force just to save her.

But that wouldn't have been necessary. For she would never have been caught up in spying. She would have been at home, where she belonged, tending to their domestic life.

It was absurd he should have to relive all this now. And with a woman completely wrong for any primale. Theron and Nyssa were wrong. There was nothing here that could bind him and Theryssa. She was just dredging up ghosts, that's all.

But she was damn good at it.

And right now, she had him walking as a man again, as a primale, for the first time in years. For her safety. And for the honor of the pirate code, which had its limits, its morals.

Those without honor. Those who abused females, who took from them what they did not wish to give in their hearts, including their own desire for slavery, were not fit to live.

Blast it, how long had he been walking the line himself? Wasn't he calling the kettle black?

"Captain," whimpered Vraka, one of Oleron's henchmen, his sword hand trembling fiercely. "I swear, I wasn't never part of no mutiny plans."

Azar inclined his head in the direction of the man's weapon. "Do you intend to use that sword on me?"

"No, sir," exclaimed the man, realizing his error. "I swear," he raised his hands in the air.

"Drop it," said Azar, the quiet intensity of his voice only heightening the fearsome sense of his power.

Vraka dropped the sword and fell crying to his knees. "Please, don't kill me," he wailed.

"You will come with me," said Azar "You will point out to me every traitor. You will reveal them all. If you exclude one, or falsely accuse any man, I shall remove your entrails and have them fed to the first dogs I run across. Is that clear?"

"Oh, yes," he cried, sweat beading on his forehead. "Oh, sir, I swear I'll not steer you wrong."

Azar lifted him by the collar, suspending his entire body in the air. "I hope not. For your sake."

One by one, they searched them out. Azar knew already who they were, but he wanted to see if the man would lie to him. In the end, he dispatched a dozen, without ever touching the hilt of a sword.

The first two sought to charge him with axes at the ready. He grabbed the handles mid air, snapping them. The men sought to run, but he grabbed them by the sides of their heads, crushing them together.

The third had a laser weapon. Azar was too fast even for this. Ducking the bright red beam he delivered a kick to the midsection, knocking the man through the bulkhead.

At this point two others attempted a cowardly attack from behind. He seized them in a bear hug, making them whimper for their last breath.

The next one begged like a baby on his knees. Azar handed him a knife, with which to dispatch himself.

Four more attacked en masse with swords. Azar cracked the blades, one by one. Then he broke their necks. The last two jumped into the airlock, in a crazed attempt to escape.

With the death of his final adversary came a return to calm. Albeit with an unspeakable desire to lie beside Theryssa, to smell her sweet skin, to kiss her lips and neck, to hear the sounds of her surrender, to seal between them the sexual bond that he must have…or die.

"You are second-in-command," he deposited the bearded information provider back on the floor when the job was completed. "From this moment on."

"Aye, aye, sir," the man saluted, his intensity unmatched in pirate history. "You can count on me."

"I know that," said Azar, his energy already shifting. To lust and conquest. "That is why you are still alive."

Vraka swallowed hard.

"I'll be in my quarters," said Azar.

"Very good, sir. Um…if I could ask a question, begging your pardon?"

"What is it?"

"The…uh…remains. What should we do with them?"

"Launch the bodies of the traitors into space. Let the universe deal with them."

He saluted again. "Yes, sir."

Azar did not think he would have any mutiny problems again for a very long time.

Unfortunately, his secret was out now. There was no mistaking he was more than a man.

Word would spread to other ships. The other captains, lesser though they might be, could decide to unite against him if they suspected that he was really a primale, a former Guardian.

He might well have to make a choice. Either surrender his command and flee to safer quarters, or else do what he had never been done before. Namely embrace both his primale nature and his pirate nature. This was what Theron was hoping for. That he would forge the pirates into a force worthy of battling the Narthians. Side by side with the Guardians.

It would indeed comprise a splendid navy. Worthy of the finest traditions of the Guardians and the pirates alike.

Now was not the time to face such decisions, however.

Theryssa was waiting for him in his quarters. Theryssa, the one woman who stirred his blood and his loins like no other. Who felt in his arms like beauty itself...and truth, and destiny.

A woman who was his equal in many crucial ways and who made up for her lack of male strength with cunning and a courage that outstripped that of anyone he had ever known.

Himself included.

The dynamics between them were subtle. Difficult to explain. It was interesting to watch Theron and Nyssa together. His authority as the male was quite evident, and he was quite sure that Nyssa yielded to him in all the appropriate ways. But she clearly had her own drive and she was not afraid to speak up and intervene when she needed.

He saw how Theron respected that, how he knew to trust her and to bow to her grace and wisdom when needed.

Azar would do the same with Theryssa, were he her mate. He would work carefully to be strong and not stubborn. Firm, but not pigheaded. He would take her submission to him as a gift, and he would never lose his humility.

A woman like that would have to be a man's partner.

She would pose challenges for her mate that even Nyssa did not. She was of a more martial nature, like her father. She would always want to fight. But with feminine strength, he had often seem, came a secret need to yield to the right man.

Theryssa responded to his power. She was turned on by his domination. Perhaps Nyssa found the same with Theron. Azar could hardly imagine Theron being less than a lion in bed.

Certainly Azar himself had requirements. Needs. He could respect and adore Theryssa, but looking at her body, seeing the flame in her eyes, he could never *not* want her as his absolute sexual possession, moaning and writhing at his touch.

In short, he would honor her as a queen in everything, but in bed, she would be his slave. All of this was a lovely theory, though. In reality, he could not see his life with her beyond today, let alone the rest of his days.

Perhaps that was his pirate nature, living for the latest plunder, always knowing death could be around the next corner. Or maybe it was his old fears. About relationships. About love.

Theryssa was not waiting for him in bed, where he had told her to be.

And why should she be? She was willful and spirited. And a bit of a tease.

Azar tried to hide his smile, affecting the serious countenance of the spurned Master. He found her still in the sanitizing chamber under the cleansing beams.

His cock sprang to life at the sight of her under the golden rays. She was like a sun goddess. A nymph, her body arched, her hands caressing up and down her body.

She was masturbating. Her mind and flesh lost somewhere far away.

For a split second he thought of leaving her to her dreams. But that could never be. If for no other reason than that his own male urges were too strong.

And not just for sex, but for bonding, too. It was literally implanted in his nature to lay hands on her such that she would forget every other man, to give her loving such that she could never lie with or even think of another.

He must chain her with invisible links.

Chains of the heart.

Azar's own heart swelled and ached with the implications.

A man did not lock a female in a golden cage of love unless he was prepared to meet her every need, to be the hero of her dreams.

She was so intent in her fantasy that she did not hear him approach from behind. One second under the rays and he was as clean as a newborn babe, the dead cells zapped from his body, his skin left tingling and refreshed, his cock twice as hard and a full two inches longer. Binding her arms to her sides, he cupped both of Theryssa's breasts. "You are not in bed," he whispered, grazing her ear.

"I lost track of time," she sighed, falling back against him.

"Are you making excuses?" he asked, massaging her nipples.

"No, Master," she breathed, slipping perfectly into her role, "I disobeyed you. I should be punished."

"We have such a backlog already," he teased. "I'm afraid I'll grow old before we're caught up."

"Worse things could happen."

Azar's heart slammed in his chest. Was she saying what he thought she was saying?

"Master...may I..." Theryssa had managed to work one tiny hand between them, her small fingers brushing his cock where it pressed into his ass cheeks.

Azar let her turn and sink to her knees.

"Forgive me," she looked into his eyes, her own moist, "my Master."

She kissed the tip of his cock, treating it as an object of worship.

"May I?" she asked again.

He laid his fingers on her cheek, lightly drawing her forward. Theryssa opened her mouth, taking him smoothly inside. He expected her to stop, but she kept on going. Inch after inch after inch.

By the gods, she was going to deep-throat him.

Azar groaned, feeling himself suddenly captivated. If he had any hope of holding on against her onslaught, it was blown to smithereens by her rapid-fire motions, sliding him out and then back in.

Like a hungry bird, she bobbed her head, holding onto his hips for leverage. She wanted him to come quickly, and on her terms.

She was going to get her way, too, for as much as he was supposed to be in control, this kneeling nymph was holding the key to his lust...and maybe his soul, too.

"Theryssa..." he exhaled, feeling like a man stabbed. Gone was his usual restraint, his ability to stretch the sex out, molding the experience for his partner's joy and titillation.

He was just releasing, his muscles taut, his pelvis pushed forward. Hell, he didn't even have to do the thrusting. Leaning his head back, he let loose with the cry of a warrior, a satisfied lion.

His semen rushed into Theryssa's mouth. She swallowed unabashedly. All of it, every last drop. He had so much of it, as though he hadn't orgasmed in months.

"Oh...baby. Sweet baby." Azar was orbiting. Launching from one mountain to another, rockets inside his cock, shooting one after another. He put his hands on her shoulders to steady himself. No one had ever brought him off like this. No one. This whole situation was getting more complicated by the moment.

Theryssa continued to suck him, getting the last available drops. Her mouth was like a vacuum, pure suction.

Were he an ordinary man, he would have been spent for the night. Out of commission for hours. But Azar was not ordinary. Besides, he was on a mission.

At last she released him, a catlike grin on her face. "I take it you accept my apology…Master?"

She spoke the word with mild irony. Probing, testing. The power had shifted again, like a sand dune, sculpted by desert winds. He could not get enough of this interaction between them. It was as though his body was coming to crave it like some drug.

Azar brought her to her feet and crushed the air from her with a kiss. By the time he released her, he had inhaled her very soul. She clung to him, whimpering, perspiring. From between her thighs, her wetness dripped. Her lips were puffy and needy. Above and below.

"Do you feel that?" he asked.

He meant his cock, pushing at her belly button, still rock hard.

"Yes," she panted, reaching for it with her hands.

Azar took her wrists and held them over her head. "That cock is going to be in you and at you. Nonstop. For as long as I wish it to continue."

Theryssa saw in this no threat, but only a promise. "Oh, yes, I want you to, Azar, I do."

"You do now. But it will change. Soon enough there will be too many orgasms and too much intercourse. You'll beg that the sex-making end," he predicted. "And there is only way I will make that happen. Do you know what that way is?"

She shook her head.

"By exchanging the sex for torture, Theryssa. Yes, you will beg for torture. You will beg for the flogger. Or perhaps we'll begin the other way around, by flogging you until you beg penetration. Do you think I could make you do that, Theryssa?"

"Oh, god." Theryssa shivered against him. Nibbling, caressing. She wanted to touch him everywhere at once. "Yes,

yes to all of it. I fucking give in," she groaned, barely able to articulate.

Clearly his words had pushed her into a new place. A place of deep masochism. Azar instinctively knew how to treat her now to maximize the experience. Turning her about, he pushed her up against the smooth, rounded wall of the sanitizing chamber and entered her from behind. She was considerably hotter inside than the beams, her accompanying wetness in stark contrast to the dry, cleansing sensation.

Keeping her hands against the wall, effectively pinning her breasts and belly, as he had with the conference table, he indulged in her pussy. Long, languid strokes—powerful, animal ruts.

The rutting of a king, a lord of beasts. And why shouldn't he feel the sheer passion and glory of this moment? After all, he had Theryssa, and he had her for all the time in the world with no one to oppose him in his enjoyment of her full feminine delights. All of them, her body, her mouth, her sighs, her blatant desire serving to heighten his sheer ecstasy.

It was good to be a primale, able to fully exploit the situation. To have at Theryssa without the fear of losing control over his sexual releases. He could come now, and then keep going. And indeed, he would. "Theryssa," he told her. "You are so fucking incredible. Do you know that?"

"Oh, Azar." She was pushing her ass out at him, practically daring him to push on, as far as his will would allow.

In time...but for now, he made quick work of things, bringing Theryssa off to another orgasm, taking one for himself in the balance. It was a fast one, lean and low, just a few microbursts to whet his appetite for more.

She was still twitching as he pulled out of her. "To bed," he said.

Azar scooped her up, cradling her. She clung to his neck, holding on as he tried to deposit her on the furs. She was no match for him, however, and he easily managed to lay her facedown.

"Hold still." He patted her ass with his palm.

She clenched her buttocks instinctively, as though he had spanked her. Finding the pink folds irresistible, he pushed a finger into her pussy, hooking it.

He had her, frozen.

"Don't move. No matter what."

"Yes, Master."

Her breath was as still as her body. He had control, completely. "Theryssa," he called her name.

"Yes, Master."

"Come for me."

"Oh...yes..." She writhed wantonly, instantly obeying him, his little spy, horny, obedient. And in training.

Mesmerized, he watched the motions of her body, her beautiful slit, the pink folds, the mysterious opening wherein his cock had found such pleasure. On and on, it went, her flesh dancing, lifting higher and higher to a peak of liquid bliss.

He'd never been so happy as to be able to please a woman. And now it was time to take things a step further, to a new place.

He waited until she had settled back down. "I'll be right back," he whispered.

Azar went to the rack, retrieved a flogger—his favorite one, long and black, with a dozen strands of synthon, a material rather like suede, but with the advantage of feeling wet and liquid to the touch.

Synthon had another advantage, which consisted of microscopic sensors that reacted on a cell by cell basis with the victim, conforming after the first blow to a pattern of personal, maximum tormenting.

He also took a piece of ice—a small cube of it—from his beverage freezing unit. It was time to confuse Theryssa's sensations a little bit.

He sat down beside her. She tensed instantly. "That's a good girl for waiting." He ran his fingers down her back. He had the flogger in his lap, and the ice on the floor.

"Thank you, Master."

He smiled down at her, building the anticipation.

"Master?" She broke the silence.

"Yes, slave girl?"

"What are you going to do to me?"

"That's an easy one, Theryssa. Whatever I want to."

"Yes, Master."

He reached back, caressing her instep.

Theryssa startled, kicking out with her foot.

"You were told to stay still." He thwacked her, hard enough to leave a glowing pink patch. The next time would be worse, as the synthon learned her pain spots.

"Ow," she cried. "That hurt."

He spanked her again, on the same spot. "Were you given permission to protest?"

"No, Master." She gritted her teeth.

"I didn't think so. I want you to hump the bed," he said, quite abruptly.

Theryssa hesitated, as he knew she would. "Master? I don't follow…"

He spanked her again, inducing a stifled cry. "Of course you do, slave girl. You are to move against the mattress as though you were making sex with it. You're to give me a little show."

"Yes, Master." Her voice shook with shame. He was pushing her to a new level.

"You can do better than that," he critiqued her first efforts, which were timid at best.

Theryssa gave a little moan of frustration. Lifting her hips, she raised them in the air a few inches, and then lowered them, her pussy touching the furs once more.

"A virgin humps like that," he tapped her back with the flogger, "not a sex slave."

She moaned at the feel of the leather brushing across her flesh.

"That's right," he confirmed her fears, "that's the flogger. It owns you, and it's quite hungry for your flesh."

Her breathing shallow and rapid, she began to make love to the bed in earnest. Her aroma filled the air as she writhed up and down, helplessly revealing her deepest carnal motions.

She was like some exotic animal scratching an itch. All she needed was a little extra stimulation to put her over the top.

"What do you think you're going to do?" he demanded, lashing her ass cheeks with the flogger. "Come all over my furs?"

"Oh, god," she reacted, her cheeks vibrating and pinkening all at once, "what's in that thing?"

"It's synthon. Special memory strands. It remembers what you like…"

"I don't…like this," she protested.

"Are you lying to me, slave girl?" Azar slapped her with the whip, strategically dragging one of the stinging strands across the crack of her pussy.

Theryssa began to spasm uncontrollably. "Oh, my fucking stars."

"I'm thinking you do like this," he teased her, whipping the back of her legs, lightly all the way down to her feet.

She wriggled, trying to get up. He held her down, as he slapped the insteps of her feet. "Bad girl."

"I'll be good, Azar," she panted, desperately trying to dissuade him from using the flogger any more. "I swear."

"And obedient?" He lifted her face, tugging her head by the hair.

"Yes…I will…I'll be so obedient," she moaned as he swished the flogger across her face, over her twitching lips and smooth cheeks.

"I don't know," he feigned uncertainty. "How can I be sure you're trainable?"

"I am. I can follow commands. I can learn."

He slapped the whip down hard on the back of her left thigh, and then again on the right. "Turn over," he said. "Hold up your breasts for me to flog."

Theryssa scrambled to comply. Her globes were so very tempting, splendid and lusciously available as she cradled them, offering them up between her lightly pressed fingers.

"Beg for it, Theryssa."

"Please, Master. Flog my breasts."

Azar delivered a measured stroke. *Let's see how easy it is for her to beg now that she's felt the sting*, he mused. "Again, Theryssa, beg for it again."

Her face was twisted in dark lust. Her eyes were lit with desire. "Again," she said after the briefest hesitation. "Please, Master. Flog my breasts again."

Azar crisscrossed the pure skin a total of five times. Theryssa's head was back, her hair hanging loose, her torso bent as a self-offering. She was the perfect picture of submission. He had to have her. As never before.

"Prepare yourself," he ordered. "Legs spread."

Theryssa positioned herself with exquisite grace, like a melting goddess, a butterfly unfurling its wings, revealing a precious colored center. In this case pink, like purest coral. And glistening drops of white. By the gods, even her pussy was perfect and beautiful. A work of art. If ever a woman could be plunder, it was she. And yet there was no price in the entire universe to redeem such a creature.

He descended on top of her, a single measured merging, flesh against flesh. This time they began with an embrace. Doing nothing more than listening to each other's breathing, and feeling the tickle of one another's sweat.

They licked each other, each dabbing lightly at the other's skin. But still, they did not relinquish the bond, like two magnets, south to north, poles inseparable.

Azar just reveled in the feel of her, making his cock as large as he could, letting her accommodate, with all the seeming practice of a lifetime. Hand in glove, that was how to describe it. Hard muscle against soft curves. Male and female. A match, yes.

Logical, even inevitable, according to Nyssa and Theron. And good for him in so many ways. He was alive with her, and he knew that in her absence he would never feel joy again. But would it make her happy to be tied to a man like him? Did she not deserve more?

She did in fact, and he had to convince her of that. The sooner the better.

"Theryssa," he said, trying not to sound too abrupt. "I realize this has been…pleasant between us. But I don't want to hold you to any commitment…sexually or otherwise. I understand that you need to go."

She wrinkled her brow, smiling oddly. "Why would you say that? No one's satisfied me like you. I don't want to be with another man. Ever."

The finality of her answer startled him…and made him a little lightheaded.

"You should be with someone younger, more like you," he said quickly. "I'm a pirate, I'm set in my ways, and that's just for starters."

"You're not that old," she laughed. "And I'm as set in my ways as they come, ask my folks."

"I'm nearly your father's age," he reminded.

"You aren't him, though. I don't think of you like that."

"How do you think of me? Outside of bed, I mean."

She thought for a moment. "You're intriguing, sexy as hell, smart, exasperating, stubborn. And did I mention sexy as hell?"

Azar laughed deeply. It felt good. Not to mention way overdue. "You're not too shabby yourself."

"For a youngster."

"You're plenty old enough, missy."

"Old enough to know better?"

"I'm the wrong one to ask."

She pursed her lips. He could tell she was thinking. He was getting pretty good at reading her like that. "Do you think the Narthians will really attack in as large a force as my father says? I'll admit it's a little scary."

"I don't know, Theryssa. Unfortunately, I can tell you your old man is seldom wrong about these things, though I would never tell him to his face."

Theryssa's pretty eyes were studying him. A lesser man would be terrified by that kind of probing. "Why wouldn't you accept my Dad's offer?" she wanted to know.

"You mean to take you as my mate?"

"No. To join your fleet to his."

Azar frowned. "It's complicated."

"It doesn't seem complicated," she insisted. "Either it's the right thing to do or it isn't. Are you holding back because of your objections to the Council's genetics programs?"

"No, you are proof that things have changed. And I believe your mother and father when they say they want to work with me to improve the world. We can all learn from each other."

"Well if it's not that," she persisted, "what is it?"

He was tempted to tell her something along the lines of "*At your age it's all black and white…*" but he quickly dismissed it as an excuse to avoid the hard truth. "You're right, Theryssa," he dared to look into his deepest heart, "I'm only hesitating because I'm afraid."

"You? What could you be afraid of?"

He heard the awe in her voice. It was flattering, if misguided. "I'm afraid of just about everything," he said. "Beginning with myself."

"You're a good and noble man," she said with all the confidence of youth.

"You don't know that," he said gently.

"Yes," she replied, undeterred. "I do."

He drew a breath as she squeezed her sex muscles around his cock, letting him know just how confident she was feeling about him.

"A woman trusted me once with her life," he tried to put her off, "and I let her down."

"You mean Solania," she pressed. "Tell me, tell me what happened."

"Why? You can't change anything."

"But I need to hear," she took his hand. "I love you, Azar."

His lip trembled slightly as he prepared to relate the story, the whole story, including the deepest part of his rage…which had never been directed against Theron but against himself.

"Solania risked everything to be with me," he explained. "She was a fem. I should only have married an obedient like the rest of my kind. I seduced her. The Council found out. They sent Theron to warn her off. She was...confused, alone. She took an air-car...there was an accident, no one will ever know exactly..."

"But that isn't your fault," she said quickly, echoing the words he'd heard so many times.

"It is my fault, though. No one knows this, Theryssa, but she tried to contact me. After Theron left. I told her...I told her I couldn't ever talk to her or see her again. The Council had sent someone to talk to me, you see, at the same time Theron went to her."

Theryssa's eyes reflected his pain. "I'm so sorry, Azar?"

"Sorry for what? That I'm a monster? A coward?"

"You did what you had to," she insisted. "You followed orders. You know, like we all do. The Council is all we have. It is what makes us human."

"Damn the Council, Theryssa, and damn your Pollyanna mentality. For god's sake, must you have an answer for everything?" He couldn't believe he was getting impatient like this. It was almost like he wanted her to hate him. And he had been so anxious to hear what she felt about him, to see if she might like him.

To his surprise, she seemed unfazed by the outburst. "Well it wouldn't be much fun if I couldn't keep up with you, would it?" she quipped.

"I think we need to be realistic about what is going on here," Azar thought aloud, succumbing once again to that veil of fatigue and grayness he'd been feeling in the months and days preceding her arrival.

"And what is that," she asked skeptically, a distinct twinkle in her eye, "oh, all-seeing Master?"

"We're making good sex," he deliberately ignored her good humor. "That's all it is."

"Really? Then why do I feel like there's a hole in my heart whenever you're gone from me, Azar? Why do I bleed to death, in my soul?"

Her words cut him to the quick.

"After a day? Theryssa that isn't possible."

What was wrong with him? His emotions were on a cascade? He needed safety, needed to be alone.

"How do you know what's possible? Do you know what my heart feels like…and my soul?"

"No," he admitted grudgingly, "I don't."

"And what about you? What do you feel?"

"Me?" Azar scowled. "I feel like hell. Confused, churned up. All twisted. Out there, with my men, I would have killed them all to save you. Damn it, Theryssa, I bonded with you. What else do you want me to say?"

There, it was out. The truth he'd been hiding from himself all along. Azar rolled off her, landing heavily on his back.

She leaned across, propping her head up with her elbow. "You mean a primale lifemate bond?"

"Yes," he glared at the ceiling.

"Well, I guess that's that." She shrugged.

"That's what?"

"We have to be mated."

"That's the most ridiculous thing I've ever heard," he retorted. "I bonded…by mistake."

"So you don't want me? You wouldn't care if I walked out and found the first guy to fuck? You would be cool with that?"

"Of course I wouldn't. I would want to rip him to shreds."

"Okay, suppose I find a nice man and settle down?"

Azar sighed, sounding more and more like a man playing a game of chess and discovering himself checkmated. "I would probably haunt you both until you had me arrested for harassment."

"I'm in the same boat," she told him. "I'm a primefemale, seventy five percent primale, remember? If you ever went near another woman, I would cut your balls off."

"How charming. Sounds like the answer is for you to stay in the Guardians, choose the path of lifetime commitment, no mating."

"No. I can't live alone my whole life. I thought I could, but thanks to you, I know I need companionship."

"So basically, I've sunk my own ship."

"If you consider mating with me a fate worse than death."

"Personally, I adore you," Azar admitted, still eying the ceiling. "You have completely swept me off my feet. But I still don't see how I can be the right man for you."

"Isn't that my decision?"

"I suppose, but I don't want you throwing your life away."

"Do you love me, Azar?"

Azar felt like a laser had been fired through his heart. "Love?"

"Yeah, you know," she quipped, "that four letter word that rhymes with above."

"Theryssa, you can't ask me a question like that."

"Why, does it scare you?"

"Look, let's leave it that I don't love you," he said flatly, "and we'll both be better off."

"But you bonded," she reminded him, mischievously fingering his cock. "We made sex, you bonded with me and now you have to love me. It's your biology."

"I don't have to do anything, Theryssa. And if you keep on pressing me, I will not be responsible for my actions."

"What will you do?" she asked, eager-eyed.

"I'll chain up these busy little hands of yours, for one thing. And I'll gag that impossible-to-argue-with mouth."

"I'd be helpless, then." She licked her lips. "And you could fuck me again."

"Damn it, no."

Theryssa was crawling on top of him, trying to mount his erection, which he could do not a damn thing about no matter how hard he tried.

"Why not, Master?"

"Because I said so."

"I'm being disobedient, aren't I? I need another flogging."

"You need to go home, Theryssa, that's what you need to do."

"You would miss me," she predicted.

"That's something we can certainly find out, isn't it...by going to different sides of the galaxy?"

"Nah, I'd rather just fuck."

Azar resisted in vain as she managed to slide his cock across her slit and between her gaping lips. His willpower pathetically low, he did little more than groan as she sheathed him completely inside her warm, tight opening.

"There, isn't that better?"

"No," he grumbled, "it's messy and complicated. And it's creating problems we will just have to resolve later."

"We can resolve them by making more sex."

"Theryssa, you are impossible," he declared.

"And you love that about me."

He had a lump in his throat. "Yes," he admitted softly, "I suppose I do."

"And you love everything else about me, too," she beamed.

"First and foremost your modesty." He rolled his eyes.

Theryssa slapped his chest, playfully.

Azar arched a brow. "I'll take care of the discipline, thank you very much."

"Aha," she proclaimed victory, "so you admit we have a relationship."

"I meant for this one-time encounter."

"Which began a half hour after we met and shows no sign of letting up any time in the next millennium…"

"I'm a quick seducer." He shrugged.

"And you have finally met your match."

"You wouldn't last a week," he predicted.

"Try me."

"There you go again, trying to make this permanent."

"Isn't it?"

"Nothing is permanent, but the stars," he said stubbornly. "And even those will burn out eventually.

"You think too much," she teased. "Tell me how this feels, not how it calculates."

"I won't speak to how it feels." Azar shifted, settling his cock an inch or so deeper. "As for you, you feel like…heaven."

"And you feel like a man with some unfinished business."

Azar smiled in spite of himself. As if one single orgasm would actually do it. Each one so far had only begged another—bigger, better and more spectacular.

Was Theryssa an addiction? Maybe, but she was the kind of habit a man was goddamn lucky to find. She was a one of a kind addiction, in a world of sleazy habits and mindless routines.

Would they make it a week together? Who knew the answer to that one? He was a pirate. He had today. And nothing more. He followed his heart and his head and right now they were telling him something.

More to the point they were showing it. And its name was happiness, in the most unlikely form of a young Guardian, the daughter of his brother turned enemy and quite possibly soon to be a brother again.

Who could argue with how alive he felt inside her, and beside her. Talking to her, making sex with her. Looking at her. Hell, just being in the same room with her, in the same ship, even, was enough to awaken him from an age-old slumber.

"Just promise me one thing," he said, grasping hold of her in preparation for riding her rapid-fire on his lap.

"Anything," she vowed.

"You won't run circles around me constantly, even though we both know you can."

"Absolutely not," she did her best to keep a straight face. "Master."

"I know I will live to regret this," he shook his head.

"I know," she bent to kiss his forehead. "I love you, too, you stubborn pirate."

The talking done, they returned to what had first brought them together, and what would always serve as their touchstone. Call it the forge of their bond, the source of their incendiary heat, the cauldron of their molten energy.

Sex, to use the technical word.

Whatever you called it, though, there was no denying they would never get enough of it. Not if they lived to be a thousand and crossed the galaxy a dozen times over.

They came together this time, their cries intertwining, their precious fluids flowing together, their fingers interlaced, their bodies moving in time, finding just the right motions to seal the gaps, to close the empty spaces. Her breast in his mouth, his cock in her pussy, their pelvises conjoined, and their flesh superheated.

Two persons. One destiny.

"That was good, lover," she whispered when she'd finally worn him out. "But I hope you have some energy left for fighting the Narthians."

"The Narthians are nothing," he grumbled, still holding her in his arms, loath to let go, now or ever, "compared to you."

"Thank you," she giggled. "I think."

"Seriously," he stroked her cheek, "thank you."

"For what?"

"For giving me my life back?"

"You're welcome. But you've had a life all along. The gods know you've been giving my father a run for his money all these years with this pirate rust bucket of yours."

He smacked her bottom playfully. "This rust bucket is older than you and deserves respect. As for my life, it was gray until you came along. Now there's color again."

"Well, I do seem to make you see red often enough."

He kissed her face—once, twice, a dozen times for good measure.

"What's that for?"

"Insurance. Against the next time I piss you off."

"Don't worry," she stroked his limp cock. "I have lots of ways to find revenge...*Master*."

"I'm not sure I like that look in your eyes."

"Is the big pirate scared of the little female?" she cooed.

"Damn straight I am."

She laughed. "You just better hope I don't figure out how to chain *you* up one of these days for a little payback."

"Actually," he grinned, "I'm kinda curious to see you in action...with a whip."

"Name the time and place," she said.

"Later. After a nap."

"Perfect time to chain you up."

"What you don't trust me to surrender willingly?"

"Not on your life."

"Smart girl. Very smart girl." He kissed her again. This time she kissed back.

"You can forget your nap idea," she murmured.

"Aye, aye," he said throatily. "Mistress."

Epilogue

ഇ

Azar watched the ship's viewscreen, his every nerve ending on high alert. For a half hour now the attack fighters had been engaging the advanced force of Narthians. It was a test battle, designed to see if the new weapons were going to work against the super bugs.

Azar had wanted to fly one of the ships, but his skills were needed as a general. Should the fighter ships fail to stop the attack, the larger cruisers, his own ships and the Guardian fleet would have to do the job.

Naturally, he was concerned for all the pilots. But he had his eye on the left side of the formation. A certain ship, flown by a certain woman.

The woman who held his heart. Who was his joy, the color in his world.

If he should lose her...

Damn it, why weren't there any transmissions coming back?

"Reconfigure the transmitters," he ordered his first mate. "Make sure we're not being jammed.

"Aye, aye, sir."

There was a sputter over the loud speakers, and then silence.

He glared at the dark stars, in the center of which loomed a gray, swirling cloud. The battlefield. Narthian nest ships and Guardian ships, locked head-to-head.

"It's not worth the risk," Azar had thundered at Theron when the plan was presented to engage the small ships. "Why not meet them with heavy cruisers? We know their advance party is limited?"

"Because we have to know," said Theron. "If our battle plans work, if the weapons work. You know as well as I when they make their main attack we will be spread too thin to use the heavy ships everywhere. We have to know where we stand. Later on it will be too late to experiment and you know it."

"Damn it, you're thinking like a bureaucrat, Theron."

"And you're thinking like Theryssa's husband," he countered.

Azar had no response. His old friend was right.

"I'll be fine," Theryssa had insisted. "Stop fretting over me so much. I'm a soldier, not a baby."

"You're my baby," he insisted. "Always."

She kissed him soundly for that one. "And you are my hero. My swashbuckling, idealistic, grumpy, domineering pirate. I know you only want to protect me, but you have to let me go. It's my job."

"Do you have to be so dedicated?" he complained.

"I had a good teacher." She patted his ass.

Azar smiled at the memory.

"Sir, we have something."

"What is it?"

"A faint signal. Over the secret channel. Number Seven."

His heart thundered. He'd had that one put in for Theryssa. At his insistence. She thought it was showing favorites over the other pilots, but he didn't give a damn. He could fight just as well with one more channel to listen to. "Can you zero in?"

"It's in code."

"Give it to me," he ordered. "Quickly."

"It says…You owe me. Have I translated wrong, sir?"

"No." He sighed in relief, too deep for words. "You have it right."

They had made a bet. Theryssa's idea. If she came home safe, he would get flogged for giving her a hard time about going. She thought it the perfect bet.

"If I lose," she'd quipped in perfect Theryssa style, "I'll never have to pay up."

"Sir, we have more signals. It's the fleet."

"I know," said Azar. "The battle is won."

Azar felt the warmth return to his limbs. All would be well. For Earth. For the galaxy. And for his heart, which was at this moment sailing in space, somewhere out there, locked in a fighter ship piloted by the bravest soul, male or female, he had ever known.

After all, who else would dare to love him?

Yes, indeed, things were going to be well all over.

With the possible exception of his ass, which was going to sting like hell tonight.

Also by Reese Gabriel

❧

A Centaur for Libby

A Filly for Doug

Chaining His Heart

Come and Get Me

Commanding Kat

Dance of Submission

His Sahvria

His Submissive

Holiday Reflections (*anthology*)

Kimberlee's Keeper

Laila's Bargain

More Than Male 1: Nyssa's Guardian

More Than Male 4: Jaxey's Master

More Than Male 5: A Dominant for Desela

More Than Male 6: Vandar's War

My Carina

Prisoner of Shera-Sa

Roping His Filly

Soul Master

Taming Delaney

Temporary Slave

Tying Tempest

About the Author

୫ଠ

Reese Gabriel is a born romantic with a taste for the edgier side of love. Having traveled the world and sampled many of the finer things, Reese now enjoys the greater simplicities--barefoot walks by the ocean, kisses under moonlight and whispers of passion in the darkness with that one special person.

Preferring to remain behind the scenes, cherished by a precious few, Reese hopes to awaken in the lives of many the possibilities of true love through stories of far off places and enchanted lives.

For the sake of love and hope and imagination, these stories are told. May they be enjoyed as much in the reading of them as in the writing. Reese loves to hear from readers.

Reese welcomes comments from readers. You can find her website and email address on her author bio page at www.ellorascave.com.

Tell Us What You Think

We appreciate hearing reader opinions about our books. You can email us at Comments@EllorasCave.com.

Why an electronic book?

We live in the Information Age—an exciting time in the history of human civilization, in which technology rules supreme and continues to progress in leaps and bounds every minute of every day. For a multitude of reasons, more and more avid literary fans are opting to purchase e-books instead of paper books. The question from those not yet initiated into the world of electronic reading is simply: *Why?*

1. ***Price.*** An electronic title at Ellora's Cave Publishing and Cerridwen Press runs anywhere from 40% to 75% less than the cover price of the exact same title in paperback format. Why? Basic mathematics and cost. It is less expensive to publish an e-book (no paper and printing, no warehousing and shipping) than it is to publish a paperback, so the savings are passed along to the consumer.

2. ***Space.*** Running out of room in your house for your books? That is one worry you will never have with electronic books. For a low one-time cost, you can purchase a handheld device specifically designed for e-reading. Many e-readers have large, convenient screens for viewing. Better yet, hundreds of titles can be stored within your new library—on a single microchip. There are a variety of e-readers from different manufacturers. You can also read e-books on your PC or laptop computer. (Please note that Ellora's Cave does not endorse any specific brands.

You can check our websites at www.ellorascave.com or www.cerridwenpress.com for information we make available to new consumers.)

3. *Mobility*.   Because your new e-library consists of only a microchip within a small, easily transportable e-reader, your entire cache of books can be taken with you wherever you go.

4. ***Personal Viewing Preferences.***   Are the words you are currently reading too small? Too large? Too… ANNOYING? Paperback books cannot be modified according to personal preferences, but e-books can.

5. ***Instant Gratification.***   Is it the middle of the night and all the bookstores near you are closed? Are you tired of waiting days, sometimes weeks, for bookstores to ship the novels you bought? Ellora's Cave Publishing sells instantaneous downloads twenty-four hours a day, seven days a week, every day of the year. Our webstore is never closed. Our e-book delivery system is 100% automated, meaning your order is filled as soon as you pay for it.

Those are a few of the top reasons why electronic books are replacing paperbacks for many avid readers.

As always, Ellora's Cave and Cerridwen Press welcome your questions and comments. We invite you to email us at Comments@ellorascave.com or write to us directly at Ellora's Cave Publishing Inc., 1056 Home Avenue, Akron, OH 44310-3502.

COMING TO A BOOKSTORE NEAR YOU!

ELLORA'S CAVE

Bestselling Authors Tour

UPDATES AVAILABLE AT

WWW.EllorasCave.com

MAKE EACH DAY MORE *EXCITING* WITH OUR

ELLORA'S
CAVEMEN
CALENDAR

www.EllorasCave.com

erridwen, the Celtic Goddess of wisdom, was the muse who brought inspiration to storytellers and those in the creative arts. Cerridwen Press encompasses the best and most innovative stories in all genres of today's fiction. Visit our site and discover the newest titles by talented authors who still get inspired - much like the ancient storytellers did, once upon a time.

Cerridwen Press

www.cerridwenpress.com

Discover for yourself why readers can't get enough of the multiple award-winning publisher

Ellora's Cave.

Whether you prefer e-books or paperbacks,

be sure to visit EC on the web at
www.ellorascave.com

for an erotic reading experience that will leave you breathless.

Made in the USA